THE WEAVER'S DAUGHTER

Books by Sarah E. Ladd

The Treasures of Surrey Novels

The Curiosity Keeper
Dawn at Emberwilde
A Stranger at Fellsworth

The Whispers on the Moors Novels

The Heiress of Winterwood
The Headmistress of Rosemere
A Lady at Willowgrove Hall

ACCLAIM FOR SARAH E. LADD

"A gently unfolding love story set amid the turmoil of the early industrial revolution. [*The Weaver's Daughter* is] a story of betrayal, love, and redemption, all beautifully rendered in rural England."

—ELIZABETH CAMDEN, RITA AWARD-WINNING AUTHOR

"Once again, Ladd delights readers with a skillfully plotted, suspenseful page-turner. As always, her characters jump from the page, each one a realistic and achingly human assembly of merits, flaws, doubts, and faith. Like all superior novelists, Ladd doesn't default to pat endings, offering even her villains a potential happily-ever-after by putting her faith (not to mention the characters' and the readers') in God's abiding mercy."

—RT BOOK REVIEWS, 4 STARS FOR A STRANGER AT FELLSWORTH

"This novel reads well and fast; its vivid imagery and likeable characters fill the pages. The well-crafted metaphors and tight sequences make for an absorbing read. Though set around the Regency period, the style is fresh and the voice genuine. The spiritual aspect of the novel does not overpower; it is woven into the plot and provides a graceful way to unite the beliefs and morals of Annabelle and Owen Locke. I want to read more in the series."

—HISTORICAL NOVELS SOCIETY FOR A STRANGER AT FELLSWORTH

"[*A Stranger at Fellsworth*] can easily stand on its own, but readers who enjoy this book will want to devour the trilogy."

—LIBRARY JOURNAL

"With betrayals, murders, and criminal activity disrupting the peace at Fellsworth, Ladd fills the pages with as much intrigue as romance. A well-crafted story for fans of Regency novels."

—PUBLISHERS WEEKLY FOR A STRANGER AT FELLSWORTH

"Beautifully written, intricately plotted, and populated by engaging and realistic characters, *The Curiosity Keeper* is Regency romantic suspense at its page-turning best. A skillful, sympathetic, and refreshingly natural author, Ladd is at the top of her game and should be an auto-buy for every reader."

—*RT Book Reviews*, 4 1/2 stars, TOP PICK!

"An engaging Regency with a richly detailed setting and an unpredictable suspenseful plot. Admirers of Sandra Orchard and Lis Wiehl who want to try a romance with a historical bent may enjoy this new series."

—*Library Journal* on *The Curiosity Keeper*

"Ladd's story, with its menace and cast of seedy London characters, feels more like a work of Dickens than a Regency . . . A solid outing."

—*Publishers Weekly* on *The Curiosity Keeper*

"A delightful read, rich with period details. Ladd crafts a couple the reader roots for from the very beginning and a plot that keeps the reader guessing until the end."

—Sarah M. Eden, bestselling author of
For Elise on *The Curiosity Keeper*

"My kind of book! The premise grabbed my attention from the first lines, and I eagerly returned to its pages. I think my readers will enjoy *The Heiress of Winterwood*."

—Julie Klassen, bestselling, award-winning author

"Ladd proves yet again she's a superior novelist, creating unforgettable characters and sympathetically portraying their merits, flaws, and all-too-human struggles with doubt, hope, and faith."

—*RT Book Reviews*, 4 stars, on *A Lady at Willowgrove Hall*

"This book has it all: shining prose, heart-wrenching emotion, vivid and engaging characters, a well-paced plot, and a sigh-worthy happy ending that might cause some readers to reach for the tissue box. In only her second novel, Ladd has established herself as Regency writing royalty."

"If you are a fan of Jane Austen and *Jane Eyre*, you will love Sarah E. Ladd's debut."

"This debut novel hits all the right notes with a skillful and delicate touch, breathing fresh new life into standard romance tropes."

"Ladd's charming Regency debut is enhanced with rich detail and well-defined characters. It should be enjoyed by fans of Gilbert Morris."

The *Weaver's* DAUGHTER

SARAH E. LADD

THOMAS NELSON
Since 1798

The Weaver's Daughter

© 2018 by Sarah Ladd

Published in Nashville, Tennessee, by Thomas Nelson. Thomas Nelson is a registered trademark of HarperCollins Christian Publishing, Inc.

Interior design by Mallory Collins

Thomas Nelson titles may be purchased in bulk for educational, business, fund-raising, or sales promotional use. For information, please e-mail SpecialMarkets@ThomasNelson.com.

Library of Congress Cataloging-in-Publication Data

Names: Ladd, Sarah E., author.
Title: The weaver's daughter : a regency romance novel / Sarah E. Ladd.
Description: Nashville : Thomas Nelson, 2018.
Identifiers: LCCN 2017049556 | ISBN 9780718011888 (softcover)
Subjects: LCSH: Family-owned business enterprises--Fiction. | Man-woman relationships--Fiction. | Weavers--Fiction. | GSAFD: Christian fiction. | Love stories.
Classification: LCC PS3612.A3565 W43 2018 | DDC 813/.6--dc23 LC record available at https://lccn.loc.gov/2017049556

Printed in the United States of America
18 19 20 21 22 LSC 5 4 3 2 1

For A. D.
In loving memory

PROLOGUE

Summer 1801
Amberdale, West Riding
Yorkshire, England

Alarm's menacing sting pricked Kate Dearborne's consciousness and hurried her steps. Clutching the note in her hand, she climbed the wooden steps over the stone fence separating Amberdale's main road from the churchyard.

The church's bell struck the eight o'clock hour as her booted feet landed on the other side with a dull thud. She was late, but it was not from a lack of effort to meet Frederica at the appointed time. Kate wiped the perspiration gathering on her brow with the back of her hand and then shielded her eyes to see in the light of the setting summer sun.

Her dearest friend was waiting in the grove, just as her note said she would be. She jumped up from the bench beneath the willow trees at the edge of the yard. "There you are!" Frederica rushed to meet her, her lips tugged into a pretty pout. "I've been here half an hour!"

I

Kate leaned forward and rested her hands on her knees, pausing to catch her breath. "Sorry. I couldn't get away."

As Kate straightened, Frederica's eyebrows shot up and her deep-mahogany eyes widened in horror. "Your gown! What's happened?"

Kate pushed her hair from her eyes and followed Frederica's gaze to the blue stains marring the front of her linen skirt. "It's only indigo. I forgot to put on my smock in the dye house today and, well, this happened."

Frederica took a step back, as if nearness alone might transfer the unsightly stain to her own white muslin frock. She clicked her tongue. "You should be careful. What will people think when they see you like this?"

Kate giggled at the assumed authority in her friend's voice and tugged her skirt away. "You sound like old Mrs. Purty lecturing me on manners." She strode to the bench that had been a place of play since they were very young and flipped her thick braid over her shoulder. "Besides, you asked me to be here at half past seven, and I didn't have time to change my gown. So what did you want to tell me?"

Frederica was about to be seated when activity in the village square captured her attention. She angled her golden head and rose to the tips of her toes to see over the honeysuckle-laden wall separating them from the square. Sudden energy seized her plump frame, and she leapt to the side of the willow tree. "Oh, there he is!"

Kate frowned and stepped nearer. "Who?"

Frederica shook her head but never shifted her focus. "Don't pretend you don't know who I'm talking about."

Kate strained to follow Frederica's gaze. She glimpsed the owner of Stockton Mill sauntering toward the south lane. "Old Mr. Stockton?"

"Of course not, silly. His grandson next to him. See?"

Kate pivoted farther to see over the wall. She'd not heard that Mr. Stockton's grandson was in Amberdale, but then again, why would she be aware of anything to do with the Stockton family?

"His name is Henry Stockton." Frederica's excitement brightened her countenance.

Kate squinted to assess the youth further. With his hands stuffed in his pockets, the lanky, black-headed lad walked in step with his grandfather. He could be no older than her older brother, Charles.

Kate sniffed and retreated to the bench below the emerald canopy of branches and leaves. Her father and Mr. Stockton were bitter business rivals, and that fact alone thwarted any interest in the newcomer she might have. "I don't see why we should care about *him*."

A pretty pink flush bloomed on Frederica's cheeks as she scurried back to the bench. "Father told me that Henry's father died last month, and now he and his sister are both moving here. Henry will inherit both Stockton Mill and Stockton House one day. Don't you think him handsome?"

Kate lifted one shoulder in a shrug. "I could barely see him."

"Well, I find him to be exceedingly handsome, probably the most handsome boy in the entire village." A triumphant smile lit Frederica's face. "I think I'm going to marry him."

"Frederica Pennington!" Kate stifled a laugh. "That's ridiculous. You've never even met him, and besides, you are too young to get married."

When her friend did not join in the good-natured jesting, Kate quieted, until the only remaining sound was the chirping of the noisy warbler flitting in the boughs above.

Frederica perched on the bench's edge and folded her hands in her lap as primly as if they were taking their tea. "I'm not going to marry him tomorrow, silly, but one is never too young to prepare for what lies ahead." A giggle bubbled from her throat. "Father says one day Henry could be a fine match for me. He will be rich, you know, just as his grandfather is." She rested her palms on the bench and leaned forward. "Do you not think about getting married?"

Kate studied her indigo-stained hands. Of course she wanted to get married. What girl didn't? But she was only ten years of age, and as her mother would say whenever such a topic would arise, there were many more practical things to think on. "I guess."

"And besides, you were mistaken when you said I've never met him before, for I made his acquaintance just last night at supper."

A chill radiated through Kate's thin frame, despite the evening's balmy warmth. Something was amiss. Weavers and mill owners never dined together. "Why would you dine with the Stocktons? Your father detests Mr. Stockton. I heard him say so myself at the last weavers' meeting."

Frederica tossed back her glossy blonde curls and bit her lower lip. "Times are changing, Kate, and if we don't change with them, we'll be left behind."

Confused, Kate furrowed her eyebrows.

"Father and Mr. Stockton have become quite cordial over the past few months." Frederica's nostrils flared in pert confidence. "In fact, Father is going to help Mr. Stockton open a new wool mill a few miles to the west of Stockton Mill."

The meaning of her friend's words sank heavy and fast into Kate's soul. She turned her face into the gentle westward breeze to regain her composure. Frederica's father was her papa's biggest partner. They had worked together for as long as Kate could recall. Could Frederica be telling the truth?

"That is why I wanted to talk with you." Frederica fidgeted with the lacy cuff of her sleeve, suddenly intent upon smoothing nonexistent wrinkles. "Father says you and I are not to be friends anymore."

The words hit her as if she'd been struck in the stomach. Kate wrenched around to face her friend. "What? But why?"

Frederica fixed her dark gaze on the courtyard. "He says your father is dangerous."

"That's absurd!" She reached out to touch Frederica's arm, pulling her friend toward her. "Why will you not look at me?"

Frederica shook her head, her curls swinging with the movement. "Father thinks that Mr. Stockton's view on the future is prudent, and if we are to thrive, we must turn away from the way things are done and look for new methods."

Kate dropped her hand. "You mean the way *my* father does things."

Frederica's silence spoke louder than any words.

Escalating hurt slid into slow-burning frustration. "But surely you do not agree with him."

"It doesn't matter what I think." Frederica shrugged and finally looked at Kate. "Does it really matter what either one of us thinks?"

Hot tears welled in Kate's eyes at the thought of losing her one friend, but Frederica remained detached, her eyes dry as stones, her lips pressed in a firm line. Kate's arms felt too heavy to move, and their weight pulled her back against the bench.

After several moments, Frederica stood and swiped a wayward leaf from her gown before facing Kate. "I do love you, Katie, but my future cannot have you in it."

Her dearest friend spun on her heels and walked away.

Kate trembled. Her mind struggled to comprehend what had

just happened, and she looked back to the village square. Through a messy blur of tears she saw the Stocktons at the gate to Stockton Mill. How dare they have the nerve to stand there, laughing and chatting as if her world had not just crumbled beneath her. She clenched her stained fists at her sides. This man had already brought so much pain to her family. And now it was even more personal.

Unsure how to quell the anguish welling within her, Kate leapt up from the bench. She sprinted down the gravel road and over the stone bridge. She ignored how her too-tight boots pinched her feet with each footfall and how the breeze ripped her hair from its plait. Tears streamed down her cheeks as she raced past the entrances to Willford House and Stockton House until she finally arrived at Meadowvale Cottage's gate.

Breathless, she paused only long enough for the blistering within her chest to subside before she thrust open the wooden door, rushed through, and allowed it to slam closed behind her.

The sun drooped lower now, dissolving into the twinkling shimmer of purple dusk, and a sleepy ambience lingered over the silent courtyard. The men would have departed for a weavers' meeting, but Mother would be here.

Wobbly legs carried Kate to the dye house on the grounds' far end. She ducked beneath the lengths of wool drying on tenterhooks just outside the thatched-roof structure and sidestepped a bundle of freshly sheared wool. Steam rose from a large cauldron suspended above a flickering flame, adding to evening's already muggy clime. Inside the small stone outbuilding, another fire blazed in the grate, giving life to an even larger pot.

Mary Dearborne straightened from the pot as Kate entered, drawing a hand over her brow, streaking damp strands of dark hair across her forehead. "What's the matter, poppet?"

"Is it true?" Kate shot back, gritting her teeth and finding it difficult to control the timbre of her shaky voice. "About the Penningtons?"

Mother stared at her for several seconds, then her face softened and her shoulders slumped. "You've heard."

"It isn't fair." Kate's kid boots were heavy against the damp wood floor as she stomped even farther into the dye house. "Frederica says we can't be friends anymore. All because of the stupid mill."

Mother rested the dye stick on the side of a chair and wiped her hands on a piece of cloth tucked into her apron strings. "Mr. Pennington is doing what he believes to be best for his family. We cannot judge him for that."

"But he is a weaver. Like Papa." She folded her arms over her chest.

"Times are hard for everyone, dearest." Mother stepped away from the fire and approached Kate. "We are fortunate. We have our own sheep. We have food. We have this dye house. We even have our own spinning jennies, which many others cannot boast. We are comfortable, and for us, things are tolerable. But things have not been so easy for the Penningtons."

Kate pulled away when her mother moved to place a comforting arm around her shoulders. "But the Penningtons are our friends. How could they change, just like that?"

With a sigh Mother tilted her head to the side and pressed her lips together. She felt the same way—Kate knew she did. Her mother tried once again to wrap her arm around Kate.

This time Kate didn't pull away.

"We cannot control what others do. We can only control how we react to it. Being angry will only hurt you, not them."

Kate stamped her foot and stared into the fire.

Angry? Yes, she was angry. Angry with the stupid new mill that took the Penningtons away from them. Angry with Frederica for rejecting her. Angry with Mr. Stockton for opening the mill in the first place.

It was impossible not to be.

And she doubted she would ever be able to forgive them.

CHAPTER 1

January 1812
Amberdale, West Riding
Yorkshire, England

*H*enry Stockton pulled his mare to a stop at the crest of the stone bridge and tipped his wide-brimmed hat low over his forehead to guard against winter's icy blasts.

The small village of Amberdale spread out before him, slumbering in frozen stillness. Biting gusts swept down from the moorland and peppered the landscape with wet snowflakes, simultaneously obscuring the view and emphasizing its beauty.

While fighting on the Iberian Peninsula, he'd had days—months—when he wondered if he would ever again see Amberdale's rows of stone cottages or hear the resonant call of its hallowed church bells. But he was here now. And it was no dream.

Had it really been three years since he'd last set foot on Amberdale soil? Three years, two months, and one week, to be exact. And now, at least for him, the days of war and uncertainty were in the past. Surely the horrific memories would dissipate now that he'd returned to England's shores. His future stretched before him, fresh and unblemished as new-fallen snow, and he could forget the nightmare and focus on his family's wool mill.

He tapped his heels to the horse's sides and they ambled down the bridge. Perhaps he should have sent word of his impending arrival, but there had not been time. Impatience to return to his grandfather and sister had pushed him forward, and pausing to pen a missive would only result in delay.

He was about to turn off the bridge when a strange cry followed by a thud caught his attention. Before him, just to the left of the road, a woman clad in a cloak of deep red was climbing down from a donkey cart. A large bundle had fallen from the rickety vehicle onto the snowy ground behind her.

She bent and struggled to lift the wide parcel, only to have it fall forward again. The wind caught her hood and blew it backward as she leaned down a second time, sending chestnut curls whipping around her face. When the bundle slipped a third time, she gave her foot a little stomp and propped her hands on her hips.

A smile tweaked Henry's lip at the sight. Once at the road's edge, he dismounted, secured his horse to a tree trunk, and crossed to within a few feet of her. "May I be of assistance?"

She jumped and whirled around, her brilliant light-brown—no, hazel—eyes wide with surprise.

Henry drew a sharp breath as their gazes locked. Something was strangely familiar about the set of her full lips and her suspicious expression. The sight struck him like a long-forgotten memory struggling for recognition.

He extended his gloved hand to demonstrate that he was no threat. "I saw you were struggling, and . . ."

Silence hung heavy between them. Was she going to respond?

Her dark eyebrow arched and her chin lifted. "Thank you, sir, but I am quite capable."

He leaned closer. "I don't doubt your capability, but the weather is relentless, and I couldn't return home and be at peace if I thought you were still in this disdainful weather, wrestling this pack. So, if you'd allow me to help you, I'd consider it a great favor of easing my conscience."

Finally a grin curved her lips, leaving a small dimple at the corner of her mouth. Her gloved finger hooked a curl and tucked it behind her ear before she motioned to the canvas-wrapped package. "Very well then."

He crouched and wrapped his arms around the thick bundle, then stood. The wooden cart groaned and shifted when he dropped it onto the bed. "That should do it. If you hand me that rope there, I'll secure it."

This time she did not protest. She retrieved a length of rope and extended it toward him.

He threaded the cord through the rusted guides, tightened the slack, and knotted it in place. "There. That won't go anywhere." He pulled his hands back, and as he did, white and gray fibers clung to his dark gloves. He plucked them off, and the damp wind caught the airy strands and carried them away. He frowned. "Is this wool?"

She nodded. "It is."

He tilted his head and looked at her again, more closely this time. He had met many of the local weavers in the years before he left for war, and the longer he beheld her narrow face and slender nose, the more familiar they became. "Are you by chance taking it to Stockton Mill?"

She gave a little laugh, as if entertained by the idea, and shook her head. "No, no. I'm retrieving the wool on my father's behalf. He is a clothier."

"Oh. I've only recently returned to Amberdale, and I feel as if we've met at some point, but I can't place when."

After a sharp intake of breath, her words flew strong and sure, almost like an accusation. Her eyes narrowed. "I know who you are."

"You do?"

"You are Henry Stockton."

He was almost amused by the authority in her voice. "Guilty as charged. But you see, now I'm at a disadvantage. I don't know your name."

Instead of offering a smile of welcome, she glanced away, her nostrils flared. She wiped her hands on her cloak and turned. "I thank you for your assistance, sir."

Puzzled by her sudden change in demeanor, he trailed her as she rounded the cart. "But you didn't tell me your name."

She climbed into the seat, gathered the reins, and released the brake, ignoring him.

He thought she was going to drive down the path and vanish, like a vaporous dream, but then she paused and pivoted. The sharpness of her gaze pinned him to his spot. "I am Miss Dearborne. Perhaps you recall my papa, Silas Dearborne."

Dearborne.

Henry stiffened, and the imaginary thread of curiosity ensnaring him snapped.

He knew the name all too well.

She slapped the reins attached to the donkey, which started forward. The cart lurched and creaked as it crossed the bridge and disappeared down the lane edging the faded forest.

Henry released his clenched fist and once again secured his hat against the wind. The Stocktons and the Dearbornes had been ene-mies for as long as he could remember. He could only assume by her cold countenance that they still were.

Henry drew a deep breath, walked over to his horse, and mounted it, hoping his first interaction in Amberdale was not a harbinger of things to come.

Could her eyes be trusted?

Henry Stockton was *alive*.

Kate forced her gaze to remain on the narrow, frost-laden road ahead. Oh, this was news indeed.

Everyone—weavers and millworkers alike—had been surprised when Henry Stockton joined the army, and when news of his death arrived a couple of years later, a tremor shook the village.

That was several months past.

Clearly there had been some mistake.

At first she had not recognized him. Why would she? He'd not crossed her mind since she'd learned of his death, and she hadn't laid eyes on him in over three years. Even prior to that, they'd rarely spo-ken. Of course she'd seen him at church or the occasional village festival, but beyond that, Papa had shielded her from the Stockton clan at all costs.

Everything within Kate yearned to cast one more glance at the tall man who unknowingly exerted such a powerful hold over her family. She resisted and clutched her cape as the wind whipped through the woodland lining the road.

His presence was not to be taken lightly. As the heir to Stockton Mill, Henry Stockton had the power to affect commerce in the area.

If he was as ruthless and determined as his grandfather, it could be disastrous for them all.

She tugged the reins to the right to avoid a snowdrift. The drive to Meadowvale Cottage was not a long one. Normally she would have taken the main road through the village, but that path would have taken her past Stockton Mill and then Stockton House, and assuming Mr. Stockton would travel that route, Kate had changed her direction. She wanted to put as much distance between herself and the newcomer as possible until she knew more.

But as she approached Meadowvale, she frowned. Night had not yet fully fallen, and Papa was not expected back from the Leeds cloth hall for hours. Despite this fact, several saddled horses were clustered next to the stable, including her papa's dappled mare. Three wagons stood unattended, and heaps of covered cloth rested in the beds.

Kate urged the tired donkey to move faster.

No sounds came from the nearby weaving house, and none of the journeymen were visible through the dye house windows. Joseph, their young, freckle-faced stable hand, appeared in the courtyard, pitchfork in hand.

"Why are all these horses here?" she called.

"Weavers' meeting."

She glanced heavenward. Pewter clouds churned in a colorless sky, and snowflakes drifted on icy gusts. The men never returned from the cloth house this time of day, let alone in weather such as this. Normally they would find a room at the public house and wait until dawn's light. "I assumed they'd still be in Leeds."

"No, miss." He shrugged with a sniff. "Been here almost an hour."

After instructing the youth to unload the wool and tend to the donkey, Kate turned her attention to the snow-covered thatched cottage. Yellow light spilled out the windowpanes, and through the wavy glass she spied masculine silhouettes.

Something significant had happened to assemble such a large crowd. Had they learned of Mr. Stockton's return, as she just had?

Kate tightened her cloak around her and rounded the cottage to the kitchen entrance, keeping clear of the windows to avoid notice.

The door squeaked on its ancient hinges as she entered. Betsy, their maid, and Delilah, the wife of one of her papa's journeymen, huddled next to the door frame, listening.

Kate shrugged her crimson cloak from her shoulders, shook off the snow, and hung it on a nearby peg. "What's happening?"

Betsy held a slender finger to her lips for silence, fixed dark eyes on Kate, and leaned close. "Burnes and Dolten sent word with a messenger that they'd no longer conduct business in the cloth halls and that all cloth would be purchased directly from the mills."

"What?" Dread sank like a stone in the pit of Kate's stomach. This rumor had been swirling for weeks, and now it seemed to have come to pass. Competing with the mills' volume and pricing was already difficult, and the cloth halls had been their only opportunity to display the quality of their product. No wonder the tones projecting from the drawing room were so terse. "Did they say which mill owners they would be working with?"

"Not specifically, but I think we can all guess who they are referring to."

Kate bit her lower lip.

William Stockton.

Not only did he own Stockton Mill, but he was part owner of at least half a dozen more.

Kate tugged the string behind her back and released her work apron from her waist. She tossed the garment on a nearby chair and smoothed a few clinging woolen fibers from the faded blue linen of her gown. She would not stand here in the kitchen eavesdropping. She was a weaver, just like the men in the drawing room, was she not?

She eased the door open and slid into the crowded space. The scents of cold and the outdoors clung to the crowd and mingled with the wood smoke puffing from the hearth. Silas Dearborne stood atop an overturned crate at the chamber's front. Despite winter's ever-present chill, he'd discarded his coat. His striped cotton waistcoat hugged his thick, barrel chest, and his sleeves were rolled to his elbows, displaying his sinewy forearms.

Papa's full, whiskered cheeks were flushed, moisture dotted his wide brow. "We must come to terms with Burnes and Dolten's defection. Whitby just received confirmation from a reliable source that they signed an agreement to purchase broadcloth directly from Stockton, Pennington, and Appleton Mills."

Kate slid against the back wall near the stone mantelpiece and scanned the men's faces. Most she knew. A few she did not. But what she did know was that these men made their living by wool—and they all detested the Stockton name.

Her father's gritty voice intensified. "I speak for all of us when I say this has gone on long enough. William Stockton must be stopped. I'll not stand by and see the life we've all toiled for dissolve into meaningless bedlam."

All around her, weavers, shearmen, and carders nodded in agreement. Her papa raised his hands, silencing the whispers racing around the room. "If Burnes and Dolten have made this deal public, we'd all be fools to think other buyers will not follow suit. The cloth hall has been a sacred place for generations. But now buyers are dwindling. They've been seduced by the mill owners and their promise of cheap prices for poorly crafted material. Men, they are stealing food from your tables and work from your hands. Are you going to allow them to plunder your livelihood? Your heritage?"

"But what can be done?" shouted a raspy voice from the far side of the room.

"Plenty." Papa pointed a thick finger at Thomas Crater. "And something *must* be done. We are stronger, louder, and more effective if we band together."

A deeper voice echoed from the corner near the door. "Word is Stockton's going to install gig mills at his factories. This true?"

A fresh rush of chatter rippled through the room.

"I heard the same." Mr. Wooden, a short, stocky man, stepped forward, his floppy hat in his hands, his shabby gray coat hanging askew on his shoulders. "I heard tell that one man and one lad can do in a single day what it takes twenty-eight shearmen to do. Twenty-eight! Recall the agreement we struck with Stockton two years ago? He said he'd not deny the local shearmen work as long as we didn't demand a wage increase. We've honored the bargain, yet he goes against his word time and time again. He values money over his neighbor, refusing to aid the men whose blood and sweat built the very village over which he lords."

The growing fervor incited alarm within Kate's chest. She'd witnessed several heated weavers' meetings, but the men's frenzied state was unlike any she'd seen. She swallowed hard. As of yet they didn't seem to be aware of Henry Stockton's return, otherwise that topic would certainly dominate the conversation.

As usual, her father's authoritative tone commanded attention amid chaos. "Gentlemen. We must remember, the law is no longer on our side. Mr. Stockton is well within his rights to employ any machine he chooses to make his cloth."

The grumbling softened, but Mr. Wooden persisted. "It's morally wrong, and every man drawing breath here knows it. The men he employs to run the looms are barely qualified to card wool, and then he pays honest, trained weavers who have dedicated their waking hours to the betterment of the field next to naught. It's disgusting how he forces young people from their homes, when they should be learning alongside their parents, and puts them to work in such degradation. He encourages men to fraternize with unmarried women. It's not decent. Pity the man who must sell his soul! I'd sooner die than see my son or daughter work in such a den of iniquity."

The muttering rose, but then her papa raised his hand yet again and the room fell silent. "I don't agree with it, gentlemen. I don't know many upstanding men who would. Let the Stocktons and Penningtons of the county bring in their gig mills. Let them see what will happen when they turn their backs on their communities. Ah yes. Let them come. We'll be waiting for them. Are the shearmen not our brothers?" Papa balled his fist and thrust it into the air. "As long as there is breath in my lungs and strength in my arms, I'll fight for what's mine and the future of all we hold dear.

"You have my pledge," Papa continued, his face shaking, "I will not rest until every weaver, shearman, and carder alike is given due respect. The mill owners and merchants may be winning this battle, but the war is still undecided."

Without warning the main cottage door flung wide and its heavy, wooden bulk slammed against the plaster wall. Jimmy Taylor, a weaver's son, filled the door frame. Black eyes wide, he swiped his slouched felt hat from his dark head and gasped for the air to support his words. "He's back! Henry Stockton's back from the grave!"

Papa pushed his way through the crowd until he towered over the youth. "Henry Stockton is dead. Killed in the war."

"No, he's not. He's not! I saw 'im with me own eyes. He rode right up to Stockton House, pushed open the gate, and headed inside. He walked with a limp, but he was as real as any man standing here."

Pandemonium exploded. Voices, anger, and frustration echoed from the ceiling's low beams.

Papa jumped back on the crate. "Men, calm yourselves. Time will reveal all, but for now, let's not forget what needs to be done."

Kate's breath seized when her papa caught sight of her.

His thick eyebrows rose and he pointed at her. "Katie girl, go now, fetch the ale. Let this be the night we remember as one when we toasted to unity. To craftsmanship. To tradition. To the future."

CHAPTER 2

*T*he Dearborne name was one Henry associated with nuisance and mischief. Yet Miss Dearborne seemed to be neither.

The contemplation nagged Henry as he guided his mare through Amberdale's familiar cobbled street toward the north bridge. He shrugged off his interest in the odd interaction as that of a man who had not been in the company of ladies for years.

He continued down the empty street past one familiar building after another: the butcher, the grocer, the apothecary. Gold light glowed through the windows of the town's public house. Even though these buildings warmed his memory, one building mattered to him most.

As he rounded the church's courtyard, he saw it: Stockton Mill.

His breath suspended at the sight, and Henry slowed his horse. He'd almost forgotten how majestic—and foreboding—it was. The massive stone building stretched three stories above the churchyard's bare trees. Years of soot clung to the structure's textured walls, and large, symmetrical leaded windows reflected the faded sky's pale light. Smoke puffing from the outbuildings and nearby cottages mingled with the low-hanging fog shrouding all the grounds in shades of silver. Save for the sound of the river rushing behind the mill and the occasional winter bird flitting overhead, the grounds were quiet.

But even in the establishment's hushed state, memories lurked behind the trees and crept amidst the rows of modest thatched cottages. Not a day had passed when he did not think about this structure and ponder his future with it. As Henry was growing up, the mill and its workings had always been his grandfather's passion, not his. But time and experience changed all. The sooner he could lose himself in the mill's business and forget the horrors of war, the better off he would be.

Henry tugged the reins to the left, and with a click of his tongue and the flick of his heel he urged his horse into a trot. The horse's hooves clopped heavily over the stone north bridge. The sights of the village faded into the grays and browns of the wooded landscape. As each stride took him closer to Stockton House, his chest tightened. How long had he waited for this? How many nights had thoughts of this very moment occupied his dreams?

Boyhood memories flashed and groaned as he drew to a stop in front of the iron gate separating Stockton House from the public road. Some of those memories were pleasant, some not, but his grandfather, his sister, Mollie, and Mr. and Mrs. Figgs would all be within those ancient walls. It no longer mattered what he had done or what he had seen in the three years that had separated him from what he held dear. What mattered now was resuming life.

Stones and bits of ice crunched beneath his top boots as he slid from the saddle and pushed open the gate. Clouds hung low over Stockton House's gray gabled roof, and an eerie mist covered the still grounds. Stockton House's pale stones blended in with the white snow, voiding the scene of life, yet yellow light winking from the windows on the lower level stood testament to activity, and to his left, an unseen horse whinnied in the stable.

As he led his horse through the opening, overgrown shrubbery scratched against his buckskin breeches. He frowned. Normally a single branch would never be out of place on Stockton grounds, but as he studied the landscape, much of it appeared unattended.

Once at the main door, Henry did not knock. He pushed open the heavy door and stepped inside. Anticipation's warmth rushed him in the cool darkness, and he stood still for several moments, listening to the familiar sounds—a distant fire's crackling, the shuffling of paper, Mrs. Figgs's off-key singing echoing from a distant chamber. Henry placed his satchel on a side table against the wall and followed the sounds to the door of his grandfather's study. He didn't know why he should be nervous, but as he approached the space, a numb weakness threatened his fortitude.

Henry turned the corner. One look confirmed that everything was the same as when he'd left. Mint's and brandy's unmistakable scents tickled his nose. The fire popped and hissed in the grate, bathing the room's contents in a flickering orange light. Ancient swords still crossed above the mantel, and heavy oak bookcases still flanked the room's two curtained windows. Even the tall clock stationed against the back wall ticked its predictable methodic cadence.

But it was not the overflowing bookshelves or the unchanged decor that captured Henry's attention. It was the man positioned behind the mahogany desk.

Grandfather.

"I'll take no brandy this evening, Figgs." The older man did not look up from the letter he was writing. "Bring me my pipe, will you?"

Henry made no motion. Grandfather clearly thought him to be the butler.

"Did you hear me? I said—" Grandfather jerked his head up.

They stared at one another, both frozen in the significance of the moment.

Henry had expected his grandfather to be pleased at his return. Instead, the older man's mouth dropped. Confusion colored his face, which deepened to a crimson red before blanching to deathly white.

An odd welcome, but his grandfather was known for his quirky manners and peculiar tendencies. It was not his habit to show affection. But even armed with this knowledge, Henry had expected a smile at least.

"Grandfather."

He dropped his quill, nearly upsetting the ink pot.

When Grandfather made no other movement, said nothing further, Henry shifted his weight from one foot to the other. This was odd indeed. He managed, "Are you well?"

But still Grandfather sat motionless. He stared at Henry as if he were a ghost—a vaporous figure returned from the grave. The clock's ticking, which moments ago had seemed welcoming and familiar, now threatened. Henry stepped farther into the room.

Grandfather inched back, the leather of his desk chair squeaking in protest at the motion. He slowly removed his wire-rimmed spectacles. "You—you're alive."

"Of course I am." A huff rushed from Henry's lips at the cold greeting. "Very much so."

"But you've been reported dead. Killed in action during a battle on the Peninsula. Months and months ago."

The hairs on the back of Henry's neck prickled. There had been times over the past few years he had *felt* dead, lifeless. But now his grandfather's expression pushed him back to a place of empty dread. "What?"

"Yes, yes, yes." Grandfather nodded, his words rushing like the water from the mill's waterwheel, faster with each utterance. "Three months ago we received word of your death. Look." With sudden energy he leapt from the chair, yanked the desk drawer open with a trembling hand, retrieved a newspaper, and thrust it toward Henry. "Read for yourself."

Henry arched his eyebrow and lunged to catch the paper as it began to drop to the Persian rug beneath his feet. He scanned it hungrily, as if it contained the priceless antidote to a deathly poison. Sure enough, his name was at the top of the second column of the list of the dead.

It was his turn for his motions to slow and his face to heat in shock. "There was some mistake, clearly. Perhaps I should have been listed among the missing. But the dead, no."

Grandfather was close now, close enough that if he wanted to, he could reach out and embrace Henry. Instead, he stood as unmoving as a statue. The fire's intrusive crackling echoed in the otherwise silent chamber. Henry suspended his breath under the uncomfortable scrutiny.

Moisture gathered in Grandfather's reddening eyes. His whiskered chin trembled.

Relieved at the subtle change in his demeanor, Henry said, "Regardless of what has been reported, I'm home now. I'm very happy to be, and I don't wish to leave again."

As if he suddenly realized Henry really was home and not a figment of his imagination, color rushed to Grandfather's face, and a gradual smile cracked his heavy countenance. "My boy, home! Why did you not send word instead of stealing into the house like a vagabond?"

"There wasn't time. As soon as I set foot on English soil and was free to do as I like, I bought a horse and departed for Amberdale."

Henry handed the newspaper back to his grandfather, who folded it crisply and returned it to the drawer. "So you were missing, then?"

"Hmm?"

"You said you should have been listed among the missing."

Henry stiffened at the question and the memory it evoked. "Briefly, but that story can wait for another time. I'd rather see Mollie. Where is she?"

Grandfather closed the drawer and straightened, then adjusted the pristinely tied cravat at his neck. "Your sister is in London with your aunt."

Disappointment surged through Henry. "You can't be serious. I just traveled by way of London to get here. What is she doing there?"

His grandfather motioned to the side table, lifted the glass decanter, and pulled the stopper. He poured himself a dram and indulged in a long swig. "Times have grown dark. It pains me to say so, but where your sister is concerned, all is bleak."

A sinking sensation commandeered Henry's thoughts. He'd not been home a quarter of an hour, and already nothing was as he antic-ipated. "Is she all right?"

Grandfather lifted the decanter and studied its intricately cut glass before returning it to the table. "I wish I could give you happy news of your sister, but it shames me to tell you that she has disgraced herself in the vilest of manners."

Mollie had always been spontaneous and a bit rebellious, but he couldn't imagine what she could have done to cause such a reaction. He stifled a huff. "I doubt that."

"She is with child."

Henry's smile faded. The words echoed in the room as if they had been shouted. Refusing to jump to a conclusion, he shook the negative assumption from his mind. "When did she marry?"

"Therein lies the problem." Grandfather drew a sharp intake of breath through his nose. "She is unmarried."

Mollie unwed and with child? Henry studied his grandfather's face, seeking a sign of jest or mistake. Grandfather was not one prone to telling tales. Guilt quickly replaced his shock. Whatever had transpired, Henry should have been here to protect her. Questions bombarded him. "But who? When?"

Grandfather's response came painfully slow. "Time and time again I asked those very questions. She would give no answers, not to me, your aunt, or anyone. Oh, you know Mollie, headstrong and vain. I had no choice but to send her to her aunt's until this business is past."

Henry pushed his fingers through his hair. If he had been here, she would have confided in him. He knew it. "Did she desire to go to London?"

"Nay. She vehemently protested the idea, but she could hardly remain in Amberdale and become the source of gossip for every idle tongue. We've more than enough to deal with, what with the mill in its current state. Adding your sister's indiscretion to our list of burdens isn't an option. Mollie will give birth to the child, send it away, and then and only then, she can return to Stockton House. As of yet, not a whiff of scandal has reached Amberdale's perimeter. If we're lucky we'll all come out of this unscathed."

An argument balanced on Henry's tongue. Regardless of his sister's action, he refused to see her as a source of shame. He was about to say as much when the sharp sound of clattering silver and shattering glass exploded, followed by a cry.

Henry whirled around.

Mrs. Figgs, their family's housekeeper, stood in the doorway, a mess of broken china and an overturned silver tray piled at her feet.

Wiry white hair poked from the confines of her cap. Her long, bony fingers covered most of her face, with the exception of her wide gray eyes.

They stared at each other for several moments.

This woman had been more like a mother than a servant. She'd reprimanded him as a boy when necessary. Comforted him when there was no one else to do so. Grandfather may have taught him about business, but Mrs. Figgs had taught him about life.

She dropped her hands. "A ghost, then. You must be a ghost."

A smile tugged his lips. "Come now, Mrs. Figgs. You know I don't believe in ghosts."

She lifted her black skirt, stepped over the debris, and stopped inches in front of him—so close that he could smell the scent of garlic that clung to her from the kitchen.

She poked his arm with a thin finger. Then poked him again. "You, you are—?" She leaned back and assessed him, as if searching for a sign of harm.

His chest tightened at the gesture. "I'm as alive as I can be."

She clicked her tongue and gave her head a sharp shake. "So thin! When did this happen? Have you not been eating?"

"Yes, I've eaten." He chuckled, comforted by the fact that her desire to care for him clearly had resumed. There was no reason to tell her the truth, of long days with little more than a morsel of bread or the occasional bit of meat when one of the soldiers managed to trap a rabbit. "But I wouldn't turn away one of your raspberry jam tarts."

Tears filled her pale eyes. "I thought I'd never see you again, and here you are, plain as day. You are a sight to see." She sniffed and wiped her nose with the back of her hand before she propped her hands on her hips. "Mercy, but look at you. Naught but skin and bones. I'll fatten you right up. And your coat! I never saw the like for its shab-biness. Fortunately we know where we can get the finest broadcloth in the area."

He no longer had to force a smile. "I don't know what I did all those years without you to take care of me."

She beamed under the praise. "Well, you're home. And scrawny or not, that is all that matters. It's a miracle, that's what it is. And happy I am to see you here."

"And I'm happy to see you."

She wrapped her arms around his torso, and he returned the sweet embrace. The top of her faded head did not even reach his shoulders, yet she hugged him with all the tenderness of a mother clinging to her child.

It had been years since another person touched him with any sort of affection. He'd been beaten. Shot at. He'd even been stabbed in the thigh. The resulting limp—albeit slight—that now accompanied his every move would serve as a constant reminder. But at the present moment, the compassionate embrace erased, for just a moment, the weight of the memories clinging to him.

After endless days and countless nights, he was home with people who cared about him. He was safe. Henry could put down his weapon without fear of attack or injury.

He was home.

CHAPTER 3

ate stifled a yawn and tightened her grip on the woolen shawl circling her shoulders as the last weaver exited the parlor. She cast a glance toward the mantel clock as it chimed the midnight hour. The impromptu meeting had stretched much later than she'd anticipated, but with such weighty topics to discuss, Kate was glad she had been allowed to remain. Normally all women were shooed away from such meetings.

The tallow candles now drooped, and the fire hissed low. Her papa and John Whitby, his lead journeyman, were seated by the waning fire, their heads bent toward each other in earnest conversation.

She pressed the back of her hand to her mouth to hide yet another yawn. She was tired. No doubt the men were tired. But there would be little rest at Meadowvale Cottage tonight.

Kate stood from where she was sitting near the back entrance and ducked into the kitchen. "Betsy, set out the stew, will you?" She retrieved two pewter mugs from the cupboard and a jug of ale before she returned to the drawing room.

"Papa, John." She approached them by the hearth. "Come to the table. Betsy has kept the stew warm. You must be famished."

Papa heaved a deep sigh, raked his fingers through his thick gray hair, and pushed his spectacles up on his nose. Initially she thought he would dismiss her suggestion, but then he stood and took two steps toward her as his mouth eased into a weary smile. He cupped her cheeks with his rough hands, tilted her head forward, and kissed the crown of her hair, just as he had done since she was little. "That's my girl. What would this old man do without you to care for him?"

Without waiting for an answer to his question, he moved to the table, his eyes red-rimmed and his coat wrinkled, and was seated. John, his youngest but most trusted journeyman, joined him.

Kate lifted the jug of ale to pour it, but her actions slowed as her father's words met her ears.

"I'll leave for Leeds at dawn's light." His words were directed to John, not her. "The clothiers' society there can help us with this situation."

"Never would have guessed that young Stockton would return." John, who was only six years her senior, spoke as if he were an old man instead of a young journeyman still finding his place in the industry. He cocked his head and huffed. "The Stocktons are the luckiest fellows who ever walked the earth."

Papa nodded. "We'll need a bit of luck of our own, the way things are going. That's why I'm headed to Leeds." He leaned back so Kate could fill his mug. "The weavers to the south are fighting a battle of their own. Even so, they may be able to offer support."

Kate moved to pour ale for John.

John offered her a half smile of appreciation before returning his attention to her father. "Are they the ones who broke the gig mills in Sheffield a few months ago?"

"Of course no one will say for sure, but who else could it be? Their actions are a bit drastic for my taste. I've no desire for violence, as I've told you. But they've traversed this ground before. If the gig mills do arrive, all the shearmen in the area may need to band together to refuse work in order for Stockton and the men like him to know we are serious, and we might need the support of our brothers in the south—financial or otherwise."

Kate placed the jug in the center of the rough wooden table and sat in the empty chair between them. "How long do you think you will be gone?"

"Hard to tell." Papa rubbed his big hand against his whiskered cheek before he spooned the stew into his mouth. "Hopefully no more than a few days."

She gave a firm nod. "I will instruct the rest of the men about tomorrow. I'll take care of everything while you are gone. You needn't worry about a thing."

Her father did not respond. His eyes flicked to John before looking to his stew.

Kate followed his glance. A strange, almost guilty shadow tightened John's normally relaxed expression, and he studied his stew and poked at the carrots with his spoon.

They knew something she did not.

"What?" she demanded, leaning her elbows on the worn table.

Papa cleared his throat. "Don't fret yourself with the working of the looms. John will tend to the running of things in my stead."

She blinked. Was he serious? She was a Dearborne, and as such should be in charge when her father was out of town, as she had been in the past.

But his drawn eyebrows and pale complexion suggested he was in no humor for arguing.

Then a realization settled.

Papa had chosen John over her. Again.

"But, Papa, are you certain? It is no trouble, really. I only want to help you."

"You can be most helpful by tending to things in the cottage." Papa wiped his mouth with his napkin and then, as an afterthought, added, "And the dye house, of course."

Anger warmed her. It was their age-old disagreement. Papa wanted her to be a lady—to remain indoors and sew, knit. Any responsibility she shared regarding their business was limited to the dye house.

She wanted something entirely different.

She'd spent her life around looms, spinning jennies and mules, dyes, sheep, and broadcloth. It was as much a part of her as the color of her hair and the hue of her eyes. Especially after her mother's death nearly a decade ago, she had been absorbed into this world more by survival than desire. The older she grew, the more Papa tried to force her into a role she was not willing to fill. Even after her brother Charles had left to go work at Stockton Mill, she thought, for a brief time, that her father would have a change of heart. But his mind was set.

John, as if sensing the mounting frustration, stood. "I'm going to make sure the sheep are bedded down."

After the door closed behind him, Papa angled himself toward her. "I know you want to help. You're not like most young women, and glad I am for it. I can hardly stand silly girls who care only for gowns and trimmings. But you need not muddle your thoughts with the day-to-day order of things. Everything I have built has been to provide for you, not be a burden to you."

"But I—"

"Quiet, and listen to me." He pinned her with his gray-eyed stare, forbidding her to make even a peep. "I had built this livelihood for your brother, but he left us. This work was never intended to be yours. It was intended to provide your dowry. Times have changed and they are dire. Now more than ever, you must know your role."

"But I enjoy it, Papa. Does that count for nothing? If it weren't for my work, what would I do? You said so yourself that I would never be content confined in the cottage with needlework all day."

He chuckled. "No, and God save us all from your wrath if ever that fate should befall you. But it's time for you to consider other things, at least until the weaving landscape settles. John will oversee the men in my stead. So don't give him or me trouble. All will be well, you'll see."

She bit back her retort—and her hurt. Papa loved her, in his own way, she knew. But she would never be her brother; she would never be a boy. And that alone was an inexcusable offense.

As per his habit, her father signaled the end of the topic by switching to another. "Did you finish the dyeing?"

She swallowed hard. "The indigo is done and drying. I just removed it from the dye wash earlier this afternoon. I'll finish the scarlet tomorrow."

"Good girl. At least one positive thing came of today's trip to the cloth hall. Trent Riley expressed interest in the indigo. He said he heard of the superior saturation. I intend to show him a swatch next week. If he likes it, it could be a nice little sale for us."

"Perhaps I should go with you to the cloth hall. I could answer any questions he might have. I could—"

"The cloth hall is no place for a woman. I'd not be able to tend to business for fear of your safety."

"But John and Benjamin would be there to keep me company, and I—"

He raised his hand. "No."

"Papa, I—"

"Don't argue with me. I've no humor for it. The cloth hall is for men. You're a *lady*."

She lowered her eyes to hide her disappointment. A lady indeed. Kate had no desire to pick a fight with her father, especially in his state. But it hardly seemed fair. She was a woman of one and twenty, and whether her father liked to admit it or not, she had spent her entire life working the wool. Dyeing it, carding it. She knew the process better than she knew how to do anything else.

She stood from the stool and retrieved his pipe from the mantelpiece and his pouch of tobacco. He'd want it after he finished his meal.

He tilted his head and smiled as she set it next to his bowl of stew. "Ah, now there. How is it that you're so good to me?"

She nodded toward his empty mug. "Would you like some more ale?"

"No, no, child. I have all I need. Come. Sit with me. Keep your old father company."

She resumed her seat at the table. For a moment all seemed as it always was, and as long as she let the topic of her helping at the cloth hall or overseeing the looms drop, all would stay well. The fire crackled in the grate. The clock ticked off the seconds. The winter wind rattled the windows in their casings. She relaxed her shoulders.

After several moments of silence while he lit his pipe, he spoke and reached out his hand, letting it hover several feet off the floor. "Do you remember when you were this high, how you would sit at my knee each night?"

She gave a little laugh. "Yes, and I remember how you always smoked that very pipe."

He chuckled. "Your mother didn't like the smell."

"It never bothered me. Not really."

The bittersweet memory tugged at her. How different their home had been at that time. It had been just her, Papa, Mother, and Charles. Their family was small, but they had been happy. Her papa had been but a journeyman and worked for a clothier on the far side of the meadow. His goal had been to better himself, and he worked toward his goal night and day.

Now he was a master clothier in his own right, respected and revered by other weavers. Three journeymen called Meadowvale their home—two of whom lived in cottages with their wives on the edge of the property and John, a bachelor, who lived in a room off the back of the kitchen. With the addition of a handful of servants, their lives couldn't be further from how they had been those years ago. But in quiet evenings like this, it seemed that she could slip back to a happier time.

She shifted uncomfortably in her seat as the memory of her interaction with Henry Stockton flashed through her mind. She had to tell her father what had happened earlier, for if he found out from another source, he would no doubt be angry.

She toyed with the fringe on her shawl. "I saw Henry Stockton on the road earlier today. I didn't have a chance to tell you before Jimmy came in."

Her papa's head snapped up. A scowl darkened his weathered face. "Why did you not say as much?"

"You were busy, with the weavers."

He lowered his pipe, eyes boring into hers. "Did you speak with him?"

She shifted. "Just in passing."

His words rushed out. "Best to stay away from him, lass."

She paused for several moments and then lowered her voice. "I will. But do you think things might change once he's in charge of the mill? He's not his grandfather. He could be different."

"No." Her father's response came sure and swift. "He has Stockton blood running through his veins. That is all you need know of the scoundrel. I'll hear no more on the topic."

In a sudden turn, his voice softened. "You look like your mother, sitting just so. I'm a lucky man, I am. I dread the day when a man comes to ask for your hand and takes you away from me."

"Oh, Papa." She laughed at the ludicrousness of it. "You needn't worry about that for a long, long time."

"I wouldn't be so certain." He pointed his pipe in her direction. "You've become quite a bonny thing, and I'm hardly the only one to notice. You must consider these things. I'll not be here forever. I need to see you settled if I'm ever to rest easy again."

"I'll not hear of you dying." She patted the rough broadcloth of his coat's sleeve. "Please don't speak of it."

"Not speaking of it doesn't make it any less real. I don't jest, Katie."

She settled back in her chair and thoughtfully wound a long, loose lock of hair around one of her fingers. "But what if the man I fall in love with is not a weaver?"

"Love—bah." He harrumphed. "Best to stay with your own people."

Her own people.

She knew what her father meant—a weaver.

He took a swig of his ale, then covered her hand with his calloused one. "Love is all fine and good, but you cannot count on love, a fickle fancy, to help you find the most secure situation. This life is uncertain. Do you not witness that every day? Security first. Happiness second."

She sobered and studied the indigo marring her fingernails.

"Weaving." His voice rose passionately, as it had when he was addressing the weavers. "It's in your blood. That's why it's so important that you find yourself a good weaver with a decent head on his shoulders. One who will work hard to provide for you, keep you safe, and preserve our way of life."

"I am safe, Papa." Her voice sounded small.

"Aye, safe today, but what of tomorrow? And the day after that? Every day men like the Stocktons are trying to prevail and force change. No. You will find a weaver. I need to know you are cared for."

She swallowed and forced a smile. "Perhaps all that will happen in good time, but you needn't worry. Besides, Charles would never turn me out in the cold."

Her father's face tightened, as if she referred to a monster instead of his own son. "Don't speak of him in this house."

Her heart squeezed within her. "But Charles is not a bad sort. He made a different decision than you did, 'tis all."

"Loyalty, girl. Loyalty is what keeps friends as friends and holds families together. Where would any of us be without remaining true to those who helped us along the way? I brought that boy up in the trade with sound values and the best education. He knows as much as I know about weaving, and what did he do? Took that information and went to work for a man who puts profits above people."

Kate winced inwardly. Would she ever be able to speak of her brother without inciting such anger? "But he's your son. Surely there will come a time when we can all put our differences aside and—"

"Stop, Katie. Your brother made his choice the day he decided to turn his back on our way of life and accepted the position at Stockton Mill. He betrayed everything our family stood for. And I will never forget it."

38

CHAPTER 4

$\mathscr{B}$y the time Henry arrived at church the next morning, the news that he was indeed alive—coupled with the important detail of his return—had catapulted through the village. Half of the people he'd encountered on the way in had welcomed him and smiled as they shook his hand. The other half glared at him, as if he alone were personally responsible for every ill that befell Amberdale. And now as he sat, stiff and straight, in the Stockton family pew, the weight of their questioning stares and hushed whispers pinned him to his spot.

The ancient oak pew creaked as Grandfather leaned close and lowered his voice. "I know you wanted to remain abed, but are you not glad you attended? See how everyone has welcomed you home?"

Henry cut his eyes toward the sea of people filling the pews. As happy as he was to be home, it still felt unbelievable after years of extreme environments, and the attention—both positive and negative—added to his skepticism. He kept his tone light and forced a smile. "Far be it from me to break your longstanding rule."

Grandfather chuckled. "Ah yes. You remember. Do you disagree that every family member and every Stockton House servant should be at church on Sunday morning?"

"No, sir. I don't disagree."

Even in a whisper, Grandfather's voice reeked of authority. "As leaders in this community, we must set an example for those whom we employ."

Come rain, sun, snow, or fog, every Sunday the entire Stockton household, from master to kitchen maid, attended church. Grandfather had demanded it for as long as Henry could remember. Even now, his grandfather was settled beside him in the family box, his expression stoic, his gaze fixed on the prayer book in his hand.

One important person was absent from the gathering, however. Henry glanced at the empty spot next to him where Mollie should be seated.

He was uncomfortable with her absence. He was even more uncomfortable with the situation she was in. Was she frightened? Did she feel alone? Abandoned? As soon as it made sense, he'd travel back to London and see her. Regardless of her situation, he'd not turn his back on her.

A sudden commotion and feminine voices, combined with Grandfather's sharp elbow jabbing his ribs, drew Henry's attention.

"Ah, there they are." Grandfather's voice rasped low. "I sent word last night letting them know of your return."

Squat, round Arthur Pennington entered through the church's arched entrance with his wife on his arm. Henry raised an eyebrow at the man's attire. The button of his checked silk waistcoat complained against the pressure of his round belly, and his white stockings and buckled shoes were altogether inappropriate, considering the inches of snow on the ground.

Nevertheless, it was not Mr. Pennington, nor his jewel-encrusted wife, who piqued Henry's interest. His daughters—one in particular— drew his eye. Miss Frederica Pennington stepped from behind her father into the dimly lit church, handed her gloves to her mother, and lowered her cloak's hood.

She had not changed a great deal in the previous three years, not really. She was slightly taller than he recalled, and her meticulously curled golden hair was gathered at the base of her neck and held in place by a pearl-laden ribbon. Having just come in from the cold, she had bright-pink cheeks, and her large brown eyes were alert and glittering—just as he remembered.

"So it *is* true." Arthur Pennington extended his pudgy hand in greeting as he rushed toward Henry. "I wasn't sure if I could trust my eyes when I read your grandfather's note, but here you are, in the flesh." Face beaming, he clamped his other hand on Henry's shoulder and squeezed. "Egad, it's good to see you."

Henry stood, shook the man's outstretched hand, and returned the smile. "And you, sir." He lifted his gaze past Pennington's shoulder, to where his wife and daughters were standing, and bowed.

The ladies curtsied.

Mr. Pennington snatched his attention. "We've much to catch up on, that's certain. But the service is about to start. We'll speak afterward, but I insist you join us at Briarton House this afternoon."

Henry grinned and caught another glimpse of Miss Pennington. How could he decline? "I look forward to it."

The Penningtons were seated just ahead of him in their family box. As the service began, Grandfather leaned toward him and whispered, "Now there, I'm not the only one in Amberdale happy to welcome you home. I daresay Miss Pennington agrees." He indulged in a knowing chuckle.

Henry followed his gaze to the eldest Pennington daughter. She smiled at something her sister said and flicked a glance back in his direction before turning her attention to the vicar.

He and Frederica had been friends since he first arrived in Amberdale all those years ago. But a friendship it had always been— nothing more. Despite this innocent relationship, Grandfather had always been vocal about the advantages of a matrimonial union between the two families. He'd mentioned it twice since Henry's return, and he was certain he'd not heard the last on the topic.

Henry cleared his throat and looked around once more. Many of the parishioners had lost interest in him and now were focused on the sermon, but as he was about to face the front, someone caught his eye.

Miss Dearborne.

She was seated perpendicular to him and he could only see her profile, but the gentle yet unmistakable sloop of her small nose drew him in. She wore the same red cloak she had worn the previous day and was seated between another woman and a man who shared her likeness.

The seconds ticked past. He must have been staring. Miss Dearborne shifted slightly, and their gazes met. Her cool, hazel eyes narrowed and lingered on him for several seconds before returning to the vicar. She offered no warm smile like Frederica, and her brief stare was as icy as the frozen graveyard outside the stained glass windows.

Henry released his breath and turned forward. Melancholy crept in like an uninvited guest, nullifying the sense of belonging that had entered with the Penningtons. His world had changed—arguably for the better—in a single day. He was home again, but with that came the realization that even though some welcomed him with open arms, this was not as inviting a place as he had thought.

A strange panic tightened his stomach. His usual routine was already resuming, so why was he so uncomfortable? The minutes and hours ticked on as if the war had never happened. As if he had not seen the horrors of inflicting harm on another in the name of survival or heard the pain of men dying.

He tried to focus on the vicar's words, but his mind focused on the past. He wanted to forget it, but doubted he ever would.

At the conclusion of the service, Kate and her brother stood outside of the church, waiting for her friend Jane Abbott to exit.

Kate tightened her cloak around her shoulders and stepped closer to Charles. Since their father did not permit him to step on Meadowvale property, she cherished their interactions, even if they were just at church.

She leaned closer to be heard above the wind's persistent howl. "So many people are here today."

Charles chuckled, his light-brown eyes wide with amusement. "No doubt Stockton's mysterious return has something to do with it. It's all anyone's talked about since he was spotted last night. Isn't that amazing? All these months we believed him dead, and then one day he's here, walking among us, like a ghost brought back to life."

While Kate certainly did not wish the man dead, she did not share her brother's joy at his return. She folded her arms within her cloak and followed his gaze to a cluster of other young men who worked at Stockton Mill. "You mustn't feel as if you need to stay and entertain me, Charles. Jane will be out soon enough. If you want to join your friends, please do not refrain on my account."

A teasing smile twitched his lips. "I know that tone. I know it well. You're sour."

"I'm not sour."

"You are." He nudged her with his elbow. "Stockton's return

has got you on edge, and you can barely contain yourself. You are a horrible liar and never could fool me."

She gave a half smile at her brother's customary playfulness and eased her shoulders. "It is just that a great deal of uncertainty comes with his return. At least for *us*."

At the subtle reference to their father, Charles's smile faded.

The crowd shifted, and Kate spotted Henry Stockton clad in winter shades of black, gray, and brown. A straight black beaver hat sat atop his head, and a caped greatcoat with a velvet collar, suitable for such a blustery day, accentuated his broad shoulders. He smiled as he spoke, and his white teeth flashed against his full lips and dark sideburns.

Feeling more pensive than unnerved, Kate tilted her head to the side. "I wonder how things will change now that he's back."

Charles shrugged. "Old man Stockton still owns the mill. I presume Henry will take the helm one day, but for now, I doubt much will change."

Kate could not deny Henry Stockton's commanding presence. During the previous day's interaction, she'd failed to notice the straightness of his nose or the vivid blue of his eyes.

"Oh my goodness," whispered a feminine voice just behind Kate, "but he is a handsome man."

Kate started and whirled around at the familiar tone, face flaming at the idea that someone might have been able to read her thoughts. Just behind her, Jane, Kate's dearest friend, adjusted her tawny leather glove, finger by finger.

Kate scooted closer to Charles so Jane could join them in the small corner near the gate. She hadn't shared with Jane the details of her encounter with Mr. Stockton, nor did she intend to. She cleared her throat. "He may be handsome, but let's not forget whose grandson he is."

Charles leaned low with a grin. "And on that note I will excuse myself and leave you ladies to discuss such important matters."

With the customary twinkle in his eye, Charles bowed and retreated to the other millers gathered near the Stocktons.

Once Charles was out of earshot, Jane turned to Kate, gave a little giggle, and adjusted the bright-pink bonnet ribbon beneath her chin. "I don't care. He's still the most handsome man in Amberdale. Even more so than your John Whitby."

"He isn't *my* John Whitby," corrected Kate before the words were fully out of Jane's mouth. "And you will care if your father hears you speak of Henry Stockton like that."

"La, these men and their grudges." Jane pursed her lips and shook her dark locks. "Look. It appears as if Mr. Stockton and Miss Pennington are reviving their acquaintance. 'Tis a shame for every other young lady, though. I've no doubt the happy couple will marry within the year."

An unexpected pang sliced through Kate at the sight of Miss Frederica Pennington drawing near to Mr. Stockton's side as they joined in mutual laughter.

Miss Pennington's childhood declaration that she would one day marry Henry Stockton leapt from the recesses of Kate's mind. Time had softened the blow of their discarded friendship, but if there was one thing she did know about Frederica Pennington, it was that she would not give up until she got what she felt she deserved.

Blistering winds howled in from the east meadows, forcing the crowd to disperse and seek shelter. She was about to suggest they depart for home when Jane shrilled, "Is that Mr. Whitby?"

Kate shifted to follow Jane's gaze. The journeyman, clad in a heavy box coat of tan wool, approached driving a cart.

"You're a mite late for services, John Whitby," taunted Jane as the cart rattled to a stop on the road just on the other side of the fence.

John lifted his square chin. "You know how the Dearbornes feel about services. Too many mill owners here for our tastes." His gaze landed on Kate, and he sobered. "Well, not all the Dearbornes, I suppose. Besides, I am not here for church. I am here for Kate."

She stiffened at the directness of his stare and the casual manner in which her Christian name fell from his lips in public. She lifted her hood over her hair and turned to face him fully. "Why are you here for me?"

"To drive you home, of course. Your father's left for Leeds, and I know he wouldn't want you walking through the woods."

"But I walk home from church every Sunday," she reasoned. "I appreciate the concern, but I fear your trip was unnecessary."

"Well, I'm here now." In an easy, fluid motion he climbed down from the cart.

Kate stepped backward to give him plenty of room and cast a glance over her shoulder to see if anyone had noticed the newcomer. Her stomach twisted. The motive behind his action was clear, and it felt as if every remaining eye in the churchyard was on her.

Papa's words of his desire for her future rang in her ears. He would stop at nothing to see her united in wedlock to a weaver, even if it took a scandal like being alone in the forest with one of them for such a union to occur.

Kate looped her arm through Jane's arm, a silent plea for her to stay, but as if oblivious to Kate's intention, Jane only patted her hand and stepped back. "I must be going too. Mama and Papa will be looking for me. Kate, be sure to come by the shop tomorrow for those extra pieces of cloth. Don't forget!"

Before Kate could respond, Jane dipped a curtsy in parting, and within moments Kate was left standing alone with John.

Only a few brave parishioners remained as the wind drove them back to their homes, but despite the fact that John cared little for most of the people in attendance, he did find interest in one of the few remaining souls. "Is that him?"

Kate shivered as an icy gust rippled her cloak. She knew full well to whom he referred, and yet she inquired, "Who?"

John cast a nod toward the churchyard. "The man himself, Henry Stockton."

Kate retied the garnet-colored ribbons on her cloak that had come loose. "Yes."

"Hmm." John held his hat on his head so it wouldn't blow away, but even from beneath the brim's shadow his eyes darkened. "I won't give him a month before his trunks are packed and he's gone. Folks aren't happy about his return. He'll have a hard go of it, mark my words."

Kate did not feel like discussing Mr. Stockton with John, or anyone, for that matter. She approached the cart and accepted John's hand to assist her to the bench. Once they were both settled, the vehicle lurched into motion.

She probably should have been more concerned with the sight they presented, riding alone into the forest. Most women would consider it uncomfortable to be with a handsome young man without a chaperone, or at the very least would fear what others might say. But in truth, anyone who knew John Whitby knew that his loyalty to her father was unshakable, and therefore, he was a trustworthy escort for his employer's only daughter.

Their relationship was an unusual one. Not a day passed when she did not see or speak with John. Normally work in the dye house consumed her days, and he could be found in the room where they housed their spinning jennies. But their paths often overlapped.

Despite their comfortable working arrangements, an unusual

tension had been winding between them for weeks and begged for resolution. Papa's declaration the previous day had only intensified it.

"You're cross with me, aren't you?" John said after a period of silence, his gaze not wavering from the road before them.

"I'm not cross with you."

He cast a sideways glance at her and raised a light-brown eyebrow. "You can't fool me. You're upset at your father's decision to put me in charge while he's in Leeds."

"It doesn't matter." She sniffed.

"It *does* matter. At least, it matters to me. I didn't have a thing to do with it. I need you to know that."

She sighed and looked to the left at the barren pastureland spread out wide, far, and undisturbed. "Papa is set in his ways."

"He only wants what is best for you."

Kate pressed her lips together to prevent unwise words from spilling out. What her father thought was best for her and what she thought was best were two different matters entirely.

He inched closer.

Kate caught the motion from the corner of her eye and stiffened. "I think the wind is blowing in more weather. See how quickly those clouds are moving? We should hurry."

John ignored her warning and angled his broad shoulders toward her. "Do you never think of the future, Kate?"

Unsure of how to respond, she looked at her glove's worn fingertips.

"Do you find it so impossible that I care about you and your safety? I have worked with your father for three years. I live in your house. I have seen you daily. I would hardly be human if you'd not come to mean something to me."

She darted her gaze around, hoping to see something—anything—that could distract them from the conversation and dispel the weight of his suffocating gaze. Nothing but trees, pasture, the distant moors, a handful of sheep, and snow. Her ears rang in alarm as his words continued to prod her.

"You doubt I care for you?"

This conversation had been looming, circling around her like the starlings that flittered overhead, searching for the perfect place to light. When she remained silent, he drew the horse to a stop.

"Why are we stopping?"

He lowered the reins to his lap. "You are not shy about sharing your opinion. Don't pretend to be now. You're clever, Kate. Clever and smart. I know you've considered every possible outcome of your future. But what I can't figure out is how you feel about me and if I'm part of it."

She could not bring herself to look at him. She wanted to jump down from the cart and run into the forest, pretending she had not heard him. Her mind would not focus. Her words would not form. Regardless of how she felt about her father's journeyman, he was still a human with feelings and emotions. She did not want to hurt anyone. Yet she would not lie.

"I—I think we'd best return home."

He remained motionless. "You didn't answer my question."

She gave a nervous little laugh, and words whooshed from her. "I don't know what you expect me to say. You are employed by my father. I'm not aware of any sort of relationship beyond that."

His body tensed next to her. "Nothing beyond that?"

Her words had been harsher than she intended, and she summoned the courage to look at him. The cold air stung her lungs as she sucked in a deep breath. "No. Nothing beyond that."

His freshly shaven jaw twitched, and a flash sparked in his dark eyes. He tightened the reins and set the horse back into motion. "I would have guessed otherwise, based on your behavior."

Heat rushed to Kate's face, and she gripped the seat's railing to prevent herself from hurling back a defensive reply. She had always been friendly to John, kind, but she could not control if he read something in her actions that was not there.

John's nostrils flared. "I'm not a man who is easily swayed, Kate. I know what I want, and I work hard to get it. You and I have that in common."

"But we are working hard for different things."

"Don't you know what your father's intentions are? What my intentions are?"

It was no secret what her father wanted, but maybe it was time she heard John's wishes spoken aloud. "Just so we're clear, what exactly are those intentions?"

He jerked the cart to a halt once more and turned to face her. He gripped her hand in both of his. "The future! Kate, I want to—no, I will—be a clothier one day. Even bigger and more powerful than your father. But I can't do that alone. I overheard you and your father speaking last night, and I know he desires you to be with another weaver who can support you and protect you. I can be that man! Just imagine how strong we will be—the two of us with years of knowledge and experience. There will be no stopping us."

Just breathe. She forced her breath to slow to counterbalance the rush of his words. Why could he not understand that she did not want to rely on another? That she was fully capable of making cloth in her own right?

When she did not immediately respond, his face dimmed, but he did not look away. "You need to have someone come alongside you.

Someone who cares about the business as much as you do. Someone who understands the way of life. And I am that man."

She stared at him. She liked John, but she had also seen a different side of him. No, if she was going to have her own income, she would do it her way.

She forced her voice to be steady. "But I am not that woman."

His eyes grew hard. He dropped her hand, gathered the reins, and slapped them on the horse's back. The cart raced to a pace far greater than was intended for such a vehicle.

She cast a sideways glance at him. This was the start of something. Of what, she did not know, but she had angered John, and there would be no forgiveness.

CHAPTER 5

The fire's warm, flickering light sparkled on the cut glass in Arthur Pennington's hand as he raised his beverage. "To the men returning from war."

Grandfather leaned close to Henry's left elbow, his voice loud and clear. "May they all return to England swiftly and safely."

Henry lifted his glass in the toast. Mrs. Pennington and Miss Frederica, along with Miss Isabella and Miss Anna, the younger Pennington daughters, followed suit.

Henry took a sip, then returned the crystal glass to the fine silk cloth covering the Pennington dining table.

Was this not what he had dreamed of, those nights sleeping on the hard, frozen ground, clinging to his rifle lest his sleep be interrupted by the enemy? Was this not the scene that pushed him forward as he rode for days on end, giving him hope and promising him that happiness would return once again? But even as his belly was full, friends surrounded him, and a beautiful woman was near, an uncomfortable restlessness churned.

He'd heard tales of men who came home from gruesome battles and were never able to shed the horrific memories. And now, as he attempted to repel his own silent tormentors and enjoy the evening, the demons remained close, fighting, demanding his attention.

Mr. Pennington's heavy wooden chair groaned beneath the weight of his stocky frame as he leaned against the narrow spindles and slapped his knee. "Thanks be to God that you've returned home in one piece. I respect you for what you've done, let there be no mistake about that. Nobody wants to see their men go to war, but where would we be if our best and brightest stayed hidden away in the countryside?"

Henry cupped the back of his neck with his hand and studied the glass in his other hand. The kind words should have warmed him, but Grandfather's ensuing silence spoke louder than any words could. They'd had several arguments in the weeks leading up to Henry's departure, and since his return, Grandfather had barely asked him about the past three years.

Pennington, oblivious to his guests' internal struggles, pointed a plump finger at Henry. "I bet you have some stories to tell of your escapades on the Continent. Come, you must share them with us."

At Pennington's request, heat rose up his chest and neck. Henry tapped his heel against the leg of his chair and glanced at the faces across the table. Pennington spoke of war as if it were a great adventure instead of what it was—an endless nightmare.

Henry wiped his mouth with his napkin and kept his tone light. "I fear my stories are quite dull," he lied. "I'd much rather hear the news of Amberdale."

"Bah." A grin spread across Pennington's wide face, and he waved his hand before him. "News of wool, machines, and the struggles against those who hate us? Nonsense."

Henry shifted and ran his finger between his linen cravat and neck. "I'm not sure my stories, as you put it, are entirely appropriate for the ladies."

"How good it is of you to consider the sensibilities of the women-folk." Grandfather's deep-set eyes glimmered with unusual vigor. "It is good to see that war has not changed your decorum."

Henry's stomach tightened at the older man's obvious attempts to convince Miss Pennington of Henry's merits.

Pennington's unkempt, bushy eyebrows gathered, and he straightened the hem of his floral waistcoat before leaning on the table with his elbow. "At the very least you must share how you came to be reported killed in action, when here you are with nary a scratch. That must be an interesting tale indeed. Besides, it will do my girls good to hear some of the ways of the world outside of their needlepoint and fripperies."

Every eye was fixed on Henry. He glanced at the other faces around the table. Mrs. Pennington, with her abundance of jewels glittering around her neck and in her faded blonde hair, was seated across from her husband, and Frederica was seated across from Henry. The two younger girls were hardly little girls anymore. They had become young ladies, and they, too, observed him with interest.

Henry swallowed to buy himself an extra moment or two. In order to tell the tale, he had to mentally revisit the event—something he did not want to do. The panic-stricken faces. The nausea-inducing smells. They were all at the forefront, clawing to be remembered and relived, like a rabid wolf howling at an iron gate.

He cleared his throat and fidgeted with the edge of his napkin. "Well, I can't be entirely sure what led to such a report, but if I recall correctly, around that time several soldiers became separated from the battalion during a battle in the north, and I was among them. It was nearly a month before we were able to rejoin our comrades. No doubt they assumed we were lost and reported us as such."

"How frightening that must have been." The pity in Miss Pennington's gaze unsettled him.

Henry did not care to be pitied.

He smoothed his neckcloth and straightened in his chair. "I'm sure other topics would be of much more interest."

At the lull in the conversation, Mrs. Pennington stood and motioned for her daughters to do the same. "Ladies, the hour is growing late. It is time we retired to the drawing room, for I am sure these men have important matters to discuss. Let us leave them to their port."

Grandfather remained silent as the ladies took their leave, but he shook his head as the door closed behind them, and a knowing grin eased over his features. "You've got quite a task ahead of you finding husbands for your young ladies, Pennington. I don't envy you the task."

Pennington's good-natured laugh echoed from the dining room's deep-blue walls and high plastered ceiling, and he motioned for the footman to leave them. But then, once the poker-faced servant had retreated, a darker, more somber expression dominated Pennington's ruddy face.

He pulled a slip of paper from his waistcoat. "Speaking of my daughters, I need to show you this. I returned from a trip to Liverpool to find this note waiting for me."

Grandfather straightened but did not seem alarmed at the man's sudden change in demeanor. After accepting the missive and unfolding it, he leaned back in his chair, crossed one long leg over the other, and rested his elbow on the chair's arm. He pressed his thin lips together as he read, then gave his head a sharp shake. "Vagabonds." Without another word, he handed the letter across the table to Henry.

Curious as to what news could have caused the drastic change of disposition, Henry steadied the letter before him.

If you have any love for those daughters of yours, you will think twice before bringing a gig mill into Amberdale.

The shaky penmanship, uneven ink strokes, and smudged paper hinted that the letter had been hastily penned. Henry turned it over, looking for some sort of distinctive marking, but found none. Not even a seal. He frowned. "Who sent you this?"

Pennington stepped to the teak side table and retrieved a cigar from a painted wooden box. "We've been receiving threats like this for months now. So have the other mills, as far away as London. Threats to kill mill owners. To kill their families. To burn their houses."

The injustice of the sinister message alarmed him. Relationships with the weavers had always been tense, but to threaten murder? "What do they want?"

Grandfather's pale-blue eyes popped wide. "To have their way! Pennington and I, along with most of the millers in the area, have plans to install gig mills in the near future. This will increase our productivity and allow us to do more with fewer workers. The process will remain entirely within the walls of our own mills instead of having to be sent out to the local shearmen's homes. If we are to remain competitive, this must be done."

Henry handed the letter back to Pennington. "Have you informed the magistrate?"

"Of course, but little can be done. With the uprisings in the south, the soldiers in the area have their hands full."

Grandfather retrieved his snuffbox from his coat pocket, flipped it open, and pinched a bit of the black substance between his fingers. "They're bluffing. They're trying to scare you. Scare *us*. Well, it won't work. None of them are willing to risk swinging from the end of a noose; it's as simple as that."

Grandfather put the snuff to his nose and inhaled. "The more we try to do for these villagers, the harder they fight. Ungrateful, the whole lot. We need all of the strong, able-bodied, forward-thinking mill owners to unite. Your return could not have come at a better time, Henry. Don't misunderstand me. Belsey, Dearborne, and the others running Stockton Mill are capable, and Pennington's men are trustworthy, but it takes a strong hand to navigate such business in these stormy seas."

Henry's attention piqued at one of the names. "Dearborne?"

"A recent addition to the mill." Grandfather tucked the box back in his coat pocket. "He joined us not long after you left. Someone needed to tend to the books, and he has a sound mind for it."

Henry frowned. He didn't doubt much had changed in recent years, but a Dearborne at Stockton Mill?

As if sensing Henry's confusion, Grandfather leaned toward him, the chair groaning under the shifting weight. "Do you remember Charles, Silas Dearborne's boy?"

Henry shook his head.

"He and Ian Belsey struck up a friendship, and Charles, being a bright lad, saw the benefits of producing wool in a mill instead of his drawing room and wanted to learn more. So I showed him. What sort of neighbor would I be if I did not?"

The situation seemed odd. "Did his father approve?"

A triumphant gleam glinted in Grandfather's hooded eye. "Of course not. To this day they don't speak."

Henry stifled a groan. No wonder Miss Dearborne had looked at him with such scorn on the bridge.

Grandfather reached for the decanter of port left behind by the footman and poured himself a glass. "I have always built Stockton Mill and its holdings to pass to you and your children. News of your death was difficult enough, but you can imagine how difficult it was to know that all we had built would pass to the hands of the Belseys. He'd have been the best choice, mind you, since he's been in my employ for decades and knows everything about the business. But still, he's not family."

Henry raised an eyebrow. "The Belseys? I always assumed that should I not return, the mill would pass to Mollie and her children. Surely whomever Mollie chooses to marry would be eager to take part in the enterprise."

Grandfather shot Henry a warning glance. "Mollie does not share the passion for wool necessary to sustain such an operation." His jaw clenched. "Whomever she marries is unlikely to understand the impact this mill has on our life. Our community. It's not just our family we need to consider, but the dozens of families who make their livelihood standing at our looms. I'll never rest in my grave unless I know the future is secure."

Pennington crossed the room and slapped his hand on Henry's shoulder. "Well, I hope you're ready to join our campaign. There's much to be done and hard work ahead of us. We must look to the future."

Henry could only nod. "Hard work, yes."

"Good." A playful smile crossed Pennington's lips. "I'm a bit surprised to learn that there is no Mrs. Stockton, with such a strapping lad as you are."

Henry smirked. "I didn't encounter many young ladies on the battlefield looking to become a wife."

Pennington threw back his head in hearty laughter. "I daresay that's the truth. But it doesn't do for a man to remain unmarried. I tell your grandfather this all the time."

"And I think he should mind his business," his grandfather grumbled.

Henry felt as if he should agree that their logic regarding marriage was sound, but he could not. For he was not the same as these men anymore. Not after what he had done. After what he had seen. At the moment matrimonial bliss seemed an unattainable—and undeserved—blessing.

Pennington cocked his head to the side, pride radiating from his expression. "My Frederica was glad to learn you had returned to Amberdale. There is insufficient polite society in these parts. She was lamenting her decision to remain here for the winter instead of staying with her aunt in Derbyshire, but now"—Pennington's dark eyes flashed in amusement, and he lifted his glass in Henry's direction—"her disposition has brightened."

Henry glanced up to see one of Pennington's gray eyebrows raised in his direction, and he lifted his glass to his lips.

Perhaps the ills of war were a safer topic after all.

CHAPTER 6

*C*ool air rushed Henry as he stepped from the dining hall to
Briarton House's main corridor. Wall lamps cast a flickering
glow on the polished wood floor, and the click of the men's boots rang
hollow. He purposely trailed behind Grandfather and Pennington as
they made their way toward the drawing room.

Gentle strains of pianoforte music swelled from the doorway. He
followed the older men into the spacious chamber and was immediately struck with the familiarity of it. Three tall, rectangular-paned
windows looked out into the black night. A large Persian rug boast-
ing hues of green and blue anchored the space, and two large stuffed
chairs and a sofa were arranged near the hearth where a cheery fire
popped and crackled.

As he suspected, Frederica was the one seated on the pianoforte's
bench, her fingers alone responsible for the haunting sounds that had
lured them. The other Pennington ladies were seated at a table in the
center of the room, their postures straight, cards in hand.

The music stopped as they entered, and all four of the feminine faces turned toward the door. "There you are at last!" Frederica
dropped her hands from the keys.

Mrs. Pennington lowered her cards and angled her head toward the door, a twinkle glimmering in her eye. "We thought you had quite forgotten about us and were about to retire for the evening."

"My apologies for the delay. How could anyone forget about such lovely company? 'Twould be impossible." Pennington stepped toward his wife and rested a hand on her shoulder before turning back to his daughter. "Frederica, don't stop your performance on our account. Gentlemen, do be seated. My daughter is quite talented. You'll not hear her equal in the county. Do you not remember, Henry?"

A charming smile dimpled the corner of Miss Pennington's mouth at the praise, and pink bloomed high on her cheeks. Something oddly alluring danced in her eyes of deep chocolate brown. Something that called to him and harkened to years past.

"Aye," breathed Henry. "I remember."

"Frederica, love, sing for us."

Henry and his grandfather were seated in the two chairs flanking the hearth, not far from the pianoforte. Pennington stood at the instrument, a doting papa prepared to turn the pages.

Under her father's watchful eye, Miss Pennington adjusted her perch on the bench and fussed with the billowy azure skirt about her. The amber glow from a nearby candle bathed her smooth skin in a honeyed shade and glistened on the shimmery comb in her golden curls.

She glanced in Henry's direction before lifting her hands to the keyboard. With a most tender touch she pressed her fingers against the ivory keys, and in moments a haunting, almost melancholy melody reached to every corner of the gilded room. Her gentle voice swelled with beauty and vibrato above the pianoforte's strains, and he switched his gaze from Miss Pennington to the fire popping in the grate.

Henry dragged his finger between his neck and his cravat, uncomfortable at how her voice's timbre unearthed long-buried memories and transported him to another time—a time before war, before death, a time of lightheartedness and ignorant optimism.

Pennington's words regarding marriage intensified the uneasiness brewing within Henry. A lovely, talented woman like Frederica would be a jewel in the crown for any man. He understood Grandfather and Pennington conspiring. A match between Frederica and himself would have many advantages.

Henry checked his thoughts, refusing to permit emotions to run rampant. She might be the same woman from three years ago, but he was hardly the same man.

The music ended. He was reminded to clap when Pennington's thick hands thudded together. "Brava," called Mr. Pennington, chest puffed, chin high. "Enchanting."

Frederica stood from the bench and made her way to the men. Remembering his manners, Henry stood as she approached.

"Do you remember that piece?" Her pointed question demanded his response.

Henry widened his stance and searched his memory. "I'm sorry, I do not."

"I haven't the slightest inkling why the memory burns so vividly in my mind, but that was the aria I played for you the night before you left for war."

His surprise that she would recall such an obscure detail nearly robbed his words. "I am sorry, I don't recall."

She did not seem upset by it. Instead, she tilted her head coyly to the side. "I didn't forget it."

Henry grew warm. He shifted his gaze in search of his grandfather or anyone, for that matter, who could provide a diversion. As fate—or an overeager mama and a business-savvy father—would have it, Pennington, Grandfather, and Mrs. Pennington had withdrawn to the far corner of the room, and the two younger girls were gone. Henry and Miss Pennington were essentially alone in the sitting room.

He drew a deep breath and looked back to his counterpart. She, too, had glanced back at her father. Perhaps she was as much a pawn in their scheme as he was. Perhaps not, but the arrangement was not uncomfortable, necessarily. She was a vivacious companion, full of the whimsical charms absent from his life the past few years.

In a sudden motion she whirled back around, her eyes wide, and clutched the sleeve of his coat. "I've an idea. You must let me sketch you."

He laughed at her eagerness. "What, now?"

"Of course." With a nudge to his arm, she urged him to a chair by the window, next to which sat the silhouette screen. "Father bought us a new shade when he was in London last. I have already made a silhouette of Mama, him, and my sisters, but I've had no one else to try it on."

When his steps slowed, a pretty pout curved her lips and her eyes locked on him with pleading insistence.

How could anyone refuse Miss Pennington?

He consented with a nod, and she patted her hands together and gave a little squeal.

"Now, you sit there." She gathered her supplies. "'Tis a pity I can't see you when I do this, but we can still talk."

He felt a bit odd, sitting behind the screen. The candle backlit him and cast a shadow against her screen, allowing her to draw his likeness.

She chatted about this and that, rarely stopping to ask his opinion or wait for him to respond to a question, but he didn't mind. It was almost easier this way—until she inquired about Mollie.

"And have you seen your sister since you have been back in England?"

Each time the thought of Mollie in her current circumstances was brought to mind, his heart pinched. How much, if anything, did Miss Pennington know about Mollie's situation? Judging by her lighthearted tone, he assumed very little. He cleared his throat. "Unfortunately, I have not. I didn't realize she wasn't in Amberdale."

"No, she has not been here for quite some time. I do miss her."

He was grateful for the privacy of the screen and rubbed his palm against the smooth buckskin of his breeches. "I wrote to her earlier today. I plan to pay a call to London as soon as I'm able."

"Don't stay away too long. Amberdale has already been deprived of your presence long enough." She rounded the screen, a smile on her face. "At the moment, all seems so lovely. If I didn't know better, I'd think that we were three years in the past, as if you'd never gone to war. How happy we all were then."

The melancholy undertone of her chipper words caught his attention. "Are you not happy now?"

"Of course I am, but time changes all, doesn't it?" Her words slowed. "And after spending the evening with you, I find you changed."

He felt inside that he was different, but he was intrigued to find that someone else may have perceived it as well. "I've changed?"

"Oh yes."

"How?"

"Well." Miss Pennington leaned against the screen and lifted her eyes to the ceiling, as if thinking. "You have not commented once on how beautiful my gown is," she teased. "There was a time when you were quite fond of blue gowns, and I wore this one just for you."

Her flirting was bold. At one time his had been too, he mused. He did not break her gaze. "I've grown up, I suppose."

"We've all grown up, and that's no excuse." Her coquettish smile softened the harsh intent of her words, and she disappeared around the screen.

He blew out his air and settled back on the hard wooden stool, turning his face to the window so the candle's light would cast his profile's shadow. He should jump at the chance to begin a romance with her. She was beautiful. Witty. Wealthy. Their lives were intertwined. She seemed eager to resume life as if he'd never left.

But something held him back.

If war had taught him one thing, it was that the things he thought mattered no longer did so. At one time nothing mattered more than having a beautiful wife, amassing possessions, and claiming power. Now his heart—his soul—longed for things not so tangible: Safety. Security. Happiness. Justice. Hope. Forgiveness.

Maybe Miss Pennington was right—he was different.

Whether or not that was a good thing remained to be seen.

Frederica shifted the edge of her bedchamber's damask curtain aside, pressed herself against the papered wall to avoid detection, and angled herself to see down to the dark courtyard.

A gentle snow fell on Mr. Stockton's and Henry's retreating forms as they crossed the main drive and made their way to the iron gate. It was easy to tell the men apart. Henry sat so tall atop his horse. So straight. A thrill surged through her at the memory of his nearness while they were in the drawing room. He was even more handsome than she remembered. The same black hair curled over his broad forehead and fringed his high collar. The same striking blue eyes drew her in with ease.

She let the thick fabric fall and took several cleansing breaths to soothe the pain of disappointment scratching at her chest. Despite her joy at seeing him again, his aloofness doused her hopeful anticipation of what his return could bring.

No, the evening had not gone as she'd planned. She'd expected him to hang on her every word and fall prey to her flirty smiles as he had in times past. But instead, his inaccessible countenance and distracted expressions robbed her of her confidence.

And that irritated her.

She stepped away from the window, moved to her mahogany dressing table, and sat on the tufted seat. Before he left to serve his country, part of her had expected some sort of declaration of love, or at least some soft words of sentiment, but none ever came. Even throughout the time he was gone, she had never given up hope—until she learned of his death. She grieved for him, as if their love had been real and not just the fodder of her girlhood fantasies.

She had almost accepted that she would be forced to marry one of the suitors her father had approved of. They were all old. Dull. Boring.

Henry was none of those things. But now fear that he no longer matched her recollection of him took hold.

The door to her chamber flung open and slammed into the wall. Prepared to reprimand her abigail, Frederica whirled around, her face flushing. She had told the silly girl always to knock before entering. But it was Isabella, not her maid, standing in the doorway.

Clad in a white linen sleeping gown and with her tawny hair in curling rags, Isabella leaned against the door frame, a smug grin on her face.

"How many times have I told you not to come in here?" Annoyed, Frederica spun back around to face her reflection in the looking glass above her dressing table.

Isabella tittered, breezed farther into the chamber, leaned on the back of Frederica's chair, and met her sister's gaze in the mirror's reflection. "'Tis a pity. Mr. Stockton barely seemed to notice you. I know you were expecting him to."

Frederica clenched her teeth with such frustration that her jaw ached. Isabella could be so childish. "Oh, will you go away?"

Her younger sister sauntered to the bed and dropped atop the silk coverlet. Her voice took on a singsong quality as she flipped to her belly and propped her chin on her hand. "You cannot fool me, Freddie. I saw the way you looked at him. Everyone did. But oh well. Perhaps he met another lady in his travels."

If there was one thing Frederica hated more than being teased, it was being mocked. She removed the comb holding her hair in place and commenced to pull free the remaining pins. "Did you come here for any particular reason, or are you just trying to be a pest?"

Isabella rolled over to her back. "Mother wants you to come to her chamber."

Frederica stilled her hands. Her mother never called her to her chamber. "Why?"

"I don't know. But you'd better hurry. You know how she hates to be kept waiting."

With a groan Frederica let the comb drop to the table, ran her fingers through her hair, grabbed her wrapper, and slung it around her shoulders. "Fine. But you had better not be in here when I get back." She paused long enough to cast a warning glare at her sister before she stepped out into the dark hallway.

Her stocking feet were soft against the plush brown carpet. Guided by the moon's light sliding through the corridor windows, Frederica made her way down the wide hall to her mother's room and knocked on the paneled door. "Mother?"

"Come in."

Frederica smoothed her hair and straightened her wrapper and did as she was bid. Her mother would notice anything out of place, even at this late hour.

Her mother was seated at her dressing table. A tray of hot chocolate and Mother's unpinned long, golden hair provided evidence that her maid had already been here.

She waited in silence until her mother addressed her, feeling more like a child than a woman of one and twenty. Her mother's casual voice did little to calm Frederica's nerves. "How pleasant it was to see Henry once again. Why, his presence is practically a miracle after what he has been through."

Frederica had suspected that Henry was the reason for this invitation. She drew a breath for courage.

With two long fingers her mother motioned her farther into the room.

Frederica complied, resisting the urge to wrinkle her nose at the overwhelmingly sweet scent of lily of the valley. The warmth from the fire was far too intense, and yet she wrapped her arms around her waist.

"Sit."

Frederica obeyed and sat primly on a padded ottoman near her mother's dressing table and clasped her hands together at her knees. Her mother had made it perfectly clear prior to Henry's arrival that Frederica should do her best to capture his attention. Judging by his eagerness to be on his way, she doubted her success.

Mother dipped her fingers in a glass jar and scooped out some salve. "You will have to do better than that, my dear, if you are to catch Mr. Stockton's fancy."

Frederica winced at the criticism. "I can hardly expect him to throw himself at me."

"Why not?" her mother shot back as she spread the cream over her face before standing and tying her pink silk wrapper at her waist. "He's a man. They are simple creatures, really. Consider what is at stake. You will soon be past marriageable age. It cannot be put off any longer. Mr. Tynes and Mr. Simmons are both eligible men, and if you fail to captivate Mr. Stockton, you will be forced to consider your fate."

The mere mention of the names of her suitors made Frederica's skin crawl. She refused to shiver—or to give her mother a glimpse of her insecurity. "These things take time."

"You do not have the luxury of time, my dear. Every day that passes is one day closer to your father's death, whenever that may be, and one day more for both Mr. Tynes and Mr. Simmons to cast their affections elsewhere."

Frederica nodded in silent acquiescence. She never cried, and she certainly would not now, but the feeling of defeat descended on her so heavily, she wondered if she could bear it. She stepped to the window, pretending to look out. "Did you notice how little he laughed?"

Mother retrieved her brush and glided it through her hair. "People always change with the passage of time."

Frederica chewed her lip, pondering the strange, subdued behavior of the person she once knew so well. "But his entire countenance was different. He used to be so jovial. He seemed so . . . withdrawn."

"Do not discount the fact that he has been at war." Mother angled her head and swept past Frederica to the wardrobe. "There is no telling what horrors he experienced."

Frederica let her shoulders slacken slightly and studied the floral carpet. She did not know much about the war. Once when she was bored in her father's study, she had glanced in his newspaper at the account about the casualties. But other than that, she had never really given it much thought. "I suppose you're right."

Her mother clicked her tongue as she retrieved a pair of slippers from the oak chest. "For heaven's sake, stop frowning. If you keep your face like that, you will wrinkle far before your time. Regarding Mr. Stockton, we must act quickly. We'll invent a reason to pay him a call. In the meantime, I will contact Mrs. Howell to inform her we shall need a new gown for the Winter's End Festival."

Frederica straightened her shoulders. The wheels were in motion, and the price of failure would be high. She had to convince Henry that she would be the perfect wife . . . if for no other reason than to save herself from marriage to a man twice her age.

She would not let her mother—or herself—down.

CHAPTER 7

*D*awn had broken raw and cold, and the sun was just beginning its ascent into the cobalt sky as Henry approached Stockton Mill. Dots of light floating across the darkened landscape caught his attention. From the south a shadowy procession of workers was arriving to man the early shift, their lanterns swinging in rhythm with their lethargic steps.

Henry's boots thudded against the frozen ground as he dismounted his horse at the mill's main gate. He led the animal through the iron barrier, through which several workers—men, women, children—also entered.

He filled his lungs with the winter air and closed his eyes to drink in the discernible scent of smoke and frost. Familiar sounds met his ears. The waterwheel's paddling whir. The varied chatter of voices. The crackling of the open fire next to the countinghouse. The seemingly never-ending roar of machinery. He opened his eyes again, and the scene in front of him matched the one he had imagined dozens of times.

"Welcome back, Mr. Stockton."

Henry adjusted the reins over his horse's neck and turned at the familiar voice. "Belsey. Good to see you again."

The mill's overlooker extended his hand in greeting. "A miracle. A true miracle. How long has it been since you were here last?"

Henry shook the man's thin hand. "Three years."

Belsey whistled under his breath before gesturing to the mill and its outbuildings. "Well? Is it as you remembered?"

Henry shifted his attention to the cottages. The storage barns. The dye house. The ever-present canopy of smoke puffing from the numerous chimneys over the grounds. He frowned. One piece was missing. "Yes, but what happened to the stable?"

"Burned down." Belsey's sparse, faded brows jutted upward. "Struck by lightning in the dead of night, two years past. Of course the weavers claimed it was a sign from God Himself. Said it was proof that the machines within these walls are evil." Belsey huffed. "Superstitious lot. Look there, to the east. There's your stable. Built up just this past year."

Henry lifted his gaze to a stone-and-timber stable and frowned. It was a great deal larger than the old structure. "So big. What's in there?"

"Four horses and two carriages for transporting cloth and supplies and the like. And two large carts and smaller ones too."

Henry couldn't recall the mill owning more than one wagon. "Can we afford that?"

"Now that's a question your grandfather never asks." Belsey tilted his head to the side, amused. "'Course we can afford it. Perhaps you're not aware, but since you've been gone this mill's become the most productive one this side of Leeds."

Henry squinted to see in the pale light and scanned the grounds. "Speaking of Grandfather, where is he? I thought I awoke early enough to accompany him here this morning, but when I came down for the day, Mrs. Figgs said he'd already departed."

Belsey's breath puffed out before him in a frosty plume as he folded his thin arms over his chest. "Your grandfather always arrives hours before daybreak, at least an hour before the first workmen."

"Why?"

"It's his way. He's developed some peculiar habits, but I'm sure that don't surprise you none."

Henry chuckled. His grandfather's quirks and obsessive patterns were well known throughout Amberdale.

Belsey gave an exaggerated shrug and motioned for a young lad to come over. "Give your horse to Billy there. He'll see to 'im."

Once the animal was safely deposited with the stable boy, Belsey turned his attention back to Henry. "Let's check the countinghouse first. He might be there still. Lately he's taken to sleeping in the back room."

"That seems odd." Henry raised an eyebrow and looked toward the tiny cottage that at one time had been his grandparents' very first home, back when the mill was just a spark of an idea. The snow and gravel crunched underfoot as they crossed the courtyard to the thatched-roofed stone building. Smoke curled from its chimney. The flicker of a waning fire winked from the paned windows. Henry nodded at a cluster of workers staring at him as he passed. He stepped aside as a dog ran across the path.

"Odd?" Belsey's word snapped Henry back to the conversation. "You don't know the most of it."

As if oblivious to the action around them and the attention they were garnering, Belsey pushed his hat back on his head, revealing a shock of wiry hair the color of aged ale. "Lately he has taken to personally checking on each of the workers individually. If they're late, he docks their pay. He said if they start the day seeing the face of the man who pays 'em, they'll be more respectful and grateful for the position they have."

Henry frowned. Docking a man or child some of their wages seemed a bit extreme. But he kept his mouth shut and focused on the countinghouse, which was growing closer with each step.

Once they arrived, he ducked his head to enter the low-beamed building. It contained only three rooms: the old sitting room, a bedchamber, and the kitchen, which now served as the pulse of the mill's office and quarters.

Intense sentimentality rushed him as he moved to the hearth. The table where he had studied his sums was to the left of it. The chair where he used to sit quietly during mill meetings was tucked next to the window. His grandfather's oilskin coat still hung on the peg next to the oak door, and Henry's own old books still lined the hearth. Despite the activity just outside the door, time had frozen this office. Even the scents of tobacco, cedarwood, and dust lingered.

Henry removed his greatcoat, shook the moisture and snow from his limbs, hung the garment on a peg next to his grandfather's, and rubbed his hands together.

Using the fire from the fireplace, Belsey lit two lamps before moving toward the large desk anchored in the center of the dark room. "Here are some letters and invoices regarding recent dealings. You'll want to get familiar with them."

Henry accepted the stack, leaned against his desk, and sifted through the papers. If he were to have a hope of succeeding now that he had returned, he needed this man on his side. "Anything else I should know?"

"Yes, we have added more jennies and mules, but I am sure your grandfather told you that. Oh, and our employee roster is up to 172—a far sight more than when you were here last."

Henry whistled under his breath.

"Yes, sir. Fifty-nine men, forty-one women, and seventy-two

children to be exact, most of them working more than seventy hours a week."

Henry frowned and lifted his head at the number. "Even the children?"

Belsey nodded. "Some of the younger ones split their shifts, but most of the families need the money, so they work right up 'til the night bell."

Henry recalled the shadowy smaller figures walking through the iron gate, but he never expected such a large number. "Why so many children?"

"They can run the new machinery just fine. With one or two adults supervising, they get the job done. Plus their wages are less, which keeps our costs low. Makes no sense to pay a grown man for what a child can do."

Henry didn't like the thought of children working such long hours and had never felt comfortable walking down the rows of looms with his grandfather, twiddling his thumbs behind his back, when children his own age toiled for hours on end. But back then, Stockton Mill did not employ very many children. Now that number had exploded.

Belsey reached over the desk, pulled a paper from a drawer, and handed it to Henry. "These are the sales numbers. Currently we are producing fourteen forty-yard superfine broadcloths a week, and we need every person to do that, including the work put out to the local shearmen to finish the cloth once it's woven. When the new gig mills arrive, we should be able to either cut back on the amount of raising and napping we are doing or reduce our overhead and increase our output."

Henry glanced at the numbers. "When do the gig mills arrive?"

"Two should be here within the next couple of weeks. Hard to say for certain. We are waiting to hear from the manufacturer. It is all very confidential. It has to be, you see. The shearmen and master weavers caught wind of your grandfather's order, and they're up in arms. With all the machine vandalism occurring north of Leeds, I'll not be comfortable until the gig mills are safe within the mill walls where the ruffians can't get to them."

Henry drew a deep breath. How had the business grown so much in his absence? He could scarcely recall the mill producing more than seven superfine broadcloths a week. Now the numbers had shifted, production had changed. "Do we have buyers for everything being produced?"

"We do. Fortunately for us, with all of the unrest, the buyers are bypassing the cloth halls altogether. We've orders to keep us busy for months, and buyers are requesting more."

"And the Pennington Mill?" The dinnertime conversation from the previous night was still fresh in Henry's mind. "Are they faring as well?"

"They get by. Master Pennington doesn't have the knack your grandfather does for figuring the working hours, but as part owner of Pennington Mill, your grandfather usually spends a day or two out of the week there. Be that as it may, it is still a profitable mill in its own right. Last I heard it was producing roughly eight or nine broadcloths a week."

The door swung open, ushering in a swirl of gusty air and the figure of a man, much too tall and broad to be Grandfather. Belsey lifted his head. "Dearborne!"

Henry whirled to face the name's owner. The man's broad shoulders nearly brushed both sides of the door frame as he entered, and he had to duck through the low opening. He swept his hat from his head, revealing thick, disheveled dark hair. His face and nose were red from the cold. Even in the early-morning darkness, the Dearborne family resemblance was strong.

Henry said, "I know that name."

"I'm sure you do." Dearborne extended his hand in greeting, letting out a good-natured laugh. "Don't worry, I'm not here spying for the enemy."

"Dearborne here oversees the ledgers," Belsey said. "Has been for, what, three years now?"

The tall, ruddy-faced man nodded and dropped a bundle on the desk. "Almost."

Henry leaned with his hip against the edge of the large mahogany desk situated in the room's center. "I had the pleasure of encountering your sister when I first arrived in Amberdale."

Dearborne lifted his head. "Met Kate, did you?"

Kate. So that was her Christian name.

"Yes. She was carting wool in the midst of a near blizzard."

Dearborne shook his head with a laugh. "Not surprised to hear it. She's not one to let much of anything stand in her way, much less a bit o' snow."

"We'll not keep you," Belsey interjected, angling himself to Dearborne. "Stop by the countinghouse later today, will you? We'll get Mr. Stockton here better acquainted with the numbers."

"Of course." And with a tip of his hat, Dearborne excused himself.

Belsey tossed another log on the fire and wiped his hands. "He's a good sort. None finer."

"But his father, Silas. I remember him. He and my grandfather weren't exactly friendly."

"And they never have been. But Charles is different from his father. He's a visionary. Your grandfather wasted no time in taking the boy under his wing and showing him the future of wool."

Henry adjusted his stance. It did not seem like his grandfather to endeavor to separate a son and his father, despite the enmity between their families. "Did Dearborne not object to his son working with Grandfather?"

"Of course he did. Nearly caused a war of our own, right here in Amberdale."

Henry glanced through the small window at Dearborne's retreating form. What else had changed while he was away? From what Belsey said, the mill had grown exponentially, but the cost had been high: Families had been torn apart. Children were being worked and treated as adults. Such methods made him uncomfortable, and he was growing concerned at what other tactics his grandfather may have employed to achieve financial success.

Henry cleared his throat and turned back to Belsey. One day he would be in charge of the mill, but for now he had to work within his grandfather's parameters.

CHAPTER 8

I confess, I don't understand why you are so upset." Jane fixed sincere blue eyes on Kate. "It seems to me it would be a relief not to have to bother with such details."

Kate shifted her attention from her knitting to her dearest friend and considered her response.

As on other Monday evenings, the wives and daughters of nearby weaving families gathered to craft items for the foundling home and the village poor. Tonight they'd assembled at the Purty home, needles, yarn, thread, and fabric in their hands. It was a comfortable group of women and girls, most of whom she'd known her entire life. Their mouths were as busy as their hands as they chatted about the neighborhood events.

Kate glanced around the modest parlor—the white plaster walls, the leather-bound tomes on the mantel shelf, the vines carved into the hearth, the tiny violets painted on a porcelain tea set, the brass lantern flickering at the window—all reasons why she had thought the Purty home one of the most elegant she'd ever seen when she attended these gatherings as a child. But then her gaze landed on the ottoman's frayed damask hem, and her ear pricked at the subtle whistle of the wind racing around a rag stuffed in the small hole in the windowpane. The past several years had been difficult for even the most successful of the weavers.

She sighed at the uncertainty they all faced. Fortunately the women gathered had been able to put aside the worries and fears, at least for the time they were centered around the Purtys' fire, laughing, fellowshipping. Kate wished she could do the same.

Jane nudged her, as if to draw a response to her comment. With a sigh Kate shook out a tangle in her yarn and lifted the mitten she was knitting to assess her progress. "It's not that I'm upset so much as I'm not sure why Papa trusts me so little."

Loose wisps of dark hair escaped their pins and bobbed around Jane's chin as she leaned closer and lowered her own sewing to her lap. "It has nothing to do with trust, I'll wager. Your father only wants to protect you. 'Tis a natural inclination. Mr. Whitby is completely capable, and what father would not want to ease his daughter's burden? You already have your hands full with the dyeing. Let the men deal with the rest of the details. After all, that is what your father is paying them for."

Kate folded the yarn over her arm. Part of her knew the truth in Jane's words. The other part of her wanted to fight it. "Papa speaks as if John will run the business for the rest of his life."

Jane raised an eyebrow. "Do you not think that is what he has planned? Everyone already assumes that you and John will marry."

Kate sniffed.

"Would it really be so terrible to wed such a man?" Jane resumed her sewing, her tone matter of fact. "He is handsome, determined, and obviously infatuated with you."

Kate's nose twitched with unexpected emotion, and she glanced to make sure no one else was watching her. She didn't care for this feeling of vulnerability and helplessness that swelled at her father's dismissal. Not one single bit.

The fact that her friend did not seem to understand her intensified it.

Since her mother's death, Kate had striven to prove her worth in her father's eyes. At the moment she felt like a rudderless boat, adrift and aimless, and she desperately desired a sense of direction, unsure where to turn for validation or approval. Could her father's intention really be to marry her off to secure the future of his business?

Jane's stitching slowed. "Don't you want to marry?"

Kate refused to meet her friend's gaze. The question brought to mind the long-forgotten conversation she'd had with Frederica under the setting summer sun and the churchyard's willow tree—the night she first became aware of the name Henry Stockton.

The lie slid easily from her lips. "I suppose."

Jane laughed and wove her needle through the fabric. "You are an odd one, Kate. Every young lady I know is desperate to find a man, and many to no avail. You have John tripping over himself for your attention, and you ignore his advances."

"It's not as it seems. He wants to secure his future, 'tis all. His feelings for me don't enter into the decision."

Jane shook her head with a little laugh. "You are making things much harder than they have to be."

"Do you not wish for something more, Jane?" Kate failed to see the humor and searched her friend's face. "Something different?"

Jane raised her brow. "I am grateful for a roof over my head, a fire in the grate, and sugar in my tea, and you should be too. If you set your mind too high on other things, you'll be disappointed. I would not discount John. He is a good man." Jane lowered her sewing and leaned close. "I am going to say something to you, and it is with a sincere desire to be of comfort. Perhaps you need to accept the fact that maybe, just maybe, someone wants to marry you because of who you are, not who you are related to."

A burst of laughter from the other women rang out, halting their conversation. Kate turned to hear the commotion's source.

After motioning for the maid to bring more tea, Mrs. Purty returned her attention to the ladies. A pale-blue shawl shrouded the shoulders of her thick wool winter gown of dark brown, despite the fact that the fire's warmth flushed her full cheeks. After several seconds her smile faded and her expression sobered.

"We must remember the potential seriousness of the present situation." Mrs. Purty's voice was thin and low. "Who would have thought Mr. Henry Stockton would be back among us, a ghost walking among the living? Mr. Purty told me the news the night he returned from the weavers' meeting at Meadowvale, and I didn't believe it until I saw him at church the following morning."

"Well, he's here, sure enough, and naught can be done now." Mrs. Wooden sniffed. "More's the pity."

Blood raced through Kate's ears as she listened to the frustrated assessments and pressed her lips together, hesitant to voice her opinion. If she spoke to the matter, she'd be at risk of betraying her brother and his chosen path. If she withheld her disdain, then she'd betray her father—and indeed, her own livelihood.

Mrs. Noon's eyebrows arched as she retrieved a pair of shiny scissors from her basket. "I've never been as shocked as I was to see him, standing there in the nave."

"Yes, it seems the Stockton grandchildren had quite disappeared, what with him gone all those years." Mrs. Wooden's gray curls danced as her head bobbed with every word. "And where is the granddaughter?"

"I believe she is living with Mr. Stockton's daughter in London," Mrs. Purty responded. "It is no surprise that she never comes to visit here. Mr. Stockton is as crotchety as they come."

"She might come back now that her brother has returned," Mrs. Noon added, almost as an afterthought. "As I recall, she and her brother were always thick as thieves."

Mrs. Thesler added, "Henry Stockton was always such a happy boy, do you remember? Always smiling. Always laughing, although I suppose that is easy to do when the world is as careless and free as his must be. But maybe he is different than old Stockton. His return could be positive. He will one day take his grandfather's place. Perhaps he will be a force of kindness."

Mrs. Noon gave a tsk. "Men like that are all the same, unfortunately."

"I don't know," Mrs. Wooden said thoughtfully. "That is like saying all the weavers are like those weavers to the west who break looms, burn mills, and murder millers. He has been away for a long time. Maybe that has had a favorable effect on him."

"Listen to the lot of you. You are talking nonsense," Mrs. Purty scolded, her mobcap atop her head flopping with each word. "He is a Stockton through and through. Nothing remains to be said on the matter. Thinking he'll be any different will not bring it to pass."

As the rush of comments subsided, Jane leaned close. "Perhaps if he were not so handsome it would be easier to think so."

Giggles circled the room.

Mrs. Purty, clearly not amused, huffed, "Well, none of our girls should care about that. Can you imagine being united in marriage to such a family? Why, I'd not wish that on any one of us. Besides, I've no doubt he will take up where he left off with Frederica Pennington."

Kate's stitching slowed. If there was one name disliked more than Stockton, perhaps it was that of Pennington. The Stocktons had hurt her family, yes. They had lured her brother away and chipped away at her father's livelihood. But the Penningtons' offense had cut deeper. Heat crept to her face, and she forced her breathing to slow. The Penningtons—especially Frederica—had hurt Kate's heart. And that could not be forgiven so easily—if at all.

"You'll not travel to London, Henry. I forbid it."

Grandfather adjusted his spectacles on his nose and leaned forward on his desk amid the tidy stacks of letters and papers. The old man didn't blink. He didn't move. His sharp eyes remained fixed on Henry. "Mollie can wait. You will remain here in Amberdale."

Jolted at the intensity in his grandfather's voice, Henry lowered his coat and pivoted on his heel.

Perhaps Grandfather had forgotten that he was a man, no longer a boy.

A chuckle of disbelief slipped through his lips, although his mood was anything but light. Henry's first full day at the mill had already been a tiring one. After spending hours sifting through orders at the desk, becoming acquainted with his grandfather's new staff, receiving news of an attack in a nearby mill, and overseeing work for hours in the cold on the waterwheel, he was in no humor for an argument. "You *forbid* me?"

Grandfather took no notice of the sarcasm in Henry's tone. "You have duties here—at this mill. I'll not have you traipsing off to London on a fool's errand, not when there's so much to be done."

Henry's boots scraped against the floor as he widened his stance and folded his arms over his chest. "My plans are firm. I'm going to London to see Mollie. I've not seen her in three years. *Three.* What could possibly need my attention here when you thought me dead not even a week ago?"

The corner of Grandfather's thin lips twitched, and the firelight cast odd shadows on his angular face. "You're here now. Your focus should be on the mill. And on your other duties."

Henry raised his eyebrows. "My other duties?"

Grandfather removed his spectacles, placed them atop a book on his desk, and inched a candle lamp to the side. "The Stockton name must be preserved, and Miss Pennington will not remain unmarried forever. Several men have noticed her charms and are no doubt vying for her hand as we speak. If you are to pursue such a union, you must act quickly, else you will be too late."

"Egad, Grandfather." Henry shoved his hair away from his forehead. "I've only just returned. I assure you, marriage is the furthest thing from my mind right now."

"Then I urge you to reconsider your priorities." Grandfather's voice was frustratingly slow and direct. "Your sister failed to do that very thing, and you can see the outcome. She's disgraced herself. I've not worked this hard to tolerate such a black mark against the Stockton name from either one of you."

Henry checked the defensive response teetering on the tip of his tongue. Grandfather may have raised him, and by doing so deserved Henry's respect, but in this instance he was wrong. Furthermore, how would Grandfather react if he knew what Henry had been forced to do in the name of war and battles and victory? The black marks against his name and the evils he had committed would make Mollie's appear irreproachable.

"Mistake or not, Mollie is still my sister. I cannot be so punitive and cast her aside so coldheartedly."

"That is a sign of weakness, boy." Grandfather shook his head, the reddening of his face betraying his cool exterior. "You've shown the flaw to me. Let no one else see it."

"She is guilty of an error in judgment, nothing more." He abandoned his position by the fireplace and stepped closer to the desk. "Are we not all guilty of such an offense at one point or another?"

"Bah." Grandfather flung his hand in the air as if to wave off a bug or another such nuisance. "There are consequences for such moral lapses, and she must pay them."

Heat rose up from beneath Henry's neckcloth. If he didn't come to Mollie's defense, who would? "She's hardly the first woman to find herself in such a situation. As her family, shouldn't we protect her?"

"I'm already paying for her keep with her aunt. I've been more than generous given her folly, and I dare anyone to say otherwise. Her actions demonstrate a dire lack of respect for this family. No." He shook his head. "My decision's made."

Henry threw his hands outward and raised his voice an octave. "But what of the child?"

"The child will be *illegitimate*," Grandfather said, leaning into the argument. "It is therefore no family of mine."

"That child will be *my* niece or nephew, and *I* will not make his or her life more difficult than I fear it will already be."

The mantel clock ticked painfully loudly in the empty space between their words, falling heavy like fat drops of rain on glass. Henry sighed. "What of the father? Can he not be found? If they marry, perhaps there is time to save her reputation."

"Nay, your selfish sister will not reveal his identity." Vehemence sharpened Grandfather's tone. "I've threatened and coaxed, yet she refuses. No doubt she keeps her secret, for if she dared to breathe his name, it would be pistols at dawn for the scoundrel."

Henry huffed and shook his head.

Clearly that was not the reaction Grandfather desired.

The old man reached for the ornately carved cane leaning against his desk and rapped it on the planked floor, then pointed his thick finger at Henry. "Listen to me, boy. I've been explicitly clear on my expectations for this family, have I not? You may be a man of five and twenty, but I'm the head of this family and will be until the day I'm buried in the earth.

"You wanted to go play soldier, be upstanding and fight against Napoleon and all the other scoundrels and villains that threaten England's borders, and I paid for your commission. *I* paid it, on the sole condition that you would return and focus on your duties, which now are tending to the family business, settling down in Amberdale, and taking a wife, not rectifying your sister's ill decisions. It's time for you to make good on your promise. You'll do it now. Am I understood?"

Henry stared at his grandfather, words frozen in his throat. The clock's ticking was now deafening. The room's shadows emphasized the deep-set creases around his mouth and the furrow of his weathered brow. The callous, pale-blue eyes that at one time were so like his own now gleamed cold and distant. It was as if Henry were looking at a stranger, not at the man who raised him.

He'd been home only a couple of days, but it was becoming clear that his grandfather was not the same man as when Henry had left. Hardness had settled over him, from the way he treated the children at the mill to the way he treated his own granddaughter.

Henry would not win this battle—not this evening. He cleared his throat. "Very well. I'll wait to leave for London for a week or so, but I will travel there within the fortnight."

A sardonic grin creased the old man's face at his slight victory. "I suppose you think you're being noble, rushing to the aid of a fallen woman. But I have lived nearly sixty years on this earth, and I can tell you with certainty that such heroics are wasted. Consider your future! This scandal will adhere to the Stockton name for years, nay, generations to come. When you learn more of the ways of the world, boy, you will see the truth in what I say."

"The ways of the world? Grandfather, I have been in battle. When you see a man die right next to you, believe me, you see full the ways of the world."

Grandfather did not bat an eye. "These are difficult times. Success depends on more than just cloth and wool. It is a political landscape that must be traversed with wisdom. If you want any future with Stockton Mill, or Stockton House, or anything else associated with your birthright, you'll give greater care to your reputation."

CHAPTER 9

*T*he cart shifted as Kate lifted her wool skirt and flannel petti-coat and climbed onto the wooden seat next to her brother. The horse at the cart's helm pawed his hoof against the frozen ground and whinnied, sending a plume of frosty breath into the black night.

"I'm sorry I'm late." Charles adjusted the reins in his gloved hands as Kate settled the sewing basket at her feet. "I was detained at the mill."

"Oh, that's all right." Kate tightened her cloak around her and tucked her hair back beneath her cloak's hood. "Thank you for driving me home. It's so cold I fear I would have frozen solid if I had walked."

"You shouldn't be out at all in this weather." He lifted a blanket from under the seat, extended it toward her, and nodded toward her basket. "What were you ladies working on tonight, stockings or muffs?"

"Neither." Kate accepted the blanket and arranged it over her lap. She retrieved her incomplete project, smiling proudly. "Mittens. For the parish to give to the poor."

"Ah." He took the mitten from her, held it up, eyed the uneven weave. "I didn't realize your knitting skills had progressed so far."

Her shoulders sagged as the playful sarcasm in her brother's voice met her ear. With a giggle, she snatched her creation back. "It isn't that dreadful, is it? It may not be the most beautiful mitten in the world, but it will keep someone's hands warm, and that's what's important. Sadly, we cannot keep up with the need."

Charles looked up to the dark, clouded sky. "Spring will be here before too much longer, and then there will not be a need for such things. At least that is something we can all look forward to."

"Ah, but then another need will replace it." Kate rubbed her hands together as the truth of her statement settled over her. So many had so little, and many had no prospect of improving their situation. Despite the uncertainty of her future, Kate had to admit she was fortunate. Her father's business remained strong. She never worried about when she would eat or feared she would go to sleep cold, like some of the Amberdale residents.

Charles urged the horse forward, and before long they crossed the stone bridge leading out of the village. He lifted his voice to be heard above the wind. "Besides the cold, there is another reason I would prefer that you not walk alone at night. There's been another attack on a mill over in Wakefield. I don't think it's safe for you to be out on your own now. Not until the violence lessens."

"You sound like Father," Kate teased, hoping to ease the worry coloring his tone.

His voice tightened. "Well, in this one instance, he would be right."

Kate sighed and let her shoulders roll forward slightly as they swayed with the jostling wagon.

After several minutes of silence, Charles continued. "How is Father?"

Normally Charles's words were strong and clear, but his voice always seemed to grow thin when he inquired after their father.

She bit her lip. She'd been warned more than once by Father and

John against sharing Meadowvale's details with Charles, but how could she not? He may no longer live within Meadowvale gates, but he was still her brother.

Kate cleared her throat. "He has gone to Leeds."

"I'm not surprised." Charles's expression remained flat. "I've heard the shearmen have been meeting to discuss how to combat the gig mills."

"How do you know that?"

"It isn't exactly a secret." Charles fixed his gaze on the dark road ahead. "I wish you'd reconsider my offer and live with me at my cottage. I don't like the thought of you at Meadowvale with all of this turmoil going on."

Kate adjusted her cape. "I thank you for your concern, but you're overreacting."

"Things are not like they used to be, Kate." He slapped the reins on the horse's back. "The situation is quite serious, and grows more so by the day."

"I am not going to leave Father." She gave a definite nod. "I could never leave him. My mind is made up on that count. It would break his heart. Besides, all has been quiet in the meadow. I'm not in the least fearful."

"Things are quiet for now, but you know how things have been. I told you that the mill over in Wakefield was attacked, and I have heard reports that the local weavers are up in arms about the recent occurrences at the cloth halls. You probably know much more than I do about that, but I urge you to be cautious of whom you trust."

"Father needs me," she stated, as much to reassure herself as him.

Charles ignored her reason. "I fear these attacks are only the beginning. With Henry Stockton back, who knows what else will change."

She straightened but did not respond. It seemed the name Henry

Stockton was on everyone's lips, and as much as she hated it, the man she was supposed to despise intrigued her in an inexplicable way.

They drove in silence, and eventually all trace of light from the village disappeared until all that remained were the sparse silvery bits of moonlight stealing through deep, shifting clouds. She'd traveled this road so many times she could make it home with her eyes closed. They passed the Noons' cottage. The gatehouse for the Wolberdon estate. The old iron gate that marked the entrance to Stockton House. She averted her eyes as they did so.

"Just keep my offer in mind," Charles said suddenly, as if the conversation had been simmering in his mind. "Besides, the longer you stay at Meadowvale, the more you will become part of that world."

"I am already a part of that world," she whispered.

"But you don't have to be. That way of life is dying, Kate. It's why I left. Before long, there will not be enough work to sustain a livelihood."

He had shared his argument with her numerous times. She understood his reasoning. And she did not necessarily disagree with them. But her loyalty to her father ran too deep. After all, they had been raised at Meadowvale. Their mother had lived there. And if—*if*—Father's plan came to fruition, she would marry and probably never leave the cottage.

Without warning, shouts cracked to the west.

Charles jerked the horse to a halt. "Did you hear that?"

Kate shuddered. Her brother's words of danger hammered fresh in her mind, and her pulse jumped. She whipped her head around to learn the source of the distress.

Another undecipherable cry broke the icy silence, and then hoofbeats thundered across the shadowed pasture to their left.

"Is that smoke?" Charles asked, the sound of a sharp inhale rising above the disrupted silence.

Kate lifted her nose and drew a breath. At first all seemed normal, but then the abrasive sensation of smoke replaced the spicy scent of Scots pines and snow. She turned. Behind her, a yellow glow flickered into the night sky. "Fire!"

"It's Stockton House," he blurted. "Hold on."

Apprehension billowed to alarm, and Kate gripped the cart's rickety seat as her brother turned the vehicle with a shout.

Her cloak's hood blew backward, and bits of icy snow struck her face. She clutched her cloak closed. A chill raced through her core as they sped down the darkened lane in the direction from which they had come. With each fall of the horse's hooves, the scent of smoke intensified.

The gate, which had just been closed when they passed, was now open. Charles yanked the reins and turned the cart up the drive. Kate struggled both to keep her seat and to comprehend the situation at the same time.

It was not the main house that was ablaze, but a building just to the east of it.

How had this happened so quickly?

Charles pulled to a stop and leapt down from the cart. "Stay here." He tossed the reins in her direction before moving to secure a length of canvas around the horse's eyes. "Don't move, you hear? This horse will spook. Hold him tight."

Kate shifted on the gig's narrow bench and coughed as the smoky air infiltrated her lungs, thicker and more invasive than the first wisps of smoke she'd encountered on the road. Transfixed by the sight, she watched for several minutes as the bright, leaping light illuminated the figures of two men and one woman battling the blaze. One of the men struggled to lead animals from the burning structure.

She should stay where she was, like Charles had instructed, but even as she held the horse steady, she felt useless.

She hated to be useless.

The black horse pranced from foot to foot. He whinnied and tossed his head back in agitation. She adjusted the reins, but without warning the stable's roof crashed in, spewing a plume of smoke and cinders. She cowered at the sudden noise, and the horse shrieked and reared. Kate scrambled to tighten the slack on the reins, but the animal bolted before she could pull them taut.

The animal raced down the shadowed drive and rounded a corner far too quickly for the ancient gig. Kate slid to the side and slammed against the low seat rail. As she did, the cart tilted. Her weight shifted and the short side rail snapped.

The reins ripped from her gloved hands. With a sharp cry she tumbled and fell against the black stone wall lining the drive. The jagged limestone ripped through her sleeve and tore her arm's tender flesh, and her head crashed against the wall before her entire body slid to the path below. Air whooshed from her mouth as she landed. White dots flurried in her vision.

The immediate pain stole her breath, even more so than the smoke. Her body fell limp, and she did not fight it. She closed her eyes until all was black, and she gasped for air.

Minutes passed. Perhaps it was only seconds, she had no way to tell. Sounds crunched toward her. Voices. She opened her eyes and looked to her side. Two blurry silhouettes were approaching from the direction of the fire.

"Don't move." Charles dropped to his knees next to her, his breath puffing out in a fog above her. He rested his hand on her shoulder. "Are you all right?"

Shaking away her confusion, Kate grimaced as pain pierced her head. The smoke stung her eyes and scratched her lungs, and her arm screamed in protest at her injury. She dared not look at the sight. "I—I fell against the wall."

"I can see that." Charles held out her arm to examine the wound and then slowly helped her to a seated position. "What happened?"

Kate blinked away the snowflakes. "The horse was frightened. I think the gig seat broke, and I fell off. Where is the horse?"

"Don't worry about him." Charles steadied her shoulders and patiently helped her to her feet, allowing her time to test each limb as she put weight on it. "He'll find his way home. Where are you hurt?"

"I hit my head." She struggled to maintain balance. "And my arm." She winced as she took a step forward. Then she lifted her gaze. Her vision was clearing. Just behind her brother stood Henry Stockton.

She could barely make out his features, not with the firelight flaming behind him, but there was no denying the straight nose and square jaw.

"Miss Dearborne." His words anxious, he stepped from behind Charles. He reached out to steady her but then pulled his hand away.

She could only blink. How she must appear. Everywhere hurt, but now, more than anything, her pride throbbed. The fall had pulled the pins from her hair, and it tumbled over her shoulders and face in pitiful disarray.

She searched for words amidst the confusion of the night's odd events. "A misstep, 'tis all." Eager to turn the attention away from herself, she nodded toward the raging fire. "The stable?"

But one look in its direction answered her question.

In the light of the dancing flames the stone walls were visible, darkened and charred. They were still standing, but there was no roof.

Fists propped on his waist, Mr. Stockton followed her gaze and turned to assess the burning structure. His breath came in huffs, she noted, and damp hair clung to his forehead. "Just a building. No animals were injured as far as we know. Could have been worse. But more importantly, you are injured. Come inside where we can tend to the wound."

Panic surged at the thought of entering his residence. She flicked her gaze to the massive estate he called home. What would her father say if he knew? "No, thank you. I only need to go to Meadowvale."

"Kate, best have a look at it," Charles interrupted, his voice soft. "You're bleeding."

She shifted uncomfortably under her brother's insistence.

Charles leaned close and lowered his voice. "This is Mr. Stockton. You can trust him."

You can trust him.

Charles's words were intended to reassure her, but how could she trust the man whose very presence was a threat to her way of life?

Despite her reservations, her options were limited. They no longer had a cart. How would she get home? Walk? A shiver traveled her spine and her hands trembled. One look at her brother confirmed his coat had gotten far too wet from the water buckets to be walking her home. She had no choice, and with each heartbeat her wound throbbed. The entire side of her gown was damp from the soggy snow covering the ground, and her cloak lay at her feet in a sodden heap.

Mr. Stockton leaned down and picked up her cloak but did not extend it to her. "Come inside, Miss Dearborne. I only mean to help."

Her body ached, and the world around her tilted. She feared she might faint if she stood up much longer. She could not spend her energy in an argument. "Very well."

Kate took Charles's arm and turned toward Stockton House. She bit her lip as her gaze climbed from the hedges flanking the door to the leaded windows above it to the slate roof stories above her. A strange sense took hold of her, as if the moment she stepped foot in the enemy's home, everything would change.

And the thought frightened her.

CHAPTER 10

$\mathcal{H}$enry's heart thudded, wild and untamed, threatening to burst from the confines of his ribs.

The stable, burned.

Miss Dearborne, injured.

Both on his property.

True, he'd hoped to encounter the mysterious beauty again, but hardly in this manner.

He squeezed his eyes shut and pinched the bridge of his nose as he traversed the familiar, frozen path of the main drive. The lingering smoke burned his eyes and clawed at his throat. Henry slowed his steps just enough to glance back at the stable. Hot, white embers popped into the night sky, spreading their scent of burning wood and hay. The horses were loose in the garden, and Mrs. Figgs was attempting to corral them. Mr. Figgs had the blaze under control, but in truth, there was little left to save.

Henry could not think of those things now. None of it mattered. He adjusted Miss Dearborne's wet cloak over his forearm. She needed assistance, and at the moment that was his top priority—whether she cared for him or not.

He opened the servants' door to the kitchen. Warm, yellow light ushered them into safety. "My apologies for bringing you in through the kitchen. Mrs. Figgs's remedies are in the pantry, and I would hate to make you walk so far out of the way. Please, come in by the fire and warm yourselves." Henry crossed the threshold.

She stopped in the doorway, eyeing the space with cautious reserve. Her long chestnut hair hung nearly down to her waist, damp and windblown, curling under its own will. But it was her expression, full of discomfort and skepticism, that caused his breath to hitch in his throat. After several moments of silent assessment, she complied and stepped next to the fire.

As the fire's glow illuminated her slender form, Henry winced. A rivulet of blood trickled down her cheek. The upper portion of her sleeve hung shredded over her forearm, revealing a messy, crimson gash.

The sight of blood unleashed a battalion of unwanted images in his mind—memories of injuries much worse than this one. He wiped the perspiration gathering on his temple with the back of his hand and willed his lungs to expand for a breath.

Would the sight of blood always affect him so?

He discarded his wet coat and hung it and Miss Dearborne's cloak near the fire.

"Dearborne, will you get that chair for your sister?" Henry instructed, finding it easier to fall into his past role of giving orders when a crisis occurred. "I'll return shortly."

Henry stepped out of the kitchen, rolling up his sleeves as he did so, and entered the pantry. He'd retrieved Mrs. Figgs's medicine box dozens of times as a boy, and constant boyhood scrapes made him familiar with its contents. As he sifted through the bottles and jars, he could hear the conversation between the siblings as clearly as if he were still in the room with them.

"I shouldn't be here," she hissed.

"It's fine," Dearborne whispered. "We need to tend to your arm."

"Father would be furious."

"He'd be more furious if you returned home in your current state."

After a pause, she whispered again. "This is a mess."

"You trust me, don't you? I trust Mr. Stockton. All will be well. You'll see."

Feeling more like an intruder instead of the house's master, Henry returned with water, linen, and Mrs. Figgs's salve. He forced a smile and knelt before Miss Dearborne. "May I? I can assure you I've had a great deal of experience binding up wounds."

Miss Dearborne flashed her wide eyes to her brother. She shifted uncomfortably in the chair before extending her arm toward him.

Henry prepared to move the fabric away from her arm and then stopped. Her brother's cautious eye would be quick, no doubt, to catch anything that might cast a shadow on his sister's feminine virtues. "Would you prefer to clean it?"

Dearborne shook his head. "I wouldn't know what to do."

Miss Dearborne flinched and straightened when he adjusted the angle of her arm.

"I'm just looking at it. I won't touch it yet." He garnered the courage to look at her again. Her lovely eyes, deep pools of hazel, were fixed on his hand. Balanced in their golden depths was an emotion—but which one? Her expression confirmed she did not want to be in his kitchen any more than he wanted to have guests. In that measure, at least, they understood each other without saying a word.

He returned his attention to the wound. It appeared as if the bleeding had stopped, or at least slowed. The arm would be easy enough to tend. He lifted his gaze to the blood trickling down her smooth cheek.

He tipped his head toward the injury. "May I?"

She exchanged a glance with her brother and then nodded.

He forced his hand to steady as he used his forefinger to angle her chin toward the light.

"You've quite a bump here." Her nearness clouded his thoughts. With his free hand he dabbed the linen in the water and washed the blood from her temple. "Your head hit the wall, correct?"

She swallowed. "Yes, sir." She leaned forward, and a tendril of hair fell in front of her shoulder, unleashing the scent of lavender, a pleasant diversion from smoke and burnt hay.

A shiver shot up his arm as he brushed her hair back with his fingers and wiped the wound. "You'll have a pretty decent bump I'm afraid, and a mighty headache I fear, but I think you'll be all right."

"How is it that you have so much experience tending injuries?" she asked.

He dipped the cloth in the water once more, then squeezed the linen. "War. Unfortunately it turns soldiers into medics, whether they desire to be or not." He managed a smile, hoping to ease the discomfort of them both.

It didn't work.

He dipped his finger into the salve and scooped up a bit of the slimy, strongly scented ointment. "This might sting." He applied it as gently as he could.

She flinched but said nothing.

Henry was grateful when Dearborne broke the heavy silence. "How did the fire start?"

Henry shook his head. "I wish I knew. I had retired for the evening, and when I looked out my chamber window, I noticed the blaze."

"And I haven't seen Mr. Stockton. Is he not here?"

"Grandfather's not returned from the mill yet."

Dearborne clicked his tongue and gave his head a sharp shake. "I was afraid something like this might happen."

"You mean because I'm here?" Henry's words were much rougher than he'd intended.

He stood and pulled up a chair next to Miss Dearborne, then sat down and returned his attention to her arm. "There is some debris. We must get it out so it won't fester. This part might hurt a little."

She winced as he dabbed it.

"I'm sorry."

"Don't be."

Henry shook his head and dipped the rag in the bowl of tepid water.

"I take it you suspect foul play?" Dearborne crossed his arms over his barrel chest, returning the conversation to the topic at hand.

Henry raised his eyes and answered the question with one of his own. "Should I?"

Dearborne shifted his weight, sweat gathering beneath his hairline. "While we were driving on the lane, just south of your entrance, we heard horses racing across the meadow. I can only imagine they were fleeing the scene."

Miss Dearborne's amber eyes flicked in his direction, but she remained silent.

"I see." Once he was certain the wound was clean, Henry pressed the cloth against it. She tensed beneath his touch, and he did his best to avoid touching her skin with his fingers. He was already too close to her. "It appears that someone—or some people—are not happy about my arrival."

At his words, her body flinched.

She was clearly a member of that group.

He was about to finish binding the wound when the door flew back against the kitchen's plaster wall, rattling the pewter plates on the shelves and the china in the cupboard.

Grandfather burst through the narrow door. He wore no cloak. No hat covered his thick gray hair. Air puffed from his chest as audible growls, and wild anger gleamed in his faded-blue eyes.

Henry jumped to his feet, nearly knocking over his chair as he did so.

Grandfather slammed his walking cane against the stone floor and pinned Henry with his gaze. "They will be stopped. Do you hear me?" After a slew of curses he looked toward Dearborne and then back to Henry.

Henry raked his fingers through his hair and cast a glance at Miss Dearborne. Her pale face and wide eyes were no longer fixed on him but on his grandfather.

Did the man even notice her? "Grandfather, I—"

He silenced Henry by pointing a thick finger in his direction. "And there is not a doubt in my head who is behind this. If they think for a moment that—"

"We have a guest," Henry blurted out, extending his arm to Miss Dearborne.

Grandfather whirled around. His brows jumped when he took notice of her. He'd never had the reputation of being a gracious host, but even Henry cringed as the old man scowled. "What in blazes are you doing here?" he thundered.

Miss Dearborne's mouth fell open.

Henry stepped in front of her. "She was with Dearborne when he came to help."

"I'll bet she was." His icy gaze pinned their feminine guest to her chair. "What's wrong with her arm?"

"She was injured while we were fighting the blaze."

Henry expected Grandfather's tone to soften. After all, the woman was hurt. On their property. But instead, he stepped two large paces toward her. "Do you doubt that I make good on my promises?"

To Henry's surprise, Miss Dearborne did not flinch. Her voice was stronger than it had been since her arrival. "No, sir."

Henry stepped closer. "Grandfather, she had nothing to do with—"

"And do you think I am so easily shaken"—his grandfather ignored him and moved closer to their guest—"that I would cower to intimidation?"

"No, sir." Her eyes were direct. Unwavering. "I do not."

"Rest assured, Miss Dearborne, that the burning of a stable will not deter me." In a flurry of anger, Grandfather turned to stomp from the room.

Her soft words stopped him, her voice cool and controlled. "I would ask you the same question, Mr. Stockton."

He turned slowly, a vein throbbing on his forehead. "What did you say?"

She stood, her shoulders pressed back, her pointed chin jutted high. She surprised Henry further by closing the space between her and his grandfather. Pink rushed to her cheeks. Perhaps this was the dogged Dearborne determination he'd heard about but never witnessed. "You asked me a question, and now it is my turn to ask it of you. Do you think that *I* will cower to intimidation?"

Henry's eyebrows shot up. He'd spent most of his life protecting his sister from his grandfather's harsh tones. His instinct was to protect Miss Dearborne.

Miss Dearborne, however, was different.

Clearly she did not need his help.

CHAPTER 11

"Where've you been, Kate?" John's voice called to her from somewhere off to the right.

Kate froze in her steps just inside Meadowvale's main gate. Clutching her damp cloak closer to her chest and clasping the borrowed blanket around her shoulders, she looked for John but did not see him.

The hairs on her neck prickled in the night air.

A lantern's glow caught her eye, and she glanced in the direction of the sheep house.

There, next to the wooden structure, stood a dark figure.

Kate turned her attention to the main gate, eased it closed to prevent it from slamming, and turned back toward John's approaching figure.

She forced gaiety to her voice. "John, you scared me. What are you doing out here lurking in the shadows?"

"I could ask you the same question." He lifted the lantern higher, and the light glinted against his unshaven jaw and prominent cheekbones. His expression held no humor. His emotionless eyes did not waver.

"I was at the sewing meeting at the Purty home." She brushed past him toward the cottage.

His long stride quickly overtook hers, and he fell into step next to her, his boots heavy and loud against the thickening layer of snow. "I encountered Mrs. Wooden in the village, and she was leaving the same meeting you were. That was two hours ago."

Kate groaned inwardly. Father may have left John in charge of Meadowvale, but he did not leave him in charge of *her*. The last thing she wanted was to be forced to give John an account of her day. "I visited with Jane afterward and it took us a while to finish our conversation."

"I heard a man's voice. There, with you, outside the gate," John persisted.

"It was Charles, of course."

When she did not slow her pace, John took her by the arm and held it firm.

She winced as his fingers squeezed her injured flesh, and she yanked her arm back. "What are you doing?"

"How is it that a brother, who is well aware of the danger in these nights, will drop off his only sister at the gate on a public road and not have the decency to see her safely to the door?"

She tightened her grip on the blanket. "You know the situation. Charles is not welcome at Meadowvale."

Without another word she continued toward the cottage, but he stepped in front of her, blocking her path. "You've been avoiding me all day, Kate."

Annoyed, she stopped and crossed her arms over her chest, holding her bundle close. The day had been long—too long for her to consider standing out in the cold for one more minute to discuss a topic that would have no resolution. At least not this night. "I don't wish to argue."

"Nor do I." He leaned closer, his scent of perspiration encircling her. His eyebrows drew together as he focused on her face. "Have you been crying?"

"No. It's from smoke." She stiffened, regretting the words the moment they left her mouth.

"I have smelled smoke on the air. Must be a fire somewhere." John held the lantern higher, then his gaze fell on the blanket around her shoulders. His eyes narrowed. Without permission he reached out and touched the fabric.

Kate froze. It was too late to step out of reach.

She was still wrapped in the blanket from Stockton House that Mrs. Figgs had given her to wear on their walk home. She need not see his face to know what he was thinking. Like any man in textiles, he could feel the unique texture of the cloth. And he no doubt recognized it was not cloth from Meadowvale.

His countenance darkened, and he nodded toward the door. "You'd best get inside, then. It's cold out, and the night will grow colder still."

Without another word Kate hurried indoors and took the back stairs to her chamber, quiet so as not to draw Betsy's or anyone else's attention. By the time she rounded the small, dark landing and reached the top of the creaky stairs, tears had gathered in her eyes.

She had seen the way John had looked at her. Desire balanced in his dark eyes. But what was the source of that desire?

Perhaps he was concerned for her and cared for her, as a man in love cares for a woman.

Perhaps he merely saw her as a means to an end, as a man intent upon securing his future.

She had also seen the way Henry Stockton had looked at her. Even though her father was his enemy, he welcomed her into his home. Tended her arm and head. Asked nothing in return.

She entered her modest bedchamber and stepped closer to the fire that had undoubtedly been lit by Betsy, poking it to revive the flame.

Once the flame leapt with life, she shed the Stockton blanket from her shoulders and held the length of broadcloth up to the firelight to assess the tightly woven fibers and the smooth color of the dye. The soft brown fabric had its own texture, but it was not so different from the fabric produced by her father and his journeymen. Her heart sank at the realization. She liked to believe, as her father did, that their process of cloth making produced a finer fabric. But the Stockton cloth was impressive. She folded the blanket and set it atop the trunk next to the window.

Kate struggled to unbutton her dress without Betsy's assistance, but after removing her soggy, torn gown and damp underclothes, she pulled her heavy flannel nightdress over a dry chemise. After donning two pairs of wool stockings and wrapping a fresh shawl around her chilled shoulders, she returned to the trunk beneath the window and sat atop it, angling herself so she could see Stockton House.

Daily she had looked out this window and beheld the intimidating structure, and for years she had believed that its inhabitants were her enemy. That was certainly true of the older Mr. Stockton. But the younger Mr. Stockton had been quite different. Based on his behavior toward her tonight, she could almost believe it when her brother said he could be trusted.

Almost.

She tucked her knees under her chin, leaned her cheek upon them, and spied the top of the black mill beyond the shadowed, frost-laden forest. How easy it would be to believe like her father. *"Security first. Happiness second."* But it seemed such a bleak outlook.

She tried to recall what her mother would have told her during times such as these, but the memories were foggy, and they grew more so by the day. How she wished her mother were here now, to help guide her through the difficult waters—to help her make sense of the attention from John Whitby and to be a voice of reason in the midst of the weavers' plight against the mills.

Since her mother's death nearly ten years prior, Kate had had no feminine guidance, and now she was at the mercy of her father and those he put in positions of authority around her. Her mother would have reminded her that anger would only be a burden to her and no one else. She would have urged Kate to forgive the offenses of others and forget them, lest she struggle under their weight. Mother would have urged her to seek the good in those around her, like John Whitby.

Kate sniffed. She had entirely too much of her father in her. His propensity to hold a grudge and cling to wrongs had skipped Charles entirely and landed solely in her character. It was a negative trait, she knew, but one so hard to deny.

She lifted her gaze from the black mill to the starless sky. She thought it impossible to forgive someone like Mr. Stockton or the Penningtons, but as she let her fingers trail over the space where Henry Stockton had bound her wound, she began to think that maybe, just maybe, a Stockton might not be *all* bad.

Henry leaned his elbow against the wooden table, stared into the waning fire, and rubbed his palm over the stubble gathering on his chin. Cool dampness still clung to his linen shirt and wool waistcoat, creating an irritating cocoon around his torso, and smoke's inescapable scent burned his nose and lungs.

He felt his chest tighten at the recollection of the evening's occurrences. His mind rushed to make sense of it all, from a physical attack on his property to Miss Dearborne's injury to Grandfather's heartless treatment of their female guest. Surprisingly, what shocked him the most was his grandfather. Henry barely recognized him. He'd always been a gruff man with sharp opinions and exacting expectations, but something must have happened while Henry was away to harden him to the point of downright cruelty.

How foolish he had been to think that he had left the war behind him and life would be easier once he returned to England's countryside. Not only did he find his neighbors engaged in a war of their own, but the battleground seemed to be the same land he called home.

Henry turned as Mrs. Figgs appeared in the kitchen's threshold. The soot smudged on her cheek and her clothing spoke to the evening's events. She carried two cups of tea and placed one of them before him. "Drink this."

Henry made no motion to drink the tea.

She nudged his shoulder. "Go on now, do as I say. You look the worse for wear, and after being out in the cold and wet night, you'll be sick as a dog if you're not careful."

Battling reluctance, he obeyed the stern order and then grimaced at the bitter taste. "What is that?"

"My special brew." She nodded. "It will keep you well, mark my words. There now, drink it all, like I told you."

He'd never win this argument, not against the stubborn housekeeper. He took another sip. The heat eased his throat, but it did little to touch the chill plaguing the rest of his person.

"Can I get you something to eat?" Mrs. Figgs propped her fist on her waist, her head tilted to the side. It did not matter that the clock was nearing midnight. If Mrs. Figgs was awake, she was busy tending something.

Henry shook his head. He couldn't eat a bite, especially after this tea. He pushed the teacup forward and leaned back in the chair. He pinched the bridge of his nose. "What a strange night it has been."

Mrs. Figgs set her teacup on the table and wiped her hands on her apron. "Aye."

If he wanted to know the true state of the Stockton estate and his grandfather, there was no greater expert than Mrs. Figgs. Henry shifted to face her. "How long has it been like this?"

She gave a comical laugh and brushed long white wisps back under her soot-streaked white cap with the back of her work-worn hand. "To what are you referring? The fighting between the millers and the weavers, or your grandfather's brashness?"

"Both, I suppose."

The chair's legs scraped across the uneven stone floor as she pulled it away from the table. She sat and leaned forward and pinned him with a direct gaze, as if taking Henry into her confidence. "As for the weavers—the Dearbornes, the Woodens, the Purtys, and the like—these are precarious times. You must understand. You were away when the law changed. In years past the millers were limited in the number of machines that could occupy their mills. Now those limits are lifted, and the weavers have lost the last thread of power they had against the mill owners. When that happened, your grandfather added more and more of those machines, which meant he discharged many of his longtime workers."

She took a sip of tea and returned the cup to the table. "To upset them further, he employed children to run the machines, which took jobs from their fathers and uncles."

Henry lifted his gaze to the copper pots and drying herbs hanging from the kitchen's low beams. He could understand why they would be upset at the prospect of children working jobs previously held by full-grown men. He was too.

Mrs. Figgs wiped her hair from her face. "Most recently he made arrangements to purchase a gig mill—one of those mills that finishes the cloth, you know, that raises the nap and trims it off. Normally this work is put out to the shearmen to do in their own homes. One mill alone will take work from the hands of more than a dozen shearmen."

Henry remembered hearing about the gig mills. They were not a new invention, but they were not common in the area. With so many other battles to fight, they had never been an issue.

Until now.

Mrs. Figgs continued, her grainy voice matter of fact. "From what I understand, your grandfather made an agreement that he would not put in gig mills if they wouldn't strike for more pay. But now it seems he has changed his mind. The weavers feel betrayed. Folks fear for their future."

"But the economy of the entire village is not our business, is it? We are in the business of making cloth. Making money."

Mrs. Figgs raised her eyebrows and shrugged her narrow shoulders. "Depends on how you look at it. Your grandfather and the other Yorkshire mill owners decide who works and who doesn't. The weavers argue that as a prominent village leader, your grandfather should be more concerned about the village's overall economy and caring for the poor. The matter's not an easy one to solve, and I fear it will not be solved any time soon."

Henry stretched out his booted leg beneath the table and crossed his arms over his chest. Grandfather had always been fiercely loyal to those who were dedicated to him and scorned those who were not. It had been one of his greatest attributes—and one of his worst faults.

Mrs. Figgs fixed her gray eyes on Henry. "If I'm being honest, this has been difficult on your grandfather. 'Course he'll never admit to such, but it's taken a toll. He's suspicious of everyone. With the exception of Mr. Belsey, young Mr. Dearborne, and a few others, he dismissed the majority of his supervisors and hired new ones. Even here at the house, you've no doubt noticed the staff is much smaller."

"I noticed the lawn seemed quite altered." Henry recalled the overgrown shrubs and the rusty gate.

"He dismissed the groundskeeper for no other reason than he was related to one of the discharged shearmen. He dismissed several of the kitchen maids, leaving pretty much myself, Mr. Figgs, a stable boy, and a housemaid. He feared they would side with his enemies and sabotage him."

Henry frowned. The behavior was odd, especially for someone as self-assured as his grandfather. "When did this begin?"

"About a year and a half ago, several weavers cut down trees and broke windows at Stockton Mill. One of the trees fell against the waterwheel and halted production for days. Mr. Stockton was furious. Soldiers were brought to town and stayed for weeks to keep the peace, but ever since they left, he's been vigilant, awaiting the next attack that may or may not come."

"So that explains his brashness with Miss Dearborne earlier this evening."

"Oh." Mrs. Figgs's thinning eyebrows rose, and she clicked her tongue. "The feud with the Dearbornes goes far beyond cloth."

"You're referring to Charles Dearborne," Henry clarified.

"The very one." She took a long sip of tea, gave her head a sharp shake, and sighed. "Cloth is one thing, family is another. Rumors are rampant, and the fact that the son of the Amberdale Weavers' Society head weaver turned his back on his own father to work at his rival's mill was fine fodder for gossip for miles around. Silas Dearborne was humiliated."

"Charles has a mind of his own. No doubt he can make his own decisions."

"No doubt he could, but that's what people are saying, and sometimes just the mere mention of something makes it truth in the minds of some."

Henry blew out a breath and forced his fingers through his drying hair. There was a greater story here, he was sure, one he was certain he would learn before too much longer.

Mrs. Figgs reached across the table and patted his other hand. "This is a fine welcome home for you. You look tired. Your room should be warm and toasty by now. You need a good night's sleep. All will look different on the morrow."

She was right. He was tired. A million other questions for her raced through his mind—questions about Mollie, about the Penningtons and the Dearbornes, about dozens of other things—but all that could wait. He pushed himself up from the table and crossed to the paned window to look into the black night. Grandfather had stormed out of the house after his terse conversation with Miss Dearborne and had not yet returned.

The snow had stopped, yet he could not see far. "I wish Grandfather would come back. I don't like not knowing where he is, especially after what has happened."

Mrs. Figgs retrieved a shawl from the hook and joined him at the window. "I also used to worry for him, but don't trouble yourself too much. He's an apprehensive man, as much as he pretends he isn't, and is wrestling with his own demons. I'd bet a month's wages he's at the mill, sleeping in the back."

Henry's jaw twitched. The irony was not lost on him. Was he not wrestling with his own demons—demons that had stowed away with him from battlefields of the Iberian Peninsula?

He gathered his things to retire to his chamber. As he did, Mrs. Figgs caught his arm, halting him in his step. "Be patient with your grandfather. For all of his foibles and shortcomings, he is searching." Her warm smile transported him back to when she would soothe his childhood fears or offer advice.

She patted his cheek with unmasked maternal affection. "God's working on him. Just like He's working on you and every one of us. Your grandfather is scared. He'd deny it to his dying day, but fear's got him in a trap with the jaws clamped tight. I can see plain as day that you disagree with him, and I'm not saying everything he does is just, but things aren't always as they seem."

CHAPTER 12

Restless, Henry stood from the chair and paced the length of his bedchamber. He pulled back the brocade window covering at the west window and peered through the leaded glass—again. Meadowvale was spread out, slumbering in the dark of night. Several outbuildings clustered around the large cottage. A thick forest separated it from the actual village of Amberdale, and several smaller pastures created a border around the rest of the property.

How had Miss Dearborne lived in such proximity all those years and he never noticed?

Smoke curled into the clearing sky, dancing with the fluttery snowflakes, making the small estate seem awake even when all was still.

She was within that quiet house—with her feisty spirit, tenacious determination, achingly beautiful eyes, and intense hatred for him and everything he stood for.

Henry hoped her injury was not too painful. The gash had been a nasty one. But the injury did not upset him as much as the expression in her eyes when she beheld him.

Mistrust.

Dislike.

Suspicion.

He dropped the window covering and slumped into the wing-back chair flanking the mantelpiece. He tried to imagine what Miss Pennington's reaction would be to the night's events. No doubt she would have collapsed with the vapors at the sight of fire, fainted dead away at the appearance of blood, and required days abed to refresh her frazzled nerves.

He pulled off his boots, careful to avoid the bits of mud still cling-ing to them, and leaned his head back against the chair. The fire's warmth and the popping embers' soothing lullaby had nearly lulled him to sleep when a sharp crack echoed.

Henry launched from his chair.

A gunshot.

But had he really heard it? Or was it a nightmare?

Eyes wide and heart racing, Henry spun to his right, then his left.

All was still and quiet, save for the soft, steady ticking of the mantel clock. He put his hand on his chest and took deep, deliberate breaths to slow his breathing.

It had been a common occurrence for months now. He would suddenly awaken from sleep in a panic and cold sweat. His dreams were so vivid he could hardly tell reality from imagination.

But then another shot rang out, equally as loud and real as the first one.

He jumped. That was indeed a pistol's fire. And it was near.

He grabbed his discarded boots, paused just long enough to yank them on, and raced down the hallway. His steps were not as certain as they usually were as he traversed the darkened corridor. He bumped into the wall and nearly ran into the door frame as he turned to the servants' stairs. At the landing he continued down the stairs.

Mrs. Figgs's harried voice met his ears before his eyes saw her. "Do be careful."

Henry rounded the corner into the kitchen to see Mrs. Figgs, in her wrapper and sleeping cap, standing next to her husband. Mr. Figgs was donning his hat, a rifle clutched in his white-knuckled grip.

"What is going on?" Henry demanded.

Mr. Figgs lowered his hat atop his gray head. "That is what I am going to find out."

"I'm coming with you." Henry reached for one of the oilskin cloaks hanging next to the door and flung it over his shoulders. "Has Grandfather returned?"

Mr. Figgs shook his head, his expression sober.

Dread wove itself through Henry's mind.

Something was not right.

"Is there another rifle?"

"Pistols are in Mr. Stockton's office. I'll fetch you one."

By the time Figgs returned with the weapons, Henry had found a hat and was waiting by the door. His pulse hammered through him. He had not been back long enough to fully understand the scope of the turmoil between the mill owners and the weavers, but he knew the situation was dire.

Once Figgs returned, the men stepped out into the night and hurried to the stables for their mounts. No sounds, not even the call of the night birds, echoed from the forest until a crash followed by a man's cry reverberated from the darkness. Wild thrashing ensued, followed by the fading sound of retreating hoofbeats.

Alarm coursed through Henry. With pounding pulse, he pulled himself up on his horse, cocked the pistol, and galloped toward the woods.

He'd been here before—not long ago—racing toward the sound of gunfire. Fear had learned its place—to wait in the shadows until the action was complete. Then, and only then, would it be allowed to emerge and claim the respect it was due.

He tightened his hold on the loaded pistol as the horse charged over the lawn and soared over a low fence.

Well aware that Figgs was just behind him, Henry pushed farther into the forest, not sure what—or who—they sought. He stayed just off the well-worn path cutting through the forest to the mill. After several agonizing moments they drew to a halt. Figgs paused next to him and whispered, "Probably just gypsies. Or poachers."

Reason agreed with Figgs, causing Henry to lean back in his saddle. The hair prickled on the back of his neck—a reliable warning sign with which he was all too familiar. He would not concede until he was certain that his family and their property were secure. "The mill's just beyond that bend. After what happened with the stable, we should check on it to be sure."

They continued on. Just ahead, Henry glimpsed something lighter than its surroundings nestled at the foot of a tree. He squinted to see in the darkness. Without a lantern or the moon's guiding light, it was difficult to see, but as he approached, it became clear: a figure was slumped in a heap on the ground.

Henry snapped to action and slid from the saddle, nearly losing his footing as his boots landed on uneven ground. In four large paces he was next to the body. He dropped to his knees, placed his weapon at his side, and leaned low. "Can you hear me?"

The masculine figure—cloaked in a dark, caped greatcoat—did not move.

Henry grabbed the unresponsive man's shoulder and rolled him so he could face him.

Horror thrust Henry back and stole the wind from his lungs.

Grandfather.

His grandfather's face was ashen in the forest's nocturnal shadows. His eyes were closed, and a smear of blood marked his hollow cheek. His entire body lay limp, like a man who'd taken leave of all consciousness.

Perspiration dotted Henry's brow in spite of the biting wind that howled down through the leafless oak branches and invaded the moment between grandfather and grandson. Henry's blood thundered through his ears and he pressed his face close to his grandfather's, desperate to feel the warmth of a breath puffing from his lips.

He felt none.

Panic gripped tighter.

With frantic movements he felt for a pulse at the neck.

None.

He didn't believe it. He lowered his hand into his grandfather's coat to feel for the heartbeat. A warm, sticky substance met his hand.

Henry's breath caught in his throat, held captive by desperate uncertainty, and he yanked back the coat, garnering courage to face whatever might meet him.

Even in the darkness, he knew the sight. It was the sort of image that would be burned into a person's brain. Blood gleamed dark on Grandfather's light waistcoat.

Henry's hands shook as he forced his mind to organize the facts at hand. He knew the proper protocol, but this was not an unknown soldier. This was his *grandfather.*

He cupped his grandfather's whiskered chin with his hand. "Grandfather."

No response.

Henry shook his shoulder again. Harder. "Grandfather!"

Again no response.

Figgs said something and touched Henry's shoulder. Henry flung his arm back, pushing the older man away much harder than he'd intended. Could Figgs not see that Henry was busy? That his grandfather needed him?

He cleared clothing away from the wound. He'd expected a bullet wound, based on the gunshots he'd heard. And with his next breath he thought he smelled gunpowder. But that did not matter. This was a stab wound.

Henry's stomach revolted at the sight of the sticky liquid. He thought he might be sick.

Figgs touched Henry's arm again, and this time Henry did not push him away. "He's gone, sir, he's—"

"Go back and fetch a lantern and Mrs. Figgs. Hurry!" Henry ripped his coat from his shoulders and jerked the sleeves free, refusing to hear the words he knew were true. He pressed the fabric against the wound, holding it with all his strength, determined to stop the flow of blood.

Perspiration—or perhaps tears—trickled down his face. He continued to apply pressure. Harder. The bitter sting of bile rose in his throat as the blood on his hands thickened. Henry's jaw ached from clenching his teeth. "Come to, Grandfather. Wake up!"

He pinned a hard gaze on Figgs. "What is wrong with you?" Henry shouted, his head throbbing. "Go now! Get Mrs. Figgs and fresh linen."

Figgs grabbed Henry's arm, firm enough this time to still Henry's movement. "He's gone, Henry. He's gone."

Chest heaving, lungs burning, Henry lowered his hands, suddenly unable to bear the weight of holding them steady.

The silence—the deafening silence—roared through him, ripping at the few remaining bits of his soul.

Grandfather was dead.

And he'd been unable to save him.

CHAPTER 13

*T*he rumors are true, gentlemen." Silas Dearborne's gravelly voice rose once again above the impromptu weavers' meeting, demanding attention and daring anyone to interrupt him. "William Stockton is dead. All eyes are now on us."

Kate chewed her lower lip, mustering the courage to glance around the room at the dozens of somber masculine faces. All was silent, save for the wind howling across the distant moors and rattling the windows in their casings. Not a single attendee moved; not a single voice uttered a whisper.

Kate refocused on her sewing as she sat in the back of Meadowvale's drawing room without really seeing her needlework's emerging pattern. Concentration was elusive, a fickle companion—one made even more unpredictable by recent morbid events. The fire to her left was becoming too warm and stifling in the overcrowded room, but she dared not move a muscle.

William Stockton had not even been laid to rest yet, and already the weavers grew nervous. Too much change had happened too quickly. The rapid change, compounded with Henry Stockton's recent return and the impending arrival of the gig mills, forced the tension among the weavers to a boiling point, like the dye vat ready for fabric.

Her father, however, stood tall and calm in front of his colleagues. If the murder had rattled him, she could not tell. Sweat beading on his upper lip was the only sign of discomfort. "I spoke with the magistrate, Mr. Tierner, on the matter. They are still investigating potential suspects and motives, but what you have heard is true. Stockton was murdered in his own forest just two days ago, not far from the mill itself."

A fresh shiver skittered down Kate's spine. She had been one of the last people to see him alive, a fact that made her feel inexplicably connected to the matter—and one she refrained from sharing with her father.

Mr. Wooden cleared his throat and lifted his hand for the floor. "Are they sure it was murder and not an accident? He'd not be the first hunter to mishandle a weapon."

"Tierner said he suffered a knife wound in his chest and a blow to his head. 'Twas no accident. A discharged pistol was found at the scene. No one seemed to recognize it, but a gunshot was heard, so perhaps Stockton was attempting to fight someone off. Regardless, they're searching for a man named Wilkes from Beltshire. He was at the mill looking for work and became enraged when he was not given a position."

"I know him," Mr. Codding interjected, his long, narrow face made to look even longer by the shadows from a nearby sconce. "His wife died last year and left two wee ones behind. I saw him in the village myself and talked to him at the public house. But what's he got to do with it? There's no shortage of men who hate the likes of William Stockton."

Father's voice remained steady and deep. "Whether it was Wilkes or someone else, something needs to be done. This is beyond mere mischief and mayhem. Cold-blooded murder will not be forgotten by the authorities or the other millers. The magistrate has sent for soldiers to keep the peace. We are being watched, gentlemen. We and the other weavers like us. I implore each of you to be on your guard."

Father's lips formed a thin line before he resumed. "This leads us to another issue. Until this time we all believed that if something happened to Stockton, that milksop of a fool Belsey would run the mill in his stead, but now that Henry Stockton is back, this will no longer be the case. Now is our opportunity to make sure that young Stockton knows his place."

Kate lifted her eyebrows at the mention of Henry Stockton's name.

"Now is the time, my brothers, that we unite. We may not be behind the murder of William Stockton, but we must take this opportunity to make our voice heard. The weavers of Amberdale are not to be trifled with, and we will take what is ours, or die trying."

The snow fell heavy on Henry's shoulders and his eyelashes, dusting his black caped greatcoat in a veil of white. The flakes dropped on his cheeks and melted as they collided with the heat of his skin.

He should go home, but the thought of returning to the empty abode seemed a lonelier option than remaining here at the graveyard. Overhead, pewter clouds churned, whispering their ominous threats to unleash more snow and sleet. And yet here he stood, his feet planted firmly on the burial ground, his hat in his hand, his hair fluttering in a dance with the raw wind.

He lowered his gaze to the fresh heap of dirt covering his grand-father's coffin. His throat constricted around a tight lump as he read the inscription carved on the polished stone:

Here lies the body of William Herald Stockton.

Henry leaned with his hand on the shoulder-high monument and sniffed. As much as he wanted to deny it, the reality of home was more garish than war. At least in war he had been able to disengage from the actions around him. But the moment his foot stepped back on Stockton property, that self-made wall around his heart began to thin. Now he wished he would have kept the wall intact, firm and impenetrable.

With war death was expected. He'd seen too much and played too much of a role in it. He'd hoped to have left all that behind him. But like a hunter stalking its prey, determined to wreak havoc and destruction, it had followed far too closely.

But what ached more was the knowledge that his final conversa-tion with the man was an argument where anger had prevailed. Guilt and regret boiled inside him, tensing every muscle to the point of pain.

When had life taken such a morbid turn?

He turned his attention once again to the sky, squinting against the fat, falling flakes as thick clouds churned amidst the wind cur-rents. How many times had he done this very thing? Looked up, as if searching for God to answer the questions holding him captive? To release him from the grip of regret? The nightmares would haunt him, he knew. His past actions would be a noose around his neck. He could accept that. But this was different. His regret extended to his grandfather, and that he could not accept.

The snow was hardening to sleet. Bits of ice rained down on him, forcing him to flip his collar higher and return his hat to his head. Standing at the gravestone would not erase what had happened. It would not give him another chance to make things right with his grandfather.

If he was to return home by nightfall, he needed to hurry. Even with the pistol on his person it was not advisable to be in Stockton Forest alone at night.

CHAPTER 14

*W*hen Henry returned to Stockton House that evening, he stepped into the front parlor, shrugged the greatcoat from his shoulders, and swept his wide-brimmed hat from his head. As he lifted his arms to hang the coat on the hall tree, light and rustling from the drawing room drew his attention.

He slowed his motions to make no sound. It was not unusual for the maid to keep the fire ablaze all day, especially in the grip of winter's deepest chill, but the light spilling from the doorway was much brighter than that from a mere fire. Furthermore, he could account for no rustling, unless one of the staff happened to be in the room or one of Grandfather's hunting dogs had found its way in.

His frayed nerves were already on high alert, and he put a cautious hand to his pistol's butt. The weapon had not left his side in days, and he had no intention of parting ways with it now.

He pulled his pistol from his waistband. "Figgs?"

No response.

Pulse thudding, he stepped toward the door, weighing his actions. Deciding surprise to be his best bet, he whirled around the corner, pistol raised.

"Good gracious, Henry!" The light, feminine voice rose from his left. "What on earth are you doing with that pistol? Put it down this instant."

He lowered the gun. A smile crossed his face—the first genuine smile in days—for there, seated on the settee next to the fire, was his very pregnant sister.

"Henry! At last you are home." Mollie put her hands on the arms of the settee, struggling to lift herself up from the cushions.

"Don't get up." He put the pistol on the table and hurried to her, then dropped to the seat and embraced her.

She pulled away and swiped at the tears gathering in her blue eyes. "I—I thought I would never see you again. And here you are." A trembling smile brightened her face. "Are you all right?"

"I am." He wrapped his arm around her once more and squeezed her shoulders before he pressed a brotherly kiss to her forehead. Her jasmine perfume unleashed a flood of memories.

As the shock of seeing her subsided, he held her at arm's length. "But what are you doing here? You are supposed to be in London. How did you get here?"

Her lips formed a pretty pout, her spark returning. "How do you think I got here? I came by coach, of course."

"A public coach?" He blinked in disbelief.

"Of course a public coach." Mollie drew her blanket protectively around her. "You know Aunt hasn't the funds for such a luxury as her own transportation."

He drew a deep breath, willing himself to ignore the dozens of unpleasant potential outcomes that swirled in his mind. "But they aren't safe. You could have been injured. You could have been—"

"It was time to come home, and I couldn't wait another day." Her words were clipped, and the smile that had graced her face moments ago vanished. "The situation was not a good one, and then with Grandfather's death, it just worsened. I had no choice, can you not see that?"

They stared at one another for several moments, the silence between them screaming what words could not.

Mollie looked so small yet so altered. She had always worn her hair in loose, forced curls pinned to her head. Now it was secured in a tight coil at the base of her neck. She had the same finely arched eyebrows and blue eyes fringed in thick, black lashes, so like his own. Now, though, dark circles formed half-moons beneath her lower lashes. There were so many things he wanted to say to her, but the words fell flat on his tongue. How did one go about asking three years' worth of questions?

He could not help but lower his gaze to the swell of her belly. He considered his words carefully before speaking. "If things were so dire, you should have sent for me. I would have come."

She placed a protective hand on her middle, and her narrow shoulders sagged. Her words rushed forth, like a pent-up explanation waiting for release. "Oh, Henry, do not be angry with me. I had to leave. I could not bear it one more day, with the judgmental stares and whispered condemnations. Who would have guessed that Aunt could be so condescending? I was an embarrassment to her, and she made no bones about that."

She clutched Henry's forearm with her long fingers, as if to retain his full attention, and met his gaze directly. "I made a mistake, Henry. Believe me, I am paying for my decisions, but I do not need to be constantly reminded of them every hour of every day. That is no way to live."

"But it is not safe to travel alone. Especially with you in, well, you—"

"With child?" Her lips pursed, and she dropped her hand from his sleeve. "I know it's hard for you to say, but it is a fact. A fact we all must accept. I cannot hide from this. And why should I? It is all how I react to it and present it, 'tis all."

Henry softened as he looked at his sister, for he saw the child he remembered and struggled to see the woman she had become. This was not the life he would have wished for her. She was a beauty, and she easily boasted one of the sharpest wits this side of Leeds. She could have had her pick of beaus. But now her belly grew with budding life, and she would be judged wherever she went.

He shrugged his doubts to the side. At least with Mollie there was no need for pretense. "Well, regardless of why you are here or how you got here, I'm so glad to see you. With Grandfather's death, I—I—" His words faltered. He ignored the shudder that coursed through him at the memory of Grandfather's lifeless form under the tree and forced normalcy to his voice, for Mollie's sake, and quickly shifted topics. "But how did Mrs. Figgs respond when she saw you? Surely you two have talked."

When Mollie didn't answer, he lifted his head. She was rarely at a loss for words.

She studied her hand, her head cocked to the side.

She was up to something.

Henry arched his eyebrow. "You *have* spoken with her, correct?"

Again, no response.

He cleared his throat and adjusted his position. "Surely she was curious. When we spoke of you earlier, she seemed to know nothing of, uh, recent developments."

Mollie sighed. "Very well, I will tell you, but I fear you will not be happy about it."

Concern prickled up his spine. Mollie had never been a stranger to mischief, and judging by her tone, that aspect of her personality had remained consistent. "What have you done?"

"Nothing." She chewed her lip and studied the blanket fringe. "I only told her that I had been married and was now a widow."

At first Henry laughed. Surely she jested.

He narrowed his eyes when she did not join his laughter. "You did what?"

"I had to!" Her cry shattered the room's stillness. "What else could I do? She looked at me so oddly. I thought that Grandfather had told her about the baby, but apparently he did not. I had to tell her something."

The reality of her words sobered him. "What about the truth?"

"I could not tell her that."

"Why?" He raised his voice an octave.

She motioned for him to be quiet. "It worked out perfectly, you see. I have not been back in Amberdale for well over a year. It is a completely believable story."

"Believable or not, it is a lie. This is not a fantasy world, Mollie. Very soon you will have another life to care for. You cannot build a new life for you and your baby on a lie. If you do, I fear it will haunt you until the day you die. Furthermore, once it spreads beyond Mrs. Figgs, the more difficult it will be to set things to right."

Her face flushed, and she looked to the fire.

He thought he saw a tear glisten in her pale eyes, but she blinked it away and faced him again. "I know you are right, but let me handle this in my own way. I panicked, 'twas all."

"But you will speak to her and set things right?"

"Yes."

He didn't like being harsh with her. He softened his tone. "I can help you, Mollie. If you would only tell me the name of the—"

"No."

"I will not judge," he added. "I will not criticize or rebuke you, you have my word. But if there is one thing I must insist on, it is honesty. With Mrs. Figgs. With me."

She shook her head, and this time he was certain. Tears pooled in her eyes. She placed her thin hand over her midsection. "I am sorry, brother. But that I cannot do."

CHAPTER 15

A storm raged outside the countinghouse as furious as the tempest blustering within Henry's mind. Tierner, the magistrate, had sent word that he would stop by this morning. Where was he?

Henry drummed his fingers on the desk's edge, glanced at the mantel clock, then adjusted the mourning band encircling his upper arm. Only two minutes had passed since his last check. He snatched up the magistrate's letter but didn't read it. Impatience pulsed through his every breath, and his toe tapped erratically against the planked wood floor. He'd not be able to concentrate on anything, not until the man delivered the news he had been waiting on for days.

After what seemed like hours, a tap sounded on the door, followed by the customary creak of the hinges. Henry jumped to his feet before the guest's identity was even known.

To Henry's great relief, Tierner appeared in the doorway. The older man's already ruddy face gleamed red from the cold, and his long oilskin coat brushed the floor with each step.

"Is now a good time?" Tierner gruffed, sweeping his hat from his head and shaking the snow from it.

An odd measure of excitement coursed through Henry. "Nothing is more important to me than finding out who is responsible for my grandfather's death. You may interrupt me at any time, at any place, if you bring news of who might have done this."

Tierner pressed his thick lips together and nodded. "Well now, I'll not take much of your time, but I do have some information you might find interesting."

"Please." Henry motioned to the chairs by the fire. "Be seated. Would you like something to drink?"

"No. Like I said, this won't take long."

Both men settled in front of the fire, the hissing and popping of which mingled with the howling wind and the patter of sleet against the pane, creating a distracting ruckus. Henry could wait no longer. "What of Wilkes?"

"I hate to disappoint you. I know you were hoping this could be wrapped up quickly, but I am afraid Wilkes's alibi is ironclad."

Disappointment sliced through Henry as sure and as searing as the blade he'd taken in battle. He wanted to be able to blame someone, to bring someone to justice.

Tierner continued. "Wilkes found work at a farm west of here. He was seen by multiple people at the public house around the time of night your grandfather was murdered. I visited the site myself and spoke with the barkeeps, one of whom just happens to be a constable. Wilkes was not fond of your grandfather, but he is not responsible for his demise."

Henry's fist clenched at his side. He wanted to grab Tierner, as if by force he could extract the truth. He relaxed his fist. But Tierner didn't know the truth. And at the moment, he was the only one Henry could trust.

Tierner's words recaptured Henry's interest. "As you know, even though a stab wound is what claimed your grandfather's life, a pistol was found at the scene."

Henry nodded, eager for information. "And? Did you find the gunsmith?"

A rusty smile cracked the old man's weathered face. "We studied the markings and have found the gunsmith. We plan to make contact with him as soon as we're able."

"This is good news, then, right?" Optimism flared within Henry as he nearly stood from his chair. "That will lead us to the man who was likely present."

Tierner drew a sharp breath and patted his hand on his chest. "I wouldn't be too sure. The weapon was a fine one, with delicate engraving. It's not likely one that our suspect would carry. Other than that, our leads are few. The weather did not help us. Any footprints were lost with the melting and refreezing of the snow, and the ground below was too frozen to retain any indentions. We did find hoofprints, but we have no way of telling how long they had been there. For all we know, they belonged to your grandfather's horse."

The faint flicker of hope that had sprung within Henry quickly dissipated.

Tierner adjusted his coat. "But the money that was on your grandfather's person—the fact that it was left behind, along with the other items—speaks volumes as to who might be behind this."

Henry bit his lip. Yes, the money. After the body was taken back to the house, it was clear that nothing in his pockets had been tampered with. Whoever killed Grandfather did not bother to take his money, nor the key ring or watch fob that hung from his waist. Indeed, even his gold ring was still on his finger. Had the attacker been a gypsy or highwayman, anything worth any value would have been stolen.

"Be honest with me, Tierner. You know this county and the people in it much better than I do. What do you make of this?"

The magistrate ran a rough hand over his chin and stared into the fire. He stared so long that Henry began to think he would not answer. But then he responded, his voice raspy and low. "No one likes to hear that their loved one was not well liked, but I doubt it's a surprise to you that many around here hated your grandfather for the mill he had built. Just as some revered him for providing them with food and shelter.

"I hate to name names since as far as we know all are innocent until evidence proves otherwise, but men like Silas Dearborne, Donald Wooden, Andrew Purty, and John Whitby have been more than vocal about their distrust and dislike. The weavers, boy. The weavers are the ones we must keep an eye on."

A sickening sensation sank within Henry as he met the man's gaze. He did not like what he had heard, but it needed to be heard nonetheless. "Thank you for taking the time to stop by with this information."

Tierner stood and repositioned his hat on his head. "No thanks needed. In fact, I wish this conversation needn't take place at all. But if I can offer one piece of advice"—he leaned close and pinned a steely stare on Henry—"whoever killed your grandfather probably didn't count on your presence at the mill. Keep your pistol close and your eyes open."

"You've heard about the attack on the mill in south Leeds, of course."

Kate fell into step with Jane as the two ladies walked down Amberdale's main street. News of attacks on mills all over the north and west of England was becoming commonplace. She held her cloak close to ward against the late-afternoon wind. "I have not."

Jane adjusted a small, paper-wrapped parcel beneath her arm and looped her other arm through Kate's. "Papa returned from there earlier in the afternoon after retrieving an order of muslin. Last night the wool mill there was destroyed. Burned to the ground! In the middle of the night."

A sliver of guilt sliced through Kate. She and Jane rarely kept secrets from each other. In fact, when Kate and Frederica's friendship ended all those years ago, the relationship between Jane and Kate had blossomed into a deep bond. Ever since Kate's mother died, Jane had been a companion and guide. But recently their relationship was different. For a reason she did not entirely understand, Kate felt hesitant around her friend. She had not told Jane about her presence when the Stockton stable burned, nor had she shared any news about her injuries.

Kate pushed her guilt to the back of her mind and kept her voice steady. "I had heard that the weavers were breaking machines, but burning the entire mill? I thought most of the mills there were made of stone for that very reason, to avoid fires."

"This one was built in an old shed," Jane said. "Work had been started on a brick structure, and it was almost complete. Apparently they wanted to destroy the machines before they could be properly secured."

It seemed every day there was a new report of violence against the mill owners. "Was anyone injured?"

"One of the workers fainted from the effects of the smoke, but he recovered. The mill owner has vowed to seek revenge. The militia has reported to the area, but what can they do? The harm has already been done."

Kate recalled her father's passionate speeches and determined positions. "I only hope such violence stays far away from Amberdale."

With her free arm Kate adjusted her grip on the basket swinging at her side and looked up to Stockton Mill. Its hum could be heard during every daylight hour. In fact, the village relied on its clock and bells to chime every hour. The sound was louder and reached farther than even the church bells. Its prominent placement in the village meant it was never far from her—or anyone's—mind.

Jane sighed. "Let us think of something happier. The festival will be here soon. I have heard back from the musicians. They have agreed to the date. Now, with the inn leased and the musicians secured, we need to make sure we're able to find enough food to feed so many people."

Kate nodded. Every year the Winter's End Festival signaled the start of the end of winter and urged spring's arrival. As of yet spring had shared no signs of budding any time soon, but then again, over time the festival had broken away from its original intent and now was a reason for the community to come together in celebration in the midst of winter's cold and darkness. It was the one time of the year when weavers and millworkers alike would come together, for neither group was willing to abandon the long-standing tradition, and the ladies of the sewing guild assumed the monumental task of overseeing preparations.

"I will speak with Mr. Dewent tomorrow about the food, but don't worry. It comes together perfectly every year. This year will be no different."

At the foot of the bridge Kate bid Jane good evening and prepared to walk home, eager to return before it grew too dark.

As her feet traversed the bridge, she cast a sideways glance at the mill. Charles, no doubt, was hard at work within those walls.

So was Mr. Stockton.

She sniffed. She should not care about such a fact. Furthermore, she should not give it any more consideration than she would have when old Mr. Stockton was at the helm, but she would be lying if she said that the younger Mr. Stockton had been far from her thoughts in recent days. Instead, it seemed the more she tried to put him to the back of her mind, the more he found his way to the forefront.

It had been two weeks since the elder Mr. Stockton was murdered. She had seen Henry Stockton twice, but they had not spoken. At church their eyes met briefly, but he broke the gaze when someone spoke to him.

It was probably for the best. She could not deny that he was different from the other young men of Amberdale, though. He was handsome, yes. But he was kind. He was also for everything she stood against, or at least everything her papa stood against. But she was curious about him. More curious than she should be.

Once she crossed to the other side of the bridge, she was able to get a better look at the operation. She was not far from the main gate. Activity buzzed around the massive brick structure, as always. The hum of the river and voices echoed, and smoke puffed into the fading sky.

Kate arched her neck. She did not seek a glimpse of Mr. Stockton. That would be foolish. But as her foot settled on the landing on the bridge's other side, she saw something she did not expect to see.

On a bench outside of a building just inside the gate sat a small figure, hunched against the wall. The small girl, clothed in a brown dress, with a head full of auburn curls, was bent forward.

Alarmed, Kate stopped. The only people in Amberdale she knew with hair that shade of copper were members of the Thomas family. And the only member of the Thomas family that small was their daughter, Adelaide.

Kate watched the scene for a few moments. Several millworkers bustled by, but no one seemed to notice the child.

Kate lifted the hem of her wool skirt to avoid a snowdrift and hurried toward the tiny figure. The Thomas family was a weaving family, or at least they used to be. Alexander Thomas had been a master weaver, but when the Stockton Mill increased its machine count, his work dwindled. At one time he and his family worked entirely from his farm on the village outskirts, but now various local mills employed him and his children.

Her steps quickened. She looked to her right. Then her left. It was not completely unusual for her to step foot on Stockton Mill property, for she sometimes came to visit her brother. But without him by her side, it felt almost wrong to be here.

She knelt next to the girl. "Adelaide. What are you doing here?"

The child looked up at her, and Kate's stomach fell. Dark circles rimmed her bloodshot eyes and stood out against her pale, clammy skin. She licked her trembling lips.

"Dearest, what is the matter?" Kate removed her kid glove and pressed the back of her hand against the child's forehead. "You are burning with fever!"

"My throat hurts," Adelaide whispered. "And my head."

"Well, of course it does. Why are you not inside where it's warm?"

"Mr. Higgins told me to go home because I am sick."

Kate clicked her tongue. "Tell me, have you been like this all day?"

The child nodded.

Heat began to rush to Kate's face as well, but for an entirely different reason. Surely an adult had been present with her while she worked. How could this happen?

She grabbed the tie that held her cape to her shoulders, and with a flick of her wrist she released it. She positioned it around Adelaide's thin shoulders and put her arm around her.

"Well, you can't sit here." She needed to find Charles. He would know what to do. She looked toward the countinghouse. He spent most of his days in there. "Can you walk?"

The child nodded, lips shivering. "Come with me and we will find my brother."

Without the protection of her cape, Kate felt the biting wind penetrate her gown, but the discomfort she felt had to pale in comparison to the child's. She stopped at the countinghouse door and knocked on it twice before taking the liberty of pushing it open.

Someone had to answer for such treatment of a child. And they would answer now.

The countinghouse door flung open, squeaking on its hinges and smacking against the wall behind it.

The wind whooshed in, pushing the door even harder and disrupting the papers on his desk. Henry snapped his head up.

The intensity of the snow swirling in the doorway was matched only by the fiery expression pooling in Miss Dearborne's hazel eyes.

Surprise pinned him to his seat for several moments, and then as an afterthought he remembered his manners and jumped to his feet. "Miss Dearborne."

Realizing he had shed his coat due to the fire's warmth, he snatched it and pushed his arms through the sleeves.

She did not return his greeting. Instead, she stepped aside, making way for a tiny figure wrapped in her crimson cloak.

"Is Charles here?" Miss Dearborne put her hands on the child's shoulders and ushered her inside.

"N-No. He isn't. He's gone to Leeds."

"Do you know this child?" she demanded, her amber eyes flashing, thin eyebrows raised in expectation.

Henry's gaze fell to the little girl. Wild curls—redder than any he had ever seen—escaped from beneath a dirty white cap, and her red-rimmed eyes and pale cheeks shook him. "I don't."

"This is Adelaide Thomas, one of the children employed by your mill." Miss Dearborne's clear voice echoed from the low beams.

Henry's stomach tightened.

"She is clearly ill, and I found her sitting out in the snow. In the *snow*, Mr. Stockton. She said her supervisor told her to go home because she was too sick to work. Surely there must be some mistake."

Henry stepped around the desk and toward the child, who cowered toward Miss Dearborne.

The girl looked up at Miss Dearborne and tugged her gown. "Papa told me not to get in trouble."

Miss Dearborne knelt next to her and rubbed her arm. "You are not in trouble, precious, you are sick. That cannot be helped."

Henry was never around children. Never. He looked to the little person, whose lip was beginning to quiver. A strange sort of panic began to creep over him as moisture filled her eyes. He searched for words. "C-Come in, child, and sit by the fire."

Adelaide clutched the heavy cloak about her neck with a white-knuckled grip. Her gaze fixed wide and true on Henry. Her small boots tapped on the stone floor as she crossed the room. Miss Dearborne's expectant gaze was also fixed on him.

He knelt next to the girl. "So tell me. What is happening?"

"My throat hurts, and Mr. Higgins told me I needed to go home."

Miss Dearborne interjected, "Adelaide's home is more than a mile from here. There is no way she can be expected to walk."

Henry gave a sharp nod. "Miss Dearborne is quite right. We will have someone drive you home and your mother can take care of you."

Miss Dearborne cleared her throat and said softly, "Her mother is dead."

Henry stifled a groan. He wanted the floor to open up and swallow him. He looked back to Adelaide. "I'm sorry. Is there someone at home who can take care of you?"

"My brother takes care of me."

Miss Dearborne interjected again. "Her brother is a twelve-year-old boy, who is also employed by your mill. Their father works over in Wester and stays there when the weather prevents him from returning home."

Henry drew a sharp breath. He was at a disadvantage. Miss Dearborne obviously knew more about the workers in the mill than he did. He needed to do something, but what?

Miss Dearborne spoke. "I will take her to Meadowvale, and she can stay with me there."

"Nonsense." He met Miss Dearborne's frustrated gaze. "While she is an employee here, she is in our care."

An argument sparked in her sharp eyes. Clearly she did not think him capable of caring for the child.

Or perhaps she thought him too uncaring.

Regardless of the reason, he was determined. "For the time being, there is a sofa in the room behind us. She can rest there until a better arrangement can be made. I will check with Mrs. Figgs, and Mrs. Belsey is close. She will be in good hands, you have my word."

Miss Dearborne's shoulders relaxed and she motioned to the child. "Very well. Come, dear, let me help you."

Henry stepped aside to allow Miss Dearborne space to pass him. Just then the door swung open yet again.

He turned his head around and stifled another groan.

Mr. Pennington's wide frame blocked the low threshold. He shifted, and Miss Frederica, bright and smiling, peered over her father's shoulder.

Henry's stomach soured. He'd spoken with the Penningtons a handful of times since his father's death, but never had they stopped by the mill without at least sending word prior to their arrival.

Miss Pennington's disciplined smile quirked as she beheld the scene, and her father's expression darkened. No doubt the sight of Miss Dearborne, here in the countinghouse without the presence of her brother, was the source.

Henry forced a smile to his face. "Miss Pennington. Mr. Pennington." He bowed. "Come in out of the cold."

"If we are interrupting, we can return at another time." Pennington's words snapped, and he arched his eyebrow.

"No, nonsense."

The deafening silence roared.

Finally, Miss Dearborne's soft voice pulled him back to the situation at hand. "Come, Adelaide. Mr. Stockton said there was a place for you. Let's go find it."

"Yes, it is just through that door," Henry added quickly. "I think there are some blankets in the chest. I will send in Mrs. Belsey momentarily."

Henry turned back to his guests. Disapproval now darkened both of their expressions.

Pennington cleared his throat and moved to allow his daughter to pass to the fire. "We stopped at Stockton House, thinking you might have already returned home for the night."

Henry jerked at the mention of Stockton House. Concern that they had encountered Mollie wound within him, but then Pennington continued with his explanation. "Should have known better, though. Your grandfather spent most of his nights here." Pennington pressed his lips into a fine line before continuing. "Seems you are quite busy."

Henry rubbed a kink from the back of his neck. "One of the young workers has fallen ill."

"But what is Dearborne's daughter doing here?"

Henry shouldn't have been surprised at Pennington's gruff response to finding her here, but he objected to the assumed authority he heard in the man's voice. The tension in the small room was as taut as the wool stretched on the tenterhooks. "She came across the child and brought her to the countinghouse."

"No doubt she loved to discover that to lord over us." Pennington snorted, rocking to the tips of his toes and then back on his heels. "They love nothing more than to criticize the way things are done within our mill walls."

Henry stiffened. "I do not think so. The child is ill."

"Then you have more faith in the Dearbornes than I. But I did not come here to speak of that. I have news for you." Pennington extended a letter.

Henry accepted it, noting the broken seal. He flipped it open and skimmed the contents. "It's an order."

"Yes, and a large one. It arrived just this afternoon." Pennington rubbed his hands together, like a beggar on the eve of a great feast. "Our mill will not be able to fill it in such a short time, but between the two mills . . ."

Miss Pennington stepped forward and placed her small, gloved hand on her father's arm, filling the silence after her father's words faded off. "I will let you gentlemen talk business. You know what a bore I think it is." She gave her father's arm another pat, and her eyes twinkled. "If you will excuse me, I would much rather chat with Miss Dearborne."

CHAPTER 16

Henry rolled his eyes heavenward and pressed his lips together as Miss Pennington's gown swished around the corner to the countinghouse's back room and the door latched closed behind her. Why Miss Pennington would want to talk with Miss Dearborne was beyond him. The thought of the two women who had been occupying his mind being in the same room made him uneasy.

He turned back to Pennington, who, judging by his ruddy cheeks, hard gaze, and wide stance, was more in the mood to fight than talk.

Henry cleared his throat and scanned the letter once more. "By the end of the month?" Henry rubbed his forehead with his index finger, as if forcing his brain to stay focused.

Pennington straightened his waistcoat and helped himself to a glass of port, which had been sitting on a sideboard next to the fire. "Uh, yes. Needs to be *delivered* by the end of the month. Orders are coming in faster than we can fill them, which is a good thing. Any word on when the gig mills will arrive?"

Henry relaxed now that the conversation had firmly shifted to business. Pennington could be prickly and snobbish, but when it came to business, they had a common ground. "Belsey assures me they will be here any day."

Pennington retrieved the letter and tucked it in his coat. "I have heard that the weavers are planning to retaliate."

Henry huffed. "From what I am told they are always planning some sort of retaliation."

"You sound a mite flippant, Stockton. This is not a joke. Lives may be at stake."

Henry met Pennington's stare. "I'm not flippant, quite the opposite, but I refuse to live in fear of what they may or may not do. Armed guards are stationed near the gate, both here and at Stockton House during the night hours. The supervisors are armed, as are the carriage drivers. And this." Henry opened the top drawer of the desk. His loaded pistol was ready to protect what was his at a moment's notice. "Trust me, I don't take anything that is happening lightly. I suggest you do the same for your property."

Pennington downed the dark liquid and gave his head a shake, no doubt in response to the taste. "In light of what has happened, I'd imagine you would take the utmost care."

"In light of what has happened?" Henry repeated. "You are referring to my grandfather?"

"I am. It is a terrifying prospect—one that I, along with every other mill owner in Yorkshire, fears. Or perhaps you are planning to deal with this in your own way? Trying to play nice with the enemy's daughter? If you are thinking to woo her and earn favor in the sight of the weavers, you are mistaken, boy."

Boy? Henry raised an eyebrow. "Well then, that's fortunate, for I was planning no such thing."

"A word to the wise: be careful." Pennington lowered his gravelly voice. "Folks will start to talk."

"Let them. I've far too much on my mind to concern myself with wagging tongues."

Pennington shrugged and poured another glass. "Consider your-self warned. Dearborne is a volatile man. You know how defiant he can be with wool. Imagine how that is magnified where his offspring is concerned. Perhaps you do not know this, but he challenged your grandfather to a duel after his son came to work for him."

Henry winced. He knew there was bad blood between his grand-father and Silas Dearborne, but a duel?

"I only mean to help you, Stockton. Your grandfather was not only my business partner but was a close confidant for many, many years. But let me be clear. I am a businessman and will look after my prospects—and my own family—first. I only hope you do the same before it is too late."

Once inside the back room at the Stockton countinghouse, Kate put her hand around Adelaide's shivering shoulders and guided her to the sofa. If it weren't such a disturbing situation, she could almost laugh at the irony. The one day she steps foot on the property, the Penningtons arrive. Attempting to dislodge the thought, she shook her head. She could not think on that now. Adelaide needed her.

Tears balanced in the child's large, soft brown eyes. She leaned so close to Kate that it was almost difficult to cross the small room.

"Am I in trouble?"

At the soft voice, Kate stopped and knelt to face the child at eye level. "No, dearest, why would you think such a thing?"

Her lower lip trembled, and fever flushed her face red. "Because Matthew told me that the only time I would ever talk to Mr. Stockton was if I was in trouble."

Kate brushed wisps of auburn hair away from the child's damp forehead. "Well, you're not in trouble. Here, lie here." She lifted Adelaide onto the sofa and then scanned the chamber. Mr. Stockton had been right—blankets were piled in an open chest at the foot of a narrow wooden bed. Kate retrieved one and spread the woolen quilt over Adelaide's tiny form. "There, is that better?"

The child managed a small smile.

"Good. I want you to rest." Kate stood. "I'll be right here. Perhaps you could close your eyes and sleep?"

The child nodded, and Kate whirled around to pull the chair closer, but she stopped short.

For there, in the doorway, stood Miss Pennington. Her pert nose was lifted in the air, and she surveyed the space as a woman who belonged there. One of the corners of her mouth lifted in what appeared to be the start of a smile, but the cool expression in her eyes suggested that her presence here was anything but friendly.

"Miss Pennington." Kate dipped a cool curtsy and intended to move past the taller woman, but Frederica stepped before her, blocking her path.

Kate lifted her face to look at her fully. Frederica was always lovely as a child, but now she was a stunning woman. Smooth, clear skin. Deep, dark eyes.

Frederica nodded her greeting, and then she tipped her head to the side, not moving to allow for Kate to pass. "Miss Dearborne. My, but it has been a long time."

Kate returned the forced smile. The words were not true at all. They had just seen each other in church the prior Sunday.

Frederica removed her cloak and laid it across the back of the sofa. Kate could see why any man—Mr. Stockton included—would be attracted to someone like her. Her gown of fine brown velvet was trimmed in light-brown fur. A gold pendant embellished the fair skin on her neck and chest, and emerald bobs hung from her earlobes. Elegant curls, gathered at the base of her neck, cascaded down her back.

The sight reminded Kate that she still wore her work gown of pale-blue linen and that her hair was pinned simply to the crown of her head. Wind-whipped and messy, she could feel it falling on her neck and shoulders.

Kate lifted her chin. "Is there something you need, Miss Pennington?"

But Frederica did not answer her question. Instead, she clicked her tongue and turned her attention to Adelaide before her lips formed a pretty pout. "The poor child. Henry said she was ill."

Kate raised her eyebrow at the use of Mr. Stockton's Christian name. "She is. I'm on my way to find the apothecary."

"I hate to see such a young child unwell." One would think that Frederica was sincere, but the singsong nature of her voice was too forced. "It is sad, isn't it? The way fate plays her cards?"

Kate frowned. "I don't follow you."

Frederica donned a sickly sweet smile, stepped closer, and lowered her voice. "How odd it is to find you here, at Stockton Mill. I would suppose your father would forbid such a visit."

"My father forbids me nothing. Besides, my brother is here, but you know that, of course." Kate stepped to brush past her, but again Frederica positioned herself to prevent it.

"What I meant to say is I am surprised to find you in Mr. Stockton's countinghouse. You never stepped foot on Stockton property until the new master arrived. Of course I do not question your motive or claim to be familiar with your habits, but I urge you to give a care to your reputation. One might think you are trying to use your, uh, feminine charms, such as they are, to sway the new master of the mill."

Frederica's insinuations surged fire through Kate's veins. "I assure you that nothing of the sort has crossed my mind. I saw an ill child, 'tis all. And a sick child has no business working, but being from a mill family yourself, I am sure you know that."

Frederica widened her eyes in feigned innocence. "And you just happened to come upon her?"

Kate narrowed her gaze. "What are you insinuating, Miss Pennington?"

"Oh, nothing. It's only that Mr. Stockton is a handsome man, is he not? Some people who do not know you as well as I might misinterpret your intentions."

Kate didn't answer.

Frederica added, "You'd best step with caution, for no one is fond of young women who fling themselves at men."

Shoulders straight, head high, and expression confident, Frederica Pennington stepped from Stockton Mill's gravel courtyard up the carriage steps and settled against the bench. She jutted her chin assuredly in the air, lest anyone should see through the carriage's glass window. Once her father climbed in, pulled the door closed, and knocked on the wall to signal to the driver that it was time to depart, she allowed her posture to sag.

A scowl commandeered her lips, and it grew more sour the farther they drove from Stockton Mill. She didn't even care that the deep lines forming around her eyes or the worry lines creasing her brow could one day leave permanent marks. For now, that did not matter. In fact, nothing mattered. Henry Stockton was slipping away from her, and if that happened, where would she be? Married to Mr. Tynes or Mr. Simmons? No, she could not let her mind go to that place.

Henry Stockton needed to fall in love with her. The sooner, the better.

She looked to her father. Judging by his hard eyes and the firm set of his jaw, the visit had not gone as he intended either.

She huffed and folded her arms over her chest. "What in heaven's name was she doing there?"

"Blast if I know," he responded, his tone flat. "William never would have allowed her to step foot in the mill's courtyard, let alone in the countinghouse."

Frederica's gaze flicked to the frozen countryside. She and her father rarely discussed Henry Stockton as a possible match. All marriage talk had been strictly with her mother, but she'd seen her father's reaction to the unexpected guest. He'd been surprised—and displeased.

She chewed her lower lip and stared out the window.

Katherine Dearborne. *Bah.*

As far as she was concerned, Kate was about as attractive and interesting as the dormant trees that flashed by her window. After all, Kate's gown had been plain at best, and her hair looked as if she had just come in from a windstorm. What man would find such a disheveled mess appealing? Yet despite her lack of refinement, Kate had been surprisingly well spoken and confident, she had to give the woman that much. Frederica had expected the shorter woman to cower. But she hadn't.

What had Henry been thinking, allowing such a woman in the countinghouse, the daughter of his sworn enemy no less?

Frederica sniffed. She had to be smart. She knew how to flirt. Very well. She would have to be bolder. More vibrant.

The carriage wheel hit a rut, and she shifted nearer the window to keep her balance. Yes. She knew what she needed to do. Her scowl began to fade, and her muscles loosened. Before long, Henry Stockton would belong to her.

CHAPTER 17

All was silent when the door to the countinghouse finally closed. Henry blew out his breath with such force that it ruffled the shock of hair hanging over his forehead. He watched through the front window as the Penningtons' carriage rattled across the courtyard, through the main gate, and around the corner.

Nothing about this new way of life was going to be easy. Not navigating the intricacies of the business, not being an employer, not helping his sister through her current situation, and certainly not understanding the delicate relationships that held this industry together by mere threads.

He scratched the back of his head as he brought to mind the exchange he'd witnessed between Miss Dearborne and Miss Pennington. Not a word had been uttered between the two ladies; none was needed.

Belsey passed the window. Henry lunged for the door and pushed it open. "Belsey! Find Dearborne for me, will you? Tell him to come to the countinghouse right away."

Belsey stopped in his tracks, the wind tugging at his coat and flipping his wiry hair. "Will do."

"And ask Mrs. Belsey to come here. One of the children has fallen ill and needs assistance. After that, call for the apothecary."

Belsey's brow creased before a strange expression crossed his face, but he nodded. "Yes, sir."

Henry let the front door close and ran his hand over his face, noting how the day's gathering stubble itched his palm. Before him, the fire's light flickered on the closed door to the back room. Miss Dearborne and the child were still just beyond that door.

He took a moment to collect his thoughts and allow his heartbeat to slow. He'd been relieved when the Penningtons left. Their visit had been unexpected, not to mention untimely. The weight of their palpable disapproval pressed on him in the very same manner his grandfather's censure would paralyze him as a child. What bothered him more than their reaction, however, was the disdain their expressions conveyed when they saw Miss Dearborne. She'd done nothing to offend them, at least not while in his company. Yet their cool, haughty demeanor would send even the most confident of people to cower in the corner. Mollie and her situation crossed his mind. If they treated Miss Dearborne with such scorn for such a small offense, how would they react when they learned of Mollie's current state?

Had it always been this way? He'd believed for so long that the weavers were at the root of the issues plaguing their industry. Did it really take years of absence for him to view the situation from another side? What was worse, time and time again Miss Dearborne had been offended in his presence, from his grandfather's verbal aggressiveness to the Penningtons' haughty speculation. It was not to be borne.

Pushing aside his thoughts, Henry cracked the back room door, quietly so as not to disturb. The child's small form rested atop the sofa, covered with a thick wool blanket. Miss Dearborne faced away from him. Her windblown, chestnut hair was pinned in loose locks atop her head, exposing the nape of her slender white neck above the collar of her gown. The natural beauty of it stole his breath. She was sitting in a chair next to the sleeping child, her elbow propped on the chair's arm and her head resting on her fist.

The door creaked as he opened it wide enough to fit through, and at the sound she turned. There was something to be said for Miss Pennington's impeccable brand of beauty. As always, her gown of soft brown had been excellently cut, her hair perfectly curled. But Miss Dearborne, with her wild unkempt hair and delicately sloped nose and high forehead, was quite an intriguing contrast.

For several moments he remained still, beholding the scene in front of him. After years of harshness and fighting, the beauty in the act of service to another struck him. He stepped in farther and kept his voice low. "How's the girl?"

"Adelaide," she said. "She's fallen asleep."

"Ah." He nodded. Miss Dearborne's tone was not lost on him. She was determined to have him see his workers as people and not just numbers. He did not disagree. "I have sent for the apothecary. He should be here soon. And Mrs. Belsey is on her way as well. We will take good care of her."

Miss Dearborne smoothed the child's hair and repositioned a damp rag on her forehead. "It is a hard thing for these children. They should not work so."

Even now she did not let her cause go.

"I appreciate your sitting with her. I've also called for your brother. He should be here momentarily and can drive you home."

"I hate to leave Adelaide. I don't want her to be frightened."

The child whimpered in her sleep and thrust out her arm.

Henry maintained a respectable distance. He did not know why he should care so much about the opinion of a weaver's daughter. Perhaps it was because he respected her opinion. Perhaps it was because he felt guilty about the way his grandfather had treated her. Or perhaps it was because he longed for someone to care about him the way she evidently cared for those around her.

He cleared his throat, leaned his back against the wall, and folded his arms over his chest. "You don't trust me, do you, Miss Dearborne?"

The late-afternoon light slid through the window, abating the fury that had pinked her cheeks when she first arrived. "I don't know you, not really. How can I trust you?"

"But even before you met me, you made up your mind not to trust me."

With slow, gentle movements, she placed the child's hand beneath the blanket and then used the back of her hand to brush her hair away from her smooth forehead. "It doesn't matter if I trust you, Mr. Stockton."

"It matters to me."

Her amber eyes studied him, as if she had the power to see right into his very heart—if she chose to do so. "Why?"

"Because I think you are judging me by my grandfather's actions."

Her retort was quick. "Do you judge me by my father's doings?"

"As a matter of fact, I don't." He pushed away from the wall and widened his stance. "I'm not my grandfather. It is important to me that you know the difference."

She smoothed a wrinkle from her skirt, angled her shoulders to face him, her expression quite serious, and folded her hands in her lap. "Do you not stand by your grandfather's business dealings?"

"It depends, I suppose. I'm still uncovering them."

"And what are you finding?"

"I am finding that the men we thought we knew when we were children can be quite different when we become adults."

At this her lip twitched.

Ah, a response.

Up until now her words had been perfect, calm, measured. If he had not been looking directly at her, he might have missed it. At last he had hit on something that struck a chord with her.

She jutted her chin higher. "I leave the arguing to the men. But you surely aren't surprised that your grandfather was the source of a great deal of pain for my family. It goes deeper than weaving and cloth, looms and jennies."

"You are referring to your brother," he clarified.

"Regardless of the mill and the machines, that offense won't easily be forgotten. By anyone."

"But you're here," he reminded her. "Inside the countinghouse of Stockton Mill. Surely you have found it within yourself to forgive on some level."

"That has nothing to do with it. I'm here because of Adelaide and nothing more. But since you broached the topic, you must know that I love my brother. I also love my father. I'll not turn my back on either of them. So I will visit Charles here at the mill, and I have accepted his decision. I can't say the same for my father, and that will break my heart until my dying day."

For some reason she had opened herself to him ever so slightly. Trusted him with a bit of her soul. "You and I are more alike than you may think."

She raised an eyebrow.

He leaned forward, taking her into his confidence. "We are both attempting to preserve a legacy that has been set out by those who have come before us. Me with my grandfather. You, your father."

"You speak as if you know me. But you don't."

"Very true."

"You also speak as if you know Amberdale, but you have only just returned. It's not the same as it has been in years past. Once you become acquainted with the way things are here, the easier it will be for everyone."

"Then enlighten me, Miss Dearborne." He waited, finding himself intrigued by the banter.

She met his gaze and drew a ragged breath. Could it be she was enjoying the banter too, or at the very least seizing the opportunity to sway him?

"Take this child for instance," she began. "She should be at home, working with her family. That is the way we have always done things here. But she's here alone, ill."

"Millwork did not cause her to fall ill. She receives hearty meals here, works in a warm environment, and is given a fair wage."

"That is good and well, but what of the values that can only be instilled by family?"

Miss Dearborne clearly wanted answers, but he was not sure he had them to give. Not at the moment, anyway. "As you have deftly pointed out, Miss Dearborne, I have not been in Amberdale for a long time, and things are indeed very different from what I remember. But from what I understand, a great deal of the problems here stem from the relationship between our two families. It is my hope that we may mend the bridge that has crumbled."

"If that is truly your goal, Mr. Stockton, then I would suggest that the best way to mend a bridge is to listen to the opposition."

"And if I were to do so, what would I hear?"

She drew a deep breath, as if trying to hide her excitement or seize an opportunity to be heard. "Over the years, your grandfather's mill—and mills like it—took jobs from the people here, the people who have built this town with their blood and sweat. First the scribblers, then the carders. Now with the gig mill, the shearmen will be out of work. And then what?"

"I have people who depend upon me for employment. I am beholden to them to see that they are cared for and that we are profitable."

"But at what cost?" Her cheeks grew florid. "While you were gone, the laws changed. People are scared. Hungry. Angry. It's not just about money, as it may seem on the surface. It's about family and love and life. Change is hard for people, and the more sensitive you can be toward it, the better it would be for everyone."

"Sensitive?" He raised his eyebrows. "I am a man of business, Miss Dearborne. If I do not bring a gig mill here, someone else will. Even if we do not agree with progress, it cannot be stopped. It has been set into motion, and either we move with it or I risk losing everything."

"Even at the cost of the destruction of others?"

He shook his head. There was no clear, easy answer.

Her nostrils flared, the pretty passion dissolving into the same hardened expression she wore when she challenged his grandfather in the kitchen. "You asked my opinion, Mr. Stockton, and there you have it."

He did not want to argue with her. "I'll consider what you have said."

Her expression softened. "Bridges can't be repaired overnight, but you are in a position, more than anyone else, to start the process. The weavers will not change. My father included. But *someone* needs to change. Your grandfather was not that man, but maybe you are."

Her words were delivered with such authority, it almost seemed as if he were receiving counsel from a much older person. For some reason he cared very much about what this woman thought of him.

He opened his mouth to respond, but the chamber door flung open and Mrs. Belsey bustled in.

Their private interlude had ended, but before Miss Dearborne turned back toward the child, she pinned him with her gaze. "You are in an interesting place. You have the power to make a great deal of difference. Consider it wisely."

CHAPTER 18

$\mathcal{K}$ate paused on Amberdale's main road long enough to raise her face to the bright afternoon sun. The crisp air still held winter's bitter bite, but if she focused, she could feel brief moments of warmth kissing her cheeks. Days, nay, weeks had passed since the sun last made an appearance over the moors, and even this brief reprieve whispered the promise of spring to come.

As much as she should like to spend the afternoon basking in the sun's glow, much required her attention. Reenergized and armed with a hatbox and news about the food for the Winter's End Festival, she continued down the lane toward Jane's family's tailor shop.

Her light footsteps traversed the cobbled walk, and once she arrived at the modest shop, she flung open the door and shrugged her hood from her head as she ducked through the door. "Jane, I just came from the—" She lifted her gaze and stopped in her tracks.

Henry Stockton.

He stood just to the left of the door. The top of his dark head nearly brushed the low-beamed ceiling, and his broad shoulders blocked her view of the counter.

What on earth would Henry Stockton be doing at the tailor shop?

He turned at the sound of her entrance.

Heat suffused her face. No doubt she was as red as the winter berries along the moor's edge. The memory of every word spoken in the small back room of the countinghouse rushed her. She was still unsure how she felt about the interaction, and seeing him sent confusion racing through her afresh. Almost of its own volition, her mouth blurted, "You're here."

After a painfully long pause, a confident smile twitched his lips. "I am. As are you."

Determined not to allow this interaction to dampen the springlike mood, Kate forced her composure into compliance and deposited her reticule on the counter. She stifled an inward groan as the heavy falls of his boots could be heard approaching her.

He stepped up to the counter next to her, shoulder to shoulder. "It is a pleasure to see you again, Miss Dearborne."

Was he patronizing her?

She pursed her lips and looked to Jane, who had stepped from the back room behind the counter. But instead of finding a place of solace, she saw a swirl of questions in Jane's shocked expression, which proved even more bothersome than Mr. Stockton.

So Kate lifted her chin and forced her gaze to meet his. She drew a deep breath, buying herself an extra moment. It would be easier to hate the man, as her father did, if his eyes were not so clear, the cleft of his chin so engaging. "Please forgive my surprise. I did not expect to see you here, 'tis all."

Mr. Stockton held her gaze for several more seconds, raised an amused eyebrow, then turned his attention back to Jane. "I will have the cloth delivered tomorrow, then. You're sure he can handle them?"

"Oh, yes, sir." Jane folded her plump hands on the counter and nodded her nut-brown head eagerly. "Will there be anything else?"

"No, that will do." He straightened. "Good day." He rotated away from Jane and headed to the door. He paused and offered an infuriating, knowing smile, as if he were acquainted with her far better than he was.

Kate huffed under her breath as the door closed behind him and waited until he could no longer be seen through the windows before she spoke. "What was he doing here?"

"It is the most remarkable thing." Jane stared at the door, her head tilted to the side. "He came in and said that he needed cloaks for the children who work at the mill."

Kate raised her eyebrows. "Cloaks?"

"Yes. He gave no explanation. He just asked if he had cloth delivered here if Papa would fashion cloaks, all sizes, for the children. Twenty of them to start." She leaned with her hip against the counter. "He did not ask after the cost either. I tried to tell him, but he said it didn't matter. He trusted Papa to give him a fair price on the work."

So he had been listening to what she'd said—about the children and the dangers to their health as a result of millwork. Satisfaction spread through her chest. She wasn't sure why. Was she happy that he had listened to her? Happy to have seen him again?

She turned back to Jane. "I think it is only right, don't you? Some of those children walk miles in the snow. It is the least he can do."

"Well, I don't care why he is doing it. We can definitely use the money." Jane lifted a bolt of cloth, returned it to a shelf, and then leaned with her elbows on the counter. Her blue eyes held a teasing glimmer. "But he certainly seemed to know who you are."

Kate shrugged. She had not told her friend of their meeting at Stockton House, nor their encounter at the mill. But he seemed to be everywhere she went. His name was on everyone's lips. She did try to obey her papa, but it was becoming more and more difficult not to become interested in Henry Stockton's actions. "He works closely with Charles. I am sure he is just trying to be friendly."

"You are lying, Kate Dearborne. Your left eyebrow always rises when you're telling a falsehood, and you know it." A wave of fresh excitement seemed to rush over Jane. She stuffed another bolt on the shelf and hurried over to Kate. "I will ask you again, why does he seem to know you so well?"

Kate sighed. It was useless to keep anything from Jane. "Very well. But you always make such an ordeal over these things. You must promise me that you—"

A sharp, angry male voice cut Kate's own short. "What was he doing here?"

Kate whirled around. Mr. Abbott, Jane's father, stood in the shop's entrance, his face bright. She would have liked to think it was red only from the cold, but his eyes flashed with what could only be rage.

Jane's eyes widened. Either she did not see—or chose not to see—her father's festering anger. "Oh, Papa, it's wonderful! Mr. Stockton has placed an order for twenty cloaks. Twenty! Can you believe it? And I—"

"I don't care if he placed an order for a thousand cloaks. He's not welcome in our shop." Mr. Abbott stomped through the low threshold and slammed his felt hat on the counter.

"But, Papa, he wants the cloaks for the children who work at his mill. That is noble, is it not? He didn't even inquire after the price. You yourself said we needed to—"

"Do you not see what he's doing?" Mr. Abbott jerked his arm from his caped greatcoat, narrowing a hard gaze on his daughter. "How he is manipulating your feminine whims? That man cares no more for the children in his employ than his grandfather before him.

This charade of his, this pretense of charity, is his way of weaseling into the affections of the womenfolk in the village. It shocks me that you do not see it. I, for one, will not allow it."

"But you cannot know this to be true, Papa." Color drained from Jane's fair skin. "He's only just arrived!"

"He's a Stockton, and that's all I need to know. That man has put more than half of our town out of work with his newfangled machines and disrespect for tradition." The neck muscles visible above his tightly bound cravat jumped, and he turned to wave a finger at Kate. "Your father would have a fit if he were to see that man in our shop. No. We must stand together, handsome payment or not."

Kate cut her gaze toward Jane. Her heart lurched as she noticed tears balancing in her friend's eyes. Kate could only stand still, silent, her mouth agape.

Mr. Abbott shifted through a pile of fabric on the counter, as if seeking something. "I'll deliver word myself that he needs to send his work elsewhere. You are not to take his business again, am I clear? Or was it a mistake to let you mind the shop while I was out?"

"No, Papa." Jane' s chin trembled as she accepted the reprimand. "No mistake."

Mr. Abbott gathered a pile of fabric and stormed to the back room.

Like a heartbroken child, Jane slumped against the counter.

Kate gripped Jane's hand. Once Mr. Abbott was out of earshot, she whispered, "Do not be upset, Jane."

"I don't understand this at all. We need the money, just like any other family in Amberdale. Why would he refuse the order?"

Empathy flooded Kate at the hurt she saw in her friend's face after her father's harsh words. "I don't understand it entirely myself. But you know your father. He's always been sympathetic to weavers, and they have always been the bulk of his clientele, am I right? Perhaps he's worried about angering them by helping Mr. Stockton. And then where would your family be?"

Jane shrugged her round shoulders.

There was no way to tell if Mr. Stockton would have taken the initiative to purchase cloaks if Adelaide had not fallen ill. But did it matter? It demonstrated a willingness to show compassion toward the weavers' concerns and complaints. Wasn't that what she had asked of him—to consider the well-being of those he employed?

It was becoming harder to hate a man who was capable of such kindness, whatever the pretense. But shame simmered low within her. She had always believed it was men like the Stocktons who infused the situation with hatred. But was not Mr. Abbott behaving equally as boorish?

Her heart strained under the thought's heaviness, and the realization that her own stance might not be entirely faultless.

CHAPTER 19

*W*ood creaked against wood. Fluffy fibers, lit like dust motes in the late-afternoon sun, flitted and floated in the air. It might be freezing outside, but the workers and steam heated the space, making it feel as hot and humid as July.

Henry paused as he walked the deck. A child caught his eye. Adelaide.

Her bright-copper curls poked from beneath the kerchief tied about her head. He didn't know the first thing about children and couldn't even guess how old she was. Seven? Eight, perhaps? Large brown eyes looked back at him. She didn't seem afraid, more curious than anything. The woman working with her touched her shoulder, garnering the girl's attention, and she turned back to her work.

Adelaide, along with several other children, worked their own machines. It was a tedious job. Large pieces of wool were passed through the machine to individualize the fibers before spinning. Operating the machine took little skill and was easy enough for the young ones to understand.

He had been so busy since his return that he had not spent much time in the actual mill, but this afternoon he strode to the mill's south side where the men worked. They were performing heavier tasks: weaving, scouring, cutting, shearing, finishing.

Whether he liked to admit it or not, Miss Dearborne's words had haunted him as of late. Furthermore, he did not want to admit that he could see the truth in her viewpoints. The majority of these hardworking men—many with families—would be replaced when the gig mills arrived. The reality was that the highly skilled clothing finishers—the men who cut and raised the cloth once woven—would be replaced by a machine that could do their work in a third of the time.

He looked at his employees' faces as they worked. He'd have to rely on his supervisors to indicate who would stay and who would lose their work, for he didn't know them. And the thought made him uncomfortable, but he was equally determined to find a way to make the mill more productive so he could continue to provide jobs.

Henry made his way to the upper level, where the spinning jennies turned raw wool into thread. The deafening roar shook the large windows in their casings, and the heat of so many bodies working in one confined space was stifling. It could not be helped. The locked windows could not be opened, lest the outdoor elements spoil the wool and thread. As it was, the wooly fiber floated so thick in the room that it almost appeared like snow falling.

He paced the length of the room, determined not to be an absent employer—to meet head-on the responsibility of such a task. Miss Dearborne's humanitarian words stayed with him as he looked at the faces of the children.

As he was walking through the narrow corridor that separated the spinning jennies from the spinning mules, a loud cry rang out behind him. His muscles tensed, and he wheeled around. Through the maze of wood and wheels and strings of spun fibers, he saw a figure sprawled on the ground. Others hovered around him.

Concern clutched him, sudden and strong, and he pushed his way through the crowd. A woman kneeled at the man's side. Two children, pale and covered in white fibers, stood at his side. Henry fell to his knees next to the man. "What happened?"

The whiskered man looked up at him, his expression darkening when he realized the owner was present. He struggled to stand, but Henry motioned for him to stay.

Though the other machines were slowing, it was still too loud to hear. Despite this, the man rolled up his sleeve. A large welt, purple and bloody red, marred his shoulder.

"What happened?"

The man jerked his head, clutched his thick upper arm, and struggled to stand. "Flying shuttle jumped the track and got my arm," he shouted. "It comes winging out of there from time to time."

Henry's gaze fell on the blood seeping through the worker's coarse linen shirt. Was the arm broken?

The man's voice gritted with pain. "Good thing it was me and not one of the young'uns."

Henry's gaze flicked to the children, and his blood raced through his ears, the sound of which competed with that of the machines. If this kind of mishap caused such an injury to a grown man, he did not want to think about what could have happened had a child been near.

Henry drew his sleeve over his brow to remove the moisture gathered there and motioned to another man. "Help him down to the Belsey house, will you? And you." He pointed to another man. "If Mrs. Belsey is not there, find her."

As the men walked away, Henry looked to the machine in question. Yes, he had heard of this happening before, but he had never seen the aftermath when someone was struck. There had to be a way to prevent future injury.

Dearborne came up behind him and shouted, "They told me to come right away. What happened?"

Henry motioned for Dearborne to follow him to the stairwell so he could be heard once the machines started up again. "He said the flying shuttle jumped the track."

"Again?"

Shocked, Henry scratched his head. "Does this happen often?"

"It occurs on occasion, but this is the fourth time this month."

Henry touched the machine, assessing its strength. He did not want to seem overly suspicious, but with all of the violence and destruction, he could not be too careful. "You don't think anyone could tamper with these, do you?"

"Anything's possible, I suppose. What do you suspect?"

Henry pursed his lips and furrowed his brow before drawing his words out slowly. "I don't know exactly, but it seems too coincidental that so many injuries have occurred in such a short span of time."

Dearborne shrugged. "It seems unlikely. The only people who have access to these machines are the ones who work them. But I can have a guard posted on each floor if it eases your mind."

"Yes, it would. After we close tonight, get Belsey to personally inspect all of the machines. This cannot happen again."

Dearborne nodded and followed Henry down the stairs, out of the mill, and to the countinghouse. The machine sounds softened as they closed the doors to the stone building. Once inside, Dearborne produced a stack of letters from a satchel. "These arrived for you."

Henry accepted the stack, dropped into a chair next to the fireplace, and sifted through the missives. "Any word about the gig mills and when they will arrive?"

"No, sir. None."

Henry groaned. He glanced at yet another order that had arrived, which now sat atop a pile of paper on his desk. Orders were coming in fast and steady, and he was betting far too much on the fact that the gig mills would arrive in the near future. They were losing time daily. With the weather as it had been, he was concerned that news of the delivery would be delayed, and he needed the mills to arrive. Soon.

Dearborne, still cloaked in his oilskin coat, had no doubt just returned from his assignment. With the excitement of the injury, Henry had almost forgotten about Dearborne's task. He crossed one leg over the other, motioned for Dearborne to be seated as well. "How was the visit to Bremton?"

With a weary sigh, Dearborne sank into the chair by the fire and shot his fingers through his thick hair, which was nearly the exact brown hue as his sister's. He rested his elbows on his knees and leaned forward. "There's nothing left inside. Not a jenny, not a mule, nothing. All of it was either burned or smashed. To make matters worse, they housed their wool in the same building. The weavers destroyed everything. Fortunately they had been building a stone mill. It even has a waterwheel of cast and wrought iron, so they have that. Just no machinery. The owner was grateful for the slubbing billy we sent over. He said he will send payment for it as soon as he can."

"Did you tell him we didn't need any?"

"Yes, but you know men like him. He's proud, and this attack has got him quite shaken. He's hired a couple of guards, but you know how that can go. It's hard to find guards who will not sell out to the highest bidder."

The attack, even though it was far away, had Henry rattled as well. No doubt it rattled every mill owner in this part of the country. Textile machines were expensive. Valuable. And relatively easy to destroy— another reason why the mill building itself had to be a fortress, ready for battle.

Henry said nothing in response but retrieved the stack of unopened letters that Dearborne had given him moments ago. As he sifted through the letters, one in particular caught his eye. He separated it from the pile and handed the rest to Dearborne. "Most of those will be expenses. Will you see to them?"

Henry turned his attention back to the letter in his hand and slid his finger beneath the wax seal to pop it open. He unfolded it, and the signature at the bottom robbed him of breath, for it belonged to none other than Vincent Warren, the man who had served beside him for years in the war—the man who had carried Henry from the battlefield when he'd taken a blade to the leg.

He angled the letter toward the fire's light and skimmed the carefully penned words, curious as to why the man would reach out to him. They'd not seen each other in more than a year, yet somehow Warren had received word that Henry was now home. One section caught his eye.

I hope the endeavors at the mill are going well. As you know, I intended to work the family farm with my father. To my horror, I returned home to find that my wife died during our last campaign. Also during that time, my father sold our family farm.

I humble myself to consider us friends, and I hope I can call upon that friendship to beg a favor. Without a farm I have no work, and I have been unable to secure any. Have you a position at the mill? Nothing is too small. I would be grateful for any assistance.

A fire lit within Henry's chest, and he lifted his gaze to Dearborne. "Have we any open positions? Any at all?"

Dearborne frowned and scratched his head. "Not at the moment. In fact, we've a list of people waiting to be called if a position should become available. Why?"

"What about at Pennington Mill?" Henry rushed on.

"I'd have to inquire. Did something happen?"

Henry arched his eyebrow. If there was one benefit of his position, Henry could help his comrade. "There is a man I wish to employ."

"Has he a specific trade?" asked Dearborne.

"I don't believe he has experience with wool, but he's a clever one." A shadow darkened Dearborne's face.

Henry knew that look all too well. "What is it?"

Dearborne held up his hands, as if innocent of any opinion. "This isn't my mill. I'll not tell you how to run it."

Henry could feel the hesitation in Dearborne's voice. "But?"

Dearborne expelled his breath as he reluctantly shared his opinion. "It will not look good for you if you bring in an outsider to take one of the villager's positions. They'll not take kindly to it."

Henry returned his attention to the letter, feigning interest in reading further while he mulled over Dearborne's concern. How clearly his mind's eye could picture the man who wrote these words. Henry could not, would not, turn his back on this man who could be credited with saving his life. He returned his gaze to Dearborne. "I'm certain this is the right course. We will find a position for him."

"Very well. When do you need one by?"

"As soon as possible." Henry dropped the letter on the arm of the chair and moved to the desk, to put as much distance as possible between him and the memories the letter conjured.

A sudden jolt of cold air and bright light swooshed through the space. Henry glanced up. Belsey poked in his gray head and tossed a letter on the desk. "Came from town."

Henry's mood grew sour. He'd already had enough unpleasantries today, and if the tide remained true, no letter brought good news. He snatched it up and opened it.

Dear Sir,

I regret to inform you that I will be unable to make the cloaks for you, as my daughter said. We do not have the workforce at the time.

Timothy Abbott

Henry clenched his teeth and slammed the letter to the desk.

Dearborne jerked his head up. "Something wrong?"

"Yes, something's wrong," he muttered. "Cloaks. I wanted to have cloaks made for the children who have to walk here to work, and Abbott refuses to make them."

Belsey smirked as he stepped farther inside. "You did what?"

Henry shot him a warning glance. "Have you seen how the children arrive? It's amazing they are not sick in their beds. It is in our best interest to keep them healthy. I had made arrangements with Abbott's daughter to have cloaks made. And now he says he can't make them."

"Well, of course he won't." Belsey picked up the letter and skimmed it. "Abbott is in with the likes of Dearborne and the rest of the weavers. He does most of his business with them."

"So you're saying he won't do business with me?" inquired Henry.

Belsey pressed his lips together and nodded.

"That's ridiculous!"

"Ridiculous or not, that's the way things work around here." Belsey returned the letter. "'Sides, it's not your business to see the children are clothed. That sort of spoiling will make you appear weak."

Henry shot him another glance.

Belsey flung up his hand. "Just send Dearborne to the tailor over in Bremton and place the order there. They owe us a favor now, the way I see it, after we sent the billy over there. Write down what you want and we'll get it there."

So this was the way the game was to be played, was it? Henry crumpled Mr. Abbott's letter in his fist and tossed it toward the fire, casting his frustration with it. Well, he was ready, and even more, he was determined to win.

CHAPTER 20

$\mathcal{K}$ate sighed at the large home looming before her, with its gabled, latticed windows.

Stockton House.

Even after weeks, the scent of smoke still seemed to linger as real and thick as the mystery surrounding Mr. Stockton's death.

Perhaps it was her imagination. Perhaps not.

Kate adjusted the heavy blanket in her arms. As much as she tried to air it out, the fabric still smelled of smoke. She had forgotten to return it to him before she left Stockton House all those days ago. She couldn't keep it—it didn't belong to her. Plus, she could not risk someone finding it at the cottage, for she did not want to have to explain how it came to be in their home.

A small gate in the low stone wall separated Dearborne property from Stockton property. It would be less likely that someone would notice her using this entrance. When she had been here the night of the fire, it had been too dark for her to take much notice of the grounds, but she had always imagined that Stockton House was pristine and lovely, like a grand castle or elegant estate. Now in the daylight, the property actually seemed a bit dilapidated. The overgrown shrubs scratched at her ankles as she walked along the path, and the lengthy grasses bent low and brown in the snow.

She gathered her skirt and stepped over a fallen log and headed toward the kitchen entrance she had entered last time.

She expected that Mrs. Figgs would be the one to answer her knock, and sure enough, the wiry woman appeared within seconds. She did not smile, did not speak, but crossed her arms over her chest and waited for Kate's explanation.

"I am only here to return this." She extended the blanket. Feeling as if she was trespassing, Kate took a step backward. As she turned to leave, someone caught her eye.

A woman, clad in a cloak of dark gray, strolled through the dormant kitchen garden. As she approached, a glimmer of recognition sparked.

Kate frowned and squinted. Could that be Mollie Stockton?

Regret coursed through her. The last thing she wanted was to be discovered on Stockton property yet again, by Mr. Stockton's sister, no less. Kate shouldn't have come.

She bobbed a farewell to Mrs. Figgs, hoping to leave by the time Miss Stockton noticed her, but it was to no avail. From the corner of her eye, Kate noticed the brightening of Mollie's face, and she waved to her from across the garden.

Kate exchanged a glance with Mrs. Figgs. Apparently the older woman was as taken aback at the acknowledgment as Kate was. She turned back to Miss Stockton and surprise smacked. Miss Mollie Stockton's middle swelled in an unmistakable manner.

She was heavy with child.

"Miss Dearborne!" Miss Stockton's voice was light with mirth. "It has been years since I last saw you!"

Kate doubted it had been years, but the fact that the other woman addressed her with such familiarity was far more shocking than the exaggeration of time. For they were not friends. They never had been. Indeed, they had not even been acquaintances. Yet Miss Stockton knew who she was.

Mrs. Figgs retreated into the kitchen, blanket in hand, but Kate remembered her manners and dipped a curtsy. "Good day, Miss Stockton."

"Oh, you've not heard!" she exclaimed, her cheeks pink from the cold air and exertion. "It is no longer Miss Stockton. It is Mrs. Smith."

"N-No, I had not heard," Kate stammered, a bit confused at the woman's friendliness. "May I congratulate you?"

Mrs. Smith's face fell. "I would gladly accept your congratulations if my tale had a happier ending, but I'm sorry to tell you that my husband is dead."

"Oh." Still stunned at the odd interaction, Kate could only stutter, "I—I'm sorry to hear it."

Mrs. Smith sniffed and offered a weak smile. "I am fortunate that my brother has welcomed me back to Stockton House."

Kate forced a smile of her own. "I hadn't heard of your return. You know how news travels in Amberdale. Nothing stays a secret for long."

"I had no intention of my return remaining a secret," she clarified, chin jutted upward. "It's only that I have not really had much desire to leave the house in my, uh, condition. And my brother is so focused on the mill, I'm sure he has forgotten about me completely."

In the few slivers of time they had shared just now, Kate liked Mollie Smith, she decided. She exuded a confidence—one that suggested that she had no trouble standing up to the men in her life.

Mrs. Smith continued. "I'm so glad you have happened upon the garden. It's so lonely here."

Before Kate had a chance to respond, Mrs. Smith's gentle rosy glow of moments ago blanched to pale white.

Kate frowned. She didn't know much about women in the family way, but she did not think the sudden and dramatic change in pallor was a good sign. "Mrs. Smith? Are you well?"

Mrs. Smith nodded with a nervous laugh, but placed a hand over her stomach and reached to the open door to steady herself.

Kate stepped forward and took the woman's arm. She didn't like the way the woman was clutching her belly. "Is something wrong?"

"Oh, I am fine." Yet another nervous giggle escaped. "Sometimes if I get too excited, I get a little pang of, well, *something*. But it's nothing, really."

"At least sit down. I'd feel much better if you did." Kate offered Mrs. Smith's arm the steadiness of her own and ushered her into the kitchen. Kate had anticipated to go no farther, but Mrs. Smith directed her through the kitchen and up the servants' stairs to the family drawing room. Not wishing to upset her, Kate complied.

"Shall I call Mrs. Figgs?" Kate assisted Mrs. Smith to the sofa, trying not to gawk at the opulence of her surroundings.

Mrs. Smith shook her head. "No, no. She will try to make me retire for the night, and I'll go mad if I do. I can't bear to be confined."

Kate followed Mrs. Smith's motion for her to be seated and sat next to her on the damask sofa. She leaned forward. "Are you sure you're well?"

Mrs. Smith nodded, and a hint of rose returned to the apples of her cheeks. Her breathing deepened and slowed. "I feel much better. I just needed to come in out of the cold air."

Kate had thought the Purty home to be elegant and refined, but it paled in comparison to the luxury around her. Windows twice her height lined the west wall, and dark-blue velvet curtains framed each

one. An imposing marble mantelpiece took up much of the wall opposite the windows, and large portraits and landscapes added shades
of green, violet, and maroon to the otherwise light space. She had
known Mr. Stockton had been successful, but she never would have
imagined his wealth amounted to all this.

"I'm so glad you happened by." Mrs. Smith's words pulled her to
the present. "It's so lonely here! Do promise me that you'll return for
another visit soon."

Kate hesitated. If Mrs. Smith's grandfather were still alive or
if Kate's father were within Stockton House walls, she doubted she
would be permitted to continue the conversation, much less prepare
plans for a future visit. But despite their differences, Kate understood
Mrs. Smith. It could be lonely being the only woman in a house besides
the servants.

"Please say you will," continued Mrs. Smith. "I shall go daft without someone to speak with."

Kate glanced at the clock and noted the lateness of the hour. "I
must go. But I promise, I will return." She bid Mrs. Smith farewell
and was shown out of the house, not through the kitchen entrance but
through the main entrance, like a proper guest.

Once outside, she quickened her steps. She was reentering her
reality, and she could not be seen leaving Stockton House.

CHAPTER 21

*H*enry kept close to the forest's edge as he rode down the lane away from the village. From Warren's letter to the injury at the mill to Abbott's refusal to sew the cloaks, the day's frustrations weighed heavy on him. Additionally, he was not sure he wanted to return home.

He was glad that Mollie was safe underneath his roof, but he was in no mood for the argument that would inevitably transpire. She would not be swayed about shedding her little lie, and as of the previous night, she still had not told the truth to Mrs. Figgs. How could she not see the folly in her action?

As he rounded the bend he spotted something—someone—on the road ahead of him, just outside the gate to Stockton House. His pulse jumped at the sight of the unexpected crimson cloak.

Could it be she?

He urged his horse into a trot, and when they drew near, the woman turned and lifted her face to meet his gaze.

Miss Dearborne.

His heart raced at the sight. The thought of a few moments with her managed to erase the day's black marks. For a moment, just a moment, he could breathe.

Was that a smile on her face?

The sight kindled a warmth deep within his chest, even amid the snow that floated around them. Somehow, over the course of their varied interactions, she had gone from greeting him with skepticism to offering a smile.

He'd take it.

He dismounted and looped the reins over his horse's head. "Miss Dearborne. Are you coming to or going from Stockton House?"

She let out a nervous laugh, her gloved hand still on the gate's iron scrolls. "I assure you, sir, I'm not in the habit of trespassing on your property. I fear this is twice now that I have been here unexpectedly."

"I never thought that for a moment. In fact, I'm happy to see you."

She diverted her gaze and looked back at the house. "I was just returning a blanket to your home—the one you were kind enough to let me borrow the night of the fire."

"That wasn't necessary." His horse nudged his shoulder, as if to ask why they had stopped so close to home. He patted the animal's neck. "You and I both know there is enough cloth between our two families for dozens and dozens of blankets."

"Be that as it may, I felt it only right to return it."

"And how is your arm?" He recalled the softness of her skin as he had dressed the wound. Under any other situation such intimacy would not have been permitted.

"I am well, as you can see." She straightened it and then returned it to her side. "Nothing permanent."

"And for that I'm glad. I'd never live with myself had you suffered a more serious injury on my account."

Her eyebrows drew together and her tone lowered. "I don't suppose you've learned who is responsible for the fire, have you?"

Henry pursed his lips. "I have not. In fact, I haven't given it much thought in light of—"

His words faded, and a silence hovered over them, broken only by the whistling of the wind through the bare birch branches and soft flutter of her cloak in the breeze.

She looked to the tips of her gloves. "I—I am sorry about your grandfather. I should have said something before, in the counting-house or at the Abbotts', but—" She flicked her amber eyes in his direction. "I know he and I didn't exactly see eye to eye, but it is a terrible thing that has happened."

His nose twitched. It was easier to look out into the deepness of the woods along the road for a few moments than to see the earnestness in her eyes. If there was one thing he was certain Miss Dearborne possessed, it was honesty. In the past few weeks, she had not failed to share exactly what was on her mind. "Thank you."

She stilled the ribbons of her poke bonnet as they fluttered along her jaw. "It is a horrible thing to lose someone you love. I lost my mother, many years ago now, but the ache still resides."

Had she really just shared a personal memory with him, her enemy?

While her attention was diverted, he studied her. Her long lashes splayed across her rosy cheeks. Tendrils of hair danced with the wind about her face. He was struck by her. Many people had offered their condolences to him, but they were always followed by sentiments for revenge. For justice. She, on the other hand, seemed to understand it was the loss of a person, a beloved family member, and that it was painful.

She drew a sudden intake of breath and met his gaze once more, brightness returning to her eyes. "I was surprised to see that your sister has returned to Amberdale."

The words refocused his attention. "You saw Mollie?"

"Yes. You must be excited about the prospect of a niece or a nephew."

He nodded, wondering exactly what Mollie had told her about her situation. "I—I am."

His horse nuzzled her arm, and she laughed and patted the animal's velvety nose. They stood for several moments in comfortable silence before her expression narrowed again. "Miss Abbott told me of the order for the cloaks. It—it was very kind."

"Then you have probably heard that her father is refusing to fulfill the order."

"I know that as well." Sincerity filled her somber gaze. "And I'm sorry for it."

He continued. "But I've heard of another tailor in Bremton who is more likely to work with a horrid mill owner."

She laughed at his sarcasm and then spoke gently. "Regardless of who makes them, it is a gigantic step. And I am grateful."

A wagon could be heard coming down the road, and her smile vanished. "I should be going. Have a good evening, Mr. Stockton."

He bowed, and as quickly as he had noticed her, she pivoted away from him just as a wagon curved the bend.

He watched as her crimson cloak disappeared from view. He no longer felt the cold or the pain from the day's frustrations. For in this moment, their simple conversation brought lightness to his steps as he led his horse through the Stockton House gate.

To Henry it seemed odd to be home in the afternoon hours. He'd spent nearly every day from dawn until the black of night at Stockton Mill since he arrived several weeks ago.

Today he'd remained home to answer letters and to spend time with Mollie. She had grown increasingly melancholy, and he thought company might do her good. As they sat in the drawing room, Mollie on the sofa reading and Henry at the desk writing, a shrill laugh echoed from the drive.

Henry jerked his head up and jumped from his chair at the sudden noise and moved to the window. Following Mollie's request, he had not shared the news of her arrival with anyone, not even Belsey or Dearborne. As far as he knew, Miss Dearborne and the vicar's wife, who had called a few days prior, were the only people aside from the Figgs who knew of her return.

He lifted the edge of the velvet curtain just enough to see past the thick fabric. He groaned at the sight of Mrs. and Miss Pennington circling the drive.

His relationship with the Penningtons had seemed to cool ever since the father and daughter called at the mill when Miss Dearborne was present. He'd only seen Frederica at church, and her reception toward him had been cordial at best. So why was she here?

He turned from the window and frowned, prepared to see Mollie distressed, but he found quite the opposite to be true.

"Visitors at last!" she cried, her blue eyes wide as the saucer she held in her hand as she sipped her tea. "Hand me that blanket, will you?"

He leaned over to the settee, retrieved the small coverlet in question, and tossed it in her direction. She draped it over her midsection and smoothed her dark curls.

A knock on the heavy oak door sounded their arrival. Mrs. Figgs's shuffling footsteps could be heard moving across the stone floor. Metal scraped metal as the door's latch was lifted. Greetings were uttered.

He and Mollie had not yet discussed how they would present the details of her presence at Stockton House. He had thought they would have time to formulate a plan, but he left before she woke and she was usually abed by the time he returned. They had not spoken much, and now it was too late.

The door to the parlor burst open, and energy pulsed into the small space.

"Oh, my dear, oh, my dear!" The female Penningtons rushed into the room, their presence and floral scents filling every corner, from the high molded ceiling to the polished floor beneath. "It's true you're here! Oh, how long has it been?"

The Pennington ladies leaned down and kissed Mollie's cheek. They fussed over her and petted her.

Henry watched with bated breath. It was clear they were not aware of Mollie's condition. In truth, he did not care what they thought about it, but he did care how Mollie would feel about their reaction.

Mrs. Pennington clasped her hands in front of her. "Mr. Pennington called here for Mr. Stockton yesterday, but he was away at the mill, presumably. He saw you in the garden. He told us last night, and we could not wait for you to call on us."

Frederica whirled around, and for the first time since their visit in the countinghouse, she turned her full attention to Henry. "Why didn't you tell us your sister was in town? We would have visited right away!"

Before Henry could respond, Mollie moved to stand. "Don't blame Henry for that. I haven't been feeling well, you see. I've been resting, but now it does me so good to see you both again."

A silence, thick and heavy, suddenly descended upon the room.

Mrs. Pennington stared at Mollie's midsection, and Miss Pennington's mouth fell open.

Henry's defenses rose at the expressions of shock on their faces. Had they never seen a woman with child before?

Their guests exchanged glances.

The silence was deafening.

He flicked his gaze to Mollie. No smile curved her lips, yet no frown did either. He waited for someone to say something. Anything.

The mantel clock marked several uncomfortable seconds before Frederica finally broke a smile, leaned over Mollie, and patted her hand. "Don't move a muscle, not a single muscle. Mother and I are quite capable of making ourselves at home."

Frederica took the liberty of tugging the bell pull to call for tea, and before Henry realized what had happened, the women fell into quick and easy conversation, as if they forgot he was in the room.

They ignored him completely.

He did not mind one bit.

"It's been well over a year since you were last in Amberdale, if I'm not mistaken."

Miss Pennington waited for Mrs. Figgs to hand her a cup of tea before finishing. "And look at you, you're glowing."

Miss Pennington's words rang with unspoken questions, and her mother edged closer to Mollie. "My dear Miss Stockton, you must tell us everything you've been about these many months. You know men are the worst to rely upon for news, especially mill men. Their minds are endlessly preoccupied with wool and broadcloth."

Mollie did not even so much as glance in Henry's direction before speaking. "Well, it's no longer Miss Stockton. My name is now Mrs. Smith."

Henry cringed inside.

So the lying had begun.

"Oh!" Mrs. Pennington's hand flew to her mouth. The awkward

pause was much shorter this time. "Well then, congratulations are in order!"

Mollie bit her lip. A demure, pensive expression tugged down her lips. "You may think that I am wearing black in mourning for my grandfather, and while that is true, I'm also in mourning for my husband."

The Penningtons gasped.

Henry's heart thudded in his chest, then sank to his stomach.

His sister was going to forge ahead with the falsehoods of her own invention.

Pity played on the Penningtons' faces.

His jaw clenched. Nothing positive could come from this.

It almost appeared as if tears were forming in Miss Pennington's chocolate eyes. "Oh my. What you must have been through! It is a wonder that this news was never brought up by your grandfather or brother. You must have felt positively alone."

"They were only following my wishes. Besides, my aunt has been most kind. But I would be lying if I said this hasn't been difficult to endure."

Mrs. Pennington patted Mollie's arm. "There is much to your story, I'd wager."

Mollie placed a protective hand over her belly. "I'd been staying with my aunt these many trying months, but when Henry returned, I thought it best to come to the country."

"As well you should." Frederica moved to pour Mollie a fresh cup of tea. "But am I to understand that you have been traveling? The journey here can be an irksome one, and in your condition? I can scarcely believe your aunt allowed such a venture."

"There will be no more traveling for me for quite some time." Mollie finally turned to Henry. He shivered at her ability to look him in the eye and lie as easily as if she were reciting a poem. "My brother is kind enough to let me stay on with him."

Miss Pennington cut her eyes toward him. "A kind man indeed, but that is what family does for each other, is it not? And the Stocktons are the epitome of family loyalty and grace."

Henry moved closer to the window so the chilly air seeping through could cool his heated senses.

"Good heavens, Mr. Stockton, you look sour." Frederica lowered her tea. "Are you not pleased your sister is here? I'd think you should be grateful for the company. It would be lonely for a bachelor in this big house, all alone."

Frederica's ability to remind him of his single state was not lost on him. He cleared his throat. "Unfortunately, I fear my sister is the one who is lonely, for the mill occupies my days."

"And often your nights," Mrs. Pennington supplied, "if you keep a schedule anything like Mr. Pennington."

Henry did not miss the hint of sadness in Mrs. Pennington's tone.

"I'm not so lonely." Mollie's expression brightened. "I have had a few visitors. The vicar's wife paid a call the other day, as did Miss Dearborne."

Henry nearly choked on his own tongue at the mention of Miss Dearborne. Not even the coolness by the window could dissipate the heat rising to his cravat and up to his scalp.

"Miss Dearborne?" Miss Pennington shot back, a frown shadowing her face. "Miss Katherine Dearborne?"

"Yes, she was lovely." Mollie's countenance gave no indication of discomfort. "I am surprised, since she lives so close, that we had never chatted before."

Miss Pennington and her mother exchanged confused glances,

and then she pivoted toward Henry. "That is a surprise. I am astonished to hear that another Dearborne has set foot on Stockton property. Has there been a change?"

All feminine eyes were on him.

How he wished the polished floor would swallow him whole.

When Henry did not respond quickly enough, Mrs. Pennington interjected, "Well, never mind that now. From now on you shall have suitable companionship, shall she not, Frederica?"

A more neutral conversation ensued, but Henry could not relax. Lie after lie slid easily from Mollie's lips. She was cool and confident in her claims. The easiness of the act alarmed him. She had not reconsidered or heeded his caution. Instead, she forged ahead.

He wanted to intervene, to set the record straight, but how could he do so now? His sister had made her decision. It was out of his hands.

CHAPTER 22

*H*enry pressed his lips shut, lest a protest slip. He could listen to no more. The Penningtons believed every word of his sister's lies.

And why would they not?

True, Miss Pennington and his sister had never been close, especially since his sister spent much of her childhood away at school or at their aunt's home. But still, there would be no reason for them to doubt Mollie's story.

He'd muttered an excuse, retreated from the drawing room, and settled in Grandfather's study to finish his letter writing. He'd been at the task for a quarter of an hour when a rapid tap sounded at the door. He lowered the quill. The brass handle jiggled and the paneled door moved. A dainty white hand gripped the door, and then blonde curls appeared around its edge.

"Henry?" Frederica's voice was soft as she poked her head inside.

He straightened at the sight of her slender form sweeping around the door as naturally as if she owned every inch of the space.

She shouldn't be in here alone.

He did not have to consider his welcome, for she sauntered farther into the room, as if cognizant of how attractive she appeared in the gown of dark-green velvet, and seated herself across from him. "Why did you not tell me about Mollie? My, if I had known of her presence here, I would have called straightaway."

Henry remembered his manners and stood as she entered. As soon as she had settled in the wingback chair across the desk, he resumed his seat, returned his quill to the inkwell, and leaned back. "She requested privacy. It wasn't my place to say anything."

"Don't be a goose. Of course it was! Why, she's one of us, is she not? We can't have her spending her days shut up here alone, now, can we?"

He tilted his head, unsure of what message Miss Pennington was trying to convey with her direct stare and playful posture. Her words were of inclusion and acceptance, and yet they lacked sincerity.

She fussed with the lace trim of her cuff and cut her eyes coyly at him. "I know you've been gone for quite some time, but it saddens me to think that you no longer feel you can trust me with such information."

"It has nothing to do with trust." Henry restacked the heap of papers before him so as not to look at her. He refused to tell lies for his sister. "As she said, she wanted privacy."

"What happened to her husband?" Her eyebrows drew together in consternation. "The poor dear must be beside herself."

"She'll tell you in her time, I am sure."

"You know, you are quite frustrating, Henry. I can tell plainly that there is something you do not wish to tell me." Her practiced, pretty pout was directed at him. "I'll get you to tell me, you know."

When he did not respond, she sobered and shifted in her padded chair. "I was surprised to hear that Miss Dearborne had visited Mollie. Of course, it is none of my business, but the way things have been going . . ." Her voice trailed off before returning with candid emphasis. "After all, you know her father and his viewpoints."

He scratched his neck and pulled at his cravat, grateful that she seemed not to know of Miss Dearborne's presence during the fire. "I believe she was delivering something to Miss Figgs and they struck up a conversation."

"But still." Miss Pennington clicked her tongue. "The Dearbornes are dangerous people. Mollie is so gentle. I fear she may be manipulated."

Henry could not help the laugh that slid from his lips. The statement was ridiculous. "Miss Dearborne may be part of the Dearborne family, but I hardly think her capable of targeting Mollie in a sinister plan."

She shivered as if disgusted. "You've heard the reports regarding the mill at Bremton. Do you really think the Dearbornes innocent of such an act? And even if they didn't have direct involvement, do you not think them supportive of it?"

Henry stared at Miss Pennington, not sure how to respond. Her opinions and questions rang hollow, as if she was repeating someone else's thoughts and words, yet they were eerily similar to the warning issued by Mr. Tierner in the countinghouse. Regardless, he could not be so quick to judge the Dearbornes, especially since he'd not even spoken with Silas since he returned.

Miss Pennington stood and walked to the window before sidling close to the desk. Her tone took on a thoughtful air, and she tilted her head to the side. "What happened to you, Henry?"

He narrowed his eyes but did not answer her question, for his response could shift the conversation to a path he did not wish to tread.

She angled closer, her scent of lily of the valley dangerously near. "You've changed."

Frederica had said the same words the night after his arrival, but this time they held none of the teasing playfulness. Memories rushed into his mind of a time when they had been younger—before war. Before death. Before the mill became the central focus of life. They would flirt and laugh, talk and dance. She seemed much the same person, though. She'd always been direct and decisive. But he felt different about her and so many things.

She leaned her hip against the desk, picked up a piece of twine that had been discarded from a parcel, and ran it through her fingers. "You know what's expected of us."

He forced a little chuckle. "You don't strike me as the sort to always do what is expected."

She did not join in his joke. After several seconds, she shifted the topic. "Why don't you call me Frederica anymore? You always used to."

He cleared his throat. "We are no longer children."

"But are we not still friends? For in my mind, you are Henry. The formality of referring to you as Mr. Stockton is suffocating."

He crossed his arms over his chest. "And what is expected of you?"

She tilted her head to the side and looked toward the ceiling. "Oh, marriage, children, a passion for all sorts of textiles, especially broadcloth, and the ability to do my needlepoint politely and without complaint." A teasing smile stole across her smooth features. "Not that I mind. It sounds like a lovely future, don't you agree?"

"I don't know how I would fare at needlework, but—"

"Don't tease me." She swatted his arm playfully. "And you? What is expected of you?"

She was investigating him, and hiding her intentions poorly.

He sobered. "Now that Grandfather's gone, the only person placing expectations on me is myself. I'd like to think my actions would honor him in some way, but I've no desire to rush into any decisions, especially with everything happening at the mill."

He looked at her and allowed himself, for just a moment, to relax. She really was beautiful. And entrancing. The attraction that had once pulled him to her, however, had weakened.

He could not help but compare her to the one who was unknowingly drawing him toward her.

Miss Dearborne.

Would Miss Pennington ever worry if a child did not have a cloak? Would she be willing to go out of her way to tend a sick child, even if it meant facing her enemy to do so?

Frederica lacked something. Kindness. Gentleness. He never thought those qualities mattered . . . until he saw them in action.

She drew closer. Her scent, at one time intoxicating, was now suffocating. She could be his, no doubt, but as much as he tried to deny it, Miss Dearborne, with her dye-stained fingers and beautiful heart, overshadowed her.

Frederica, oblivious to the war in his mind, twirled the long satin ribbon adorning her gown's high waist. "Both Mother and Father told me I should not ask you about what happened while you were away, about what made you change so. They said it could be difficult for you to talk about. And yet I'm so curious."

The conversation was too much. He stood and moved to stoke the fire, hoping to distance himself from the memories that came rushing to him at her words. He returned the poker to the stand and turned.

She was next to him. She stepped closer still, fanning the flame of a different sort of memory; one much preferable to a gunshot and a battle cry. Oh, if he could turn back time four years, back to his own innocence.

But those days were gone.

"Do you think it is possible to recapture the past?" Her voice was barely above a whisper.

"I don't know."

She reached out and smoothed his coat lapel with unabashed intimacy and then rested her palm on his chest. Brazenly. She looked up to him with wide, dark eyes. Hopeful.

In that breathless moment his arms ached to hold her. He longed for something familiar. For something that made sense in a world that was ever changing. To kiss her as he had once before, and to feel her return that kiss.

She seemed willing, but such an action would require a promise—a promise he was not certain he could give.

He placed his hands on her shoulders and ran his hands down her arms. He could kiss her now and lock the plan in place. He could marry her soon, and the future of the Stocktons and the Penningtons would be secure.

He hesitated.

"What is it, Henry?"

When he did not respond, her fair eyebrows arched, and she sighed and pulled back slightly. "You know, I saw you looking at her."

"At whom?"

"Miss Dearborne."

The clouds outside the window shifted, casting a shadow over them. Henry stiffened. "You're mistaken."

"Am I? Perhaps you have forgotten how fast news travels around a small town like Amberdale. It's absolutely ravenous for a tale."

"My interest in Miss Dearborne is not what you think."

"Then what is it?"

Again he did not respond.

"Whatever happened to you during the war must have been quite an ordeal, and I'm sorry for it. But I miss you, Henry. The old you, the one full of laughter. If he ever comes back, please have him come and see me. I'll be waiting for him." She withdrew her hand from his chest and left the room, leaving it quiet and still in her wake.

A strange emptiness ballooned within him. He was accustomed to being alone. He'd spent years with dozens of men but knew none of them. It hadn't bothered him then, but now a strange loneliness blew over him, just as it had when he stood at his grandfather's grave.

He looked out the window toward Meadowvale. Gray smoke plumed from the cottage and outbuildings. He lived so close to the Dearbornes, but they could not be farther apart. He could have pretended he was not looking for her, but he stood for several moments, watching the landscape between them blow and sway in the wind.

And then he was either rewarded or tortured for his spying. For a glimpse of crimson flashed. He did not think, did not contemplate what he would say or do. He simply grabbed his greatcoat and hat and headed toward the door.

Where was Ivy? Kate heard the ewe bleating, but with the wind and the brush, she could not determine her location.

She glanced up at the late-afternoon sky. Thick pewter clouds swirled against a colorless background, warning of possible rain.

The sound of Ivy's renewed flailing recaptured Kate's attention, and she sloshed along the melting snow near the tree line, then peered through the bare scrubs and brush.

It was not unusual for the sheep to free themselves from the pen. But did it always need to be when it was so cold and wet?

She cupped her hands around her mouth and called again. "Ivy!"

The sheep baaed, and Kate spied the wooly animal deep in the bare brambles. She pulled her small knife from her pocket and prepared to cut through the thicket when a man called her name.

She groaned without lifting her head. John had been following her for most of the day. No doubt he wanted to help her with another task.

She adjusted the small blade in her hand, then swept her hair away from her face with the back of her opposite forearm. A protest ready to spill forth, she turned, only to snap her mouth shut.

Mr. Stockton.

Kate straightened, immediately aware of the dirt clinging to her work apron. She brushed it clean. "Mr. Stockton. I didn't hear you."

He sat tall and straight atop a horse, his square jaw shadowed by his wide-brimmed hat. "Are you having trouble?"

She propped her hands on her hips and looked back at the wooly animal. "My sheep is stuck in the thicket. I fear she'll injure herself."

"May I help?"

She was about to decline his offer, more out of fear that someone at Meadowvale would notice him than anything else, but before she knew it, he'd dismounted and tethered his horse to a nearby tree. He looked at the knife in her hand and extended his palm.

She should refuse his help. She'd seen to this task dozens of times. But bits of rain were beginning to fall from the shifting clouds, and the wind raced through the trees, growing in intensity.

She handed it to him. "Be careful." Kate shifted her position to watch him kneel down and cut through the thicket. "She's a skittish one."

"Come now, sheep." His voice was surprisingly soothing, and he knelt to one knee and ducked to look through the brambles. "You'll be free in a few minutes."

Ivy bleated and flailed.

Kate could stand it no longer. Ivy was her pet. Kate knelt next to Mr. Stockton, pulled away the thorny brush to allow him a better view, and winced as a thorn sliced through her glove. "How did you get in here, Ivy?"

"Her name is Ivy?" Mr. Stockton snipped another wiry branch.

Kate nodded, pulling a long branch straight so he could clip it.

"Don't worry, *Ivy*," he murmured, emphasizing the name. "You'll be out of here and eating your dinner in no time."

"Watch her legs. She's liable to be frantic when she's free."

After several minutes of careful cutting, Ivy pulled free and burst forth with all the energy her pregnant body could muster. Kate jumped to her feet, stumbling on her gown's hem in the process. She lunged at the animal to keep her from getting loose again.

She doubted anyone at Meadowvale would give her unladylike actions a second thought, but even as she secured Ivy, heat crept up. Mr. Stockton was a gentleman.

Pushing embarrassment aside, she knelt and looped a lead around the animal's neck and then stood.

Once the sheep was still, he reached down and offered her his hand to help her to her feet. She accepted his assistance, finding it much more difficult than she thought to regain her footing in the spongy, frozen moss underfoot.

His hand continued to steady hers as she pushed her hair away and straightened her cloak. Then he dropped his hand. "Is Ivy all right?"

"She'll be fine. I worry for her, though, stuck in the bramble and thrashing around so. It could have been much worse."

"I didn't realize you had sheep at Meadowvale." He extended her small knife back to her.

"We have a few." Kate tucked the blade in her apron and motioned to the east. "They are put out to pasture in our meadow on the other side of the cottage, so I doubt you've seen them."

Ivy jerked her head, as if eager to be free, and Kate rubbed her gloved hand against the ewe's soft fur.

He brushed his dark hair away from his forehead and adjusted his hat. "You seem to care a great deal for her."

"She was orphaned at birth more than ten years ago, and my mother and I nursed her to health. Now Ivy is quite an old lady, I fear. But there seems to be no harm done."

Mr. Stockton sniffed as the animal pulled against Kate. "She seems quite out of sorts to me."

She laughed. "All sheep are that way. Do you not know their nature?"

"I confess, I don't. For as long as I can recall, wool always came on a wagon, never directly from an animal."

"Well, Papa prefers to control every aspect of the cloth-making process. Ivy here has been giving us wool and lambs for quite some time."

Her words fell silent.

He was staring at her. Even as she looked down to Ivy, she could feel the warmth radiating from him, almost as if she could feel his very presence drawing her to him. Kate did not want to be affected by the blueness of his eyes or the softness in his expression, and yet she could feel it weakening her knees and quickening her pulse. She smoothed her hair, feeling self-conscious. It was not proper for her to be alone with him in the fields, yet the thought of walking away sent a surprising jolt of hesitation through her. "I should be getting her home. Feel the rain in the air?"

She turned to leave, but he reached out to halt her, stopping just short of touching her arm. "Wait. Please."

An unexpected flutter started in her chest. She didn't want to feel a response to him—she wanted to feel nothing but coldness and hatred for him, like her father and the other journeymen.

But something inside her prevented it.

He spoke abruptly. "The cloaks will be here. Soon."

"Cloaks?" She lifted her head, jarred by the sudden change of topic.

"Yes. For the mill children. Your brother took the cloth over to another tailor several days ago. I thought you'd be happy to hear it."

The annoyance that had lodged in her heart the day she saw him on the bridge was melting, she could not deny it. Either she had grossly misjudged him, or he was a master of manipulation. "You've been kind. After all that has transpired between our families, I can't help but wonder why."

His Adam's apple bobbed as he swallowed. "Because I like you, Miss Dearborne."

Kate blinked, not sure she had heard him correctly. Her power of speech had momentarily left her. She wanted to believe that his words were in earnest. What woman would not like to have such a handsome man think positively of her?

She opened her mouth to respond when the sound of footsteps echoed.

Someone shouted her name.

She turned, and John emerged through the trees.

CHAPTER 23

*A*nger simmered in John's dark eyes, but his focus was not directed toward Kate. His glare pinned Mr. Stockton. Boldly. Unwavering.

At first no one moved, despite the manner in which the bitter wind whipped down from the pasture and swirled at the tree line. Kate held her breath, awaiting—almost fearing—the words that would pass John's lips. The journeyman's fierce loyalty to her father made him unpredictable—a trait that frightened Kate.

Tightening her grip on the ewe's lead rope, she rallied the courage to glance at Mr. Stockton. Moments ago his countenance had been friendly, but in the span of a second, coolness descended over his features.

Mr. Stockton clearly did not share the sense of fear that wound within her.

Kate blurted out, "John, what are you doing here?"

"I've been searching everywhere for you." His words were directed at Kate, but his eyes narrowed to slits as he stared at Mr. Stockton.

"I've been out looking for Ivy." She sounded more like a child caught in a mischievous act than a woman of one and twenty.

"And it seems you have found her. Stockton, you must have lost your way. This is Dearborne property. You aren't welcome here."

Kate jumped in. "He was passing by and helped me free Ivy. She was caught in the bramble there."

"I don't care why he was here. I know I speak for my master when I tell you to keep off our land."

Mortification sank its teeth into Kate's soul at the rude treatment. What bit even more was that she probably would've treated their guest in a similar manner a few weeks ago. What had changed? She pressed her lips together and dared to glance at Mr. Stockton from the corner of her eye. Would he be angry? Offended? Would he retaliate?

A smile toyed with Mr. Stockton's lips. "My mistake. I'll be taking my leave, then." He looked toward Kate with the same disarming smile, one that dimpled his cheek and brightened his eyes. "Good day, Miss Dearborne."

She managed to squeak, "Thank you for your assistance."

Mr. Stockton glanced back at John with a raised eyebrow and then returned to his horse, which he mounted in one easy motion, urging him into a canter across the snow-clad countryside.

When he was out of sight, Kate braved a glance at John.

Without a word, he turned and stomped down the path, his heavy boots splashing up bits of frozen mud with each step.

She tugged Ivy's lead and followed, careful to lift her skirts above the slush.

After several steps he stopped unexpectedly, and Kate jerked to a stop for fear of running into his back.

"What was that, Kate?" He folded his arms across his chest.

"What was what?" Her tone was sheepish. She knew exactly what he meant.

"Pause for a moment and imagine what would have happened if it had been your father who happened upon that little interlude instead of me."

"There was no interlude." Kate lifted her chin and brushed past him.

He halted her steps by wrapping his fingers around her forearm. "He is a Stockton, Kate. Need I remind you what that means?"

She whirled around to face him, forcing herself to remain calm. "Believe me, I know better than anyone the impact they've had on my family. But that doesn't change the fact that he's our neighbor. He offered assistance, and I accepted it."

He pointed his finger at her, a vein throbbing in his temple. "Don't do that again."

She laughed. "You have no authority over me. May I remind you that you work for my family? It's not the other way around."

"Your father seems to think otherwise." He clenched his fist and released it, as if he was calming his nerves.

John sighed, softened his stance, and rested his gloved hand on her shoulder. "I should tell your father that Stockton was on his property. But I won't. Do not put me in this position again."

"Tell him what you will." She jerked her shoulder away. "It matters not to me."

His jaw twitched, stubble shadowing his square chin. "There will come a time, Kate, a time very soon, when you must decide. Battle lines have been drawn. You can't continue to have it both ways: adoring your father and supporting your brother. It doesn't work that way."

"I don't recall asking for your opinion on such matters."

He chuffed out a laugh. "Like it or not, Kate Dearborne, my opinion may matter much more than you realize."

She narrowed her eyes. "What do you mean?"

"I have been more than patient in indulging your whims. But we both know what's in our future."

Kate scowled and took a step, but he moved to block her.

"Your father's a powerful man. Once he declares that we're to marry, do you think any man in his right mind will go against him?"

His words stung.

John dug deeper. "And are you really so naive that you don't see what this wolf in sheep's clothing is doing? The first day he arrived, he came to your aid. Now this. He is grooming you to turn on your father. Doing the same thing his grandfather did with Charles."

"That's ridiculous."

"Is it? The quickest way to break a man like your father is not to beat him at his game. It's to crumble his foundation—you, your brother. Piece by piece the Stockton family is coming after him, and you, Kate, are his pawn."

Kate swallowed. The memory of Mr. Stockton's kindness burned a sharp impression on her heart. But was he sincere?

She did not know what to believe. Not anymore.

Henry had never spoken to John Whitby before today, but rumors of the man's brash nature and passionate disposition wagged on the tongue of nearly everyone in the industry, weavers and millers alike. Now that he had witnessed Whitby's threatening tone for himself, a simmering anger burned within his belly. He did not take kindly to men who employed such tactics. Furthermore, Whitby's presumed authority over Miss Dearborne—and the harsh manner in which he wielded it—unsettled him. She had not appeared afraid of him, but the spark in her hazel eyes and the flare of her nose communicated that she was well versed in the lectures.

When Henry had returned home from his ride, the Pennington women had departed, leaving behind the promise of another visit very soon. But to Henry's pleasant surprise, another visitor had called: Vincent Warren.

Warren's face had not changed—not much, anyway. He still boasted high cheekbones and narrow-set eyes, but now his straight black hair was cut short, and he'd resumed what was likely his natural weight.

It was amazing how different a man could appear with regular meals and without the constant threat of death at every turn. But even though he appeared healthier, a hollowness radiated from him. His face was paler. His eyes looked more like a man in the winter of life instead of one just beginning.

"Mary had been dead two months by the time I returned home," Warren explained as he sat across from Henry in Grandfather's study. "I had no idea."

Henry listened as his old friend recounted the events of his return home. It was a difficult story to hear. Henry shook his head, unsure of how to respond. Death was a painful yet dismally expected outcome of war. Generally one would expect the person fighting to succumb to its bitter sting, not those at home. Yet the life of Warren's young wife had been cut short by a sudden, vicious fever.

"It was humiliating to write the letter and ask for a position at your mill." Warren leaned forward with his elbows on his knees and fixed his gaze on Henry. "I wrote a letter and destroyed it a dozen times."

"When you've been through what we've been through, how could you even question it? I am indebted to you, Vincent. I doubt I'd even be sitting here if it weren't for your levelheadedness. You will always have my support."

"Enough of my dreary story." The fire's light cast flickering shadows over Warren's angular features as he indulged in a swig of brandy and then lowered his glass. He leaned back in the chair. "I rode past Stockton Mill on my way here. Very impressive."

Henry nodded.

"And this house." Warren raised his head to view the molding at the ceiling's edge and let his gaze travel down the painted walls and marble mantelpiece. "Quite an improvement over sleeping on the forest floor and washing in a river, I'd say."

Henry cleared his throat, eager to get to the topic at hand. "As I said in my letter, I've a position for you. It is not at Stockton Mill but Pennington Mill, working the looms, about a mile from here. It's not a glamorous position, but it's steady work. And we have a row of cottages on the property for the workers. A handful of them are vacant, and we can get you settled into one of those when you're ready."

Warren smiled and shook his head. "I am grateful, even if I am a bit ashamed to take such generosity."

"Don't be ashamed. If our circumstances were reversed, I've no doubt you would do the same for me."

Kate stood back from the dye pot. Steam rose from the scalding liquid, and she used the edge of her apron to wipe the moisture from her brow and cheeks. With her stick she stirred the wool in the mixture, eyeing how the colored liquid danced and swirled with the fabric. It would be indigo soon, dark and deep.

She strained to see in the day's gray light, watching for signs of unevenness in the color.

It was imperative that the dye set permanently and perfectly.

Sudden sharp hoofbeats outside the window drew her attention, and she lifted her head from her task. Even though the light was beginning to fade, she could make out the hook of Mr. Wooden's nose. He was speaking with another one of Papa's journeymen. She could not make out their words, but their tones were sharp enough to cut glass.

Betsy bustled in with an armful of raw yarn.

"What is Mr. Wooden doing here?" Kate resumed stirring.

"I don't know." Betsy shrugged and cast a glance toward the window. "They seem out of sorts, don't they?"

Kate eyed the men as she tended to her work, but something akin to alarm coursed through her as her father joined the conversation. "Here, take this." Kate handed Betsy the stirring stick, pulled off her heavy work apron, and hung it on the hook next to the door.

Her skin burned as she stepped from the steam of the dye house into the frigid, early-evening air. An icy breeze swept down from beyond the meadow, and she hugged her arms in front of her for warmth as she approached the group.

The men did not notice her. She took advantage of the oversight and strained to hear their words.

"Time is running out." Wooden's broad back was to her, his gruff muttering barely audible. "Either we confront him now, or the opportunity is lost."

"I've heard he's a mite softer than his grandfather," responded Thomas Crater, swiping a thick paw of a hand over his nose. "Might work in our favor."

"I'll never cower or beg in front of a Stockton." Papa glowered. "Neither should you. Where is your pride? Your fortitude?"

Wooden shifted, angling away from Kate and toward her father. "The time for pride is dwindling. We've enough poor and hungry in Amberdale already."

"Send a letter, then?" Mr. Crater suggested. "Outline our arguments that way."

"No, we haven't time." Papa studied the ground and rubbed his chin, as if formulating a plan. "I'll not beg, but I will talk to him. Let him look us in the face, eye to eye, and then we'll see what sort of man we are dealing with."

Kate held her breath, listening intently to hear over her increasing pulse. The thought of Papa talking with Mr. Stockton sent an uncomfortable chill through her, partly because she knew her father would meet his match in the younger man, and partly because if she were honest with herself, she felt guilty because of her budding sympathy toward him.

"It's decided. Wooden, you, Whitby, and I will ride there this evening. We'll pay young Mr. Stockton a visit and see if he's any more sensible than the fool who came before him. But if he's not, I've no hesitation to remind him what our brothers to the south have done to other mill owners seeking to do harm to their villagers."

The threat seared her ears, burning away the day's coldness and sending a surge of energy through her. As the men dispersed, Kate gathered her skirts and ran to catch up with her father. "I can help. I'm going with you."

He did not slow, nor did he look in her direction. "No, you can't, and no, you aren't."

"But, Papa, consider." She raised her voice to be heard over the sounds of their machinery coming from their own loom room. "I care about these people as much as you do. I think—no, I know—I could be of assistance. One day the future of this place will rest on my shoulders, and—"

"No, one day this place will rest on your husband's shoulders, and in the meantime, I still make the decisions." He did not even grant her the courtesy of facing her as he spoke. "John and Wooden will go with me, and you will stay here. You can mind the fires if you like."

Her steps slowed. *Mind the fires indeed.*

He called to her over his shoulder as he retreated toward the stable. "Get inside, girl. You'll catch your death out here in this cold. Or perhaps Thomas can drive you to the village. Isn't the Winter's End Festival coming soon? Surely you and Miss Abbott have some work to do for that."

Kate's steps stopped entirely as her father's dismissive words shrouded her as heavy and uncomfortable as a wet blanket. She blew out a breath and propped her hands on her hips, looking around the courtyard. Perhaps she was mistaken to feel so integral to this process, for the truth was painfully obvious: her papa would never see her as more than an assistant, an extra hand for the work.

CHAPTER 24

$\mathcal{H}$enry lifted the missive from Silas Dearborne and tapped it against his palm. The cryptic message was little more than an interview request for himself and two of his men with no hint as to the topic. It had arrived at the mill earlier that day when he had been in the countinghouse, and with it came uncertainty's dark cloud.

Henry had responded immediately with instructions to meet him at Stockton House that night. Henry wanted them nowhere near his mill—not when plans for the gig mills' arrival were under way.

If he were honest, he was actually glad to have finally made contact with Silas. He'd been back in Amberdale for many weeks now and as the two major influencers of Amberdale's broadcloth production, they needed to speak. Even now as Belsey, Dearborne, and Henry were gathered in the Stockton House study, he repeated his question to Dearborne. "Are you sure you want to do this? If you want to wait in the other room, I'll not hold it against you."

The fire's light flickered off young Dearborne's determined expression, the same indomitable fire he had seen flicker in Miss Dearborne's expression on more than one occasion. "I'm not a child, nor am I afraid of my father. I'm more than capable of handling such a conversation."

The fine hairs on Henry's neck pricked as the crunch of wagon wheels echoed from the gravel drive outside. A knot formed in his stomach as a vision of his grandfather flashed in his mind. Old man Stockton would not have even entertained the idea of such a meeting, much less in his own home. But times were changing, and Henry's motives were twofold.

He could not forget his pledge to find the person—or people—responsible for his grandfather's death and bring them to justice. Mr. Tierner was having no success on the matter, and Henry was growing impatient. Additionally, he was determined to protect the legacy his grandfather had built.

Henry tapped his finger against the desk's polished surface as the main door creaked open and guttural male voices rumbled in the night's stillness. As heavy footsteps drew nearer to the study, his fists clenched. By the time the men entered the room, Henry was standing.

He picked Silas Dearborne out from the trio immediately. He was tall, like his son, thick and barrel chested. His hair, gray only at the temples, hinted at the same dark undertones as both Miss and Charles Dearborne, but it was the shape of his eyes that tied the three together. Behind him, John Whitby wore the same furrowed brow as he had the other day in the pasture. Henry did not know the other man. But it did not matter.

Henry steeled his expression.

"Mr. Dearborne." Henry motioned for the men to be seated. "Good of you to come."

No one sat.

"We're not here on a social call," muttered Dearborne before his steely gaze, for the briefest moment, flicked to his son. He pursed his thin lips, widened his stance, and returned his focus to Henry. "I'll come right to it. We've received word that you are set to install gig mills. Is this true?"

Henry raised an eyebrow. There was no need for lies. "It is."

After a sharp intake of breath, Silas fixed him with a hard stare. "And so we are to understand that you intend to no longer hire out any of the shearing then?"

Henry nodded. "As our machinery becomes more efficient, we will not need as many extra hands. You're correct."

The vein in Dearborne's temple began to throb. "Are you aware that those men depend on the work from your mill for their liveli-hood, to support their families?"

Henry squared his shoulders. "Mr. Dearborne, you must under-stand that a great many families depend on work from my mill for their sustenance. Am I not indebted to them as well to preserve their livelihood?"

"By cutting off the livelihood of others?" Dearborne's voice rose. "Sir, you are going against centuries of tradition. We can go around and around about this, but we are here to tell you that your gig mills are not welcome in Amberdale."

Henry would not be shouted at in his own home. He kept his voice low and strong. "I have the law on my side stating that I am quite welcome to house any sort of machine I choose."

"Bah! What is the law of man to answering to God for the actions you take on others? What of tending to the widows and orphans and giving to the poor? A man whose only interest lies in lining his pock-ets is a sad sort of a man."

Dearborne whirled around to face the two men accompanying him. "Listen to him, gentlemen. We thought we would come here for a rational discussion, not to listen to pathetic excuses. We have come to urge you to abandon this idea and consider your fellow man. I respectfully ask you, one last time, to reconsider."

At this, Henry stepped forward, tempering the frustration building. He would not become excitable.

Henry cleared his throat. "I've listened to you, and I hear your argument. But I have an argument of my own, which, contrary to your statement, is not all about money. I must adapt constantly, otherwise another mill will take my place, then another. Then another. I appreciate the respectful nature of your request, but I intend to move forward with the gig mills."

Dearborne's eyes hardened. The two men shifted behind him. "Perhaps I did not make our position clear, Mr. Stockton. Our request was not so much a request as an expectation. We, as the elders of our district, have a responsibility to do whatever's necessary to protect the people and the values that are the cornerstones of our community. We are not the only ones who feel strongly about this, boy. Our brothers all over Yorkshire are ready to rise up in arms against people like you, seeking to destroy the fabric of our lives."

"Rising up in arms? Like burning a man's stable to the ground within hours of his arrival in the village?"

Dearborne's jaw twitched. Did he know about what happened that night with the Stockton House stable? But just as quickly his eyes hardened once again. "I can see you are every bit as stubborn and unreasonable as your grandfather before you. I only hope you have enough sense to avoid a fate such as his."

"Do you have specific knowledge of my grandfather's *fate?*" Henry challenged.

"I do not. But it doesn't take much to conclude that your grandfather crossed the wrong path one too many times."

"I can't imagine there's anything else to be said. I appreciate your more-than-friendly introduction, gentlemen, but—"

Dearborne silenced Henry's words by leaning forward aggressively and pointing a thick finger in Henry's direction. "Mark my words, Stockton. This is not over, far from it." He cast a final condemning glance at his son, who, unlike his father, had remained silent through the ordeal.

No one spoke until the visitors' footsteps could be heard through the front windows and the sound of hoofbeats retreated into the night. Henry unclenched his fists and turned to face Belsey and Charles. He blew out his breath and moved to the fire. "That went well."

"Makes me sick," muttered Belsey. "They speak of preserving the community and taking care of the poor. What they care about is preserving the money in their own pockets and not an ounce more."

"If we don't bring in the gig mill, someone else will." Dearborne shook his head. "It is only a matter of time."

Henry slapped his hand on Dearborne's back. "Hope that wasn't too uncomfortable for you."

"It's fine." Dearborne shrugged. "Father is the one who doesn't wish to speak with me, not the other way around. I've made my choices in my life, and he's made his. It has never been written anywhere that the son must follow the father."

The words struck Henry as a hand across his face. He could very well have said that it was not written anywhere that the grandson must follow the grandfather. And yet here he was, running his company, living in his house.

Henry hoped one day he would find the clarity that Dearborne possessed. But for now, he had to keep his goal in mind. He would find the men responsible for his grandfather's death. He would find the men responsible for the stable fire. And he would defend his work against Silas Dearborne and his men.

CHAPTER 25

*K*ate rapped her gloved knuckles on Stockton House's kitchen entrance, tucked her hand back into the warmth of her cloak, and cast a glance around to make sure no passersby noticed her presence.

Days had slid into weeks since she and Mollie Stockton had become acquainted, and now winter's harsh bite on the barren landscape was just barely beginning to weaken. Kate's visits to Stockton House had become more frequent of late. Of course, Papa knew nothing of them, and Kate intended to keep it that way. It didn't exactly feel like a betrayal. Not really, for her visits were to Mrs. Smith. Mr. Stockton was never home during the daytime hours, leaving the women free to chat as they pleased. Kate was fond of Mrs. Smith, and their friendship, although unexpected, was a bright spot in her days.

At length Mrs. Figgs appeared in the doorway, her thin lips pressed into a firm line. She, too, stuck her head out the door and looked to the right and then the left before stepping back and giving Kate room to enter.

"Mrs. Smith told me to see you up to her chamber." Mrs. Figgs clutched her skirts as they climbed the back stairwell.

"Mrs. Smith is well, is she not?"

"Ah, she is as well as one in her state can be expected." Mrs. Figgs gave her head a sharp shake, tipping the white cap on her head to the side. "The days are growing long for her."

Kate rested her hand atop the ornately carved newel post and pivoted to follow Mrs. Figgs up several more treads. Her steps were barely audible on the carpet runner protecting the staircase landing, and as Kate turned the corner to ascend another flight of steps, she caught sight of stair-step portraits lining the paneled wall. Her interest piqued as paintings of a boy and a girl came into view.

They had to be Henry Stockton and Mollie.

Both children boasted vibrant blue eyes and dark hair. Kate paused long enough to fix the images in her memory before hurrying to follow Mrs. Figgs to the next landing.

Mrs. Figgs breezed into a chamber, and Kate poked her head in afterward. "Mrs. Smith?"

"Thank goodness you are here!" Mollie's pallid expression brightened, and she struggled to sit up amid the abundance of white linens and myriad pillows. "I've been about ready to die from boredom. I knew you'd come."

Kate smiled at the woman's dramatics as she removed her cloak and let it fall to a chair. She approached the bed. "I came as soon as I received your note. I was worried you had fallen ill."

"No, nothing like that. I have been dizzy of late, and the midwife thought it best if I stay in bed." She turned to Mrs. Figgs and requested that tea be brought before she motioned to the chair at the desk. "Pull up that chair there, and sit."

Kate did as she was bid. A little warmth settled over her. It felt good to have another woman she could be friendly with. She and Jane were close, of course, but other than her there was no one she could truly relax with.

The cool light of afternoon slid through the filmy white curtains. In a quick sweep of the space, Kate took stock of the room. Floral wallpaper with birds and delicate pink flowers clad the walls, and a large bed draped on all four sides with thick brocade curtains sat in the center of the room. An intricate Persian rug, not entirely unlike the one in the drawing room, covered the planked wooden floor. Opposite the bed, a mantelpiece framed a cheery fire, flanked by a chaise lounge and a small writing desk. Against one wall was a wide dressing table, cluttered with glass jars and silver canisters. A giant oak wardrobe stood guard against another wall. It was a perfectly comfortable space, but despite the smile gracing Mrs. Smith's face, her pale cheeks and red eyes spoke to her discomfort.

Kate forced cheerfulness to her voice and adjusted the pale-blue coverlet over Mollie's maternal form. "So how are you feeling, really?"

"Very, very large. But I am well, I suppose."

Kate leaned back in her chair and waited for Mrs. Figgs to close the door before speaking. "Does the midwife think your time is near?"

Mollie shook her head. "One cannot tell these things, but I do think it will not be long."

"You must be eager to meet the little one." Kate warmed at the thought.

Mollie's smile faded, and she tilted her head to the side. She nibbled her lower lip and frowned. "We're friends, are we not?"

"I'd like to think so."

"Good. Then I can confide in you." Mollie's voice grew quiet. "If I am honest, I am frightened of what is to come."

Sympathy tugged at Kate. She knew little about children and childbirth, but she had heard stories and knew of more than one woman who did not survive the experience. "Of course you are."

"I'm not so much frightened for the birth, mind you—God will protect us through that—but I am frightened about what comes afterward. My baby will have no father. I have no husband. What will become of us?"

Kate reached out and clutched Mollie's hand reassuringly. "Your brother will not let harm come to you. Surely you know that."

"Yes, I know, but how long can I—we—rely on his kindness?"

A cloud seemed to cover the sun outside, for a shadow traversed the room. Could she not say the same thing? It seemed every woman she knew was dependent upon a man for her provisions. In that moment her underlying yearning for independence surfaced. Was this why she worked so hard in her own right? "That will all work itself out in due time."

"I wish my mother were still here." An apprehensive laugh whimpered from Mollie's lips. "I suppose every daughter who has lost her mother says that during times like this."

Kate searched her memory but could recall no details about Mollie's mother. "I don't remember her. When did she die?"

"It is no wonder you don't remember her. I don't think she ever set foot in Amberdale after she married my father. You see, Grandfather did not approve of her as a match for his son. When she died we were living in London. My father was teaching in a small university there."

Kate was far from an expert on Stockton family history, but this sounded odd. "I thought your father worked with your grandfather at the mill."

"He did when we were very young, but my mother refused to join him here. We—my mother, brother, and I—stayed in London while he worked here with Grandfather. I don't have to tell you it takes a certain kind of man for this kind of work. Being separated from his family began to wear on my father, and it took a toll on his relationship with my grandfather. Anyway, he and my grandfather parted ways when he accepted the position at the university. Grandfather never forgave him. It was only after my parents died that my grandfather took an interest in us."

It was difficult to imagine Henry Stockton as a child. She vaguely recalled Frederica pointing him out the evening she told her they could no longer be friends. Kate shook the memory away and returned her attention to Mollie. "I'm so very sorry. It's hard to lose a parent."

"But you've lost your mother too, have you not?"

"Yes, many years ago." Kate swallowed. Would it never be easy to speak of her? "Scarlet fever claimed her. Life has never been the same."

Genuine concern curved her friend's eyebrows. "You poor dear. Oh, how the story makes my heart ache! I wonder if I will be a good mother to this child. I pray I will be. I'm all he or she has."

"What of your husband's family?" Kate adjusted her back against the sturdy wood chair. "Surely they would be eager to welcome the child."

Mollie shook her head and looked to the window. "He had no family. None to speak of, anyway."

"You will be a wonderful mother, I've no doubt. And you'll not be alone. You have my friendship."

A little laugh bubbled from Mollie. "I told my brother of your visits. He asked if your father was aware you were spending time here. He said that he and your father were not exactly on friendly terms."

"That is a polite way to put it. But Father never asks where I go, so I feel no need to divulge the information."

Mollie adjusted her coverlet. "Well, I'm grateful you see fit to visit me, vile though my family may be."

Kate giggled at the exaggeration. It felt good to laugh at the serious aspects of life, especially when so little could be done about them. "I can't believe our paths didn't cross more when we were younger. We were neighbors! How did we never see one another?"

"I recall seeing you at church on occasion, but remember, I was away at school for many years, and for several years I lived with my aunt. I do believe that my grandfather loved me, but I just don't think he knew what to do with a young lady about the house. He was much more comfortable with Henry than me."

To this Kate could relate. Had not her own father poured his efforts into her brother? How odd that women from such different walks of life could have such similar stories.

Kate cleared her throat. "I find it odd that you have had no other visitors. What of Miss Pennington?"

"Mrs. and the eldest Miss Pennington have visited twice, but I do not have the same relationship with the Pennington family that my grandfather and brother enjoy. Since I was away at school much of my youth, we were never close. I think the only reason they visit now is because of Henry."

Kate swallowed, pushing the rumors she had heard about a union between Frederica Pennington and Henry Stockton to the back of her mind, rebuking herself for caring about the topic in the first place. Her voice sounded small. "Why?"

If Mollie noticed any change in her demeanor, she did not let on. "Grandfather always desired for Henry to marry Miss Pennington, from the day we first moved to Amberdale from London, and I believe the Penningtons regard Henry as an advantageous match. Part of me believes that if he hadn't gone to war, they would be married by now."

A queer pang of jealousy stabbed Kate's chest. She recalled how Mr. Stockton's hand had held hers as he assisted her with Ivy and how her heart leapt at his nearness. Kate looked down at her fingers. "Why did they not marry?"

"I cannot say for sure, but I think the war had a great deal to do with it. Henry was always so eager to prove himself."

"And he thought that becoming a soldier would satisfy that desire?"

"I don't know." Mollie shrugged and toyed with the fringe on the shawl resting about her shoulders. "I fully expected that he would return and marry immediately. I tried to ask him about it the other night, but he said he had too much work to do to think of such things. Sometimes I barely recognize him. In years past he would sit with me for hours and talk on any subject, serious or frivolous, it didn't matter. Now he clutches every thought so close to his chest. He used to be an open book. Now it seems as if his time on the Peninsula robbed him of some piece of his soul."

Kate could only imagine what tortures he endured. "Perhaps he has just matured with age."

"No, it is something different." Mollie leaned back against the pillows. "The other night I heard a shout in the black of night. It took me quite a while, but I managed to get up and walk down to his chamber. He was awake, pacing the space. I asked him what had happened, and he said he had a nightmare, nothing more. There was the strangest expression on his face, like a caged animal, trapped and afraid."

Kate lowered her gaze. Her own father had fought in battles when he was a young man, and even now there were nights he would wake up shouting in his sleep. Her heart ached at the sights he must have seen and the things he must have done.

"But that is such a dreary topic." Mollie sighed. "Mrs. Figgs told me the Winter's End Festival will soon be here and that you are quite involved in the process."

A nervous twinge tweaked Kate. With the tensions mounting, there had been talk of canceling the event in its entirety. But as of now, it would proceed as planned. "It is only a week away. Everything is in place."

"I do wish I could attend. Perhaps next year. Henry is going. He has promised to share every detail with me."

Kate ignored how excitement replaced trepidation at the realization that Henry Stockton would indeed be attending. "As will I."

After Mollie and Kate passed a pleasant afternoon, Kate gathered her cloak and turned to her friend. "Do let me know if there is anything I can do for you or bring to you."

"Just your company. Promise you will return soon."

"You have my word."

Bits of ice and sleet stung the exposed skin of his cheeks and jaw. Henry's every muscle twitched, ready at high alert, poised to react in a split second. The horse beneath him thundered across the arctic moor, its hooves grasping the frozen grass and heather, propelling him farther. Faster.

He flicked a glance toward Charles Dearborne, who rode in a similar fashion, body hugging low on the horse, gaze fixed ahead.

The moon was white and full in the predawn hours, its light flashing on the icy terrain below. At the speed he was traveling, its glow reflected and glimmered like diamonds on the hoarfrost.

Just ahead of them, two wagons, each conveying a gig mill, jostled over the uneven gravel road. In the distance a handful of yellow lanterns swung, guiding the wagons toward the safety of the mill's stone walls. He and Dearborne had lagged behind the caravan as they made the midnight journey from Leeds to Amberdale to watch for any attackers who might come from the rear. But none had come.

They'd done it. Everything had gone as planned—so far. Cautious satisfaction spread through his chest, broadening and deepening each breath. With a shout, he urged the horse beneath him to a quicker pace.

He'd not ridden like this since his time on the Peninsula, but instead of riding away from something, he was rushing *toward* something—toward the first taste of success since he'd arrived in Amberdale. Toward the fulfillment of the unspoken promise he had made to his grandfather and the people he employed. He licked his lips, blinked away bits of snow, and kicked his heels against the horse's belly.

Ahead of him, one of the lanterns rose in the darkness and moved from the right to the left and then back again. The signal indicating that the mill was uncompromised—that the weavers were not waiting for them.

The caravan began to slow at the sign, first the wagons and then the riders flanking them. The closer they drew to Amberdale, silence was essential. Henry and Dearborne followed suit, drawing their horses to a trot.

A glance toward Dearborne confirmed that his counterpart was as breathless as he. Frosty plumes puffed with his every breath, and he leaned his arm across his legs as he rode, as if to give his body a rest.

Henry squinted to see in the shifting mist. His heart threatened to burst from the confines of his ribs. He felt alive, truly alive, for the first time since the early days of the war.

Even though a wide-brimmed hat shadowed Dearborne's face, his white teeth flashed in a smile. "Congratulations, Mr. Stockton. Looks like we've done it."

Henry nodded. "I'm not ready to celebrate quite yet." Expected shadowed figures began to swarm the wagons as they crossed the bridge. Only a few hundred more yards.

Henry hurried ahead so he was even to the wagon as it traversed the mill gate. Familiar faces rushed forward—trusted millworkers—standing ready to usher the gig mills inside the safety of the mill's sturdy brick walls.

His future transformed before his very eyes in this moment. Yes, everything was changing. And the change started this dawn.

CHAPTER 26

_B_utterflies danced within Kate, and she anxiously ran a hand down the front of her embroidered muslin gown and stroked the lustrous fabric. She whirled to see her reflection in the small looking glass hanging on Jane's bedchamber wall. Candlelight shimmered against the silver threads embellishing the neckline, and she smoothed the ribbon along the gown's empire waistline. An unguarded smile bubbled up before she could censure it.

The night of the Winter's End Festival had arrived. After weeks of planning, after months of uncertainty. Her gown of pale yellow glittered in the light, and she pivoted to see how the bodice's back gathered in a column of tiny fabric buttons before releasing in a flow of fabric reaching to the floor.

Jane, who was pulling a pair of gloves up to her elbows, stepped behind Kate. "I remember that gown."

Kate did not look away from her reflection and brushed a piece of lint away from her sleeve. "Yes, it's the same gown I wore last year, but it's the best gown I own. Do you think anyone else will notice? I added some embroidery and made a few other adjustments."

"I'm sure they won't." Jane dug in a small box atop her wardrobe chest, retrieved two earbobs, and secured them to her earlobes. "Can you believe it has already been a year since the last festival? My, time passes so quickly. I wonder where life will find us one year from this very night. Perhaps another Winter's End Festival?"

Kate smiled at the thought, but it also made her stomach clench. Where would she be in a year? Would she still be at Meadowvale dyeing cloth? Would she be married? Instead of exciting her, thoughts of the future and what it might bring brought a sense of dread. She fought it and jutted her chin in the air, meeting her own gaze.

Her friend retrieved another trinket and approached her, extending the necklace. As if reading Kate's mind, she muttered, "I hope I shall be married this time next year."

Kate silently accepted the trinket and looked back to the mirror to fasten it about her neck.

Jane leaned in front of Kate to view her own reflection and continued. "It is a lovely thought, but I do think it is much more likely that *you'll* be married this time next year, not I."

"Who would I marry?" Kate shot back, amused at the banter.

"John, of course."

At the name and the matter-of-fact tone of her friend's voice, Kate sobered. "Well, we needn't speculate about any of that tonight. I only want to dance until we can dance no more. For one night we can put work and expectation behind us and enjoy being young."

Conversation faded as Jane tended the wild mass of brown curls atop Kate's head. As Jane wove a wide ribbon across her crown and braided it into the arrangement, Kate's mind wove ideas of its own.

Henry Stockton.

She shouldn't care for him. But she did.

Mollie mentioned that he had a new coat made for the event since none of his coats from before the war fit anymore. It was a trivial detail, but one that Kate clung to, as if she was apprised of some great secret about the man that no other person knew.

She gathered her reticule and a cloak of pale cream wool that had belonged to her mother. With its pink satin ribbons and silk hem, the cape was far too delicate for the everyday demands of Amberdale, but for one special evening she would don the billowy fabric. She thought her mother would want her to do so, and it made her feel as if her mother were with her.

Armed with the memory of her mother, the anticipation of perhaps encountering Mr. Stockton, and the promise of a night of revelry, she withdrew from the Abbott home and stepped into the night.

Bright light filtered from the inn's windows facing the village street as Henry approached, the yellow glow spilling onto the melting snow outside. Boughs of evergreen and holly adorned the windows and doors. Already, lively notes of violins and flutes sang from within, and the chatter of excited voices floated on the strains.

His heart pulsed, and his shoulders relaxed. The sound recalled simpler, happier times—a time before he knew the horrors of war or the weight of responsibility.

Henry eyed the villagers making their way to the venue. Villagers from every walk of life—the foundling children from the poorhouse, the rustic farmers in their rough linen coats, the perfumed and powdered Bremton ladies—all were present. Hundreds had gathered, and since there was not enough space in the inn to accommodate such a large crowd, the festivities had spread out to the town square.

Yes, nearly everyone in town was present.

And that meant *she* would be here.

He scanned the gathering crowd for the familiar crimson cloak she often wore, and he pressed his lips together in disappointment when he did not see her. Miss Dearborne had been on his mind far more than he cared to admit. She seemed to be more a part of the fabric of Amberdale than anyone else, and it captivated him.

Often she would visit her brother on the mill property, and he found himself scanning the courtyard in the midst of every day to catch a glimpse of her. He would see her at church, and even though they rarely spoke in public, she would smile and nod, and the simple acknowledgment would feed his lonely heart for days. He knew she was visiting Mollie regularly, and the thought of her in his home warmed him. But it was the chance meetings on the road that connected their homes—the sudden, unexpected moments when they were free to speak and laugh and interact without fear of condemnation—that sent his imagination soaring.

And she would be present tonight.

Dearborne and Warren both walked next to him in casual company, one on each side. Warren had been in the village a couple of weeks. He'd been working at Pennington Mill, but other than church, this was his first real introduction to the villagers of Amberdale—and the weavers. Henry was a bit nervous at the prospect. Even among the millers, the welcome Warren received had been a cold one. He was an outsider.

Dearborne was the first to speak since starting the short walk from the mill to the inn. His burly voice was barely audible above the merriment. "Well, Warren, what do you think of our village now?"

Warren laughed. "It is quite a bit larger than the village I am from."

"Rest assured, there are normally not so many people in the square. This is Amberdale at her finest." Dearborne swept out his arms in mock formality, like the carnival performers Henry recalled when he was a child. "People from every walk of life come out for the Winter's End Festival. It's been a tradition for as long as I can remember. Take a good look at it now. There'll likely not be another gathering like this until next year."

As they walked Dearborne's voice lowered. "Hope there will be no trouble tonight. Word's gotten out about the gig mills. Before we left, Belsey told me he heard two men talking of the mill at the public house. No doubt every weaver in the village knows about it now."

"At least they're safe in the mill's brick walls." Henry sidestepped a frozen puddle.

"We hope, anyway."

Attacks on mills all over Yorkshire had multiplied over recent weeks, and the frequency and intensity of them increased with each blow. He couldn't pretend that Stockton Mill would be immune.

Henry glanced back at the mill. Normally all would be dark this time of night, save for any light coming from the cottages or the countinghouse, but torches lit the space, reflecting their light on men with rifles slung over their shoulders who had been hired to protect the mill. "We've done what we can. The most important thing we can do now is attend this gathering tonight. If we didn't, that would send an even louder message of intimidation. No, I'll not live in fear of what they may or may not do."

Dearborne nodded as they approached the open door. "Let's hope it's the right decision."

Inside the inn, heat rushed Henry. Dancers whirled by at dizzying speeds. People, young and old alike, were pressed against the walls and tables, squeezing out room for the dancers in the middle. Voices, laughter, and shouts echoed from the broad, exposed timber rafters and carried down from the balcony surrounding the room.

A barmaid shoved a beverage in his hand, and Henry swept his beaver hat from his head. "I told Pennington I would find him. D'you see him?"

Dearborne gestured toward the corner. "I don't know where he is, but there can be no overlooking *her*."

Henry followed the direction of Dearborne's nod. Miss Pennington stood next to a beverage table, surrounded by a group of ladies and gentlemen. The women all paled in comparison, and the men gaped as starving men would stare at steak.

She was fit for the assembly rooms of London, not the humble inn of a local festival. She shimmered in a gown of emerald-green silk, and a sapphire pendant glittered from her white throat. A tiara glistened atop her golden curls, and diamond earrings bounced about her heart-shaped face at every movement. The cut of her gown accentuated the curves of her figure, and she fluttered her painted fan playfully about her face.

He was staring. Along with every other man in the room.

"She is a force to be reckoned with, isn't she?" Dearborne laughed. "Look at those sorry chaps, at her beck and call."

At one time the sight would have entranced Henry. They would have flirted. She'd have smiled coyly. He would have teased her. They would have spent the entire event at each other's side. But everything had been different lately. Would it remain so?

She turned, smiled, held his gaze, and then turned back to her company.

Henry expelled his breath.

This could be an interesting night indeed.

CHAPTER 27

$\mathcal{K}$ate stood next to her brother, shoulders beginning to sag. She glanced around the open space, distracted, eager to be free from his story about the new foal at the mill. His gathered friends were enthralled with the story, but how could she concentrate?

Mr. Stockton stood just behind her. She had accidentally made eye contact with him when she was looking around for Jane, and now she sensed his nearness. She strained to hear the conversation he was having with Miss Pennington, but the music and animated voices covered his.

He'd nodded in her direction and smiled, and that had been the extent of their interaction.

It was one thing to spend time with her brother, even though he was a millworker. But speaking with Mr. Stockton here would be out of the question.

She caught a flash of emerald from the corner of her eye and tilted her head slightly. The caller had announced the longways dance, and Mr. Stockton led Miss Pennington to the floor for the lively event.

Her heart sank at the sight. She pulled her gaze away and looked back to her brother, whose eyes were fixed expectantly on her.

"Did you hear me?" Charles prompted.

Apparently the foal story was over. His friends had moved on to another topic, and he took her arm. "I asked if you'd dance with me." A grin eased onto his face.

She hesitated and looked back to the dance floor. Women lined up on one side, men on the other. The row had grown quite long, a line that consisted mostly of millers.

"But there are only millworkers at the ready," she protested. "Father would—"

"Don't be so poky," teased Charles, taking her hand. "Father will just have to control himself. Let's have fun tonight. Come, little sister, join me." He pulled her toward the floor.

Was this not what she had wanted out of this night? To laugh and dance and find reprieve from the cares of everyday life? To enjoy those around her and feel free? As the music began, she forced the fear of what it would look like for her, a weaver, to be dancing in the millers' line.

The dance was not a calm one, nor a short one at that. Her face flushed with the heat of the active bodies in such a tight space. She clapped her hands when bid. Called "hey" when the dance demanded it. Laughed at the people trying to keep pace with the melody driven fast by flutes and flying violins.

Charles, cheeks flushed, made a funny face at her as he passed her, and she giggled as she had when they were children. The music whirled faster and faster, spinning her cares away and weaving a fresh attitude. More than once the ladies wove their way through the line of men. First as a group and then individually. Even in the midst of the excitement, she noticed—and relished—the flutter in her heart as she found her hand in Mr. Stockton's, even if for fleeting moments.

Despite her present mirth, Kate was keenly aware of Miss Pennington's presence during the dance, as one would be aware of a rival. The tall blonde captured the eye of every man and the envy of every woman, and as the dance drew to a close, Miss Pennington was next to her.

The recollection of her words from the countinghouse back room momentarily dampened her spirits. *"Some people who do not know you as well as I might misinterpret your intentions."* Miss Pennington said nothing to her after the dance. Indeed, she barely glanced in Kate's direction, but the possessive manner in which she wrapped her arm around Mr. Stockton's sent a clear and direct message to any lady who might dare to cast an admirable glance toward her partner.

At the conclusion of the dance, Charles swept the wool sleeve of his coat across his brow, chest heaving with exertion. "I'll go find some ale. Wait here, I'll be right back."

Charles disappeared into the crowd, and a fresh group of dancers—weavers this time—gathered on the narrow floor for another set.

She took a moment to catch her breath, her own chest heaving from the dance. She spied John leaning against a support beam and talking with a weaver from Wester. She had avoided him so far this evening, but her skin prickled. She would not be able to avoid him forever, with the weavers lining up in squares for the cotillion.

"Will you dance with me, Miss Dearborne?"

The voice, a soft tone behind her, caused her to jump. She'd been so focused on watching John that she had not heard anyone approach.

She had expected one of the weavers to be at her elbow, but Mr. Stockton stood just inches from her.

Fresh heat rushed her face, and she pushed the long locks that had come loose during the last dance away from her face. "Mr. S-Stockton. I did not hear you. Or, I mean, I did not see you."

She looked around, making sure that her papa or John or any other weaver was not witnessing the exchange.

His face was flushed too. The color brought attention to his high cheekbones and freshly shaven jaw. His eyes were bright with the exertion of dancing.

Her heart raced in girlish exuberance. Had he really just invited her to dance? She could not help the smile that sprang to her lips. How her heart wanted to accept the offer and spend more time in his company. But reality trumped her heartfelt wishes, and she raised an eyebrow. "I don't think that would be the best idea."

"Why?"

She tilted her head to the side. His handsome features and the intensity of his gaze made it difficult to concentrate on words. "The weavers are dancing now, and you—you are—"

He gave a good-natured huff. "Not a weaver."

She looked around again. There were so many people. What could a short conversation hurt? They had spoken several times in passing on the road since the day he helped her with Ivy. Each interaction had tightened the invisible thread that seemed to pull them together. She had seen him when she went to visit Charles. Their paths crossed every Sunday at church.

But every interaction, however small it was, always left her wanting to know more about this mysterious man who held such an iron grip on his mill yet cared enough to provide his young workers with cloaks.

Perhaps he was wanting more too.

His presence was commanding, as if she were unable to walk away. He was close enough she could smell the sharp, intoxicating scent of sandalwood.

He leaned closer. "And how do you feel about that, this division of the weavers?"

She looked up at his clear blue eyes, a bit surprised by the question. At first she thought he was making fun of her or making light of the situation, but the expression on his face was earnest. His question was a sincere one.

It unnerved her. She was rarely asked about her thoughts and feelings on any topic. In fact, she was often told how she was supposed to feel and act. She attempted, in that small sliver of time, to remember the last time her opinion on anything had been solicited. She normally had no problem freely giving it, but had anyone cared to listen?

She drew a deep breath. "I find it sad, actually. Very sad. My father is on one side and my brother on the other. I will forever be suspended in the middle."

"Must be difficult. You see, Miss Dearborne, I loved my grandfather, but he was a stubborn old goat. He'd not deny that statement either. I see no reason to continue a grudge, especially when I have little knowledge of the beginning of it. And if dancing the weavers' dance will mend that division, so be it. Besides, if the grudge remains, then how shall I better make your acquaintance?" His gaze did not waver.

Was he flirting with her? Teasing her? Grooming her to hurt her father, as John had suggested?

She smiled, reminding herself what was at stake if she misjudged his intentions. "That would take a significant shift of perspective. But it is an admirable thought."

He lifted his gaze to the crowd before fixing his eyes on her again. "Do you think it possible to overcome this prejudice?"

A dozen questions rested within that one question. She had to be careful how she answered. "I like to think it is possible."

"Despite what you may think, I am on your side, Miss Dearborne. I hope that you and I can overcome this and maybe even become friends." The inflection in his voice rose, and his gaze blazed with intensity. "I do hope one day you will accept my invitation to dance."

She could get lost in this moment, lost in his words, lost in the picture he was painting, lost in the suggestion of a life that was different from the one she had now. She could believe he wanted to know her better, and the prospect sent warmth flooding through her, tingling the tips of her fingers and making her head dizzy.

"Kate."

The sound of her father's voice snapped her from the moment. She whirled around and stumbled back, nearly bumping into Mr. Stockton.

Her papa's hard eyes pinned her, his brow furrowed. "What are you doing?" he thundered, garnering the attention of the villagers around her. His resolute gaze lifted to Mr. Stockton.

Mr. Stockton dipped his head in a greeting. "Mr. Dearborne."

"I'll not pretend I'm glad to see you," huffed Papa. "You have a right to be here as much as the next man, but you're hardly welcome."

Mr. Stockton raised his eyebrow. "At least we are clear on that count." If he was rattled by the rude greeting, he did not look it. He stared her father dead in the eye, an act not many men could do. Strength and confidence radiated from his firm stance.

Kate bit her lip and sheepishly glanced around. People were taking notice of the interchange. Her father never spoke to Stocktons. *Ever.* And yet here he was doing just that.

Questioning gazes were focused in their direction. John and Mr. Wooden stepped threateningly near.

Panic began to encroach. Kate looked in the opposite direction. Her brother and Mr. Belsey were approaching.

Her father's voice rose over the crowd. He was a master at persuading others to follow him, and it was clear—his goal was to further label Henry Stockton as the enemy. "But since you are here, there is a conversation that needs to be had."

Kate leapt in. "Papa, I really don't think this is the time. Perhaps you will—"

"Quiet, girl."

She snapped her lips shut at the rude dismissal and flashed her eyes toward Mr. Stockton.

His calm gaze slid from her father, to her, and then back to Papa. "I don't think it's necessary to speak to a lady in such a fashion."

Her father leaned in toward Mr. Stockton as a man leaning into a fight, daring the other man to strike the first blow. "You'll not tell me how to speak with my own daughter, and you'll not take a highbrow tone with me."

Mr. Stockton's eyes narrowed to slits, the act of which delivered a threat of its own. His very deliberate gaze shifted to both of the men behind her father before he spoke, and his tone reeked of sarcasm. "Very well. If that is how you feel she deserves to be spoken to. What did you wish to discuss?"

Her father's expression darkened, and a bead of moisture that had gathered on his creased brow dripped over a flaming cheek. "We know the gig mills are here."

Mr. Stockton crossed his arms over his chest and broadened his stance, creating a more intimidating presence. "They are. Just as you, I have every right to do what is best for the future and sustain my business for my employees."

John pushed his way forward from behind her father's comrades and stepped in front of Papa. The wild glint in his eyes suggested he had been waiting for a moment just like this to provoke Mr. Stockton into breaking his composure. He fairly spat his words. "For your employees? You mean for yourself."

Mr. Stockton stepped forward. Kate resisted the urge to grab his arm to hold him back. "Every man who is in business for himself seeks success. Only a fool chases after failure."

"But success at what cost?" goaded John. "To the detriment of the community you live in?"

"Stockton Mill provides employment for more than 150 people in Amberdale."

Papa cackled. "Listen to him, boys. He speaks of the mill as if it's the fruit of his own labor, as if it were something he built from the dust with his own hands. It was built by your grandfather, who would employ any means necessary to squelch the competition and trample anyone in his way."

"Yes, my grandfather built the mill, but it is mine now. I'll run it as I see fit."

Her father was shouting now and pointed a thick finger at Mr. Stockton's chest. "It's a disgusting lack of humanity. Let me be clear, boy. There are those of us concerned with the welfare of those whose livelihoods you are so quick to destroy."

Color flamed to Mr. Stockton's face. His square, clean-shaven jaw twitched, and he stepped forward another pace. "I am not a boy, sir. And I have no need to answer to you or to anyone for the decisions I make. I will not be swayed."

"So you will continue with this cruel, ill-advised decision of yours?" John stood shoulder to shoulder with her father. "Be careful with your answer, for the room is full of people here who have short tempers and long memories."

Mr. Stockton glared. "I will proceed."

Charles, no doubt drawn by the harsh shouts, now stood behind Mr. Stockton. How Charles could look their father in his tenacious face was beyond her, but he had made his opinions clear time and time again. Perhaps it was growing easier for him, but every time the two were in the same vicinity, the tension tore at Kate's already fragile heart.

John turned his attention to Charles. "You. You're as guilty as he is. You are a part of this."

Charles pressed forward, fists balled at his sides. The muscles up his arm flinched.

Please don't, Kate mouthed, a silent plea for her brother to stand down.

He did not look at her.

Kate whirled. John was just behind her now, close enough that she reached out and pushed against his chest, trying to create space. If he cared for her in the least, like he said, surely he would listen.

"John, don't. Please." Her voice grew louder. "He's my brother, I beg—"

A shove stole the breath from her lungs, then she heard the eerie sound of fist meeting skin. She wheeled around and, to her horror, saw blood smeared across Charles's face.

Suddenly shouts and screams replaced the musical strains. The noise of scraping chairs and breaking wood filled her ears. Fists flailed and bodies writhed, so much so that she could barely tell who was who.

On instinct, she stepped forward, but someone had her by the waist. "Let go!" She struggled against the tether, but the arm held firm. She looked back and found none other than Mrs. Figgs holding her steady.

The older woman tightened her grip, but her words were gentle. "It's not your place. Let them beat each other senseless. You stay strong."

Stay strong.

She could almost laugh at the bitter irony of it. How could she stay strong if her family fought before her, severing her heart and destroying her future?

Even though the brawl seemed endless, it was only a matter of seconds before bystanders—both weavers and millers—drew the men off each other, their huffs and grunts the only sound in the now-still room.

She could not look at their faces. Not her brother, not her father, not Mr. Stockton, and certainly not John Whitby.

She did not have time to consider her next step, for her father grabbed her by her wrist, wrenching her from Mrs. Figgs's grip. He dragged her through the dispersing crowd. Blood from his hand soaked her white glove.

She cast a single glance backward, and Mr. Stockton caught her eye. He was leaning on a table, looking down at his arm. His black hair fell over his forehead, blood trickling from his brow.

Gone was any hope of what he had spoken of earlier. He would never want to know her now. Never want to dance with her. Never want to make her better acquaintance.

Their romance, or at least the one she secretly imagined, was over before it had begun.

CHAPTER 28

*I*t did not matter that a solid hour had passed since the brawl. Kate's chest still burned. Her head pounded. And her broken heart stuttered. Even as she walked alone behind the stable in the alley, cloak wrapped tightly about her shivering shoulders, her mind struggled to make sense of what she had witnessed.

For the most part she was alone. A few stable boys tended carts and horses belonging to the guests inside, but no one noticed her, and more importantly, no one here had witnessed the scene between her father and Mr. Dearborne.

At the conclusion of the vile argument, her father had marched her over to the corner and deposited her in a chair, like a child. She sniffed defiantly. She had refused to be ordered about and made to sit on a chair, and at the first possible moment, she escaped through the inn's kitchen and out the gate.

Resting along the inn's back wall, she allowed the cool air to wash over her like a balm. With searing tears gathering in her eyes, she spied the festivities through the window.

She could see Mr. Stockton's back, and Miss Pennington was at his side. Looking up at him. Speaking earnestly. Holding his arm possessively.

How Kate wished she could see his reaction, but all she could see was that he leaned closer to say something to her. Did he really want to better make her acquaintance, or had he been attempting to use her as a pawn?

Kate drew a shuddering breath.

She had done what she told herself not to do. Somehow, in the cracks of daily life, she had let the wall around her heart crumble. It had happened so gradually she hadn't even noticed it, but now, as she stood watching Mr. Stockton in the presence of the charming Miss Pennington, the stinging in her chest threatened to expand to every inch of her being.

Mr. Stockton was her family's enemy. Entertaining the thought for even a moment that there was a possibility of something more was a misjudgment. After what had just happened, there would be no future between them.

Jane burst from the door, her eyes wide, expression panicked. "Oh, I've been looking everywhere for you." Her friend gasped for air between words. "What a turn of events that was! I don't know how you can handle it."

Kate dabbed at the corners of her eyes with her knuckle and sniffed. It would not do to show anyone, even a friend as dear as Jane, how deeply she was affected by the exchange. "I should have known better from the beginning. I never should have spoken with him."

"Why *were* you speaking with him?" Jane drew to a stop next to Kate.

"It was all quite innocent." Kate shook her head. "I finished the dance with Charles, and then after he went to fetch a drink, Mr. Stockton approached me. He's not like his grandfather, and I wish Papa would see it. Mr. Stockton seems intent upon mending some of the broken bridges."

Jane leaned against the stone wall next to Kate and folded her arms across her chest against the cold. She gave a little laugh, her attempt at lightheartedness falling flat. "You deduce this from one conversation at a festival?"

Perhaps it would be good to get her friend's perspective. She weighed each word, measuring exactly how much to reveal. "We've spoken before, on occasion."

Interest brightened Jane's eyes. "On occasion? Oh, Kate, you must tell me all. How could you keep this from me?"

Flashes of their interactions blinked before her, but she could not—would not—share everything. "All I will say is that he is not as Papa believes him to be."

Jane toyed with the sleeve of her gown. "And here I was, thinking it was John who had captured your heart."

"No one has captured my heart," Kate shot back.

"Sorry. My mistake, then. But you are having quite a reaction for someone claiming indifference."

Kate looked into the wind, allowing its cool steadiness to dissipate gathering moisture. "I am in a difficult situation, that's all. I—" She stopped short as the door behind Jane creaked open.

There stood Henry Stockton. Alone.

Kate reached for Jane's hand and gripped it in a plea for her friend not to leave.

But Jane, as if sensing the tension between the two, stuttered, "C-Come and find me, Kate. I must go tend to the food. It seems we never have enough."

And just like that her friend was gone, leaving her alone with the very man who had been at the center of the evening's humiliation.

They stared at each for several moments. She did not want to be affected by his nearness, but the pale bruising beneath his eye ripped at her. Was she to blame for this? Was it her fault her father had approached him and mayhem ensued?

A horse from the stable whinnied, and Kate jumped. Her raw nerves were not ready for this. Suddenly the cool air that had been so inviting was now prickly and painful.

She wondered if he was going to speak, but then his words tumbled forth, low and raspy. "I am sorry you were put in that position. I hope you can forgive me for the part I played back there."

And that was it. He offered no attempt to deny what had happened. He only offered an apology with an expression so sincere it could not be untrue.

It was easier to become angry with him than to try to sort out her feelings. "I don't know what you think of me, Mr. Stockton. And truthfully, I don't care. But if you think you can affect my father through me, you are sadly mistaken. Now, seeing as our interaction has caused quite enough frustration for one evening, I will thank you to go back inside."

Henry winced at the sight of her red-rimmed eyes. She bore no bruise, but he surmised that her wounds from the brawl were the deepest of them all. He would not go back inside. Not until he made things right with Miss Dearborne.

His actions, his words, had hurt her. Embarrassed her. He should have turned away and refused to engage with her father. Silas Dearborne had been intoxicated, angry, and looking for a fight. At the very least Henry should have insisted they take their conversation outside.

But he had not.

And Miss Dearborne was the casualty.

He saw her emotions—her fear, her sadness, her confusion—balancing in her eyes. He was doing the very thing that had been a source of pain by insisting on speaking with her, but he could not help himself. She was as an injured bird, needing assistance. Needing *his* assistance.

She sniffed.

He retrieved his handkerchief and extended it to her.

She eyed it but did not accept it.

He returned it to his pocket.

She tightened her arms across her chest and met his gaze boldly. "I fear that somewhere along the way I've given the impression that my interest in you and your family is from a place other than congeniality. And if that is the case, then it is my turn to beg for forgiveness."

Her words burned in his ears. He did not believe her. He did not *want* to believe her. He shifted and hesitated a few moments to bolster his courage. "Let me be blunt. I don't care who your father is, nor do I care who your brother is. I've watched you, Miss Dearborne, in these months since my return, and you've captivated me. I find myself thinking of you, hoping to catch a glimpse of you. I'm mortified at tonight's events, not for the inconvenience they've caused *me*, but for the pain they've caused *you*. I wasn't lying when I said that I want to better make your acquaintance. In fact, I hope I can impress upon you my sincere and growing affection for you."

He stepped closer. "I am asking a great deal of you. Perhaps I would be wiser to keep my thoughts to myself, but after witnessing what happened tonight, I cannot."

She said nothing, but her gaze did not waver. A tear slipped down her cheek.

Emboldened and energized by the fact that she had not pulled away, he reached out his hand. It hovered near her skin for a few moments before he wiped the tear away from her velvety cheek with his bare thumb.

"Have I hope, Kate, that you might return my regard?" Her Christian name escaped his lips. He could not take it back.

Another tear escaped. Her chin trembled. She cast her gaze downward, her wet, black lashes fanning over her flushed cheeks.

As if touching a priceless treasure, he tucked her billowy strands behind her ear. He stepped closer, mere inches from her. His thumb lingered on her cheek until she looked at him again.

Amid all the uncertainty, all the sadness, all the fighting, his hope sharpened. What did it matter if he won or lost against the weavers? She may be the daughter of his enemy, but she seemed the only person to understand the struggle. They were alike, painfully so, both fighting for a future. And his future needed her in it.

He lowered his hands to her upper arms, resting them there gently. He was no longer a miller; she was no longer a weaver. Providence had brought them to this moment—a moment that, if he did not act now, might never present itself again.

So he followed the command of his heart. Wordlessly, pulse racing, he lowered his lips to hers, and the feathery touch infused him with glowing fire. She rested her hands against his chest, melted against him, and returned his kiss with increasing intensity. He lowered his arm and wrapped it around her waist, pulling her closer.

Words were not needed. They were two people fighting the same battle on different sides of the war.

But then something snapped. She stiffened beneath his touch and shoved against his chest, putting space between them. Even in the night's shadows, he could see vibrant pink flush her cheeks, and the cold breeze whipped long strands of chestnut hair about her face. "This cannot happen." Her voice was barely above a whisper.

He stammered, surprised at her abrupt statement. "I—I—"

"What did you hope to accomplish by doing that?" Her eyebrows drew together. "Are you mocking me?"

He shook his head, confused at the sudden change. "I thought that—"

"Are you making fun of me? I don't know what you think I am—" She stopped talking and pinned her sharp gaze on him. "That was a mistake."

She started to push past him, but he caught the crook of her arm in his hand. "Wait, Kate, it's not what—"

Every muscle in her arm stiffened beneath his touch. "My name is Miss Dearborne."

"Kate," he repeated, softer, hoping to calm her. "It wasn't a mistake. I would never—"

She jerked her arm away. "I will not be played for a fool. I saw you, just now, through the window, talking with Miss Pennington."

"Miss Pennington?" Frustration began to mount. "Kate, I—"

"She is clearly your choice."

"She is a family friend. At one time, yes, things might have been different. But time and circumstances change everything."

Fresh moisture pooled in her topaz eyes. "Do you really think me so naive as to be swayed by a moonlit kiss and a fancy apology? Like I said, I'm not a fool, and I'll not be used as a pawn in this war you are fighting with my father."

"My feelings for you have nothing to do with your father and everything to do with you." His words rushed from his mouth, so desperate was he to make her see. He stepped forward. "Oh, Kate, there is something between us. You *must* feel it."

Her words slid through gritted teeth. "You know nothing of my feelings, my heart, or anything else to do with me."

"I know plenty. I know that when I kissed you just now, you returned my kiss, and I know that I will never again stand by while another man speaks to you as your father did."

Her eyes narrowed to slits. "You overstep your bounds."

"You deserve more than to be treated like that."

She stepped back, allowing the cold air to rush between them. "I don't know what your intentions are in telling me this, Mr. Stockton, but I assure you, I am not one of those silly girls whose fancies can be turned by affectionate words."

"But I—"

She straightened, as if finding a fresh source of determination from somewhere deep within. "And now, allow me to make *my* intentions clear. I love my father. Regardless of his actions, I will be loyal to him."

Henry stepped back. He was treading on dangerous ground. Loyalty was an admirable trait—a trait she possessed in abundance. The realization that she was not going to change her mind slowly blotted out his earlier optimism.

His expression began to sour. "Forgive me, Miss Dearborne. It appears I have misinterpreted the situation entirely."

Her jaw twitched as she stared at him, but anger no longer fueled the sharpness of her tongue. For tears gathered in her eyes once again.

He did not want to leave her alone in the alley, even after what she had said, but how could he stay after she bid him go so bluntly? Feeling strangely numb, he stepped back and bowed. "I bid you good night, Miss Dearborne."

He withdrew back into the inn, where festivity and merriment surrounded him. But his countenance was far from merry.

Frederica Pennington straightened her shoulders, her gaze blazing a trail as Henry entered through the back kitchen entrance, stomped through the dancers whirling the Scotch reel, and stormed through the main entrance out into the night.

What on earth was he up to?

She told herself that normally she would not care, but she had spied him, immediately after the dance they had shared, speaking with Miss Katherine Dearborne. Again.

His head had been inclined toward her, as if they were lovers engaged in intimate conversation.

The memory of it sent a bolt of anger through her. He shouldn't be talking with her like that. Not a weaver. It was not decent.

Head throbbing with questions, she barely noticed when a milk-faced young man appeared at her elbow, a glass of punch in his bony hands. "What do you want, Mr. Bryant?"

"Here is your punch, as you requested." His words were bright and hopeful.

Exasperation pulsed through her with each heartbeat as the back of Henry's tailcoat disappeared through the crowd. Horrid man. How would he ever have the opportunity to propose if he kept disappearing like he did?

The evening was growing tiresome, and Henry was probably embarrassed from the ridiculous fight that had happened. But to ignore her? *Bother.* If she didn't need to marry him so badly, she would write him off once and for all.

"Oh, Mr. Bryant." She huffed just loud enough to be heard over the crowd's incessant chatter, waving her fan furiously in front of her face. "I'm in no humor for punch. Please leave me be, will you?"

"But the dance is about to start, and you said you'd dance the next reel with me."

Drat. She had promised that she would dance with the man, but that had only been because Henry was present, and what better way to spark jealousy in a man's heart than to be happy in the presence of another? But now she did not need him. "La, I fear a headache is afoot. You will forgive me, won't you? I'll not dance another step tonight."

The man's nostrils flared.

She didn't care.

He sulked away, like a child pouting over a withheld toy, but as he melted into the crowd, suddenly she wished she had not been so quick to dismiss him, for coming her way was the portly Mr. Reginald Simmons.

She looked to her right, then to her left, curls bouncing as she did so. It was at times like this she wished she had a female friend who could rescue her, for she was certain not a single person in her family would do her the favor—not when a marriage to the oaf would bring financial security not only to her but to each of her sisters as well.

Frederica shrank against the wall, hoping to blend in, but it was useless. Who could ignore the dazzling emerald of her gown or the elegance of her hair? No, this was her lot. She straightened her shoulders as he approached, bracing herself for the deluge of flirting and flattery that was soon to come her way. But even as she bolstered herself, sadness cloaked her.

In her fantasy world someone handsome, strong, and wealthy, just like Henry, would sweep her away, but she almost choked on the sad reality that all the beauty in the world could not protect her now. Nobody could protect her now.

CHAPTER 29

The morning following the Winter's End Festival dawned gray and dismal, which suited Kate's mood perfectly. Her head throbbed and her heart ached—at least the pounding rain and sleet blocked out the angry crying of her own heart.

Clad in her flannel nightdress and wool wrapper, Kate sat atop the chest and looked out at the chilly drops pelting the brown earth below. By the time she had finally returned to Meadowvale after the festival, dawn was beginning to creep over the distant moors. Her body cried out for sleep, but how could she rest after all that had happened? Over and over she thought of the events of the previous night. The fight. The conversation. The kiss.

Oh, the kiss.

She'd never been kissed before. Even now she could still feel the warmth of Mr. Stockton's—Henry's—lips on hers, the warmth of his arms about her. Now that she had experienced it, her heart cried for more. But it was not to be. Especially now.

With a sigh she moved from the window and dropped to the bed and shut her eyes, as if by doing so she could hide herself from the world.

What had she done?

Never before had anyone spoken such tender words to her. And what had she done in response? She accused him of mocking her. Of using her as a means to an end. Even now she did not understand her behavior. His affectionate words had frightened her.

But what if he was as earnest as he seemed?

It had been easier to lash out at him than to admit her feelings for him were intensifying. And whether they were feelings of infatuation or genuine affection did not seem to matter. The fact that he was her father's enemy should be enough to keep her far from him, and yet that particular reason seemed to become less and less compelling.

She groaned and tightened the covers about her. Part of her wished she could take back the words she'd hurled in his direction. The other part of her knew the words were just. Regardless, all of her heart was confused and weary. The concept of loyalty was becoming a messy blur.

Kate eventually succumbed to a restless sleep and awoke several hours later. Upon rising, she moved to the window to assess the day. What she saw surprised her. Several men were gathered in the courtyard, their coats shiny and wet with rain. She frowned. What were they doing?

She squinted to see their faces. She recognized John's thick frame and Thomas's distinctive pug nose, but many of them she did not know.

She pushed herself away from the window and dressed quickly in a high-waisted gown of light-brown linen. She looped her hair in a low chignon, secured it with pins, and exited her chamber. Voices wafted from the floor below. Even though she could not make out the words, she recognized her father's unmistakable brogue.

Something was not right—Kate sensed it. Excitement hovered in the air, charging the cottage's cool atmosphere.

"You sure she's here?"

Kate stiffened at the unknown voice. They were talking about her.

"Of course she's here, but she's abed and has been since we returned home," Papa said. "Needn't worry about her. She'll not wake, not after a night like last night."

Kate held her breath, fearing she would not be able to hear them above her own exhale.

"You know her reputation, Dearborne. That episode last night proved it."

She gripped her skirt tightly in her hand, sat on the step, and leaned against the wall.

"What do you mean, her reputation?" Her father's voice was gruff.

"It pains me to tell you this, Silas, for I've nothing but respect for you. But the other members of the weavers' society are questioning her loyalty."

"That's preposterous," Papa boomed. "My daughter is as loyal as I am, if not more."

"Is she?" A pregnant pause followed the question.

Surely her father was not listening to this man.

"You saw her," continued the other voice. "Everyone saw her. She was speaking openly with Stockton. Dancing with the mill folk as she pleased. We all know where Charles's loyalties ended up landing. Do you not think it possible that his sister followed in his footsteps? We are asking for discretion on this matter."

"Very well. I will make sure she stays inside until this passes. I will say nothing to her about our plans."

She frowned. What plans did they mean? She strained to hear the muted words.

"It's for the best. In a mission like this, if we are to be successful, complete secrecy is vital. This may be the only opportunity we'll have to take Stockton by surprise. Then, with any luck, he'll know that the weavers are not to be ignored."

She was hearing their words, but she had a hard time believing them. Tensions had been high. Anger had reached a boiling point. Were they really planning to attack the mill?

Could *her own father* stoop to such a cowardly level? To burn it down, as they said? To destroy the machines?

Panic raced through her. All this time she had been defending her father. To her brother. To the Stocktons. To herself.

Kate leaned forward as the voices continued.

"The Wester men will be joining us after midnight tomorrow at the crossroad south of the village square. There will be two score of them. The men from Bremton and Beltshire will be there too." The man's voice broke with excited laughter. "Mark my words, Stockton will have no choice but to heed our demands after this."

"Are you sure we can count on them?" Papa asked. "Those boys from Beltshire are a shady, brawlin' lot. Always have been. I've never trusted 'em."

"They take the accusations against Wilkes personally. Claim he'd nothing to do with old man Stockton's death, and they are going to fight to prove it."

"Good. And what of the magistrates?"

"Bah. They won't expect a thing this close to the festival. Therein lies the brilliance of our plan. They are sleeping off their drunken stupor, and I know for a fact that the soldiers in the area have been sent to Leeds to manage the crowds there. The timing is perfect."

Her ears throbbed. Without the magistrates and soldiers, Stockton Mill would be like a sitting duck, waiting for the hunter's shot.

She sat back. Charles would be at the mill, his cottage just a few steps away from the main gates.

Could her father really participate in an act of violence that could potentially harm his own son? Did they not see by damaging the mill, they would do the exact thing they were fighting against? No mill would mean fewer jobs. Even more of Amberdale's villagers without work. In a time like this, they needed to promote as many jobs as possible, not add to the numbers of the unemployed.

The men stopped talking and began to stir, and Kate lifted her skirts and crept back up the stairs. Still not entirely sure she believed what she had just heard, she returned to her chamber.

A war raged within her. The way she saw it, she had but two choices. She could confront her father, but she doubted he would listen. She could warn her brother, but by doing so she would expose her father.

Could this have been how Charles felt in the days leading up to his decision to leave Papa's business? This horrific severing of ties and tearing of loyalties? This hurried need to decide whom you would betray and whom you would defend?

She didn't want to betray her father, but she didn't want to see her brother or Mr. Stockton attacked. Perhaps she was the one being disloyal. Yet she could not live with herself if she did nothing.

CHAPTER 30

*H*enry winced as he gripped the newel post and pivoted from the stair's landing to the next flight of stairs.

He had not realized exactly how hard he'd been hit in the ribs until today. Every muscle around the injury protested his movements. But did he not deserve his current discomfort? He could have—and probably should have—refused to react when John Whitby's fist pounded against his jaw.

He hated to admit it, but satisfaction had been sweet with his retaliation in the form of a swift punch to Whitby's belly. Despite the discomfort, he adjusted the tea tray on his hip and stepped up the next flight. He traversed the hall and paused outside of Mollie's chamber before rapping his bruised knuckles against the door.

"Come in."

He pushed the door open. Mollie was abed, tucked in a cocoon of white linens with pillows propped around her at every angle. She was clothed in her nightdress, and a heavy black shawl hung askew over her shoulders. Her dark hair was gathered in a single plait flipped in front of her shoulder, and the gentle gray light highlighted the shadows beneath her eyes and emphasized the pallor of her cheeks.

Her red-rimmed eyes widened only slightly at his arrival. "You've returned! What on earth took you so long? You must tell me every-thing about the festival."

"I will, but first you must drink this. I encountered Mrs. Figgs on my way up here, and she said to make sure you drink your fill." Henry rested the tray on a small table near the bed and poured his sister a cup of steaming tea from the pot. He extended it toward her. "Here."

Mollie scrunched her face and lifted her hand. "I don't want it."

He lowered the cup. "She also tells me you've not been eating. How do you expect to have strength for the coming days if you don't eat?"

She shrugged and then looked toward the window, as if searching for faraway thoughts.

The sadness on her face tore at him. He hated to see her in such a state. He wanted to say something to ease her discomfort. He cleared his throat. "If you tell me what is bothering you, perhaps I can help."

She fussed with the coverlet over her legs. Her small voice was barely audible. "Nothing can be said or done to help the situation I am in." A tear slipped down her cheek.

He put the cup of tea on the table before he drew a chair up to the bed. He didn't know what to say or do. But at least he could be present.

She swiped her tearstained cheek with the back of her hand. "I fear I have ruined not only my life but the life of my baby."

"Soon this particular state will be just a distant memory." He leaned forward and rested his elbows on his knees. "You'll have your babe in your arms and all will be well. I promise."

"How can you promise? It's too late. Can't you see? All because of one foolish decision."

He clutched the small white hand on top of the coverlet. "Everyone makes mistakes in their life. It is how you respond to them and learn from them that matters."

"And you think me a liar and a fool," she blurted out.

It would not do to upset her further, yet he could not pretend to feel something he did not. "I don't think you a fool, but I don't understand the reason behind the lie you've told. The longer you live in it, the tighter the grip this mistake will have on you. It will be a constant reminder."

"I know, I know. But too much has been said. I've lied to too many people. Mrs. Figgs. The Penningtons. Miss Dearborne. Even the vicar and his wife. It'll be like unraveling a tangle. I fear it will not be easily undone."

Henry nodded and looked at his hands. "No, it won't be easy. But you'll not be free until you cease the lie. Then the forgiveness can begin."

She huffed a sarcastic laugh. "They'll never forgive me."

"I wasn't referring to them forgiving you. I was referring to you forgiving yourself."

They locked gazes for several moments. Fresh tears gathered.

He wanted to erase the pain and humiliation she suffered, but could that ever really happen without truth's full disclosure? "I've asked you this before. And I'm not asking to embarrass you, but perhaps if you told me more about what happened, you might feel better."

He thought she was going to refuse, to shut him down as she had other times this topic had come up. But instead her chin trembled.

"While I was living with Aunt, I met a man, a soldier. He was a relative of one of Aunt's friends. We became quite close, and after a while, he declared his love for me. He spoke of a future so lovely, I should have known it couldn't be true. He spoke of how we would be married, and when he was done being a soldier, we would move to the country where he would run his family's shop. I believed him, Henry. Like a fool, I believed every word he said. Until one day I realized I was with child. I—I was so frightened. I could tell no one for the shame of it. Now everyone knows."

He forced his brotherly defenses down. "Did you speak with him about it?"

"I did. He grew angry. Said he did not believe me and that he wasn't responsible. I knew he was, but he was indignant. And then he disappeared."

"Have you tried to find him?"

"To what end? He became cruel. He'll never own up to his actions, but I will live with the consequence of mine until the day I die. And my child will suffer for it too. I had to lie—I had to! Do you not see it?" Her eyes pleaded with him for understanding.

He sighed and scratched his head. "Part of me wants to hunt this man down and make him pay. But the more practical side of me knows that will do no good. In the end, you need to find the strength to deal with this. It is in you, Mollie."

"But I am all alone! Who will love me now? I shall die just as I am—alone and relying on the charity of others."

"You aren't alone. You are still the same person, and you are still worthy of love and affection. But I fear you'll not be willing to accept it until you can forgive yourself. And you'll never be able to truly forgive yourself if you cannot be honest about what happened. You don't want your baby growing up believing a lie."

She sniffed again.

"Just promise me you will consider what I've said."

At this she nodded and sighed. "I suppose you think me dreadful."

"I think you are my sister, and I love you."

CHAPTER 31

$\mathcal{K}$ate could wait no longer. Tonight was the night Stockton Mill would be attacked. Something had to be done.

She dressed quickly, skipped the morning meal, and tended her sheep before making her way to the dye house to set the crimson wool. She kept her eyes low, but never had she seen so many men in the courtyard. Their eyes were fixed on her. They said nothing, yet their questions hung thick in the air, like an ominous rain cloud threatening to spill forth.

She'd been branded the enemy.

Perhaps she was. Even John would not make eye contact with her.

She went about her duties as normal, but by late morning her head throbbed with such distraction that her hands began to tremble.

How she wished she could have heard the news and let it pass from memory as quickly as a mundane bit of gossip. But the information was lodged in her mind. In her heart. From the window she spotted her father heading away from the loom house. She ran to the door and flung it open. "Papa, will you come here, please?"

Annoyance shadowed his face, but he stopped, looked toward the cottage, and then headed in her direction.

She ushered him into the steaming room and closed the door

behind him. They'd not exchanged a word since the Winter's End Festival, which shouted louder than any whisper could. Silence was, and always had been, his heaviest weapon.

Once the door was closed, she wiped her hands on a cloth and pushed her hair from her face with her forearm. "We must talk."

"About what?" he barked. "Make it quick, there's much to do."

She did not have his attention, she knew, so she blurted out the words. "I heard you talking about the plan to attack the mill."

Father jerked his head up, but the intensity of his eyes belied his words. "You're talking nonsense."

She skirted around the dyeing bin and deposited the cloth on a table. She drew near enough that he could not look away. "Yes, you do, Papa. I heard that you are going to be meeting the men from Wester and Bremton and Beltshire."

"Are you eavesdropping on me now, Katie? Is it not enough that you made a spectacle of yourself with Mr. Stockton, pining over him like a little puppy, and now you have to meddle in weavers' affairs?"

"But, Papa, I'm a weaver just like you, and—"

"You're not a weaver. You're a woman. And you will remember your place."

He moved to step past her, but she sidestepped and blocked his path. "Fine, you're right. I'm not a weaver like you. I'll always be a woman, and I'll never be able to take Charles's place in your mind. But attacking a mill is not the answer."

"You've done enough. You've no right to speak to the current affairs. You and you alone are responsible for why the weavers are questioning my loyalty. *My* loyalty! I lack a great deal of positive characteristics, but at least I'm loyal. A trait that did not pass to my children, I see."

She winced at his words, but she could not back down now.

"Don't you see that I worry for your safety? For Charles's safety? Nothing good can come of this."

"Safety is nothing. Pride and loyalty are what matter. And if you are loyal, you will claim your rightful place and take your path."

She planted her hands on her hips. "And what place is that? In the cottage, sewing and knitting?"

"Don't be cheeky. It's in marriage, girl. Marriage to John. How can you be so blind that you don't see what is right before you? You must secure your future. I know he has broached the topic and you denied him. Foolish girl! Do you not see the harm you are doing?"

"But my loyalty is to you, not John."

"I trust John. He is a good man. He shares our vision."

"He shares *your* vision."

"I've had enough." Her father's face shook. "You've pushed me to a limit that can't be ignored. You will reconsider a union with John. You will cease communication with Charles once and for all. You'll do both of these things immediately, or you're no longer a daughter of mine."

With this he pushed past her and jerked the dye house door behind him, shaking the glass in the panes and the walls of her own breaking heart.

At the door's slam, tears flowed unchecked, then dissolved into sobs. She sank onto the chair next to the hearth. The heat suffocated her, adding physical discomfort to the turmoil churning within. She cried tears that had built up for so long—tears of sorrow over her papa and brother.

Tears of frustration over her feelings for Mr. Stockton.

Tears of fear for the future.

She sniffed and wiped her nose on a cloth. How easy it would be to just give in and comply with her father's demands. She should be a dutiful daughter. If only she would do his bidding—stay quiet, keep to the house, and marry John—her life would be so much easier. Why could she not cease striving? Why could she not be content, like other ladies, to live a life that was dictated to her by those in charge of her?

As much as she tried to convince herself that was the path she should follow, her stomach clenched in fretful disagreement. She had to believe she was here for more than that—that God had given her a heart and soul, and she needn't just blindly accept what she was told to do.

Forcing her thoughts aside, she finished her dyeing, cleaned her work area, and prepared to leave.

As she shrugged the apron from her shoulders, the door flung open. John hurried in and closed the door.

She frowned. She had avoided him since before the Winter's End Festival, and she'd hoped it would stay that way. But instead of looking cross, as he had so often of late, his eyes were bright.

She turned to hang her apron on the hook. "What is it?"

He swept his hat from his head. "I've just spoken with your father."

She pushed past him to return the glass dye jars to their spaces on the shelf. "Oh?"

"I—I know you're confused about the current situation, and you do not agree with me or your father right now. But I'm asking you to trust me." His words were soft and slow. The sincerity in his eyes made her pause. "Not your father, not the other weavers, but *me*."

"Trust you?" Was he in earnest?

"I know you have feelings for Mr. Stockton."

She shook her head again at his blunt words and stepped back. "You don't know anything."

"I may not be the cleverest man, but I can recognize when a woman looks at a man with love in her eyes."

She stared at him, searching for a response. But none came.

"There." He pointed at her. "You've no clever comeback, which proves my suspicions correct."

She turned back to the table. What good would it do to argue?

He slid his fingers through his hair. "I had hoped that over time you would grow to care for me as I care for you. But dark times are upon us, and lines must be drawn in the sand and decisions must be made. Kate, if this operation is to thrive, to survive the stormy seas ahead, we must present a unified front."

She refused to look at him, and he drew close to her.

"Have I not been patient? Have I not waited while you look for whatever it is you are searching for? Whether you like it or not, you are a Dearborne. Your brother may have abandoned your father, but you haven't it in you to do something like that to one you love."

She eyed him. The words, such as they were, should have felt like a compliment. But there was something deeper to them, a condemnation almost. A challenge as to whether she dared to go against her father's wishes.

"Why are you resisting?" he continued. "It's important to your father to know he is leaving a legacy, and you and I are that legacy. You, his daughter. I, the man in whom he has instilled everything he knows about the business. He has been planning for this since the day I arrived at Meadowvale. Do you not feel it?"

She met John's gaze fully. He expected her to answer, but words would not form.

John's intentions could not be clearer, but to her, nothing seemed easy or sure. She may not understand her heart at times, but she did know right from wrong, and that knowledge needed to be her guide.

Instead of donning her cloak of deep red, Kate selected a cape of dark gray from her wardrobe. The last thing she wanted was to attract attention. As she tightened the cloak about her shoulders, she eyed the men in the courtyard making their way to the stable. No doubt they were meeting in preparation for tonight's attack.

She drew a shuddery breath. If only there was some way to know for certain that she was making the right decision.

She stood for several moments in the threshold to her chamber, listening, making sure the cottage's main floor was quiet before descending the stairs and stepping out into the night. The full darkness of a moonless night would soon be on her side. If she was going to leave Meadowvale unnoticed, now was the time.

She did not take a cart or even a horse. Instead, she set out on foot, cutting through the familiar forest behind Meadowvale Cottage, avoiding the main road altogether. Careful not to leave footprints, she sidestepped the snow. She did not anticipate anyone following her, but she didn't want to take any chances.

As she hurried through the woods, she practiced in her head what needed to be said. She had to talk to Charles. He was the key to spreading the word. She had no idea what she ultimately would say to him or how much she would reveal, but the pressing weight of responsibility was too much to keep within. Enough people had suffered. If she kept this information to herself and something bad did happen, she doubted she could live with herself.

At this time of evening, her brother would be at the counting-house. There was a real chance Mr. Stockton also would be there. The thought of seeing him again after their last interaction chilled her.

She kept her eyes focused straight ahead and ignored the inquisitive gazes that followed her and the clusters of millers who halted conversations to watch her. She tightened her cape and lifted her gloved hand to knock on the countinghouse door.

"Come," a male voice responded.

She mustered her courage and opened the door.

Mr. Stockton looked up from sorting letters, and his hands stilled in midair when his gaze met hers.

He looked tired. His left eye was bruised, dark circles shadowed his normally bright eyes, and his neckcloth hung untidily about his neck. His disheveled hair hung low over his brow, giving him a roguish appearance, and his eyebrows narrowed briefly, as if he was confused.

Neither of them spoke for several moments. Neither moved.

She had ruined the rapport between them, and that knowledge tugged on her already raw emotions.

"Miss Dearborne." He straightened at last and lowered the papers to the desk. "How may I assist you?"

There were so many things she wanted to say. So many things she wanted to explain. But she needed to stay focused on the task at hand. "Forgive the interruption"—she lowered her cape's hood—"but I need to speak with my brother. It's an urgent matter."

He pressed his lips together. "Of course."

He disappeared in the back room, and several moments later he reappeared with Charles just behind him.

Charles frowned and drew close to her, concern creasing his brow. "What is it, what's wrong?"

She winced at the garish scab on his lip—a result no doubt of the brawl. "I must speak with you."

Mr. Stockton started to retreat. "I'll give you privacy."

"Wait." Her word was a surprise even to her. She rose above the embarrassment. "This concerns you too."

His expression sober, Mr. Stockton stepped back inside the main room, hands clasped behind his back, stance wide.

She looked to make sure the door was closed behind her. "There is going to be an attack on this mill. Tonight."

Charles dropped his arms that had been crossed in front of his chest.

Mr. Stockton winced.

Her throat grew thick, and she lifted her hands. "Don't ask for details. Just please, take precautions."

Mr. Stockton sucked in a deep breath, and he and Charles exchanged glances.

Her brother stepped forward and took her arm. "Are you certain?"

She nodded. "It is to happen just before midnight." The words rushed from her, but they offered no release. She'd done it. She'd betrayed her father. "Men are coming from Leeds and Bremton. That's all I know. Please, just take precautions."

The sting of tears pricked her eyes. She could see the questions balancing in both their expressions.

She clutched her cloak, but before she turned to leave, she met her brother's gaze. "Charles, please. I'm in a terrible situation. This is all I can tell you, but promise me you'll be careful."

CHAPTER 32

$\mathcal{H}$enry watched the hem of her dark-gray cloak clear the frame and the door slam closed.

Had she really said what he thought she'd said?

Despite what had happened between them, could it be possible that she would notify him about an attack on his mill?

The gravity of her words, and the implication they held, grabbed Henry by the throat. After several seconds, he turned to Dearborne. "Is she serious?"

Dearborne dragged his hand down his face and propped his hands akimbo before lifting his shoulders in a shrug. "At one time I never would have thought my father capable of this, but now, I don't know."

Henry paced the small space, growing increasingly troubled with each passing second. The familiar knot in his stomach—the one that would always tighten before a battle—cinched within him. It was not just the war for his mill that concerned him. By coming to them and sharing this news, Miss Dearborne was putting herself in harm's way. "Your sister has declared time and time again that she's loyal to your father, at least to me. Would she really warn us?"

"Kate's loyal, yes, but she is also rational, and she's also loyal to me. She must really believe us to be in danger."

Henry combed his fingers through his hair. Sudden energy took hold. Was this why his grandfather had taken to sleeping in the mill room? Suddenly he had a new understanding of the man. He was starting to feel the tie to the people, to the grounds, to the industry. Henry stared into the fire. He thought of the letters his grandfather and Pennington had received—threats to his land, his property, his life. These people—these cowards—had already taken his grandfather from him. He'd not allow them to take his mill and everything it stood for.

"Let's notify the guards and tell them to look out for anything unusual," he directed. "Fetch Belsey in here and let's notify the magistrate. He may be able to call the militia. And get some of the male workers to stay tonight," he continued as his thoughts took more definite shape. "We will put together a schedule for them to stand watch throughout the night until we are out of danger."

Henry hated the memories of war, but perhaps his experiences were training for just this moment. He may not fully understand all the inner workings of a mill, but he understood soldiers. Yes, he was ready for this. "I'll be staying here for the time being as well. If it is a fight they want, we'll give them one."

Kate raced through the familiar forest. She needed to get back home before anyone discovered her absence. Twigs snapped beneath her feet, and the thickets tugged at her cloak. She couldn't see much in the snow, but she could see the yellow lights of lanterns moving around Meadowvale.

What have I done?

All was eerily quiet as she stepped through Meadowvale's gate.

Dark-blue light shadowed the loom and dye houses, the stable, and the cottage. Before she left, the courtyard had been swarming with people and horses, but now only a few men lingered, talking by the stables.

Once inside the cottage, she called out, "Papa?"

The fire was burning low, and all was still. She stepped farther into the still space, her wet boots clicking heavily on the wood-planked floor. "Betsy?"

Still no answer.

Using the fire from the hearth, she lit a candle. The light cast bending shadows on the wall as she rounded the staircase, and the stairs creaked as she made her way up to her chamber. Once in the safety and silence of her room, she paced the narrow space.

How could she rest in light of what might happen? Possible scenarios rushed her. She could go to the mill. But if the weavers did attack, what could she do?

Her pulse still racing, she reached to pull the bow that secured her cloak when her eye caught on something on the wardrobe. A letter. Kate stared at it for several seconds.

It was not often she received letters, but when she did, it was not uncommon for Betsy to place them here. She lifted the missive and turned it over. Her name was written on the front, but there was nothing else. She placed her candle on her table, ran her finger under the wax seal, and opened it.

Dear Miss Dearborne,

Mrs. Smith's time has arrived, and she has asked for you to come. She is in a great deal of pain and could use your friendship.

Mrs. Figgs

Kate lowered the letter. Guilt washed over her. She had told her friend she would visit after the Winter's End Festival, and she had failed to do so. And now Mollie was in need of comfort and care.

She had to go. She tucked the letter in a small pocket within her cloak and tightened the ribbons fastening her cloak, then raced into the night.

CHAPTER 33

The clouds had parted, and silver moonlight streamed down. It reflected off the remaining patches of snow, the brightness seeming to turn night into day.

Kate's stomach churned with nerves and the thought of what would meet her when she arrived at Stockton House. She'd heard tales of the horrors of childbirth but had never witnessed it. She had seen ewes give birth, but that would hardly prepare her to be of much assistance.

She hurried her steps along the frozen road. Small bits of ice and mud kicked up on her cloak, but she could not stop.

At the Stockton House gate, she placed a gloved hand on it and creaked it open. She ran to the servants' entrance, just as she always did, and did not bother to knock. Once inside, Kate made her way through the kitchen and around to the foyer, where she noticed light seeping from the study. Not wanting to be detected, she hurried down the corridor, but a familiar voice slowed her steps.

"Figgs, fetch the hunting rifles from the library, will you? And I think there is a pistol in the chest on the bottom shelf of the wardrobe. We'll need every one, I'm afraid."

Henry Stockton's voice froze her feet to the ground.

"Figgs!" Urgency tightened his timbre. Muttering and swift footsteps soon followed, and the door jerked open.

Their eyes locked instantly; neither moved. Neither breathed. His hair fell disheveled over his somber face. His lips were parted. The bruise on his face—not to mention the pistol clutched in his fist—contributed to his sinister presence.

At length she drew a breath and knitted her fingers together in front of her. "I—I thought you would be at the mill."

"I've just returned from there." He motioned toward the stairs. "But Mollie's time is upon us."

"I know. I received a letter asking me to attend her."

His expression did not soften, nor did his tone. "At least you can be with her. Unfortunately I'm needed at the mill."

Her gaze shifted from the pistol in his hand to the rifle on the table behind him. Her heart sank. "Do you think you will need those?"

His gaze followed hers. "I hope not. Time will tell."

Silence filled the space between them. She felt as if she should offer some sort of explanation for her sharp words the night of the Winter's End Festival, but she didn't know what to say or where to begin, especially in light of the situations they both were now in. Besides, with so many important things to tend to at the mill, she did not want to detain him.

He finally broke the silence. "Thank you for coming to be with Mollie."

"I'm not sure what help I will be."

"She esteems you. Just your presence here will be a comfort, I know."

Kate stepped back sheepishly as Mr. Figgs descended the staircase.

Mr. Figgs eyed her with wordless suspicion before he crossed the foyer and handed another pistol to Mr. Stockton. "Good. Is that all of them?"

"There are two hunting rifles in the library. Fetch them for me, will you? Then we'll be off."

Mr. Figgs hurried away, and Mr. Stockton turned the bulk of his attention back to Kate.

Her heart ached at the pain evident in his expression. This would not be an easy night for him—for so many reasons.

She cared for him.

The realization jolted her.

She cared that he was frightened. She cared that he was passionate. She wanted to tell him as much, but what right did she have to do so? She'd already denied him. Perhaps if he would repeat his declarations, her responses could be different.

But it was too late.

Too late for it all.

In a quick sweep he gathered his things and reached for his oilskin greatcoat. His words were almost an afterthought as he reached for his wide-brimmed hat and jammed it on his head. "Please take care of her."

"I'll not leave her side." Her voice cracked. "Be careful."

He nodded, bowed slightly in parting, and left.

Dread settled over her as she stared at the empty space where he had been. Not only did she fear for his safety, but she feared for the safety of Papa and Charles. How was it possible that the men she cared about most were likely to be locked in battle soon?

An anguished cry rang out in a chamber behind her, and she returned her attention to the task at hand. She could not worry about those things now. She needed to focus on her friend.

After leaving Miss Dearborne, Henry met Figgs in the courtyard. The old man had brought around the wagon, and as they loaded the weapons, Henry glanced up at the yellow light spilling from the windows.

He had not expected to see Miss Dearborne at the mill earlier today, let alone at his house this evening. Every aspect of his life seemed in a state of upheaval. A shadow crossed past his sister's chamber window, and a pang of guilt thudded harder than Whitby's fist against his ribs. He should stay with her. He'd heard too many stories of women who faced death during childbirth. But how could he expect others to fight to protect his property if he was not willing to be present?

Decisions were not always easy to make, but he was certain this was the right course.

He climbed up into the wagon and signaled Figgs to proceed, and the cart crunched over snow and ice. They arrived quickly, the ride but a few minutes, and a menacing silence covered the grounds.

No one was visible. Not a soul stirred. All was quiet.

With every sense heightened, he scanned the blackened tree line. Was he being watched? It would be easy for men to hide out in the woods. If they were planning an attack, it was likely they would be conducting some sort of surveillance.

They arrived at the mill entrance, and several men, including Belsey, were at the large door, waiting.

"Anything?" Henry jumped down from the cart.

Belsey shook his head as he accepted the crate of weapons. "No, sir. Not a thing."

Henry could see the shadows of men just inside the mill's windows, standing near the looms. In the past the attackers had gone for the windows and the doors to gain access to the machines inside. With the walls of thick stone, they were the only way in.

They simply would not allow that to happen.

With preparations in the mill ready, Henry made his way into the countinghouse. Despite the cold, perspiration beaded on his forehead and dampened his shirt. Miss Dearborne had told them the men would be meeting at midnight. He glanced at the clock. The hour was past midnight; the night was still. Not even the wind dared to disrupt the reverent calm.

Henry looked around the black room. There was not even a fire in the grate. No one spoke. No one moved.

Two magistrates, including Mr. Tierner, had joined Henry, Belsey, and Dearborne in the countinghouse. They had been able to secure three soldiers, all of whom stood with their weapons at the ready, and Pennington had dispatched a few of his men to offer support. They all knew that this building—the countinghouse—was the most vulnerable. It was made of stone, but portions of the frame were made of wood. It would be easy to gain entrance, especially if someone was familiar with the layout.

Minutes ticked by in agonizing slowness.

Perhaps Miss Dearborne had been misinformed?

He lifted the edge of the window covering.

Nothing.

He was about to turn to the other men when he heard it—the deafening crack of iron against iron.

The gate.

He snapped his head away from the window to avoid being seen. Belsey's brows were raised.

He'd heard it too.

And then the footsteps started. Slowly. Steadily.

He'd heard the footsteps before. Just like the ones he'd heard in battle. But instead of fighting for their country, these men were prepared to fight for their livelihoods.

His heart thudded, and sweat dripped into his eyes. He blinked it away before reaching for his pistol on the table.

With a furrowed brow and lips pressed to a firm line, Dearborne stepped next to him, shoulder to shoulder. "That's them."

Behind him, grave expressions painted the faces of all gathered, and one of the magistrates withdrew out the back door, no doubt to connect with the men in the mill.

The time had come, and there would be no turning back.

CHAPTER 34

$\mathcal{K}$ate gripped Mollie's hand and winced as the young woman cried out.

Pain twisted Mollie's face. Her jaw clenched. Perspiration dampened her hair, clumping it in thick, black locks over her pale forehead.

Tears burned in Kate's own eyes at the sight. It was not easy to watch another in such pain. The night's darkness added to the uncertainty of the evening, although she doubted sunlight would make much of a difference. She squeezed Mollie's hand back and looked to the midwife, who stood near the foot of the bed.

"It will all be over soon, Mollie," Kate whispered, even though she had no idea how long the labor would last. "Soon."

As another pang seized Mollie, she clenched her teeth and squeezed her eyes shut. Perspiration trailed down well worn paths on her face, and she flailed her hand and grabbed Kate's arm. Her fingernails dug into the flesh, but Kate didn't pull away. She obeyed the midwife's every order. She wiped Mollie's brow. She fetched clean linens when bid to do so.

The hours dragged on mercilessly and excruciatingly for the young mother. When the midwife withdrew from the room, Mollie clutched Kate's skirt. "Don't leave, Kate," she panted. "Please."

"I'll not leave."

The fire's light reflected off the moisture on her brow. "Do you promise?"

Before Kate could respond, a sob from another spasm of pain seized Mollie. Anguish deepened her cry.

"You're strong," Kate encouraged. "Your husband would be so proud of you."

Kate had expected the words to be a comfort, but as they passed her lips, fresh sobs shook Mollie's form.

"I'm sorry." Panicked, Kate reached for her and pressed a linen cloth to her forehead and reached for words. "Please don't cry."

Mollie pushed the rag from her face and lay back on the pillow, the strands of her long, dark hair clinging to her face. She ran her hands over her face and covered her eyes as she spoke. "I've deceived you."

Clearly the woman was talking out of her mind. Kate put her hand on her shoulder. "Hush now. You've not deceived me."

"Yes, I have." Mollie's voice punched with sudden strength, and she jerked her hands away from her face. "You have been kind to me. A friend. And I've deceived you. I've deceived everyone."

Confused, Kate stared at her. Did she know what she was saying?

More tears flowed from Mollie's blue eyes. "Why am I lying? Have I really gone so far?" Tears merged with the perspiration on her face and tracked down her cheeks.

Kate moved a pile of damp linens to the floor. "I don't understand."

"My name is not Mrs. Smith."

Kate straightened and then frowned. Surely the pain was altering her thinking. "Of course it is."

"No. My name has never been Mrs. Smith. I have always been Mollie Stockton. Just—Stockton."

Surely she was delirious. "We can discuss this later. Just focus on—"

"Do you not understand?" she hurled back. "It means that the baby's father couldn't care less about how I'm doing."

As the meaning of the words sank in, Kate let out a slow exhale.

Mollie had never been married.

She had no husband.

Not knowing how to respond to the sudden, breathless admission, Kate remained silent. She was torn. She had been lied to. Blatantly. But as she watched the woman writhe in pain, did it even matter? She knew how women who had a child out of wedlock were treated. Had Kate not been treated as an outsider by others at times? The harsh rejection of her childhood friendship with Frederica Pennington and the recent dismissal of her by her own weavers burned.

These were hardly on the same level as what Mollie would endure.

Kate forced a smile and wiped perspiration from her own brow. "Well, at this moment that doesn't matter. Nothing matters but staying calm. It will all work out in the end. You'll see."

"But will it?" A different emotion flashed in her eyes. "Please don't hate me. I couldn't bear it. You're the only friend I have here. You're the only friend I have anywhere."

A fresh wave of pain broke over Mollie, and her words stopped. Instead, between groans and cries she gasped for air.

Kate watched helplessly and waited for this round of pain to pass. As she did, she held Mollie's hand again. She thought of Henry's request for her to help take care of Mollie. Did he know all of this?

At the thought, she could not help the worry seeping into her mind. Were Henry and Charles safe? What was happening with the men at the mill? Mollie had no idea what the men were facing this night, for the battle she was fighting required her full concentration. But the knowledge that an attack could be under way nagged Kate. Toyed with her. Frightened her.

She could not let Mollie know that her brother was in danger. She breathed a little prayer, then returned her full attention to Mollie. "Does your brother know about the—the—"

"Yes. He knows I've been lying, and he's been cross with me about it." Every word was exhaled as a breathless pant. "But how can he possibly understand what this means for my future, my baby's and my future?"

"I don't know, but I do know that your brother will not betray you. He loves you."

The midwife bustled back into the room.

Mollie clutched her arm. "Please. Keep my secret."

"Of course." Kate rubbed Mollie's hand. "It isn't my story to tell."

Henry's heart thumped in his chest. Erratically but strongly, alertly. He stood at the countinghouse window, his body shielded by the window frame.

He sensed their presence. The hair on the back of his neck stiffened. He swallowed hard. His finger flexed near the trigger of his pistol.

"What do we do?" Belsey whispered.

"We wait."

A sudden, sharp crack, like wood splitting, echoed in the night. Henry jumped.

"It came from over by the stable." Belsey pressed his body against the wall and peered out the window.

And then Henry saw them. Shadow people, perhaps fifty of them, moving silent and slow toward the mill like a great black wave, weaving in and out of the silhouettes of trees and outbuildings.

Suddenly, the sharp *ping* of a stone crashing through a window shattered the silence and showered glass to the ground. Henry whirled around.

Without warning a rock sailed through the window next to Henry. First one and then another. The glass exploded. Henry ducked and covered his head. The rock ricocheted from the rear wall.

A slew of curses spewed from the magistrate's mouth, and one of the soldiers stepped forward, filling the space just to the left of the window. "Take notice," the soldier shouted, his side pressed against the wall. "This is a member of His Majesty's army. I'm charged with keeping the peace in Amberdale and defending the legal rights of this establishment. You are ordered to disperse and return to your homes. If you fail to do so, force will be used."

Henry held his breath.

But mere seconds later, another rock flew and shattered another window. A cheer rose from outside.

The soldier cursed this time. He aimed his rifle through the broken window toward the black sky and fired. The muzzle flash flared in the dark night, and the shot echoed from the outbuildings. "This is your final warning. Disperse!"

Instead of discouraging the weavers, the warning incited the crowd.

Henry widened his stance and tightened his grip on the firearm.

Shouts and calls thundered. Faceless silhouettes stole across the yard. And then he saw it—a flash of fire across the courtyard. It grew from a flicker of a flame to a roaring blaze.

"They've set the wagon on fire!" cried Dearborne.

Henry exchanged a sober gaze with the magistrate. Their only retaliation would be to fire upon the crowd. That he would not do until fired upon first. Flames engulfed the wagon. A horse's silhouette raced in front. Had they gained access to the stable?

The fire illuminated some of the attackers. He had no idea there would be so many. They wore wide-brimmed hats, and black handkerchiefs covered their faces.

And then it happened. A series of gunshots—sharp, clear, and loud—rang out in the night. Two of the men in the countinghouse dropped to the ground at the sound, and Henry pressed against the wall again. Perspiration stung his eyes. His mouth grew dry.

The line had been crossed from mere vandalism to something much more sinister.

He looked out the window. Two more fires had been started, one at the north end of the courtyard, the other at the south. The north end ran against the river, and next to it, the waterwheel.

Another shot rang out.

Tierner pushed past him, leveled the barrel of his rifle on the jagged glass of the windowsill, took aim, and pulled the trigger.

"What are you doing?" Henry grabbed his arm once the shot had been discharged.

Tierner's annoyance flashed. "The animals will pull your mill down brick by brick. Is that what you want? You'll not have all night to decide if you are going to act or not."

Before he had a chance to respond, a volley of gunfire rang out over the courtyard. Shot after shot bellowed.

Battlefield images rushed him as real as an enemy wielding a knife. Henry struggled to separate the vivid memories from the sights, sounds, and scents he encountered now. Just as a war raged in his courtyard, another raged in his mind.

Then he saw it. Across the courtyard, the fire's light illuminated a man hammering at the waterwheel. Only half of the huge wheel was visible, and he squinted to make sure his eyesight could be trusted. The waterwheel powered several of the machines within the mill.

He had thought they would be after the machines themselves, but destroying the waterwheel would halt production completely.

Confident he saw real men and not just shadows, Henry motioned for Belsey to follow him and crept out the countinghouse's rear door. The cold air rushed him, stealing the air from his lungs and pricking his fevered skin.

Under the cover of darkness, he and Belsey rounded the back of the mill and crawled through a small tunnel that ran the length of the mill's wall and provided access to the waterwheel at river level.

Then his suspicion was confirmed—two men crouched near the wheel, hacking at the wheel with axes, sending chunks of wood flying into the rushing water below.

Next to him, Belsey seemed less affected and more angered by what was happening. He, too, brandished a gun, only he was less hesitant than Henry. The older man took aim and fired. The men dove to the ground.

Now that the perpetrators were alerted to their presence, Henry snapped to action and lurched from the safety of their tunnel. He pointed his pistol at the man. "You there!"

The closest man jerked up his head and yanked a pistol from his coat.

To Henry's surprise, the man was pointing his pistol not at him but at Belsey.

Henry did not think. He just responded. He would not have a man fighting for him injured or, worse, killed. He knew what he needed to do. He aimed for the man's leg and pulled the trigger.

The man screamed and fell backward, the pistol tumbling from his grip onto the muddy ground. In the confusion, the other attacker retreated back to the courtyard, leaving his fallen comrade.

Henry nearly dropped the pistol from his hand when the man

rolled over. The light from a nearby fire shimmered on the face of none other than Silas Dearborne.

Dearborne cried out in pain and clutched his leg, fixing his eyes on Henry.

One glance at the location of the wound told Henry that the shot was not a mortal one. He would survive.

Henry had a choice. He could drag the wounded man back to the countinghouse, where the authorities would be ready to take him captive, or he could let the man return to the other weavers.

Belsey nudged him in the arm, his rifle now pointed at Dearborne. "What do you want to do with him?"

Henry stooped to pick up Dearborne's dropped pistol. "Let him go."

"What?" cried Belsey. "Have you gone mad?"

Henry did not take his eyes off Dearborne. "Yes. He and his men will not be successful, not on this night or any other. I am not frightened of them, and I never will be. Let him nurse his wound. We've other matters to deal with."

Belsey grumbled under his breath, but complied and backed away from the wounded Dearborne.

Henry had no doubt that the other man who had fled would return for the wounded Dearborne, but he could not—would not—return to the countinghouse with Silas Dearborne as a prisoner. Not with Charles within those walls, and not after what Miss Dearborne had risked to warn him.

He and Belsey returned to the countinghouse. The fighting waged for hours. At times the activity would lull. At other times the activity would stir into a frenzy, punctuated by gunshots, crackling fires, angry shouts, and showers of stones. Several hours into the battle, the weavers felled one of the larger courtyard trees, sending it crashing against the roof of the stable and dye house, but even then, they did not relent.

With the exception of protecting the waterwheel, the millworkers never left the safety of the mill and the countinghouse. The weavers scurried around the courtyard like ants around an anthill, bent on destruction and mayhem, but throughout it all, Henry, the magistrate, the soldiers, Dearborne, Belsey, Pennington, and the various millworkers pressed forward, answering every gunshot and thwarting every attempted entry.

After hours of fighting, the weavers, little by little, retreated into the forest. Men wounded by gunshot or fire were carried off. Soon the silver light of dawn revealed a smoke-filled and badly damaged courtyard. Not a single window remained intact, but the mill, the waterwheel, and, most importantly, the machines inside were safe.

There were still unanswered questions. Despite strong suspicions, he did not know with perfect certainty the identity of the man who was ultimately behind this attack. He still did not know who had killed his grandfather. But he did know one thing: The weavers would not take his mill. Not tonight.

CHAPTER 35

*K*ate pulled Stockton House's iron gate closed behind her and jogged down the lane. Relief and fear mingled in every thought. She'd not slept the entire night, and even in her fatigued state, apprehension still fueled her steps.

After hours of relentless labor, the babe arrived: pink, plump, and healthy.

But several hours into the night, staccato gunshots had shattered the silence. As if watching Mollie grip life during childbirth had not been difficult enough, Kate had to wrestle with the fact that the men in her life were engaged in an entirely different battle.

Hours had passed since the last shots rang out. The fighting—or whatever it was—had to be over. If there had indeed been a battle, she would be wise to return home. But was Meadowvale even a safe haven anymore?

She stood in the lane, chewing her lower lip. The wind swept down from the trees, fluttering the ribbons on her straw bonnet and filling her lungs with its freshness. If she turned left, she would arrive at Meadowvale. If she turned right, she would cross the bridge into Amberdale and, in essence, be at the mill's doorstep.

Despite the exhaustion begging her to rest, her soul would not be quieted. She turned to her right, and before long she stood at the base of the stone bridge. Smoke teased her nose and burned her eyes, and that fact alone sent a chill up her spine. Kate clutched her cloak and ran over the bridge and past the churchyard to the gates of Stockton Mill.

Not a soul was in sight. She put her hands on the locked iron bars and looked to the courtyard within. This time of morning it should be alive with activity, but the only motion she saw was the flickering of several small fires scattered around the courtyard. Two large trees had been felled, one of which had landed on the thatched roof of one of the outbuildings. Debris and splintered wood littered the soggy ground, and the light from the fires glimmered off the shattered glass.

Horrified, Kate saw all that she needed to see. She staggered backward and turned to run—and she did not stop until she reached Meadowvale's gate.

By the time she arrived home, she was gasping for air. She peered over the wooden gate, looking for more detailed clues about what had transpired. There were not nearly as many weavers as there had been when she left, but a few remained, sitting on overturned crates or standing just inside the stable. Other men moved to and fro, but their steps were slow, their clothing damp and dirty. Gone was the buoyant energy that had lit everyone's steps and expressions. What had happened?

Kate inched the gate open. Determined not to draw attention to herself, she stole behind the loom and dye houses to the kitchen entrance. She needed to change her gown before she encountered anyone. But as she strode toward the stairway, Betsy intercepted her steps.

"Where have you been?" Betsy demanded, her eyes wide. "Everyone's been looking high and low for you."

Kate turned. "Why? What is it?"

"Your father. He's been shot."

"Shot?" Alarm sliced through her, and she clutched the maid's forearm. "Is he all right? Where is he?"

"He is abed. Resting."

Kate pushed past Betsy and ran up the stairs. She never went into her papa's private chamber. Ever. Panic seized her when she thrust open the door. He was in bed, just as Betsy had said, a blanket pulled to his chin. His face was white, his eyes closed, his mouth open. He was still.

Several men, including John, were gathered in the low-ceilinged space. She hurried past them and dropped to her knees next to her father's bed. His eyelashes fluttered at the motion. Tears flooded Kate's already burning eyes and she gripped the edge of the blanket. "What has happened?"

He drew a deep breath. Annoyance—not pain or fear—scrunched his face. He surveyed the men in the room. All were silent.

Kate's breath caught in her throat. He wasn't going to tell her.

This was no time for games. In a sudden burst, she clutched his arm, as if to demand his attention. "Tell me immediately! What has happened?"

Her mind rushed to every possible garish conclusion as the silence persisted. If he had been shot, who else had? How many?

"It was the mill, wasn't it?" she blurted out, heat creeping up her neck. Her throat felt almost too thick to speak. "Papa, I begged you not to go. I—"

"Silence!"

She snapped her mouth shut at her father's blunt order and leaned back from the bed.

He fixed hard, narrow eyes on her. She had been afraid of her father, but the coldness in his eyes caused her to shrink back even farther.

At length, his raspy voice filled the chamber. "Like I told you earlier, what I do does not concern you. Nothing of what any of us does concerns you, especially after what you've done."

The situation came into hard focus. He must know that she had alerted Charles and Mr. Stockton. What else would initiate such coolness?

Her hands began to tremble with trepidation.

"Don't lie to me, girl."

Almost by accident she glanced at the other faces in the room. John. The man from Leeds. Thomas Crater. Mr. Wooden. They were all fixed on her. Angry. Unmoving.

"Someone notified the mill of our intentions."

Kate swallowed. Hard.

He continued. "This was orchestrated from Leeds, organized by the society leader there. And yet someone who knew the Stockton workers well enough let them know. Professional soldiers were there, ready to meet us. Do you think that a coincidence?"

Kate didn't respond. She didn't blink. She didn't breathe. The situation's gravity pressed in on her.

"You did it, didn't you?" The pallor of Papa's face was replaced by anger's red fire. "Do not lie to me, lass."

Kate's lack of sleep and fear of her father's response faltered her words. "P-Papa, I—"

He appeared frail in his bed, but his voice rang out strong and forceful. "This is your doing, Kate. We had a mission, a unified front. We were to take back what belongs to me and every other man who makes a living by honest means. To take back dignity and respect. And what did you do, you selfish, ungrateful thing? You informed them! You could have been responsible for the deaths of dozens of people who counted you as family."

"I didn't betray you, Papa. I—"

"How is that not a betrayal!" he thundered, the suddenness and intensity of the words making Kate jump. "I have suffered the betrayal of one child, but now two? You could have cost me my life."

Emotion tightened her throat. He was right. But if she had not done anything, could she have caused the men at the mill their lives?

His face deepened to almost purple. "And for what? Because of feminine whims and female fancies that your brother somehow still cares for you? Bah!"

A tear trailed down Kate's cheek.

But her father did not stop. "Or perhaps it had nothing to do with Charles at all. Perhaps it was Stockton himself. I have heard rumors, sickening rumors, that burn my tongue even to say. It has been whispered that you have formed an attachment to Stockton. That you find yourself infatuated with him. Is this true?"

She did not respond. Humiliation twisted her stomach.

"I have been wounded, shot like an animal," he roared. "Would you like to know who pulled the trigger? Would you?"

She stared at him with wide eyes.

"It was your Mr. Stockton. The man you flirted with at the festival. The man who enticed you away from your family. He shot me in cold blood, Kate. How do you feel about him now?"

She shook her head slowly from side to side. He couldn't be telling the truth.

"You have a choice, and you'll make it this minute, with these fine men as witnesses. You'll create a path for your future, marry Whitby, and put an end to these sickening rumors. Then and only then can things go on as they have."

She flicked her gaze up to John. Her fists clenched at her sides at the obnoxious expression of victory on his face. She looked back to her father and jutted her chin. "And if I don't?"

"If you fail to prove your loyalty, you can go to your brother then, since you have such a fondness for him. But if you choose to do so, my door will be forevermore closed to you."

"Papa, you cannot mean that!" she cried, pain shooting through her.

"Have I ever wavered on such things? Over three years have passed since I last had a word with your brother, and it will be fifty-plus more years before I consent to speak with him again. So the choice is yours."

She shook her head as a frustrated huff escaped her lips. "Papa, you are not well. You're not thinking clearly. I—"

"Your options are known," he snapped. "Think carefully and choose wisely. This offer will not be made again."

She leaned back and stood. Papa looked fragile as he lay in his bed. She narrowed her gaze. "I don't feel I need to marry anyone to prove my loyalty. I will not consent to marry John. I am your daughter. Either that is good enough, or it isn't."

If she had not been staring directly at him, she might have missed the flash of surprise in his pewter eyes before they hardened once again. "Then 'tis done. Go to your brother. You're the same, the two of you, and I'm glad to be finished with you."

Tears blurred her vision at the quickness with which he dismissed her.

His pride had always been his greatest downfall, first with Mother, then Charles, and now her. Stunned, she turned and somehow managed to walk from the room.

She was three steps into the corridor when someone grabbed her arm from behind, disrupting her balance and pulling her back in the darkness.

John.

She forced herself to meet his gaze, willing her heart to slow its beat.

A single flickering corridor sconce highlighted his profile. "It wouldn't be so bad, would it?"

His gaze had softened. If she did not know him so well, she might think that genuine concern shone from his eyes. But she knew him to be a deceiver. He possessed the gift of being able to earn trust easily. He had found her father's vulnerability and played to it.

"We could have a good life, you and I." His hand did not leave her arm. Instead, his rough thumb caressed it, as if to soothe her. "Your father will leave all this to us. To us! Our life can be full and happy."

"Can you really be so blind?" She laughed incredulously. "I am not even sure I want this life, especially after what occurred last night."

"So you are aware of what has happened." His gaze narrowed. "Perhaps your father was right, then. I never thought you capable of turning on your own, and yet see what you caused as a result."

"I want no part in destroying what another man has worked for, regardless of who that person may be." She shrugged her arm away. "Good-bye, John."

CHAPTER 36

*D*isbelief robbed Kate of breath. Had her father really ousted her from their home?

She half expected him to call to her and say that he had changed his mind, that his temper and pain had gotten the better of him. But the other half of her knew better. He was a hard man. After all, he'd not spoken to his own son for years, and Charles had been the one on whom he had pinned the future of the Dearborne clan.

Through tear-blurred eyes, Katherine assessed her small but beloved bedchamber. Was she really going to leave it and never come back? Was this really the last time she would open her trunk, gaze in the looking glass hanging on the wall, or sit at the little desk and write a missive or read a book?

She moved to her wardrobe and pulled out a satchel. She stuffed every gown, petticoat, stay, and chemise that would fit. She tucked in boots, slippers, and trinkets, her hairbrush and toothbrush. But all the other things that had surrounded her since childhood—the bed, the dresser, the trunk—would remain behind.

Was this how Charles had felt after Papa placed the ultimatum on him?

She could not stop to think about that now.

With every passing second she felt the need to move faster, to be quicker. When she could not fit a single other item into the satchel, she layered her crimson cloak over top of the gray one, donned her straw bonnet, and stole outside.

She tried to be as quiet as possible, but to what end? No one tried to stop her. No one detained her.

And it stung.

Could she be released so easily?

By the time she stepped onto Amberdale's main road toward her brother's cottage, the day was clear and bright. The village's atmosphere was unusually quiet. It was late enough in the morning that the shops should be opening. Millworkers should already be at their stations. Shopkeepers should be selling their wares. But no one was visible.

She paused in front of Charles's cottage door and looked around. A face peered out of the window from one of the adjacent cottages, but as Kate met the nosy gaze, the spying woman dropped the curtain.

Kate knocked on the door. No response.

She tried the doorknob. Locked.

She tucked her satchel in a large crate next to his door and stepped toward the mill's gate. As she rounded the corner and the mill's courtyard came into view, nausea washed over her, for the sight confirmed what she had seen at dawn.

Smoke and mist hovered over the grounds; a fire still glowed in the yard. Dozens of windows were shattered, and the ever-present hum of water and machinery was eerily absent. No millworkers were visible earlier, but now people scurried around the courtyard, sifting through the debris.

Male workers had started the task of cleanup, and the bright-red coats of two soldiers across the yard caught her eye. Two men leaned over a body lying on the ground, and two more were seated by the battered waterwheel at the edge of the courtyard.

As she stepped farther onto Stockton property, she gaped at the splintered wood and discarded weapons littering the ground. She had never been in battle, but was this what the aftermath looked like?

She stepped over a large branch and headed toward the counting-house. All the windows were shattered. Glass and leading lay at her feet, jumbled with the remaining snow and mud.

As the reality of the situation set in, panic joined it. She frowned as she sought a familiar face. Where was Charles? Henry? After all, Papa had been shot. Who else shared his fate?

Once at the countinghouse door, she knocked before taking the liberty to push it open. She was not sure what to expect inside, but she couldn't have been more shocked to see Mr. Pennington seated behind the desk.

"Miss Dearborne." A scowl scrunched his round face, and judgment flashed in his dark eyes. "What are you doing here?"

"I am here to see my brother."

He huffed and stood. "I am surprised you have the audacity to come here."

Her tired, muddled mind could not formulate a response quickly enough.

When she did not respond, he stepped closer to her. "You and your kind are responsible for this. What makes you think you would be welcome to step foot in this office?"

She wanted to spew a clever retort, but her mouth was so dry no words would form.

"Either you leave now, or I will see that you—"

"Pennington!" shouted a deep male voice, halting Mr. Pennington's threat.

Her already taut nerves tensed at the harsh tone. She whirled to see Mr. Stockton in the doorway of the back chamber. His brow furrowed, he stomped into the room.

Kate darted her gaze from his soot-smudged cheek to his torn coat to the white bandage on his hand. His eyes were red-rimmed and bloodshot. Dark circles balanced beneath them. His hair hung in damp clumps over his forehead, and a bloodied scratch marred his unshaven cheek.

She resisted the urge to run to him and put as much distance between herself and Mr. Pennington as possible, and instead planted her feet firmly on the wooden floor. The battle-weary man did not look at her. Rather, his attention was fixed firmly on the Pennington patriarch.

The odd interchange confused her. She understood the Penningtons and the Stocktons to be allies. But the hard stare between the men, the silent challenge, was obvious.

Mr. Stockton did not break his gaze. "I must be mistaken at what I am hearing. It seems you are insinuating that Miss Dearborne was responsible, at least in part, for what happened."

Mr. Pennington laughed sardonically. "Come now, Stockton. You're a rational man. You cannot think for a moment she is innocent in all of this. We all know who is behind this garish display."

Stockton stepped farther into the room. "Surely you do not think Miss Dearborne to be one of the men wielding rifles and bearing flames."

Pennington retrieved his pipe and drew a long breath of tobacco smoke. "Perhaps if you concerned yourself with the needs of the mills and the people in them instead of flirting with the weaver's daughter, things would have ended differently."

Mr. Stockton stepped closer to Kate, almost as if to shield her from Pennington's harsh words. He crossed his muscular arms over his chest. "Mr. Pennington, you and I have enjoyed a friendly relationship since my return, but I do not recall asking for your opinion on how I operate my mill or with whom I choose to speak."

Mr. Pennington sneered. "Your grandfather never would have been so foolish as to allow an emotion to come between him and the success of his business."

"That is your opinion."

Mr. Pennington gave his head a hard shake. "I fear for the future of this establishment. All of your grandfather's hard work, to what end? A true pity. All could have such a different outcome."

Still smoking his pipe, Mr. Pennington pivoted toward Kate, gave a mockingly low bow, and glared back at Mr. Stockton before he exited the countinghouse and slammed the rickety door behind him.

Silence, heavy and deafening, once again descended on the chamber. Now was not the time for shyness, but she did not feel strong enough to feign bravery. Hours without sleep and unsettling words and circumstances were eating away at her resolve, making her question every decision she had made over the course of the past several weeks. And yet in spite of the night's occurrences, she found strength in his nearness.

"Are you hurt?" Her voice sounded small. She rubbed the cloak over her arm.

"No, and your brother is fine as well." His dark eyebrows rose. "And my sister? I've heard no news."

It seemed like days had passed since she'd left the Stockton home, when in fact it had been only hours. Kate smiled. "You have a beautiful nephew, a fine, sturdy baby boy, and your sister is as well as can be expected."

"Thank God." His posture slumped as he ran his hand down his face and then cupped the back of his neck.

She wanted to go to him, to comfort him in some way, but one question in particular was poised on the tip of her tongue and prevented her from taking a single step. Perhaps she and Henry could be friends one day, perhaps not. But until one matter was clarified, she doubted she would ever have peace. She steeled herself, preparing for an answer either way. "Did you shoot my father?"

Hand still behind his neck, he blinked at her. His eyes, the blue of which was enhanced by the redness around them, transfixed her. But he did not respond.

She said louder, "Did you do it?"

"I did."

She stared at him, her mind wrestling with the information she had just received.

"I had no choice," he continued. "He was going to—to—"

Heat rose to her face. "He was going to what?"

He stared at her.

Suddenly, she did not want to know. Instead, she wanted to cry. To scream. Would this nightmare never end?

The door to the back room opened. "Who's this I hear?" Charles appeared, a good-natured—if not forced—smile on his stubbled face. Besides the dirt on his face and clothes, he seemed relatively unharmed.

She rushed to her brother and flung her arms around him. "I am so glad you are safe!"

He released her. "Are you crying? There is nothing to cry about! All is well, see?"

"You have not heard, then." She shifted her gaze to Mr. Stockton.

"Heard what?"

"Father was shot."

"I know." Charles's face darkened. "How is he faring?"

Shock robbed her of speech. She'd assumed Charles must not have known, or he wouldn't be so calm and collected.

When she did not respond, he blurted bluntly, "It was a leg wound, wasn't it?"

Kate nodded, barely noticing that Mr. Stockton had slipped from the room, no doubt to give them privacy.

Still shaken by the news, Kate waited until the door latched to continue. "But why would Hen—I mean, Mr. Stockton shoot Papa?"

Charles sighed. "He had to."

"What do you mean, he *had* to?"

Charles sat down in one of the chairs by the desk and cast a glance into the fire. "Because Father was going to shoot Belsey. Mr. Stockton prevented our father from becoming a murderer."

Kate sobered. She had not considered that.

"And there's more," Charles added. "Stockton could have turned Father over to the soldiers after he wounded him, but he didn't. Machine breaking and the attempt to do so are punishable by death. Hanging. Stockton saved Father on two counts."

Kate swallowed and looked to the toes of her muddy boots.

"Don't judge Stockton so harshly. He's not the enemy here."

Yes, she knew all too well who the enemy was.

And the fact broke her heart.

Charles folded his arms across his chest. "But I must say that I am surprised. Why are you here, exactly?"

With a hesitant sigh she dropped down to the chair next to him. "Papa said I am no longer welcome at Meadowvale."

"He did what?" Charles's face reddened, displaying the first sign of anger Kate had seen since her arrival. He rested his elbows on his knees, fixing an intent gaze on her. "Unbelievable. It is one thing to disown a son, but a daughter?"

"He found out somehow that I was the one to warn you."

Charles shook his head. "If I have told you once, I have told you a thousand times, you will always have a home with me." In a sudden burst of energy, he stood and reached into his pocket. He extended a key toward her and dropped it into her outstretched hand. "Go back to the cottage and get some rest. I've no idea how long I will be here, but after a good rest we'll get to the bottom of this."

As her brother retreated to the countinghouse's back room, Kate tucked the key in her pocket, looped her hood over her head, and stepped back into the daylight. She'd obey her brother, and no doubt, her body did cry for sleep, but she feared no rest would come to her this day.

CHAPTER 37

*H*enry had not slept in more than two days, but somehow energy coursed through him. The battle had been a long one. Some of his men had been injured, and one of the weavers had been killed. But through all of the drama and tension, a glimmer of light shone through.

He should be optimistic. Mollie had safely delivered her baby. The damage to the mill was extensive but reparable. The machines, which had no doubt been the target, were untouched.

But the dark cloud hanging over his head was his recent interaction with Miss Dearborne.

He wanted so much to please her. To impress her. He wanted to see her smile, and he wanted to know that he was the reason for her smile. But time and time again, he'd failed. How he'd wanted to defend himself when she asked him about her father's shooting. But how could he look her in the eye and tell her that her father could have been a murderer? Or worse yet, boast about setting the man free?

No, some things shouldn't be said.

Perhaps everything was as it should be with Miss Dearborne. Perhaps she had been wise to refuse him that night at the festival.

Some boundaries weren't meant to be crossed, and this might be one of them.

Henry continued his walk from the countinghouse to the north end of the mill's main building. He glanced at three weavers lined up against the wall. With the help of the magistrate and the soldiers, the law would be on his side. If these men would divulge who orchestrated the attack, they could bring the man or men to justice, and by doing so, they might be one step closer to discovering the identity of the man who killed his grandfather.

The prisoners' injuries were not life threatening. Two had been shot, and one had broken his leg after falling from his horse. The men had each received medical attention, and now the magistrate was preparing to take them to the village lock, pending Henry's orders.

"It is up to you, Stockton." Tierner scowled at the three men. "I've no patience for cowards like this. Do you want to press charges? If you let 'em go now, you'll never see them again. If you want justice, you'd best get it now. Judge will be 'round in a few weeks."

The men looked dejected and scared, their faces smeared with dirt, soot, and mud. The black handkerchiefs that had been tied about their faces now hung around their necks. They were a pitiful lot, but he didn't recognize any of them. They were not Dearborne's men, he was certain. Nor did he think they were from Bremton. They were out for trouble, men who wanted to blame anyone—anything—for their dire circumstances and not take ownership for the situations in which they found themselves.

He'd heard the story of how these unemployed men would get scooped into the plans of the weavers' societies at large. These were not the men he was fighting against. Not really. He was fighting against a much larger organization. Someone had to orchestrate this attack. Someone had to unify the weavers across the towns.

Henry stepped forward. "The three of you could feasibly be charged with vandalism, attempted murder, and a host of other charges."

The men exchanged uncomfortable glances but remained silent.

Henry paced in front of them. "I know the weavers have a code, and they will not turn on one another or reveal another's wrongdoings, but I have a code too. I'll not pretend that I sympathize with you. I'd like nothing more than to see you punished for the crime you have committed against me, against my family, but I'm willing to come to an agreement with you."

He flashed his gaze toward Belsey. "You provide the magistrate with the men leading the society, and once they have been apprehended, you'll be given your freedom. Until such a time as that, you'll remain incarcerated."

He blinked away the smoke stinging his eyes and stared at the men. "If you don't provide the names, you will be charged, and with the shift of tides in cases such as these, I'd not want to be on the wrong side of the law."

Grateful to be home—not to mention alive—Henry climbed the staircase to his sister's chamber. Eagerness to meet his newest family member infused his tired steps with energy. After dealing with hatred and destruction, he could hardly wait to meet him.

He rapped his knuckles against the open door and ducked his head inside. Rare, fleeting sunlight flooded the tidy space with a cheery glow and fell upon Mollie as she sat in her bed. In her arms, a dark-haired baby with rosy cheeks slumbered.

His raw emotions would get the better of him, he feared. His chest swelled with affection for this brand-new being, and his eyes stung with an unfamiliar burn. The babe may not be his son, but he was still his flesh and blood, and his birth marked the dawn of a new Stockton generation.

Was this not what his grandfather had desired?

A smile lit Mollie's face, and her dark hair streamed over her shoulders. She motioned for him to draw near. "Come see!"

He went to her side, his eyes not leaving the angelic face.

"I'm so glad you're here at last." Mollie beamed. "Henry, I'd like for you to meet your nephew, Henry James Stockton."

Henry jerked his head up at the name. *His* name. A much-needed smile cracked his face.

"Do you want to hold him?" Mollie adjusted her position and started to extend the bundle.

"Oh, no. He's sleeping and I'm filthy." He pulled a chair up next to the bed and sat down. The thought of his dirty hands and clothes next to someone so precious and clean seemed an absurdity. Instead, he angled himself so he could watch the child. "How are you feeling?"

"I'm much better than I was. I'm almost glad I didn't know how dreadful it would be—I would've been even more frightened than I was." The slumbering babe wiggled as his mother laughed. "Thank goodness Kate was here with me. I don't know what I would have done without her."

"Kate?" He repeated her name. He didn't want her to pass from the conversation. Not yet.

"Yes. Miss Dearborne. She didn't leave my side. Not once. The midwife was as sour as could be. I'm so glad Kate was here. I would have been so frightened otherwise."

Every time Miss Dearborne crossed his mind, guilt descended.

He tensed. Would he always feel responsible for the situation the lady was in?

Mollie's face grew somber as she looked down at little Henry. Her words grew soft and her eyes narrowed, almost as if she were about to divulge a great secret. "I told her about my husband or, rather, my lack thereof."

"You did?"

"Yes, I confessed everything. It is amazing what one will say while in childbirth."

Henry didn't know much about childbirth, but he did know how cleansing the truth could be. "And what was her reaction?"

Mollie tilted her head to the side, her gaze fixed on the tiny cherub. "She was gracious, especially considering the fact that I'd deceived her for all these weeks."

He leaned back in the chair. "How do you feel now that the truth is out?"

With the softest touch she smoothed the baby's hair. "All right, I suppose."

"And Mrs. Figgs? Does she know yet?"

"Yes. I told her. You know how she is—she became all growly and gruff, but what's done is done. She said that lamenting the fact won't change the matter, and she could understand my actions. I'll need to have a conversation with the vicar's wife and the Penningtons, but hopefully once that is settled, all of this business can be put behind us."

Henry stiffened at the reference to the Penningtons. The relationship had been tense for some time, and now, after Pennington's rude treatment of Miss Dearborne just a couple of days ago in his countinghouse, the relationship was dissolving. Henry doubted there was any way to save it, even if out of respect for his grandfather.

She lifted her gaze. "Mrs. Figgs told me there was trouble at the mill."

Henry crossed one leg over the other, attempting to appear calm for his sister's benefit. There was no need to worry her, not with what she had endured. "Everything is under control. Nothing to fret over."

But Mollie refused to let the matter go. "She said the weavers attacked and there was a great deal of damage."

He smiled. "Nothing that cannot be fixed."

"Is that how you hurt your hand?"

Henry glanced down to the bandage on his hand, flexed his fingers, and nodded.

"Miss Dearborne was by earlier today and told me all about how her father asked her to leave his house and how she was staying with her brother. Isn't that terrible? I can hardly believe a man would treat his own child so coldly."

Henry frowned and stilled his hand.

He hadn't heard those details of the story.

Dearborne had traveled to London to see about a few replacement parts shortly after the conversation in the countinghouse. He'd seen Miss Dearborne around the courtyard from time to time, but he never would have guessed she was staying at his cottage.

"You didn't know?" Mollie raised an eyebrow as if reading his thoughts. "I must say, I'm surprised. You seem to be very familiar with the Dearbornes."

"How would I know something like that?"

A knowing smirk tilted her lips. "Come now, Henry. I'm not a fool. I may get quite a few things in life wrong, but I know love when I see it. The two of you are the most stubborn two people I know."

"Bah. Love."

She adjusted the child in her arms. "Just now, when I mentioned her name, you got all flustered and strange. And yesterday, when I mentioned your name to her, her face flushed such a becoming shade of pink. It's just a shame that the two of you are so pigheaded you refuse to see what is right in front of you."

He could only stare.

"I know you think me a fool, Henry, but I had that feeling once, that feeling that would make me blush the moment his name was mentioned. It turned out that I had fallen for a man of poor character, but that is not the same for the two of you. She is smart and kind. You could do worse, big brother."

He waved his hand as if to shoo away his discomfort with the topic. "You're talking nonsense."

"I am not, and don't look so annoyed at my recommendation. I have taken my fair share of advice from you over the past few months, and it's only fair that you take time to consider what I've said."

"Very well, if it will make you happy, I'll consider it." He turned his attention back to the sleeping baby. He was swaddled in a blanket of yellow wool, but his tiny hand had poked out and now rested against the side of his pink face.

As the child's small chest rose and fell with each breath, he began to understand, for the first time, what his grandfather had meant about legacy. Henry would show his namesake the ways of the mill, as his grandfather had shown him, and hopefully teach him the lessons he had to learn along the way. The child was perfection—the ideal image of purity and innocence. Each finger so tiny and precious. He was something good born out of something perceived as disgraceful. Henry hoped he would have children of his own one day, and his incentive to continue to fight and grow burned even brighter.

CHAPTER 38

$\mathcal{T}$ ierner rushed into the countinghouse and slammed the door. Henry lifted his head from his letter at the sound.

The magistrate's caped coat was shiny with rain, and his round face was ruddy with cold. His face beamed bright with triumph. His smile fell slightly as he pointed his thumb out to two workers in the small room. "What's going on here?"

"Repairing, and in most cases replacing, windows." Henry stood from his desk as the two workers continued repairing the glazing bars in the countinghouse window. "I never stopped to consider how many there were in these buildings until they all needed to be repaired. Quite an unexpected expense."

"Well, I have news that might ease that pain, if only for a bit." Using his hat, Tierner pointed toward the back room, forged inside, and motioned for Henry to follow. Once inside the private space, the hefty man removed his wet coat and moved next to the small fire. "They've agreed to it."

"The weavers?" Henry's pulse thudded. Could it be they would share information so soon?

"The very ones. Turns out a few days in jail was enough for them.

It's a bleak prospect, and even some of the toughest crumble when behind those iron bars. They've given us the names of the men who organized the attack from Leeds. Of course, men from Amberdale participated and will no doubt have to answer for their actions, but it is the men from Leeds who will face most of the charges. The weavers in Amberdale never would have been able to pull this off on their own, as tough and stern as they may be. Soldiers are on their way to Leeds to help the magistrates take them into custody as we speak."

Satisfaction spread fast and warm through Henry, but even as welcome as this news was, it was not really the one answer he was looking for. "Did you question them about my grandfather's death?"

Tierner nodded, but the smile that had lightened his expression faded. "Aye, I did. The men had no knowledge of who was responsible."

Henry widened his stance. "And you believe them?"

"Aye." Tierner met his gaze. "I do."

Disappointment quickly replaced the optimism that arrived with Tierner's news. Yes, he wanted justice for what happened to his mill. But the mill could be replaced. His grandfather was flesh and blood, and meant more to him than any mill ever could.

With a sniff, Henry reached for his coat on the nearby hook. "Not much more work will get done here today. I'm taking my meal at the inn tonight. Care to join me?"

His request was not a social one. He wanted to find out more about the men who were being arrested. He had no interest in punishing the mass of men who attacked his mill. They were as sheep following their shepherd. More importantly, he was interested in finding out exactly what role Silas Dearborne played in the attack.

Tierner patted his round belly as if he were full and then gave his head a sharp shake. "Well now. It's never a good idea to turn down a meal. Sir, lead the way."

The inn was always busy this time of night. Many of his millworkers, especially the unmarried men and the families living in the millworkers' cottages, took their meals here.

Outside, darkness had fallen, and inside, warm light flickered from a dozen low-hanging lanterns strung from the rough wood beams that ran the length of the room. A large fire roared from the hearth, and chatter and laughter welcomed them. Henry should be able to relax in such a place, even for a bit, but tension pulled his shoulders back and screamed through his neck.

No, this was not a place of rest.

For Tierner had more information, and Henry needed to hear every bit.

He leaned back long enough for the scrawny barmaid to place a bowl of lukewarm mutton stew and a mug of ale in front of each of them. When she'd retreated to the kitchen, Henry leaned with both elbows on the table. "Listen. I'm done waiting. My grandfather's dead. My mill and home have been attacked. I'll not stand by while another catastrophe occurs. I've a sister and a nephew under my care, and I'll take no more chances."

Tierner forked a bit of mutton and tore off a piece of bread with his teeth before responding. "I understand your impatience. I do. But we've gotten a confession and names. Best to let it play out. Once the leaders start to crumble, the men following them will dissipate. If the weavers are behind your grandfather's death, someone will know something. There are no secrets among the weavers."

Henry pressed his lips to a fine line and smoothed his neckcloth to dispel the energy gathering in his limbs. "It's too late for that. Surely there is something we're missing. Some clue. Some bit of information that will lead us down the right path."

"The authorities in Leeds are involved now. They have many more resources. Now that they're on the case, we should see faster movement."

"But the murder is so far in the past." Henry pushed his pewter mug away. Like a dog with a bone, he refused to let the matter drop. "The pistol—the one found beside Grandfather. What of it? Did you find out anything about the gunsmith?"

"The gunsmith's a man out of Liverpool." Tierner swiped his heavy wool sleeve over his mouth before taking a noisy swig of ale. "Says he remembered the weapon and made it specifically to order, but the pistol was retrieved by a messenger, not the buyer."

Henry searched his memory. Liverpool. Pennington had mentioned a trip to Liverpool, but that was nothing unusual, seeing that many shipments of wool came in and out of the docks there.

"It just doesn't make sense. Whoever did it was not after money; otherwise it would have been taken."

By the time Henry had finished his musing, Tierner was almost done with his meal. Henry was about to take his first bite when he noticed the Dearbornes, Charles and Kate, at a table on the other side of the room.

He took a swig of ale and studied her from the corner of his eye. Mollie's news that she was now living with her brother seemed to be true. He had never seen her taking a meal here before, but Charles did often. Part of her hair was loosely pinned atop her head, and long, wavy brown locks fell over her shoulders. A loosely woven shawl wrapped around her narrow shoulders, and her crimson cloak puddled at her side. A gown of blue muslin hugged her curved figure, a gown, he noted, he'd never seen before. An easy smile graced her lips, and her head tilted to the side in relaxed amusement. At one point she threw her head back in laughter at something her brother said.

The sight tweaked a smile from Henry. The last several weeks had been hard on her. She deserved a few hours of carefree gaiety, even if in a tavern. His optimism was short-lived, however, as two mill-workers stopped by the Dearborne table. They immediately focused their attention on Kate, nearly ignoring Charles completely.

Jealousy tightened within him, and he took another drink, his gaze never leaving the lady.

"What's captured your attention, man?"

Henry jerked back to Tierner. He wanted to slap the knowing grin from the old man's face.

Tierner leaned with his elbow on the table. A chuckle rumbled through him as he nodded toward Miss Dearborne. "Ah, to be young again."

Henry did not wince. He didn't even look back over his shoulder. But he'd be a fool to think that male millworkers would not take notice of their beautiful newcomer, especially now that she had parted ways with the weavers. Even his ears burned with the frustration of it. Charles was suddenly the most popular man on the property, for he was guardian to the most charming girl in the village.

Henry forked a bite, gulped down a swig, and rose. He dropped a few coins on the table, grabbed his coat, and punched his arms through the sleeves.

Tierner's laughter rumbled loud and true. "If you're going to act, now's the time. She'll not stay single long. The pretty ones never do."

CHAPTER 39

The countinghouse was quiet. The glaziers were finally go ... for the night. The men chopping the felled oak had stilled. ... enry sat at his desk, stared into the leaping flames, and contemplated, ... cent events.

He'd fix what had been broken.

He'd make sure the workers had jobs.

He'd do his best to grow the business.

But the numerous unsettled matters wrestling about in his ... distracted him.

He glanced at the clock atop the mantel, noting the hour's lateness. Miss Dearborne would be just down the street, nestled in Dearborne's tiny cottage, and she'd likely still be awake, sewing or reading or engaged in another such activity that drew a woman's attention.

He grimaced at the manner in which the two brutes had ogled the young lady in the inn, and what made it worse was that she didn't seem to notice their intentions.

He forced his fingers through his hair, growing annoyed with the clock's incessant ticking. At one time, not so long ago, life seemed limitless. The world had been his to take. Love and life were easy. There was no gray, simply the stark contrast of black and white.

Now he could easily become lost in the murky shades of gray, where ideas were wrong for some and right for others; black for one side and white for the next. Never before had his decisions held such weight and impacted so many.

He tapped his foot against the leg of the desk. Grandfather never had qualms about his decisions. Decisions were always made for financial gain, and he never questioned his method.

Grandfather also had been black and white about his approach to relationships.

Henry had no doubt that despite the argument that had transpired between him and Pennington, if he were to propose to Miss Pennington this very day, she'd accept. It had nothing to do with love or feeling, but everything to do with money.

He huffed. At the day's end, what did money matter? War had hardened him to such a point that the only way to feel human again was to find the beauty, find the peace.

To him, the one person who possessed both of those was Miss Dearborne—Kate. No, time and circumstance had not softened his growing affection for her, as he'd hoped they might. If anything, the events of the past few days deepened the resolve to a point that it could no longer be avoided or ignored.

He pushed himself up from the desk, lifted a lantern, and headed into the night. He could wait no longer.

He had to speak with her again.

Kate sat at the table in her brother's humble cottage, her elbow resting atop the smooth surface and her chin resting in her hand. She nodded at the game of dominoes filling the space between her and Charles and gave a tsk. "Are you going to play?"

"Give me time." Charles leaned back in his chair and surveyed the game. Again.

With a sigh Kate pushed herself back and slumped her shoulders. The cottage was small, with only one living space and a bedchamber, but it was large enough for the two siblings. A modest fire flickered in the grate, and two wavering candles provided enough light to see the black-and-white tiles in the darkness.

Kate had to admit it was nice to spend time with her brother. Games like this were never played at Meadowvale. Wool had been the primary focus at any hour of every day. She glanced up at the concentration furrowing Charles's brow. He seemed more relaxed, happier than she had ever seen him.

At length, Charles placed his tile, and Kate set her domino in place and blew out her breath.

"You used to make that sound every time Mother would tell you to corral the lambs." Charles lifted a domino and tapped it against the table.

The reminder of Meadowvale—and of family—touched a place in her soul that she was attempting to avoid. "Do you never think of him?"

"Who?" Charles shifted in the wooden chair.

"Papa." Even the mention of his name exposed a tender wound. "I've never gone this long without seeing him."

Charles drew a deep breath before placing another tile, as if his patience was being tested at the mere mention of the name. "He is a stubborn man, Katie. I know it upsets you, but if he said that he doesn't want to see you, then you won't see him. I'm testament to that, am I not? Best forget it and move on. You can have a good life outside of Meadowvale. Can you not just embrace it?"

Kate chewed her lip. "But this is different."

"How? We both chose a different path than he would have chosen for us. And that he cannot abide."

She considered his words. "I hope his wound is recovering."

"I'm sure word would have gotten to us if it isn't. Haven't you spoken with Jane or any of your other friends?"

The mention of Jane's name wrapped a cord around her chest. "I have tried to call on her, but her father will not permit her to speak with me. It appears I have been branded the enemy. Again."

The stark similarity to the way Frederica's father would not permit her to remain friends with Kate chafed. The situation was repeating itself. When she was a child, she'd stomped her foot and demanded answers, but now the slow burn of rejection cast long shadows to the corners of her heart.

"This will pass."

"Was it difficult for you when you left Meadowvale?"

Charles set his jaw before drawing a deep breath. "Of course. But I had support. Mr. Stockton and Belsey took great care of me. I, too, at one time was branded the enemy, but they were quick to overlook it. I was given access to this cottage, an income. It was especially hard to leave you, but in my gut I knew it would all come to this—the mill owners versus the weavers—and I knew that the production advances embraced by the mill owners were the future."

"Did you miss Papa?"

"I did, especially my first year away from Meadowvale. After all, Father taught me everything I know. But when he did not return my letters, when he refused to see me, and when he passed me in public without acknowledging me, I hardened to it."

Kate looked down at her hands. "The hours just pass by. I am so used to being busy. I miss my work. I suppose it sounds silly, but I miss my sheep. Especially Ivy."

"If you want a sheep, we can get one," teased Charles. "With all of our pasture space."

Kate smiled at his little joke. "You know what I mean."

"At the risk of sounding like Father, perhaps it is time you turned your attention to something besides weaving and cloth."

She raised an eyebrow, not sure she liked where this conversation was going. "What did you have in mind?"

Charles shrugged and played a tile. "I always thought you would make a good mother. Perhaps finding yourself a husband and settling down wouldn't be such a bad idea."

"Are you trying to get rid of me?" She played a tile of her own.

"Listen, Kate. You have always been independent. Far more independent than any other woman I've known. But there is a rhythm to life. Perhaps this is your time to consider a different purpose."

Charles placed another tile. "In just the week that you have been here, I have already had three men inquire after you. I fully intend to beat them away with a stick if I must, until you tell me you are ready to consider such a future for yourself."

Silence continued for several minutes. Tile after tile was played in the quiet, but Kate's mind wasn't on the game. Not really.

Charles crossed his arms over his chest. "And what of Henry Stockton?"

Kate flicked her eyes up at the mention of his name. "What of him?"

Again, Charles shrugged and stretched his booted foot out before him. "Perhaps I only imagined it, but I thought I noticed a *friendship* developing."

Kate sniffed. She'd smack him if he were closer. And yet she could not deny that she was equal parts unwilling and yearning to talk about the man who was never far from her mind. The recollection of his kiss on her lips was also never far from her thoughts, and a strange heat settled over her. And even though he had declared the opposite to be true, she could not help questioning the rumors that he intended to marry Miss Pennington. Knowing Charles would have at least some knowledge on the matter, she stated, "I was under the impression that he and Miss Pennington would marry one day."

Charles frowned. "Since old man Stockton's death, things between Stockton and Pennington are tense. I'm not sure what it is about, but something's not right. None of the Penningtons have been by the mill since the attack. In the past Mr. Pennington would be by the countinghouse every other day at least. No, something has changed."

Her mind mapped to Henry's hard censure of Arthur Pennington when he had spoken harshly to her. Could she be part of the reason the relationship between the families was crumbling?

The words were far from definitive, but her heart gave a little leap at the mention of it. Perhaps Henry Stockton would be a part of her life, or perhaps things would continue on and his declaration of affection would be forgotten. But at least for now, a small glimmer of hope fought to be recognized, and she would cling to that.

Henry could no longer handle the unsettling restlessness within him.

A heavy moon cast dark shadows over the haphazard mill courtyard, and he sidestepped a large pile of debris. It had to be nearing midnight. Kate would probably be asleep. He should wait until the morrow to seek her out, though he knew his soul would find little rest until he spoke his piece.

He assessed the row of cottages. Yellow light winked from a handful of them. Maybe, just maybe, the Dearborne cottage would be one bearing a sign of activity.

As he traversed the broad lane to the millworkers' cottages, a shuffling sound slowed his steps and caused the hair on his arms to stand on end. He patted his hand over his pistol and drew close to the hedgerow along the shadowed lane. He'd not taken a step without it in weeks, and he was glad he hadn't forgotten it tonight. His muscles tensed and his breath grew shallow. With all the violence brewing the past several weeks, caution was vital.

For a moment all was still, then the scraping sound returned—louder. Stronger. He whirled as the sound of a deep, muted voice fought against the windy sounds of night.

And then a gunshot cracked the night's cool stillness.

Poised to respond, Henry jerked his pistol free.

A man's cry rang out, and then more shuffling.

He squinted into the darkness, searching for the source.

The sleeping cottages leapt to life. Light flamed where darkness had once been. Doors flew open. Voices rang out.

Henry gritted his teeth. How would he find who was responsible with the bodies flooding the street?

He raced toward the direction of the scuffle, past cottages and onlookers. At the end of the row, shadowed figures wrestled on the ground, their struggle illuminated by naught but moonlight. He pushed through the other men who had gathered and stopped short.

He put a heavy hand on the figure on top, employing every muscle, and yanked the flailing figure backward.

There on the ground lay Arthur Pennington, eyes wild and mouth agape. Blood and dirt mingled on his face. Profanity spewed from his lips.

Henry swallowed his shock and whirled to identify the man he'd just peeled from on top of Pennington.

Vincent Warren, his old comrade, stood firm, his chest heaving, but the expression on his face was hard and unmoving as the mill itself.

Henry reached to help Pennington sit up, cognizant of the blood trickling down his thick arm and pooling on the ground beneath. Two millworkers now held Warren, each gripping an arm. The cold, hard glint of battle gleamed in his eyes, and the pistol, reeking of discharged gunpowder, lay still at the toe of his boot.

Henry dropped to his knees next to Pennington. "What happened? Have you been shot?"

"It grazed me." Pennington cut sharp eyes toward Warren. "Fortunately the man *you* brought to our village is a poor shot."

Obscenities and threats spewed from Warren, and Henry's stomach clenched. Yes, he had brought Warren to Amberdale, but he also knew that the ex-soldier's shots were sure and true. He'd not miss unless he intended to.

Henry helped remove Pennington's coat, yanked his own cravat from about his neck, and used it to put pressure on the wound.

"Someone go for Tierner. Now," Henry ordered, shooting a glare over his shoulder at Warren and pinning him with all the condemnation he could. Regardless of what had happened, there could be no excuse for pulling the trigger on an innocent man.

"Don't you dare look at me as if I'm the one in the wrong," hurled Warren, perspiration beading on his brow. "I was defending myself."

Pennington snarled. "You're a fool. How could I attack you? I've no pistol."

"He's not who you think he is, Stockton. He's a murderer." Warren spat the words, eyes wild, jerking his arms against the restraint of the men holding him. "If you're looking for the man who killed your grandfather, look no further, because you've found him."

At the words, Henry's head grew light, but his limbs felt weighted like stone. Surely Warren was mistaken. He snapped his attention back to Pennington, whose ashen face trembled with anger.

"How you lie, you pathetic man." Pennington turned to Henry, his stare hard and his words full of condemnation and censure. "You fool. Did you not even consider the nature of this man? Why, you gave him the key! He's a murderer in his own right. You want to know who informed the weavers' society of your every move?"

Henry pressed his eyes shut for several seconds, trying to make sense of what he was hearing. It was hard to believe either of them when trust was rare and loyalty was scarce. He opened his eyes again to see Warren still struggling against the men binding his arms, the moonlight slicing sharp shadows on his angular face.

He met Henry's gaze fully, his words tumbling forth. "I've nothing to lose, so why would I lie now? Consider, Pennington's got nothing to lose and everything to gain if Stockton Mill failed. Your grandfather's business was growing too large, and Pennington feared that your grandfather's success would impede his own, so he stopped at nothing to make sure your grandfather did not grow too confident. He never saw your grandfather as a friend. He saw him as the competition. All the letters threatening your families and the mill? Those all originated with Pennington—a figment of his imagination to further gain your grandfather's trust and unite them against the perceived enemy. Pennington was the one responsible for burning the Stockton stable—all to create the illusion that the weavers were more dangerous than they are. But that night of the fire, your grandfather stumbled on Pennington's role in the blaze. Your grandfather promised to expose and ruin him, and that is why Pennington killed him, in cold blood. You've got to believe me. Pennington's even befriended some of the weaving chaps from Leeds to try to cover his tracks. He's chipping away at the situation to strengthen his mill and ruin Stockton Mill. Why can you not see what has been right in front of you all along?"

Warren stopped struggling, gasping for breath after the rush of words. "I'm not innocent in this. I'll admit, I could have stopped it, but I didn't. Pennington did his research and found out that you and I served together. He contacted me and promised a handsome sum to make my way close to you. To inform on you. But now it seems he's had a change in plans, for his pockets do not run deep enough to pay me for my services. When I threatened to go to you with his plans, he told me his intentions for framing me for old man Stockton's murder and as the informant to the weavers. Yes, the weavers are angry in their own right, but they are not nearly as big of an enemy as this wolf in sheep's clothing. God help me, I may be guilty of lying and betrayal, but at least I am not a murderer."

"I killed no one. The accusation is ridiculous!" spat Pennington, cutting off Warren's words. "And what do you mean you're not a murderer? You shot me in cold blood."

Henry drew a sharp breath, his blood throbbing through his veins and Warren's words pounding in his head. "I have seen the man handle a pistol. If he wanted to kill you, you'd have a bullet in the center of your chest."

The clues were coming together, like a puzzle nearing completion. Now he understood why they could find no fault with the weavers in Grandfather's death, for they were never involved in the first place.

Nausea settled over him. As if a veil had been lifted, he suddenly saw Pennington in his true light.

Pennington grabbed Henry's arm, clutching it, as if sensing that his defense was slipping. "Surely you do not believe this man, do you? I have known you all your life, and this is how you treat your grandfather's closest friend?"

Henry jerked his arm free and stepped back from Pennington.

Within moments Dearborne and Belsey were both at his side. "What do you want us to do with them?"

"Take them both to the lockup," Henry ordered.

Pennington shouted and fought, but Henry scanned the crowd. Every expression showed on the faces of those surrounding him. Horror. Shock. Even amusement on some as they beheld how the mighty had fallen.

As the men were led, fighting and flailing, down the cottage lane, the crowd began to disperse. Dearborne had found his way to the center of the activity and clasped his hand on Henry's shoulder, gently urging him away from the scene.

Stunned, Henry put one booted foot in front of the other.

It was not a weaver who took William Stockton's life, as Henry had suspected, but one of his grandfather's closest friends.

Friend indeed.

How had he not seen it? It had been right in front of him.

He wanted to be away from the mill. Away from everything it stood for. There was no reason to stay here, in the street. He turned to stomp down the road but then stopped in his tracks.

Kate.

CHAPTER 40

*W*arren had said he was a man with nothing to lose.

Henry felt completely different about his own situation, for he had much to lose.

Despite the past, Stockton House gleamed with new life and a promise of things to come. The gruesome mystery around his grandfather's death had been solved. He knew who was responsible, and he knew who was *not*. Why did he not feel a sense of satisfaction? Why did it all seem as dire as the day before?

While some ties had been severed, others had grown strong, like iron forged in fire. Perhaps he'd trusted the wrong people and mistrusted those he shouldn't have. His prejudices and assumptions had proven to be wrong in some instances. All would need forgiveness, and that forgiveness needed to start with him. Yes, he bore scars that would likely haunt him until the day he died, but he didn't need to carry hate for the men who put them there.

He yearned for a new beginning and closure to the past. But there was more reason than ever to continue fighting for a future.

And his future was right ahead of him—if only she felt the same way.

The cottage alley was now empty, save for Kate. All the onlookers had returned to their homes, but she stood in the shadows. Watching silently. Was she relieved at this development? Was she shocked, as he had been?

She rubbed her hand over her arm as he drew near. "Are you all right?"

He did not respond. He only reached out to take her hand.

It was a simple touch, but the warmth of it soothed the jagged edges ripping within him.

She did not resist his hand. Instead, she allowed him to lead her to the space between two cottages. There was not much room, but he preferred it that way.

Her eyes were downcast, and her long lashes fanned her cheeks. She shivered. In a moment of boldness, he reached out and placed his hands on her upper arms to warm her.

She stepped closer. "That must have been difficult for you to hear."

"What was difficult was not knowing. At least now I can rest assured that justice will be had."

"But the Penningtons." She lifted her wide eyes to meet his. "With everything between you and Miss Pennington, well, I thought that you—"

"Why do you not believe me when I say that time has deadened that relationship? And now, well, nothing will ever be as it was."

"But are you saddened by it?" Her eyebrows drew together in question. "My mother once told me that we cannot control what others do. We can only control how we react to it. Being angry will only hurt you, not them. And yet, lost affection can be painful."

He smiled. The fact that she was concerned for his feelings gave him reason to hope that her attitude toward him had changed since the night of the Winter's End Festival. "*Affection* is not the word I would use to describe my relationship with the Penningtons. She causes me no pain. The only pain I feel now relates to you."

"To me?" She gave a little laugh. "How?"

"I meant every word I spoke the night of the festival. If anything, the events of the past few days have only deepened my feelings. I have seen you be kind. Strong. Giving. Brave."

She trembled in the cold. Perhaps she did not believe him.

He inched closer still, the warmth of her body now reaching through his coat, infusing him with bravery. "I can't help but feel responsible in some way for the position you are in, and I want to spend my days proving to you that love can be loyal and that it will never go away."

"I've never known never-ending love." She looked to the cobbled path beneath them. "I'm not entirely sure it exists."

The wind blew a curl over her forehead, and he reached up and brushed her hair from her eyes. Fire rushed him at the touch, intensifying every sense. "Oh, Kate." Her Christian name slid easily from his lips. "If I thought for a moment that your opinions from the festival night had changed, I'd be complete."

She leaned closer. Her voice was barely above a whisper. "I was frightened that night."

Her skirt swooshed against his legs. He was so close now he could feel the soft flutter of her breath on his neck where his cravat had been. "I should have, well, I should have—"

"Are you still frightened?"

She placed her hands on his chest and lifted her face. "No. Not anymore."

He closed the gap between them, lifted her chin with his forefinger, and pressed his lips against hers. Warmth radiated from the union, wrapping him in a peace like he'd never known.

This was what he wanted. Not mills or money or wool or power. He wanted Kate.

She melted against him, filling the empty spaces in his soul.

Then gently, she eased away. The moonlight, now fleeting behind the gathering clouds, illuminated tears in her eyes.

Concerned, he brushed the hair from her face once more. "What is it?"

"It's only that I am happy." She smiled. "For the first time in a long time, I can see a future ahead of me. And I never want to look away."

He drew her close and kissed her forehead. He, too, could see his future before him, and it glowed much more brightly than he ever thought possible.

Frederica balled up her fine taffeta ball gown and stuffed it in the trunk. Once it was settled she gave it an extra punch to relieve the tension mounting in her slender frame.

It didn't work.

She propped her hands on her hips and surveyed her bedchamber. Sadness, anger, and fear jumbled within her. In four short hours she would be leaving Briarton House for the last time. And she would likely never return.

Normally her abigail would see to a task like packing a trunk, but her maid, along with half of Briarton's other servants, had abandoned her post when news of her father's crime surfaced.

As it turned out, no one wanted to work for a murderer.

She wiped her nose with the back of her hand and sniffed. Crying would do no good now. Her best chance for a decent future was to do as her mother had said: leave Amberdale behind and relocate to her grandmother's in London. It would take months, maybe years, for the scandal to reach the distant neighborhood. Perhaps she would have time to secure a husband before the news caught up with her.

Frederica reached for another garment in the wardrobe and paused when her hand landed on the emerald gown she had worn to the Winter's End Festival. With a deep breath she let her finger run down the fine, shimmery silk and traverse over the fine pearl beading. It truly was a magnificent gown. She had best take care with this one. It was the last fine garment she had made before her life fell apart, and with the creditors even now beating down their door, she doubted she would be able to afford such luxury for some time—if ever.

She knit her fingers together so tightly it was a wonder they didn't break. What if their plan didn't work? As they had all discussed, her sisters were traveling to live with distant relatives, each hoping to outrun the scandal, and her mother would stay at Briarton alone to deal with the fallout of her husband's actions. Father's reckless spending and foolish investments had drained their funds. Everyone in Amberdale—nay, everyone in Yorkshire—knew the story of Arthur Pennington's betrayal by now. His full confession of burning the stable, murdering Mr. Stockton, and attempting to bribe the weavers' society had left no doubt.

Even now, as she packed up as many earthly possessions as she could fit in the traveling trunk, she did not understand it. How could the man she loved, her father, do such things?

Frederica drew a shuddery breath. She had to prepare herself. He would likely face the end of a noose for his crimes. The thought forced bile up her throat. That was what happened to murderers.

Murderer.

The word echoed hollow in her mind and tasted bitter on her

tongue. Anger burned afresh, clenching her stomach and numbing her fingers and feet. Perhaps what hurt the most, even beyond the betrayal of her father, was the fact that his actions destroyed any chance she had to become Mrs. Henry Stockton. Henry would never speak to her again. And she did not blame him. He would never believe that she knew nothing of her father's deceit.

Before long a tear slipped down her cheek. Then another, and another. If she thought it would do any good, she would throw herself to the ground in a tantrum to rival that of any child. But there was no one to see her. No one to care.

In the past, pouting and feigning distress was the surest way to get what she wanted, but now she doubted it would have even the slightest effect on anyone—not even a fool like Mr. Bryant, who had fussed over her at the festival.

She'd been an idiot not to accept Mr. Simmons when she had the chance. Even though he was old and portly, he was safe. For now, who would want her? She would even trade places with Mollie Stockton, who became pregnant out of wedlock and then lied about it.

Mollie Stockton's humiliation was great. But Frederica's was greater. At least Mollie's sin could be forgiven. But to be the daughter of a murderer?

No. Society would never forgive that. And without society's approval, what options did she have?

Frederica tucked the last items in her trunk, let the lid fall, and glanced around her room one final time. The moment she stepped out the door, her life would never be the same.

CHAPTER 41

*I*t had been four months since the attack on the mill. Four months since Kate had last spoken with her father. Four months since her engagement to Henry Stockton had been announced. And four months since her heart began to find freedom.

It was hard to comprehend how much her life had changed in less than a year. Life had been plagued with uncertainty and feelings of inadequacy. Now she was making more friends. Finding new purpose. But there was something that needed to be done.

The skies were clear and vibrant above the pastures flanking the public road leading to Meadowvale's gate. Summer's warmth had replaced winter's snow, and the heather dressed the distant moors in shades of violet and lavender. Pastures now hosted lambs and sheep, and the sun's light blanketed all.

She tightened her grip on Henry's arm. He looked down at her and smiled, and her heart swelled at the sight.

How her life was altered because this man was in it.

Charles fell into step next to her, and he tilted his head to the side. "Are you sure you want to do this?"

Nervousness surged through Kate. But yes, she was certain. She had resisted her mother's words for so long. Not forgiving her father would only hurt her. She nodded. "We need to."

Henry patted her hand on his arm. "This is the right course. You need closure. At least now you will know you've done what you can to set things right."

The trio stopped in front of the gate to Meadowvale Cottage. In the blue skies above, warblers and robins darted about, their chirping cheery and optimistic. Butterflies fluttered in Kate's stomach. It would take a miracle for her father to even speak with them, especially after the months that had passed and the events that had transpired. But what did she have to lose? What did any of them have to lose?

Kate pushed open the gate, just as she had done a thousand times before. The familiar sound of it creaking on its hinges cast a melancholy shadow over her anticipation. Her hand trembled as she released the gate. And her heart sank when she assessed the grounds.

Normally summer marked a productive time at Meadowvale Cottage. Her father had always taken great pride in maintaining his property. But now all was overgrown. In fact, there were few signs of life.

Charles whistled under his breath. "Look at this place."

Kate could only stare. If the grounds were any indication of how her father was faring, all was dire indeed.

She quickened her steps, suddenly desperate for answers to the questions that had been simmering within her. Now that she was considered a traitor by the weaving community, no one, not even Jane, had spoken to her. For all she knew, Papa could be sick, or hurt, or worse.

She broke away from the men and hurried to the cottage door. An eerie silence permeated the space that once had been so full of activity. No sound of looms running met her ears. No cloth hung from the tenterhooks on the south edge of the property. No chatter echoed from the stables or dye house.

Where was everyone?

She pushed open the door. Betsy, who was standing in the parlor, jerked her head up. She dropped her armful of linens to the table. "Miss Dearborne!" Her eyes widened when she noticed Charles and Henry behind her.

The sight of her old friend tugged at her, but Kate needed to keep her emotions steady. "We need to speak with Papa. Do you know where he is?"

Betsy's face blanched. "I—I do. Just a moment. I'll see if he is available."

Betsy disappeared through the doorway, leaving them alone in the drawing room. No fire lit the grate. Kate tapped her fingers along the bare table with nervous energy. This room used to be the heart-beat of weaving in Amberdale. It was always alive with visitors and meetings. But now it seemed almost dead.

Henry stepped beside her, lifting her hand from the table and squeezing it. She was about to suggest they move to the sofa when uneven footsteps clomped in the corridor. She turned just in time to see Papa's bulky frame fill the door frame.

She gasped at the sight of him. A full gray beard hid the lower half of his face. His graying hair was in need of a trim. He leaned heavily on a cane, no doubt a result of his gunshot wound. He wore no coat, and his wrinkled linen waistcoat hung askew on his frame.

Kate dropped Henry's hand and stepped toward her father, but when he made no motion to receive her, she stopped. Her father's cold expression shivered her spine.

Perhaps Charles had been right.

Maybe this was a bad idea.

She swallowed. "Papa."

His hard gaze shifted from Charles to Henry and back to her. "Why are you here?"

Kate stiffened. She had thought about what she would say. She had planned it out in detail. But now that she was standing before her father, her mind was blank. "Can we sit?"

She expected Papa to reject the idea, but he pointed to the worn sofa and the chairs next to the fireplace. Once seated, Papa set his cane on the ground next to him. "I suppose you've won, then. Is that what you have come here for? To gloat?"

Kate shook her head, and her words tumbled forth. "It's not about winning or losing, Papa. I miss you. I want our relationship to be as it was."

"Nothing will be as it was, Katie."

She could not help but ask. "Where is everyone? John? The other journeymen?"

"John is in prison. Seems he had accompanied the shearmen in Leeds and was arrested for breaking machines. He could hang. The rest of the men have other employment."

Kate's stomach churned. She and John may have had their differences, but they had a long history together. She did not want to think of him in such a situation, regardless of what had transpired between them.

Papa cast a hard glare at Henry. "You've done it. Your grandfather would be proud. The weaving industry is all but destroyed in Amberdale. Besides John, four other of our men now sit in prisons."

"I cannot be happy about that, sir." Believable sincerity rang in Henry's tone.

Papa huffed. "I have a hard time believing that."

"Please, listen." Kate reached forward and clutched her father's large hand in both of her own. "It isn't what you think. Things are improving at the mills. They aren't like you believe them to be. I've seen it with my own eyes. Henry is changing things. The children are not permitted to work such long hours. A tutor has even been hired. After work the children go to classes and are being taught reading and sums."

Henry leaned forward. "My grandfather and you did not see eye to eye, but I hope for a different outcome. Obviously, Pennington no longer runs Pennington Mill. He's been bought out, and Charles will be overseeing operations there."

Kate looked at her brother. She thought he wasn't going to say anything, but then he looked up. "I'll need help, Father."

Papa laughed and rolled his eyes to the ceiling. "Are you suggesting that I work in a mill?"

Charles shrugged. "The cloth halls are closing. Where are you going to sell your goods? It could be worse. We could start over."

She knew what Papa was thinking. Too much time had passed. Too many words had been exchanged. Too many stones had been cast.

He shook his head. "I can't do that."

"Well, if you can't do that . . . perhaps you can accept my apology."

Her father's face fell as he stared at his son. "Your apology? For what?"

"When I left Meadowvale, I did so because I believed it the right thing to do. And I still do. But I disrespected you. And for that I'm sorry. I was headstrong, and our relationship crumbled to this enmity we have today. I'd like to think that it could be repaired. I'm not sure how to start that process, but I'm willing to try if you are."

Their father continued to stare at him but said nothing. Kate could stand it no more. "Papa, please. This has gone on long enough.

I don't want to start the next stage of my life without you in it. I'd like to think that you could also forgive me for alerting the mill to the attack, but I hope you can see now that it was the best way to proceed. If not, you could be in prison. Or hung. Many more lives could have been lost. And for what? Pride? Is it really that important?"

Papa shifted toward Henry, his gaze frustratingly cool. "I have heard word that you are to be married."

Henry leaned forward. "Yes, sir. Your daughter is an incredible woman. You should be very proud of her."

Kate gripped her father's hand tighter to recapture his attention. She had to make him understand. "At least listen to me. We are making changes at the mill. It is not such the vile place you assume it to be. Henry is raising wages, not cutting them. Now that Charles will be in charge of Pennington Mill, we can make the work environment better. Can we not resolve this?"

Papa reached for his cane and stood. Kate held her breath and looked at Charles. But instead of accepting their apology, Papa's face darkened. "I think it is time for you to leave. I cannot forget—or forgive—what you have done."

EPILOGUE

*K*ate bit her lips and smiled as she assessed her reflection in the looking glass. A new gown of cream silk hugged her frame. Her hair was curled and pinned atop her head, and summer's last dainty flowers of pink and violet were tucked amid the pins. A flush graced her cheeks, and her eyes shone brightly.

She felt beautiful. She felt complete. She felt happy and needed.

To her left Mollie fidgeted with her bouquet, and across the room, Mrs. Figgs retrieved a necklace from the chest.

"Here." Mrs. Figgs motioned for Kate to turn so she could fasten the necklace. "Who would have thought, all those months ago when you were injured the night of the fire, that you would be the one to capture Henry's heart."

Kate smiled. It was true. She never would have dreamed during that time of uncertainty that her future could be so full. She looked out her brother's cottage window to the church's spire. It would be her last day as a guest before she would move to Stockton House. She had been a woman without a true home since her father threw her out of Meadowvale, but tonight she would have a home of her own. A husband who loved her. And the promise of a future that set her imagination on fire.

When the time came, the women made the short walk to the churchyard. Henry was inside those walls. So were Charles and all the people who had welcomed her into their way of life.

Not even a year ago, many of those attending her wedding would have been considered her enemies. But times were changing, and the hope of a new future spread before her—before them all. Even some of the weavers had come around. While she had not yet spoken with Jane, her heart was hopeful than one day her dear friend would consent to visit her.

Adelaide and several of the other girls from the mill were waiting outside the church, excited and eager to catch a glimpse of the bride. Kate smiled and waved at them.

As she paused at the church door, waiting to go in, one shadow fell over her. A few weeks had passed since Henry, Charles, and she had visited Meadowvale. She had not heard from her father since. She'd even written a letter to him but received no response.

She pushed it to the back of her mind. She'd allow nothing to dampen the happiness in her heart and the optimism within her soul. With a deep breath, she stepped into the reverent, cool church.

She'd barely entered the church when someone caught her eye. She looked to her left. There, in the back row, sat Papa. Her hand flew to her mouth, and tears rushed to her eyes. The day was already ripe with emotion, and the sight of him cut to the core of her very existence.

He'd shaved. Trimmed his hair. He was dressed in his tailcoat of dark-blue broadcloth—the same coat he used to wear when he attended church, before Charles left Meadowvale. The corner of his mouth lifted in a small smile, and he nodded at her.

Happiness flooded her, and she turned her gaze toward Henry.

She floated past her father. Past the millworkers who had welcomed her into their family.

Past the Figgs who now treated her with parental affection. Past her new sister and the dark-haired baby who would be her nephew by the time she left this church.

She was grateful to have these people in her life, but it was the man who was waiting for her at the altar who set her soul ablaze. With the glimmer of hope for a reunion with her father and the promise of a new life as Mrs. Stockton, her heart brimmed full.

Henry stood before her, as handsome as the day she had met him. His blue eyes gleamed brighter and his smile flashed broader.

Kate breathed a prayer of gratitude. If her life had gone as she had hoped all those months ago, she would have missed the gifts God had given her.

She looked to the man who would be her husband in a few short minutes. Her soul felt at rest, for now she knew the true power of love, the unbending strength of loyalty, and the eternal beauty of forgiveness.

ACKNOWLEDGMENTS

*W*riting *The Weaver's Daughter* was such a joy, and there are several people I would like to thank for their support along the way.

First and foremost, to my family: It is because of your endless encouragement that I am able to follow my love for storytelling. I am so grateful for you.

To my incredible and insightful editor, Becky Monds: Thank you for guidance. And to the rest of the team at HarperCollins Christian Publishing—from marketing to design, from production to sales, you are all spectacular!

To my writer friends Kristy and Katherine: I am blessed to share this journey with you and call you both friends.

To my first readers: Thank you for reading the early manuscripts and helping me get the story just right.

To Tamela Hancock Murray, the agent who helped make this book possible: Thanks for believing in this story!

To my author pals, "the Grove Girls"—Cara, Katie, Melissa, Courtney, Katherine, Kristy, and Beth: Thank you for the brainstorming sessions and encouragement!

Last but not least, a huge thank-you to my readers. I am so grateful for each and every one of you!

DISCUSSION QUESTIONS

1. Which character did you identify with the most? Why?
2. How do you think Henry's experiences in the war shaped his life after he returned to Amberdale?
3. Let's talk about Frederica. Her behavior had a huge impact on both Kate and Henry. Do you think she was a happy person? Do you think she influenced Kate or Henry in any way?
4. If you could give Kate one piece of advice at any point in the story, what would you tell her? What advice would you give Henry?
5. In the prologue, Kate's mother says, "We cannot control what others do. We can only control how we react to it. Being angry will only hurt you, not them." Based on your experience, have you found this statement to be true? Can you think of an example in your own life that demonstrates this?
6. How do Kate and Henry change over the course of the story?
7. Both Kate and Henry are very loyal to their families, but there comes a point for each of them when they must consider if remaining loyal is the best course or if they must follow their own consciences. Do you think Kate and Henry were justified in defying family expectations?

8. Mollie had difficulty forgiving herself for her past actions and decisions. What advice would you give her?

9. What comes next for Kate and Henry? If you were to write a sequel, what would happen?

CHAPTER ONE

Iverness Curiosity Shop,
London, England, 1812

*C*amille Iverness met the big man's gaze.

    Bravely.

Boldly.

She would not be bullied or manipulated. Not in her own shop.

Camille recognized the expression in the man's eye. He did not want to speak with her, a mere woman. Not when the owner of the shop was James Iverness.

But James Iverness—her father—was not present.

She was.

She jutted her chin out in a show of confidence, refusing to even blink as he pinned her with a steely stare.

"As I already told you, Mr. Turner, I have no money to give you," she repeated, louder this time. "Any dealings you made with my father you will need to take up with him. I've no knowledge of the transaction you described. You had best return at another time."

"I've seen you here, day in, day out." His voice rose in both volume and gruffness. "How do you expect me to believe you know nothing about it?" The wooden planks beneath his feet groaned as he shifted his considerable weight, making little attempt to mask his effort to look around her into the store's back room. "Is he in there? So help me, if he is and—"

"Sir, no one besides myself is present, with the exception of my father's dog."

It was in moments like this that she wished she were taller, for even as she stood on the platform behind the counter, the top of her head barely reached his shoulder. "If you would like, I will wake the animal, but if you have seen me here often, as you claim, then no doubt you have also seen Tevy and know he does not take kindly to strangers. You decide. Shall I go fetch him?"

Mr. Turner's gaze snapped back to her. No doubt he knew of the dog. Everyone on Blinkett Street knew about James Iverness's dog.

His whiskered lip twitched.

A warm sense of satisfaction spread through her, for finally she had said something to sway the determined man.

Mr. Turner's face deepened to crimson, and he pointed a thick finger in Camille's direction, his voice matching the intensity of his eyes. "Tell your father I've a mind to speak with him. And tell him I want my money and won't take kindly to his antics. Next time I am here I will not be so willing to leave."

He muttered beneath his breath and stomped from the store, slamming the door behind him with such force that the glass canisters on the near shelf trembled.

A shudder rushed through her as she watched him lumber away, and she did not let her posture relax until the back flap of his gray coat passed the window and was out of sight. How she despised such interactions. As of late, Papa seemed to be angering more patrons than he obliged, and he always managed to be conveniently absent when they came to confront him.

She needed to speak with Papa, and soon. Awkward conversations like the one with Mr. Turner needed to stop.

Camille tucked a long, wayward lock of hair behind her ear and drew a deep breath. Once again her father's dog had come to her rescue, and he was not even in the room.

"Come, Tevy," she called. In a matter of moments the massive brown animal was through the door and at her side, tail wagging enthusiastically.

"Pay heed!" she laughed as he nudged her hand, forcing her to pet him. "That tail of yours is likely to knock every vase off that shelf if you're not careful, and then Papa will blame—"

The door to the shop pushed open, jingling the bell hung just above it. She drew a sharp breath, preparing to deal with yet another customer, but it was her father who appeared in the doorway.

He was a short man, not much taller than she herself, but that was where their physical similarities ended. His green eyes made up in intensity what he lacked in stature. His hair, which in her youth had been the color of sand, was now the color of stone, and years spent on a ship's deck had left his complexion ruddy. His threadbare frock coat, dingy neckcloth, and whiskered cheeks made him appear more like a vagabond than a shopkeeper, and despite his privileged upbringing, he often acted and spoke like an inhabitant of the docks where he did much of his trading.

"Good day, Papa."

He ignored her welcome and bent to scratch Tevy's ears. After pulling out a bit of dried meat and handing it to the dog, he reached back into his coat. "This came for you."

He stretched out his hand, rough and worn. Between his thick fingers he pinched a letter.

Camille stared at it for several moments, shocked. Clearly she could make out her name—in her mother's handwriting. The edge of the paper was torn. She could not recall the last letter she had received from Mama.

He thrust the letter toward her. "Don't just stand there gawking, girl. Take it."

Camille fumbled with the missive to keep it from falling to the planked floor below, but for once, she found herself unable to find words. Unprepared—and unwilling—to deal with the onset of emotions incited by the letter, she blinked back moisture and shoved it into the front pocket of her work apron.

"Are you not going to read it?" Her father nodded toward her apron.

Of course he expected her to read it, for he himself devoured every one of his wife's scarce communications the moment they arrived. Though they both felt her absence keenly, they reacted to it very differently—and they never, ever discussed it. Over time, Camille had made the topic off-limits in her own mind, and a letter crafted by the very person who was the source of the pain was unwelcome.

"I'll read it later. There is far too much to do at the moment." She sniffed and gestured toward the curtain that separated the shop from the back room. "There was a crate delivered to you by cart in the alley, but it was too heavy for me to lift."

She was a little surprised at the quickness with which her father let the topic of the letter drop. "Why did you not have the men delivering it bring it in?"

"I tried, but they refused—said it was not their duty. They left it in the courtyard out back."

"When are you going to learn that such things are your responsibility? You should have persuaded them to bring it in." Her father shifted through the papers on the counter, not pausing to look up. "Had you been a boy, this would not be an issue."

Camille folded her arms across her chest. "Well, I was not born a boy, and there is precious little I can do about that. So if you will fetch the delivery in for me, I shall tend to it. Or it can spend the night hours where it sits. But the sky looks like it holds rain, so whatever is inside that box will just sit there and soak."

The story continues in *The Curiosity Keeper* by Sarah E. Ladd.

Don't miss Sarah Ladd's Treasures of Surrey novels!

RT Book Reviews calls Sarah Ladd a "superior novelist" and the Treasures of Surrey novels "Regency romantic suspense at its page-turning best."

9780718011888-A

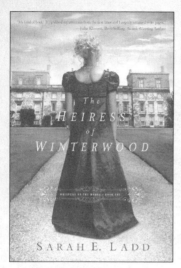
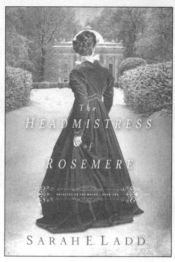
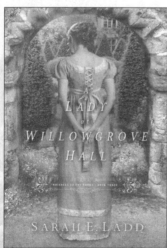

ABOUT THE AUTHOR

Forever Smiling Photography

*S*arah E. Ladd received the 2011 Genesis Award in historical romance for *The Heiress of Winterwood*. She is a graduate of Ball State University and has more than ten years of marketing experience. Sarah lives in Indiana with her amazing family and spunky golden retriever.

Visit Sarah online at SarahLadd.com
Facebook: SarahLaddAuthor
Twitter: @SarahLaddAuthor